P9-ELQ-570

A MEMORY OF WAR

**Center Point
Large Print**

**This Large Print Book carries the
Seal of Approval of N.A.V.H.**

A MEMORY OF WAR

FREDERICK BUSCH

CENTER POINT PUBLISHING
THORNDIKE, MAINE

For Judy Ann Burroughs Busch
from *Once upon a time*
to *The End.*

This Center Point Large Print edition is published in the year 2003 by arrangement with W. W. Norton & Company, Inc.

Copyright © 2003 by Frederick Busch.

"The Red Wheelbarrow" by William Carlos Williams, from *Collected Poems: 1909-1939, Volume I,* copyright © 1938 by New Directions Publishing Corp. Reprinted by permission of New Directions Publishing Corp.

All rights reserved.

The text of this Large Print edition is unabridged. In other aspects, this book may vary from the original edition. Printed in Thailand. Set in 16-point Times New Roman type by Bill Coskrey and Gary Socquet.

ISBN 1-58547-350-2

Library of Congress Cataloging-in-Publication Data

Busch, Frederick, 1941-
   A memory of war / Frederick Busch.--Center Point large print ed.
     p. cm.
   ISBN 1-58547-350-2 (lib. bdg. : alk. paper)
    1. Upper West Side (New York, N.Y.)--Fiction. 2. Psychotherapist and patient--Fiction.
3. Lake District (England)--Fiction. 4. Missing persons--Fiction. 5. Married people--Fiction.
6. Psychologists--Fiction. 7. Adultery--Fiction. 8. Brothers--Fiction. 9. Refugees--Fiction.
10. Large type books. I. Title.

PS3552.U814M4 2003b
813'.54--dc21

                               2003051498

NOTE

WHILE THEY ARE not to be held responsible for my errors of fact, my lapses in judgment, or my failures of expression, I do wish to note of the following that I am indebted to them for assistance, information, guidance: Det. Sgt. Joyce Baldassari, New York City Police Department (Ret.); Dr. Eleanor Mallach Bromberg; Gerald Conroy, Esq.; Dr. Eileen Brockman Goggin; Dr. James E. Goggin; Elsie Mackey of Torver, Cumbria; Det. Austin Muldoon, New York City Police Department (Ret.); Margaret Proctor of Coniston, Cumbria; Ewa Rodzik; Elise Vogel.

Recollections by Roy and Lilian Cooksey about the Lake District during World War II led to the writing of this novel. The Cookseys, he a painter and she a writer, are also intrepid mountaineers and our dear friends.

FB

IT WAS THE weather he remembered, as much as the faceless men who were said to come to the door. So often, when Ann Arbor was gray and damp in the earliest days of winter, when the sky was low above their high, gaunt house, when it nearly rained and when the rain, had it come, might have rapidly turned to a kind of driving snow that Januscz, Alex's father, always called filthy, that was when—it seemed to Alex that was *why*—his father, the least talkative of men, seemed compelled to chatter. He made vegetable soup for them by opening a can and adding water and boiling the mixture in a small white enamel saucepan, then pouring it into broad brown coffee mugs, splashing the stove and the counter. They ate it without spoons, sucking at the hot metal-and-tomato-tasting liquid until, his mouth tender from the heat, Alex could tilt his mug and induce the vegetables and noodles to slide from the cup to his mouth. His father did the same. Then, the empty cups still steaming, his father would tell Alex something new—about Januscz's childhood in rural Poland, or his arrival in a teeming, terrible city of Europe or America, or his courtship of Sylvia, Alex's mother, who slept upstairs on this Saturday afternoon because the weather—or a social encounter of the day before, or a clumsily narrated recipe in a cookery book, or an overheard conversation, or a word she had mispronounced with especial clumsiness—had pitched her into a headache that crushed her temple bones into her brains, as she seemed to enjoy describing it.

In the dimness of their kitchen, in its order—the neatness of an abandoned room—Alex, at six, heard his father ask him, "What to you is a Jewish boy, sweetheart?"

"To me?"

"If I ask you what is a Jewish boy, how do you reply?"

Alex shrugged.

Januscz folded his immense workingman's hands, with their thick, clouded nails, on the edge of the Formica-topped table. He smiled his slow, adoring smile. "Why am I bothering my baby boy with such questions?"

Alex nodded: yes, tell him why.

"In Europe, at home, when in my Poland your mother and I could say 'my Poland,' same as when we could say 'my God,' but *that* we don't discuss today. In Europe, in Germany, *that* place, the place where the disease began, there was a time, men in brown shirts could come to a door of a house and knock. Bang-bang! Understand?"

Alex didn't. He nodded.

"They took people away! Because they were Jews! In the religion, you understand, of Abraham. Not so much Abraham the father, Isaac the son. Not for me, if you please: that is a terrible story of a father, what he would do to his boy. But not for you to bother!" Januscz shook his head, shook it again, then regarded Alex. "You are bewildered, as they say! Poor child.

8

What kind of conversation?" He shook his head again. "Still. This: if a man can come to the house on a horrible day like this—mostly, though, *this* was the weather in Barrow. You remember Barrow? When we lived in England? You were tiny-small, I held you in one hand." Januscz separated his fingers and spread his immense right hand on the table as if he cradled Alex's head. "Sweet child," he said. "Can you remember?"

Alex shrugged.

"And if they knock—"

" 'Bang-bang,' " Alex whispered.

"Exact. And if they take you away—"

"Where, Daddy?"

"Away!"

Alex nodded.

"Then you are a Jew. You understand, now."

Alex nodded.

"You do not," Januscz said. "But this is true. Your mother," he said, and he moved his eyebrows up, as if pointing with them toward the beautiful, unattainable, volatile woman who cradled her pain to herself as she slept. Januscz nodded, and Alex nodded in return. It was how they spoke without speaking. "Once upon a time, your mother was a Jew. So, to those people, in the shirts, it is always. If once, then always. She quarrels with her God. What do they know? What do they care! Once—always: the door."

In school, after they pledged allegiance to the flag of the United States of America and the Republic for which it stood, they chanted, twenty-six first-graders, *Oh, beautiful four spaceships skies*, and Alex, one of

9

them, had assumed that God's shedding of his grace meant that the song was a Christian children's hymn about those who could not be taken away by a man, wearing a brown shirt, who came to knock on the door of a house like theirs. Billy Boudreau, who, after high school graduation, would be drafted by the Boston Red Sox, and who would play two seasons for their farm club in Pawtucket before returning to Ann Arbor with a permanent limp to sell appliances for his father at Boudreau's—*"Home on Your Range!"* was their motto—had whispered that a fruit was a boy who caught a disease and his penis fell off. As Alex sang *above the fruited plane*, he saw a vast airliner filled with such boys who sat unhappily beneath the supervisory gaze of the Christians' God.

And now Alexander Lescziak, Ph.D., having survived to Manhattan's icy spring in 1985 without a visit from the brown-shirted men, greeted a new patient in his Upper West Side practice. The patient's name was William Kessler, and Alex, as he spoke and as he listened, heard, beneath their tense, parrying language, the treble voice of a six-year-old who murmured about God's good crowned with the brotherhood this Kessler claimed to bring him.

He did not enter, but stood on the edge, the heels of his expensive shoes back in the anteroom—three chairs against a wainscoted wall, a standing lamp, a coat tree, a table with dull magazines—and his toes in the office, at the door of which Alex stood to welcome him. Kessler, short, slender, with a strong nose and fierce, dark eyes, brandished the clipboard holding his intake material.

"What if I have no insurance?" Kessler asked, without prelude. "What if all I have is money?" His voice was deep, his pronunciation careful. He sounded like someone who knew that what he said would provoke you, and who wanted, therefore, to be certain that you disliked him for the right reasons. This was a man, Alex thought, who wants to be understood.

He hadn't Alex's Slavic beak, but his nose was long, and his cheekbones, Alex later thought, could have been described as analogous to his—high, prominent, though thicker in the doctor, who was taller and broader by far. You could have thought them relations, once it was suggested, of a distant sort.

"Direct payment is acceptable, Mr. Kessler," he said.

It was four in the afternoon of a day early in February. Alex was wearing tan slacks and a Donegal tweed jacket woven of dark putty colors. His brown loafers were shined and the collar button of his almost-khaki shirt was fastened beneath his tie. He was ready for business. And that was what Kessler, in his black broadcloth suit, his light brown shoes, his double-strapped brown briefcase, had brought.

"Do you think that insurance is an issue?" Alex asked him. "Do you worry about being uninsured?"

He stepped back from the door to give his patient room to enter. When Kessler moved, Alex stepped around him to close the door. Kessler went directly to the Gustav Stickley chair beside the head of a cordovan leather chaise longue covered with red, gray, and black American Indian blankets. Across the room, near the windows, beside the table with its box of tissues, was the matching cordovan chair for patients. Alex stood an instant at the door, wanting to leave this patient behind and not return. He was almost panicking, he thought.

No, he thought, panicking—without the almost—would do.

"I am here about you," Kessler said, standing at the chair. "About our parent. The mother. The story of her life, and yours, and mine. And I must speak, of course, about my father."

He had been right to panic, Alex thought. He smiled, however, and said, "Mr. Kessler, it's customary for patients to sit in that chair, over there. I usually sit where you are."

"Oh, I see I've already created a threatening situation," Kessler said.

"Did you want to?"

"Excellent," Kessler said. He carried his briefcase to the chair twenty feet, diagonally, away. Sitting, opening the briefcase, he said, "Are you ready? Right. Right, then. I am not unwilling to consider that my historiographical view is part of my pathology, if you discover and can prove to me I'm ill."

Alex sat slowly, opened his notebook, uncapped his pen. Berating himself for the pursuit of little victories, he said, "Sorry? Would you repeat that?"

"No," Kessler said. "I've thought better of it."

Alex said, "Do you know why you've come here, Mr. Kessler?"

Kessler sat forward, his feet straddling his briefcase

as if he were riding it toward Alex. "You're my brother," he said. He sat up straighter, a rider who rose in the saddle to stop his horse, and then he leaned back. As if overwhelmed by his own news, he opened his mouth and eyes very wide, paused, and then said a strangled, hoarse *"Brother."*

"My brother?"

Kessler swallowed, but only bobbed his head.

"Which parent? Both? Impossible."

"Sylvia Shber Lescziak," Kessler whispered. He seemed almost in syncope, and, noting that, Alex reminded himself that he, the doctor, was to navigate these sessions, even moments like this. Whatever he did, he thought, would be appropriate: shriek, leave the room, smile casually, write—as he was writing—on his notebook page, *Brother Brother Brother Brother Brother*. Kessler said, his voice gaining strength, "Sylvia Shber of Cracow. Married to Januscz when she was little Sylvia Shber. Fled to England. A Land Girl, of sorts, in Barrow-in-Furness through 1944."

" 'Furnace' as in heater?" Alex could not stop himself from asking.

"F-u-r-n-e-s-s. A small city to the west of what is known as the Lake District in the north of England. As you know, doctor. Where, as you very well know, Vickers now manufactures atomic submarines. And where, during the war, as you very well know, your father worked for them in the manufacture of ships. Whereas *my* father, an interpreter for the SS—"

"Ah," Alex sighed, writing *Brother* again, "the sainted SS."

13

"Conscripted," Kessler said, his chin high, his face a shiny crimson. "He was in training to be a pastor, he served Dietrich Bonhoeffer's Confessing Church. You must know it. Their people, often, were conscripted to eliminate dissension, resistance."

Alex said, "They were said to have smuggled Jews from Berlin."

"That is true," Kessler said. "That is known to be true. My father was drafted to keep him from resistance work."

"Why not kill him? Why not send him to one of the camps?"

"They needed interpreters, and my father could speak several languages."

"Convenient for him."

"And for our mother," Kessler said. "Why must one leave a telephone message at this number, then wait for you to telephone back, and only then receive an appointment? Is the practice of psychology so much about aloofness? Why, I am asking, create such *distance*?"

Meet my wife, Alex thought: she asks the same question.

He said, "I prefer to make my own appointments. To speak with patients and prospective patients. That, too, I think, is part of the practice. Why—you didn't mention this alleged—possible—relationship when we spoke."

"I mentioned anxieties," Kessler said. "I have them."

"To be human is to be anxious. If you breathe, you are anxious. Is that what you meant? I cannot cure you

14

of humanity."

"Of what, Dr. Lescziak, *can* you cure me?"

"We would have to talk awhile. And 'cure' was the least accurate word I could have chosen."

"I've made you nervous," Kessler said. "Upset your apple cart. Thrown your whole life's history into doubt, perhaps." He smiled, then wiped at the smile with three fingers of his left hand. The muscles in his jaw seemed to ripple. Alex wondered, as he turned on the table lamp to his left, whether the pale yellow light that fell across the room was brightening his actual brother.

"You record your occupation as historian. Do you teach?"

Kessler shook his head. "I haven't the disposition for it," he said. "I am an independent scholar. I write history. I am presently writing my father's story. And I have sought you not because of pathology—although you are welcome to find it and . . . what do you do if you don't cure? Would you prescribe for it? Help me, I suppose, to *cope* with it? Well, whatever it is you do, Dr. Lescziak, I invite you to do it. As for me, I am here because you are my brother, and what I intend soon to publish will undermine who you think yourself to be. It's bound to."

Kessler sat back as if suddenly exhausted. He permitted his legs to relax away from the briefcase he had nearly sat upon.

Alex said, "So you might say that *I'm* consulting *you*."

Kessler shrugged. "I've no idea what you mean. But

I *would* say that you're learning something new from me."

"Interesting," Alex said.

"Frightened?"

"Are you frightened, Mr. Kessler?"

"Actually, it's Dr. Kessler. I have the doctorate in modern European history from the University of Chicago."

"And you prefer that I call you 'Doctor'?"

"Oh, that's up to you."

"But you wanted me to know," Alex said.

"We both deal in histories, and I thought you might appreciate the confluence of our stories. Of our careers."

"What *is* your career?"

"But I told you. I am an historian. I have a little money. My parents—I was adopted when I came to this country."

"And you came here how?"

Kessler smiled as if with actual joy. "Why, they brought me here. Januscz and Sylvia. Mostly Sylvia, of course. She was the vessel in which I traveled."

"Can you clarify?"

"May I wait?"

"It's your story, Dr. Kessler. So your adoptive parents gave you money."

"Left it to me. They died. They drove off Route 90 in a snowstorm outside Rochester, New York. Somehow, they managed to freeze to death. It seems such a nineteenth-century death, doesn't it? Trapped in the car and frantic for hours and dying." His bony face showed nothing. He shook his head.

"The Kesslers," Alex said. "Good people?"

"Fine people," Kessler said, "fine. Actually, though, they were not the source of this name."

"I ought to get it straight for my records."

"Kessler was my father. The prisoner in England. Otto Kessler. Two *t*'s, of course, then two *s*'s in the surname, followed by the one *l*. Otto Kessler. My father. By our mutual mother. Straight enough?"

"Thank you. And your adoptive parents?"

"Diamond. Stan and Betty Diamond. Greek Jews. Diamanitis when their parents came over. Diamond in the New World. He made his money importing olives and oil and sour wine from the Old."

"Miss them? Mourn them?"

"I'm not an unloving son, Doctor. They loved me fiercely, and I loved them fiercely in return. We were a family. I'm not renouncing them, God knows, to cleave to my father's story."

"And name."

"True."

"But is that *not* a renunciation, Mr. Kessler? Dr. Kessler? Renaming yourself instead of keeping the name they gave you with their love?"

"Well," Kessler said, "we all see how *you* feel about it." His small hand on its short arm swept the air before him, as if he made the point to a room filled with note takers.

Alex said, "How do *you* feel about it?

"They were my parents. We loved each other. They died. I took my doctorate in history. I visited Barrow-in-Furness. I sat in the Cumbria Public Records Office and read the old Lancashire documents. I read every newspaper from the time he spent interned there. I know about our mother and her husband, and I know about you. Sometimes, one is called by his own story. Do you agree? By his history? And one goes where he is called. I was Kessler's and Sylvia's. Then I was Mom and Dad's. Now I am Kessler. Do you see that as mental disorder?"

"I see it as your story. Just as you said."

"And you disapprove of my story."

"Why do you think so?"

"You pursed your lips."

"No, Mr. Kessler, I never purse my lips. Perhaps because I am trying to write while you speak—"

"No," he said, "you pursed your lips—like this." Kessler grimaced very slowly. "And I can hardly blame you for being . . . upset. Let's say upset."

"If you wish," Alex said. "But I don't believe I've a right to approve or disapprove of what you say is the story of your life."

"It isn't what I *say,*" Kessler said. "It's what the case is. It's what my life is. And what *yours* is. What will it take for you to believe, Dr. Lescziak, that we are brothers? Do you wish documentation? Birth certificate, for example? The one that says I was born in Ann Arbor, Michigan?"

"You needn't prove anything to me. Let's say I believe you."

"Let's say you do."

"All right. I do."

Kessler tilted his small head and cocked it back, so that he aimed along his nose to stare at Alex. Finally, he smiled ruefully and said, "No. No, you don't. I can tell."

Alex nodded his head and, almost simultaneously, reprimanded himself. The motion, the arresting it, made his head ache. He had suffered a kind of whiplash effect, he thought, as if a speeding car in which he rode had suddenly stopped. He wondered if he had just described his life. But he was thinking, he knew, of the end of his sixteenth year and his date with April Navarre. While her cousin Constance sat in the front with Daniel (never Danny) Victor, April sat on Alex's lap in the backseat of Daniel's father's high green Volvo and nipped at Alex's neck and jaw with her even white teeth. Then she leaned over and around—and he could feel the shell of her panty girdle, the hard, pointed brassiere—and she bit the lobe of his ear.

The Volvo shuddered, then picked up speed as Daniel worked his uneasy way through the stiff gears. April had been drinking Schenley's Reserve in her room at the back of her mother's apartment, and Alex smelled its harsh fruitiness. He had asked her out because she was known among the seniors in school to drink and because she had dropped out to work as a secretary in a real estate office. She was older and dangerous, short, bosomy, and reputedly careless with herself; Alex was feverish with hormones while as repressed by his fears as April was sheathed by the panty girdle. But every such thing, he remembered promising himself, could be taken off by someone who worked hard at the catches.

"I used to watch you when we rehearsed for *Oklahoma!*" she said directly into his ear. Her tongue worked there, and then her voice roared inside his head again as she said, "You were so shy. I thought you were cute. I thought: I could get something working on that one." What was working on him was what she wriggled upon. He thought that he felt the flesh of her thighs and buttocks, and he considered that panty girdles might be thinner than he'd imagined.

The car tilted hard, and he and April were pressed into the quarter panel. Constance said, "Daniel!"

"Daniel has departed the premises," Daniel said. He had accepted several drinks of April's Schenley's Reserve with 7 UP.

The car rocked again, and this time Daniel swore as he tried to work at the gears.

"Shift *down*," Constance told him.

"I am," he said.

"When, Daniel?"

"Shut *up*," he told her.

Alex tried to become lost inside April's mouth. That was the feeling her lips and tongue on his ear gave him. He felt a surging, and then—as the police later told them—they hit the sapling and took it down, and then they hit the Canadian hemlock that bordered the front porch, and then they inserted the car in the porch itself at possibly forty miles an hour, the Volvo roaring in second gear, April's tongue at work, Alex thought, inside his brain, and the friction of her buttocks on his lap having brought him, at the instant of their impact, to his first ejaculation that was not self-induced.

He cried out, as they hit, with wonder and distress. April's body cushioned him when Constance hit the windshield and Daniel hit the steering wheel. Alex and April clung to each other as they slammed against the back of Constance's seat. Everyone survived, and everyone was hurt, and Alex's mother, summoned by a fatherly sergeant of police, managed to pass out, gashing her forehead on the tiles of the ER waiting room even as the sergeant murmured his assurances. When Alex was discharged, Sylvia was admitted.

That was almost thirty years ago, Alex thought. Kessler was speaking, and Alex had again lost minutes of a patient's time. He wasn't listening to anyone, was he?

Oh, no, he thought: you're listening to *some*one. Unfortunately, it happens to be yourself.

Alex felt that he must speak. He could think of nothing to say. Then he surprised himself by saying, with what sounded to him like real regret, "You know, I'm afraid," he said, "that our time is up."

Kessler lifted his wristwatch, a large oblong stainless-steel face on his thin wrist, close to his eyes. He tilted his head again, then slowly shook it. "Really? It's—well, no matter. Though I've hardly—"

"If you'll telephone, we'll see about an appointment."

Kessler sighed, then leaned to close and strap his briefcase. Then he stood, and reached to the inner breast pocket of his jacket.

"No," Alex said, "the accountant sends out bills."

"You control time, and he controls money, eh?" Kessler said.

"Well," Alex said, "let's say that he controls money. Goodbye, then."

"But I'll see you again," Kessler said, his taut face anxious.

Wondering about that, but trying not to lie a second time, Alex said, "We'll do it by phone."

"Life at one remove," Kessler said. He stood before Alex, holding his briefcase.

Then Kessler extended his hand and Alex felt he had to take it. The hand was light, the palm damp, the grip briefly and surprisingly powerful. Kessler smiled, as if they had agreed. "So here we are," he said. "Brothers."

When, several years before, he had sat in the Packard Road nursing home in Ann Arbor, either sleeping or waking to watch his father sleep, Alex sometimes thought he heard the air leak squeakily up from his father's flattened ribs and rattling chest. Sometimes, with his eyes closed, he listened to what he would describe as oxygen passing through the transparent nostril tubes. But what he really thought he heard was a whispering, through the walls or from the room above, of the same sentence—it meant nothing, it addressed no one—over and over and again. Sometimes he thought that he could hear the leathery lungs as they faltered, but then drove on. He squinted at the sunlight that lay against the white cotton curtains and the tilted plastic blinds. He smelled the dampness of the hot room, its peppery, sweet odor of steam and astringents and skin. He watched the gray-white face and especially the large eyelids that were never still. The eyes seemed to roll and surge beneath them, or perhaps, Alex thought, the lids were on the verge of sliding up so that Januscz's eyes would be fully upon him, staring with the power of knowledge gathered and saved over more than seventy years to be given now, a truth about a father's love that his son could use against the hugeness of the coming death. But the eyelids were locked, the breathing difficult as if through baffles of wet cloth, and nothing came from his father that either man could use.

Alex thought of his wife, who complained that she no longer could reach him. He recalled with distaste his unfunny little joke that if *he* could reach him, he would set himself before her as an offering. Liz had answered, "I don't want offerings, Alex. But I'd love your company." He closed his eyes and imagined whom Liz might be looking to for company.

His father moved and the bed shifted. Alex opened his eyes and his stomach pulsed when he saw that Januscz had opened his. But there was no message on his father's face. It was shadowed, it was bloodless, and it was—he would swear this afterward—contemplative.

Looking at the corner of the wall behind Alex, or at some time remembered, or some place imagined, his father raised his head from the pillow and said, in his lovely, deep voice, a barbed consonantal knot that meant nothing to Alex. He said the thorny syllables as if intending them reasonably, in reply to a reasonable question. Then he lay back and coughed, gagging, and then he grew quiet, and then his breathing became regular, and then he was deep in the long tilt toward nothing of his sleep.

Alex took his notebook from an inside pocket of his sport coat and he did as in his practice he was supposed to: he took notes. He wrote phonetically what he thought he might have heard. He would not ask his mother about the words he guessed had been Polish, for her face went angry, almost cruel, when he spoke to her of his father. Or, somehow worse, she grew pale and very still, wary with a knowledge she refused to share, when Alex described him in the nursing home or asked about their shared past, So, several weeks later, he asked the genial, squat Solly Vinokur, the translator fluent in several languages, who lived in his building, for help. Over a pot of green tea that Solly insisted on brewing, in the blue-white light of the lamps that warmed his plants, they reconstructed the sounds, and Alex now had in his notebook *Niemiecki wiezien.* He had the phonetic mess he had taken down, and he had this: his father had possibly said, in Polish, "The German prisoner."

So, he'd thought, he had nothing. For his father had never spoken to him, or to his mother in Alex's hearing, about such a person. His mother had not mentioned a German prisoner. She would die alone, to be discovered in the morning curled, like a child, around her pillow. On her bed would be photographs, one of her mother, a sturdy woman in a figured dress with wide skirts, and one of Alex in a wicker pram on a street in England where they had lived a few years of the Second World War. The street on which his mother stands unsmiling behind his pram stretches away from dark brick apartment buildings beneath rows of clotheslines suspended between the upper windows of the building nearby and the windows of the building across the street. Wrinkled laundry suspended above the child and his mother appears heavy and unmoved by the wind against which they seem to squint.

Alone now in his office, clenching and unclenching the hand that Kessler's little hand had gripped, Alex scorned himself for believing in ghosts. But he knew that he had, in a manner of speaking—"Life at one remove," in Kessler's words—just touched the German prisoner.

NOW, AT SIX P.M., the patient was Anthony Slowacki, Transit Authority patrolman, who was there because his watch commander required that he see a therapist. He was a contract assignment which Alex had received at the recommendation of a civil servant known to Teddy Levenson, who was Alex's closest friend, the psychiatrist who prescribed for Alex's patients, and possibly—possibly—the man who was consoling Liz, who needed consolation precisely, Alex thought, because she *was* his wife. Slowacki was there because his watch commander had required it. A very old Filipino man, dazed and wordless, apparently lost on the 42nd Street shuttle and traveling its loop from East Side to West for hours, was observed and then questioned by Slowacki. Receiving no response except a staring, expressionless face, Slowacki had begun to shriek and point and threaten him until the old man had fainted. *Brother*, Alex had written at the start of Slowacki's session, and then he'd crossed it out, not with a single horizontal line but with a diagonal stroke through every letter, and then with a furious vertical scribble that looked like the stuttered theta waves on the EEG of a damaged brain. His pen broke through the page on which he was to note what his patient had said, and Slowacki paused, looking up, as if he had heard the pen against the page. But he hadn't, Alex knew. Just as the therapist was locked inside his thoughts, so the patient heard only his own: the rote and largely disbelieving defense of what was, more than likely, another routine rape by Anthony Slowacki of Maureen, his wife.

Alex nodded, and Slowacki closed his eyes again, and leaned back into the broad, thick armchair, and said, "And that's because it is not rape. Easy. Simple. No argument. Because it's not. Doc, I'm in fucking *law enforcement*! You think I don't know what is it, rape? I pull the animals off of these women in the subway! I don't know what's rape?"

This man, Alex thought, and all of the others—the wife beaters, the child abusers, the women outraged at being called dykes, the psychotics equipped with sidearms who trembled with rage, and of course the civilians in his practice who were constant blinkers, or insomniacs reliving all night their long day's failure, the affectless in their terror, the loveless in their despair—each of these people was, according to his training and commitment and oath, to receive his attention. He was to listen to their every word. And he no longer did, no longer could.

As now. He sat up and leaned his pen upon his page. For he had lost Slowacki and had heard, again, his moments with the tall, pale, elegant woman who had come to his practice only several months ago. She had wished to be healed, and had despaired of any healing.

"Why," he remembered her asking, "does an adult really *need* a father? Fathers die, after all, and we go on."

He said, "I'll call you Nella if I may. Or do you prefer Ms. Grensen?"

She shrugged, and he reveled in the stiff, balletic dip of her broad shoulders and tense, long arms.

He said, "Why a father is what *you* have to answer. I'll try and help, of course."

"I know," she said, not knowing. How could she? How could he not? He was the doctor, Alexander Lescziak, Ph.D., and he was going to be her lover. Even in this first session, he was thinking ahead to a time when he would speak of her as a vast event in his past. He heard, in his voice, *had to have her*, and he despised himself. It was the forty-fifth year of his life, a busy time in a crowded practice, the year—he thought it would happen quite soon—of the end of his marriage, and, according to the *New York Times*, the year when his President would fly to Europe to lay a wreath on the graves of several dozen Waffen SS. The Republic, he thought, was lost to this cunning, stupid man, and Liz, his wife, was lost to Alex, as was

Nella—vanished, and possibly dead—and Slowacki had said, "I could kill for a cigarette, Doc."

"Don't kill for anything," Alex answered.

Slowacki, slender and strong-looking, with long arms and broad hands, said, "No."

His hands were still, and so was his narrow face. But the lip on which his dark brown mustache lived—Alex thought of it as a separate creature—jumped, from time to time, and Alex watched it: Slowacki's betrayer.

You get to work, Alex said to himself, and he heard himself project a thin, unthreatening voice: "May I ask, do you hold your wife's arms during sex?"

"She says to." The mustache moved.

"Before or during?"

"What's the difference, Doc? You want to know how to question somebody? I'm a professional. It's one of the things I have to do. It's a professional activity. I don't ride fucking subway trains all night to, you know, *get* someplace. I apprehend felons. I ask them what I need to know. Why not, for example, ask me if my wife knows I'm here?"

"Good question," Alex said. "Does she?"

The patient's tinted glasses kept his face unreadable. It would be the mustache, Alex knew.

"No," Slowacki said. "That tell you anything?"

"Not necessarily. But you need to know this. I am not trying to find you guilty of something. I don't think you did something wrong."

"Then how come I'm here? Who does?"

Alex said, "Maybe you."

"*I'm* the perpetrator, I thought."

"Maybe it's an idea you have."

"And I apprehended myself?"

"It happens."

"Not to a Polack named Slowacki it doesn't."

At a similar point in another patient's treatment—Regina Zimmerman, who was a professor in her forties, very thin, her eye sockets hollowed by sleeplessness and the flesh about the fingers torn to scabbed stripes—she had scolded, "Why haven't you asked me about my childhood?" As with Slowacki, the patient had signaled readiness, had held the door, with courtesy, ajar. Instead of walking through, however, Alex had thought of the heavy front door of his childhood house in the middle west, and he thought again that it should have been a house filled with wailing, a chambered cave of Polish sorrows, and instead it had been a two-story silence in which they waited. There were human noises, of course, but the dominant sound, he thought, had always been the audible gathering intensity of his mother. He remembered waiting for his father to sigh or to clear his throat whisperingly, and for his mother, in turn, to move a platter, or a pen, as if it were the next phrase in a wordless conversation.

I was an only child, he thought he heard himself think. Closing his eyes, and closing out one patient, and the memory of another, he realized what he had possibly said to himself: *I was only a child*. He pitied the boy, cold in their rooms even in the damp, sultry August of the middle west, waiting for the waiting to be over with, for something he could recognize—say, grief—to have begun. Something did, he thought. It was anger, the cousin to sorrow, our oldest living relative, perhaps, and the one we always wished to eschew like, say, an unsuspected and even perhaps—why not admit it?—unwanted brother.

But he hadn't heard Regina Zimmerman until she was well into the recitation of her story. As if the wavelength, at last, had been tuned, he heard her say, "But it wasn't, you see? It was my sister." He did not see. He did not hear. Obviously, he thought, it was her sister *again*. Once more, the sister was favored—was perceived to be favored. You get to choose a direction at the forking of the paths: illusion to the left, history to the right. Or: to the left, an error in perception which had grown into a habit of seeing and to the right, what someone authoritative—parents, maybe her doctor—would claim had actually occurred. Though maybe they were shits, her parents, and they had played favorites and mistreated her. And maybe he, Alexander Lescziak, was a shit, and was failing to help her understand why she had needed to see her sister as the favored one.

He thought this as Slowacki argued his innocence. He loved to talk, this man who claimed to feel forced by his commanders to consult with the therapist. As with Regina Zimmerman's and too many other sessions, he was steering the hour from habit, as a drunk paws the wheel to roll his car up the proper driveway at night. He should have found her another therapist. He should find one for Slowacki. He should turn himself in to the Ethics Committee. Or take a long vacation. Or have Teddy Levenson find him someone to talk to. Or get himself dosed on a tricyclic, he thought.

Claims she wants to be held down in bed, he wrote.

Possibility, he wrote. He was about to ask Slowacki whether he thought his wife might affect to enjoy, for the sake of his attention, what she might not desire. But, instead, he thought of what he had said to Regina Zimmerman—"When did you and your sister most recently speak?"—and of what she had replied: "Do you think of me as a client or as a patient, Dr. Lescziak?"

"Which would you prefer?" he'd asked her. And they were off. And he was in command again, apparently. But of course he was failing her, as, this afternoon, he was failing this tough, angry, stymied policeman.

"That," Teddy Levenson would say, "is what makes therapy sessions. And the minutes of the Liars' Club. It's how the record gets written," Teddy would say, "so come to terms with it, Alex."

But, Alex remembered, he had bailed the water from his little boat, he had steered by the compass and the stars, saying to Regina Zimmerman, "Could we return later to how I think of my patients"—not just how I think of you, my volunteer for transference—"and could we perhaps talk a little more about your sister?"

"Your speech," she said, "it's so—careful. Is that a foreign accent?"

"Indeed," he told her. "Michigan. And now, your long-awaited sister, if you will. She's possibly why you're here."

And he had rescued some of the hour from himself for her. He tried it, as well, with Slowacki. He noted,

Agitation re suggestion that she dislikes the violence he says she wants.

"Does she ever strike you, Mr. Slowacki?"

"You can call me Anthony. Tony, if you want. Officer, even."

"Thank you. May I ask: do you ever ask your wife, at intimate moments, to be rough with you?"

"You mean, you know, pull on this, pinch that—that kind of thing?"

"Maybe."

"No. I don't like to be distracted. And it wouldn't be proper. You know? A man asking for that?"

He didn't respond.

"The man does the man thing, the woman does the other."

"The other?"

"The stuff you were talking about. You know."

"Would you object to being specific?"

"Doc. It is not right for the man to let his voice get shrill, he loses his bearing and begs the woman to do something for him. He tells her, if it's one of the—you know: 'Do this,' he says to her. Nice. You're making love, after all. But he says it, she does it, and that's the end of the conversation."

Tell it to Liz Lescziak, he thought, missing Slowacki's next few sentences, vowing, as he began to listen again, that he would make up for the lapses in their next session, if he could convince him to return. Thinking of returns, of failures to return, he continued to fail to listen. He was hearing Delilah Rose, a sweet, beaten patient who had married a prisoner of New

York State. She was a widow by the time her brother had convinced her to see someone. Alex Lescziak was the someone. She sat in the Gustav Stickley chair now occupied by Anthony Slowacki, who spoke unheeded, and she told her therapist of bloody handprints on the floor: the décor of her dreams. The handprints were hers, she dreamed, and they were, in fact, hers. For her late husband had beaten her palms and arches when he tied her still and flayed her with a choker chain designed for large dogs. He began on his second night away from prison, on parole. They had married after she visited him for a year, as part of what she saw as her Christian mission. She had been a Seventh-Day Adventist of her own special sort, and he had been a nonobserving Jew. He had beaten a man almost to death while committing armed robbery.

And they had made no progress. "I think you're right, in a sense, to be having these dreams," Alex had told her. "He was brutal and cruel in his repayment of your generosity. I think he must have been damaged irreparably. Like many abusers, he was condemned to pass the damage along. Unfortunately, he had access to you."

Her reading: "He was ill. He needed to learn to trust. I couldn't teach him how. I failed."

"Well, you certainly paid for your so-called failure. Why do you think it was you, of all people, who was responsible for teaching your husband to trust? Does Henry agree that you were responsible?"

"My brother has nothing to do with this."

Everything, everything, everything. But how to

define a brother? "I see."

"I don't think you do."

"You don't?" Anthony Slowacki again, because Alex, it seemed, had spoken to him instead of to Delilah Rose. "What?"

"Sorry," Alex said. "Maybe I didn't understand you."

"You looked like you were someplace else, Doc."

"No," he said, "not at all. I'm wondering—"

"Sure. Go ahead. You can ask me anything you want."

"You're enjoying this process," Alex said.

Slowacki's mustache lay still, but the face around it moved a little, tightening. He smiled for the first time in the hour, which was up. "Yeah, I have to say you're right. You could be right." He nodded once, then again, then again.

"So come back," Alex said. "We'll talk some more."

"You think we're making progress, Doc?"

"How do you feel?"

Slowacki took his tinted glasses off and rubbed his eyes. They looked exhausted, weak. He nodded as if in agreement. "Tired," he said.

"Because you're working," Alex said.

"I am?"

"I believe you are."

"Well, that makes two of us, Doc. I'm not easy. My wife says that to me all the time. 'You ain't easy, Tony.' I guess I'm not. But there you are, analyzing me. This is analyzing, right?"

"Analysis."

"Right."

"Yes," the therapist told him, "yes, it is, in a way."

"You sound discouraged, Doc."

"Oh, the time's up, now, I'm afraid. But, no, I'm not."

"Hang in there, all right? I mean, if I do have some kind of a problem, which I don't believe I do, I should get it corrected. You agree?"

"I do."

"So do I."

"That's a fine first step."

Slowacki looked pleased, as if by an accomplishment, and Alex thought of the patient called Pal—"Call me Pal," he'd instructed—who was really Solomon Soderkrantz. He was a hive of anxieties, and of course he came each week a half an hour early, to sit in the tiny anteroom, once a very large closet, what the English called a box room, and chew on his fingers, tighten his tie, line the edges of his shoes up, clear and clear and clear his throat. He endured the discomfort he constructed for himself, he kept his job as a clerk in the Herald Square post office, and he mourned the loss of his wife and two children. They had left, she to live in sin—Soderkrantz's language: sin—because she hadn't, said she couldn't have, waited to divorce him. The lover, who owned a bottled water delivery service for the Oranges, in New Jersey, was raising the children as his own. And Soderkrantz was no one's Pal.

As early as he came, Alex came late. He crushed a forefinger in the door, one day, and therefore was delayed. He took a nap in their adjacent apartment and overslept. He lost the pen he favored for note taking, so had to search lengthily, delaying another session's start. He forgot an appointment. How does a doctor *forget*? He doesn't. Or: he wants to. So of course he had to dismiss him, Soderkrantz who was already so thoroughly dismissed. It was textbook countertransference, and Pal was Alex, and Alex was his Pal: the man whose family had fled him. "For your own sake," he had told him, "I am suggesting that another doctor see you. He agrees to. He's very good. Dr. Chandrai, a lovely fellow, and very competent. You'll be fine."

Soderkrantz squatted in the chair, his thick thighs pressing at his trouser legs, his wide feet in frayed sneakers planted, as if the turning of the earth might pitch him from his perch. He gripped the wooden chair arms. He squinted out of thick smudged lenses, peering as if at Lesceiak's language, as if he interpreted an alien tongue. Even his oval, hairless head was smudged, with something purple, perhaps from the post office.

"But he won't know about me."

"Yes, he will, Solomon. I'll tell him everything."

He cleared his throat and gripped his hands, then seized again at the arms of the chair. "Everything," he said.

"You've done nothing wrong."

"Good."

"Sometimes things occur in the course of therapy, and it's wise to acknowledge them early, and then to move on."

"It's something you—"

"Yes."

"Something *I* didn't—"

"Right."

"Right," he said.

"Okay, Pal?"

He beamed like a boy on his birthday. And Alex, alone in his office, Slowacki gone, now, for several minutes, remembered remembering Soderkrantz's broad face, as innocent as some of childhood, and a birthday party in Ann Arbor, for Madeleine Cohn, the suzeraine of his preadolescent dreaming, and then his mother on a stormy middle western night, and, somehow, inevitably, Nella Grensen—missing from the city, now, and from his life—when, months before, they had first made love.

His patient become his transgression, his betrayal of his studies and his ethics and his oaths, lay facedown on their damp bedclothes, and he ran his fingers on her buttocks and thighs. She spread her legs, and he wished that the room weren't dark so he could see his hands on her.

"This is delicious," she said, "but are you sure? At your age, remember, it takes a lot longer to heal when something's broken."

"I am so sure." His hand gripped at the buttock muscle it was stroking before he sensed that it would. "I'm sure," he said. She flexed the big muscle against his hand and then let it lie slack. He kneaded it like bread. She gave him her undefended softness by moving toward his hand. His penis felt sore, his lower back ached, and he luxuriated in his complaints—in the simply having acquired them—by saying, too smugly, "Anyway, I don't think anything's broken."

"Oh, Alex," she said, as if she had just learned terrible news. "Your heart," she said. "You wait and see."

Alex waited. Now he saw. And he remembered now, alone in his office, the practice of counseling suspended as his thoughts were, of the iciest end of March in 1985, less than a month ago, as he and Teddy Levenson, a couple of burly shapes in overcoats worn against the dirty lingering slush and the slick, hard mud of almost-spring—he closed his eyes, in his office, and he saw them, heard them—went around and around the reservoir in Central Park. Their pace was slow. It was no health walk, unless the health was mental. Teddy, the almost unrepentant Freudian, taller and broader than Alex, and huge beside Liz, large in their lives, said, "I am thinking of Anna O."

Alex said, "Do you think Breuer was dipping it in Anna and Freud was jealous?"

"She died a virgin," Teddy said. "And smut hasn't ever become you. You're too formal for it. Too self-protective. Dirty talk, with you, comes across as gesture, a clumsy machismo."

"Liz says I sound like an asshole when I tell dirty stories. Would that be your implication?"

"Asshole will do it, fundamentally. I was thinking of what Anna called the process."

" 'The talking cure,' " Alex said. "Of course, I see the direction we're going in. The answer is no. But thank you."

"She also called it time travel, Alex, but what Breuer wrote to Freud, what I have in mind, was that his

38

patient called it, also, 'the chimney cleaning.' You could use a terrific chimney cleaning."

"You want me on some analyst's couch."

"Don't you sound like a patient instead of a doctor! Alex, fine: I want you on some good doctor's couch. I really want you on a small, elegant, purple pill."

"Why not just addict me to Valium?"

"Imipramine is what I have in mind. Seventy-five milligrams b.i.d., to start."

"Because I need a chimney cleaning."

"Alex, you need a chimney *fire*."

"My doctor in graduate school," Alex said, "was turning against Freud."

"So was everybody else. Why was your analyst confessing to you?"

"He was boasting, Teddy. He was crowing. Cock-a-doodle-doo: he thought Freud abandoned a lot of kids who were complaining they'd been abused. Freud was diagnosing them as cases of repressed sexual desire because *Freud* was repressing his own, for Fliess and for other men."

Teddy said, "Don't be offended if I yawn, all right?" He gave a great, exaggerated, theatrical yawn. "Old news, of course. You know that. Because what if he was? It doesn't matter. Whatever he was, whatever he wasn't, he was a great philosopher. He saw the Dead Sea inside of everyone, and he described it. He was the one who saw the only way to survive it. You know the words. *Love*, he said, and *work*. Do you have them, Alex?" Teddy had stopped, with his hand on Alex's sleeve, but Alex pulled away.

"Probably," Alex said. "Of course. I mean— But you know, I'd rather not have this conversation, Teddy, if you can bear to avoid medicating me on the spot."

"I apologize," Teddy said. "I was—"

"Worried. I know. Liz is worried. You're worried. I have to tell you, sometimes I'm worried. But worry: that's what you get by living an adult life, Teddy. Let me—I wanted to tell you about an *actual* patient. Not me, but one of mine thanks to you. A transit cop. Very violent guy, and early in the intake he says something about how 'every shift's a patrol, and every rider's a dink.' That, he said, was how he saw it on especially bad days or nights—hazardous-feeling tours of duty, or times when he was tense."

"Dinks. Very nice," Teddy said.

"We haven't gotten to it yet, but we're clearly talking about Vietnam. Yes?"

"Or a Vietnam pretender. A number of those are coming into the literature. All males, so far—no surprise—who claim to have served with distinction and hazard but who really never came close to active duty or to Southeast Asia," Teddy said. " And why *not* wish to be a hero?"

"Why, on the other hand, live a fantasy?"

"Because you feel better?"

Alex said, "Did you mean *I* feel better?"

As they stepped solemnly among the runners and the health walkers, Teddy shrugged and Alex, close beside him, felt the motion. "You may be *wanting* this patient to have been in Vietnam. Maybe he's just an average racist. Some sort of functioning paranoidal fascist with a manic rage and a need for significant doses of an antipsychotic. Is he acting out?"

Alex said, "Yes, in a sort of controlled but very dangerous way. But hold on. Wait a minute, Teddy. I may *want* this? I'm projecting with this patient?"

Again, Alex felt the shrug of the long arm, the heavy shoulder, the bulky coat.

"Why would I do that?"

"Alex, you're thinking this fellow is repressing a war he was in. I'm suggesting that—*possibly*, now, far from certainly—*you're* projecting on him the war you *haven't* been in but *feel* that you have. I don't mean in Asia, fifteen years ago. You know. An embattled state is like a war. You think he's transmitting to himself the memories of the war he hides from. Well, sure. Yes. Textbook stuff. All I'm saying is it's possible—*possible*—you are feeling at war and his is a screen for your own. Your patient's a doppelganger, and you're coping with a war you've not participated in historically, externally. But in the real combat zone—" Teddy had stopped walking, and Alex turned to see him point at his own belly, then up at his own forehead. Then he aimed his great hand with its long forefinger at Alex.

Alex said, "In the chimney, you fucking Freudian monster bastard?"

Teddy smiled broadly, then resumed his pace, passing Alex, who turned to follow.

"You love my insights," Teddy said.

"You're six times too wide to be a chimney sweep," Alex said.

But it was not the image of the chimney that stayed

with him; it was time travel, that sense of jumping, like slides in an old-fashioned viewer, or the frames of an 8mm movie. He remembered it, and he remembered the suck of their city man's street shoes, the heavy leather soles and stylish, narrow toes, against the icy mud of winter's slow conclusion. And he remembered the concern in Teddy's voice, contained at a level below his banter, and how it frightened him then, as it did now. Because he thought he might be falling, in a clinical tailspin. He thought of airplanes shot down by peasants with SAM missile launchers that crashed into the canopied rain forests of Southeast Asia. Because he often wished for something—purple or light blue, small, tight, potent—that might keep him from marching the neurotic's mental quickstep, with no destination, on streets where he hadn't errands or pleasure, but where he stared at pedestrians because, apparently, he continued to believe he would pitch up against Nella's narrow body, her long legs and short trunk, her big hands on long arms, her neck that went on and on—the dancer gone bad, he had teased her. It was a drunk's favorite love song, he thought, a witless lyric about the loss of his final romance. But he saw no doctor except among the hospital staff when he ran a group or visited patients, and except for Teddy, who could not treat his closest friend, but who nevertheless informally tried. He saw his own patients, and, also, he saw his life as Anna O, the Ur Psychiatric Patient, the virgin mother of them all, had described the process of seeing her own: time travel.

Which brought him, in his office while he considered

patients and his conversations with his friend, to the thirteenth birthday party of Madeleine Cohn of Ann Arbor, Michigan, in June, he thought, of 1954. There was a chimney fire of sorts, the one on her parents' massive brick backyard barbecue. Her father cooked kosher hot dogs and fat hamburgers which were served with grainy mustard instead of the yellow ooze preferred by kids. Later, in what her parents called the family room, vast and cold, littered with large, bright cushions on the blue slate floor, the children squirmed, and the boys jockeyed for proximity to Maddy and her full breasts, her round thighs, her feet so almost naked in her ballerina shoes, her pimpled face scarlet with embarrassment and appetite under her bright blond hair tied back. They watched movies shot by her father. Maddy, oh, Jesus, naked at six months (and screaming, now, into a pillow not too far from Alex's), Maddy at four and boring, Maddy at five, and on, until, at half past eleven, her breasts began and the movie, awkwardly edited so that it jumped and sprocketed without transition, from vacation home out east to Ann Arbor backyard, from then to now to a little after before and then to nearly just this minute, made its crooked way from place to place, from time to time, every new image leaping into sight before he could prepare himself to see. It was not so different now, he thought, except that his lust was directed at slender and strong instead of pudgy and pubescent. Except that Liz was in the adjacent apartment, in all her power and woundedness. Except that *this* time travel seemed to have nothing to do with the talking cure, with any cure at all.

"Ma," he had asked, after he ached his way home from the party and had come upstairs to their room, where his father read in his bed, his mother curved around her headache in hers, "how come we don't have any picture albums? Or movies? Did you ever shoot movies?"

"We carry pictures here," she had answered, pointing at her head, then his. She touched his forehead gently, and he closed his eyes. When he opened them, hers were huge and dark and pained, then closed. Tapping at her forehead and wincing, she said, "In here, we are seeing every moment."

"We see," he corrected automatically.

"Of course," she'd replied.

LIZ SAID, "I'm all right. But how are you?"

"Are we business associates? We ran into each other in the, I don't know, the club car of the Westport train?"

Liz looked at him with her enormous pale blue eyes as if to discover who was talking. She shook her head. "No," she said. "We've kept missing each other, the last couple of days. I was just wondering, really, how you were doing."

"Oh, fine, sweetheart. I'm fine. Excuse me for— Jesus, Liz, anything you'd care to excuse me for I'd accept." He heard himself snicker a nervous, social laugh and he watched her keep her expression bland. She was frightened for him, he thought. This bold woman with her fan of stiff, gray hair and her alarming attentiveness—she made people nervous, he knew,

44

when she listened hard and watched them while they spoke—this woman to be reckoned with was scared.

He lost his own courage. He had thought to tell her something of Slowacki's story, and how he was guessing—after Teddy's comments, hoping—that he would learn Slowacki had served in Vietnam or had seen terrible carnage underground, in the subways. He wished to say nothing about William Kessler and his remarkable, but really quite credible, story. Nor, of course, did he want to speak of Nella Grensen. But all of them, and others, were in the air. And Liz was frightened for him—possibly *of* him. And Nella, he thought, might be dead. And here they were, suspended above 90th and Central Park West, vessels of illness anchored in the sky. He wondered what his face looked like to Liz, or to the pedestrians he stared at as he walked and walked, staring because one of them might be the patient he had committed adultery, malpractice, and despair with before she disappeared, in what he feared was an act of vengeful self-destruction—you kill two for the price of one—and whose voice he heard, as he tried to hear his patients', and as he so frequently failed.

"You all right?" he asked Liz.

"You already asked me, honey."

"Sorry," he said, "sorry. Sorry, Liz."

Her face made clear to him that she knew, as he did, that he was out of control. She let her head droop on its strong neck, but then she sat straight again, on their tobacco-colored sofa which was centered under one of her most powerful paintings from the late seventies.

He was grateful to see that her eyes were not running with tears, for weeping made her eyes look even paler, and he thought of them as a hunting bird's, feral, merciless, although he knew they weren't meant to be. He had damaged her, yet she had not left. Her loyalty or perhaps decorum punished him. He thought she did not mean to. It was who Liz was: the person who stayed with you. If she were a mother, he thought, some child would live with profit in the lee of that persevering, hopeful emotion.

"Liz," he said, "don't let it turn to despair."

"What? Turn what?"

He shook his head. He didn't dare say it. That was where they were, now: in the echo of syllables, in the eddying of unspoken words. He betrayed his patients and his wife. He was faithful only to his sorrow. He was wasting their time. He was doing far worse. And even at such a moment, he thought. Even at this moment, he thought, while Liz managed not to weep, crystals of color slowly popped on the grainy, bright, overexposed movie frames, and the images jumped— from Liz, her long, curly, gray-white hair and bluest of eyes, to Nella Grensen, dark in the darkness, pale against the pallor of the sheets, her eyes invisible, her voice muffled but insistent as he labored to hear her, to understand what her skin meant on his at that disappearing instant. He pierced her and pierced her, in every way he could, and she permitted it, encouraged it, and yet she remained impenetrable. She was always sorry, even when he thought her jubilant, breathless, triumphant.

"It is so sweet," she said. "You are so sweet."

And he, his breath whistling and his chest wet, his heart hammering like a hand at the hotel door—rapid, regular, malevolent—he managed to say, "No, Nell. *You're* sweet. You."

And even then, in the darkness, her head would shake, the fleeting glimmer of her eyes would escape him as she finally closed them and turned, beneath him, away, so that he would shift off her, and lie alone in bed with her, and think of how many codes he had, a moment ago, violated. So she was a virgin every time.

"As much fun as dying," he wanted, once, to tell Teddy, so that Teddy could somehow tell Liz that he was deceitful and that he hated himself and that his pleasure was no fun. It was Nella's language. It was what she said, and more than once, when she called him at the hotel where he sat away from the bed and waited for her, and then waited, reading the bound magazine, supplied with the room, about the attractions of New York. When she called, he was sick with disappointment and need, but he was not surprised. And he welcomed the punishment, he understood.

It would be on the night of such a day, having staggered through his practice, having received the last-minute call from Nella, that he would drift through the apartment after a sandwich and a glass of wine, then stand at the threshold of their door when he heard Liz turning the lock after working with her graduate students at Hunter or, he had thought more than once, after pursuing with Teddy in his apartment or her

47

studio on Greene Street a kind of comfort he found too easy to imagine. This time he kissed her on the mouth and bit her lip a little, and she stood stiffly and then, suddenly, relaxed against him and returned the kiss. Then she stiffened again. Of course, he thought. She was confused. After weeks—after months, he thought—of bruised, embarrassed separateness, he had used a different vocabulary of manner and touch. Now he must seem like somebody else. He sensed her fatigue—not the tiredness of teaching, but the flulike weariness, the throbbing head and smarting eyes that were caused by trying to sense the emotions of someone far removed. It was, in a sense, what he did every hour or so in his practice. Once, he thought, it had exhilarated him; now, often, it seemed an intrusion.

"I'm so hungry," she said. "Would you like a salad?"

He smiled and shook his head.

"Sandwich? I think there's flank steak left."

"I ate it," he said. "I'm full."

"Anything?"

"You," he said.

"Oh, Alex." She closed her eyes and shook her head.

"No, Liz?"

"Honey, I wasn't saying no. I was saying . . . I'm puzzled, let's say. And I'm not crying. Don't worry. I am not going to cry."

"God knows you're allowed to cry, Liz."

She shook her head. She looked at the floor and then at him. Her eyes were magnified by the tears she wouldn't acknowledge. The pain in them, and the distance of which they spoke, dried his mouth and stung his eyes. They stood before each other at their doorway, and Alex waited for Liz to speak. He didn't think, that instant, of Nella. He thought of all the words that he and Liz had exchanged, and how he thought he knew which words she'd choose. But he would wait to hear, as if the words were new, and he would repair them as a couple. That was his work. He listened to the narrative, he heard its sense, he culled its truth, and he helped to make repairs. It was what his work required. It was what he wished to do, he thought.

He cupped his palm beneath her chin, as he often had done, and, as she often did in response, she leaned the weight of her head—with all its conscious, unsaid language, as well as the forgotten dreams she dreamed in the separateness of her sleep—and closed her eyes, and so, for an instant, did he. But then he was alert and watching her, and then pitying her, and then he was thinking that even those few sleeplike seconds of repose were never available to Nella. The betrayal must have moved in his nerves and through the temperature, the tremor, of his hand. For Liz blinked as though he had shouted, and she looked at him as if she thought that he might wish to make an announcement. But of course he didn't. And of course she sensed his reserve. She smiled a grateful, sad smile, and he was hurt, as if by a gash that opened the skin, to see how she had welcomed his hand. Then she stepped back from it, and he returned it to his side and leaned against the wall, closing the door as she went past him down the hall.

"It's pouring. My clothes are soaked," she said, in a tense, friendly voice. "I need to change." So she had told him that she'd be naked briefly, and that he still could follow her down the hall and turn off to the bedroom instead of walking back toward the living-room sofa and something to drink or nothing to drink and a book he would forget as he read, or television dementia, and then the silence afterward. He hadn't known that it was raining. Liz was home, so their failure would not be consummated, tonight, by her leaving. She was safely home. Liz was safe as houses. He heard his mother's voice, at night, in the gray, humid August heat of the 1950s in Ann Arbor, when lightning storms were brilliantly reflected on the bright white paint of the woodwork in their hallway and danced on the light green linoleum of his bedroom floor. His mother sat beside him in her nightgown, the ample flesh of her arms cool, her breath a dark intimacy carried from her sleep, and the furrows at her mouth invisible until the lightning exploded. Despite the heat, she pulled his sheet up and she lay briefly—shockingly, he thought—upon him, so that he felt the weight, the reality, of her breasts.

"You are protected," she had intoned in a whisper. "Safe as houses," she promised him.

"Ma," he asked her, not knowing that he would, "how can you be safe if men can come to your door?"

"Men? No men coming here."

"The ones because of Jews who knock on the door." He whispered, "Bang-bang." Then: "They take you away, Daddy says."

"Daddy," she said, "is knowing *nothing*. You see? Nothing." She explained, in her husky rasps and thick vowels, that she had learned about safe-as-houses during their years—*our* years—in the northwest of England, when she and Januscz were among the few hundred who sailed from Warsaw aboard the *St. Louis* and were permitted by the English to disembark.

"No men are coming to door, it means," she said.

"Houses are really the safest?" he asked her.

The lightning jumped, the room flickered. "What is being safer?" she asked.

"What *is* safer, Ma," he said, even then.

And she, of course, replied, "Of course."

Liz was out of sight, and Alex continued to stand in their hallway as if, he thought, he were awaiting an arrival at the door.

HE COULD NOT telephone an elderly Lescziak aunt, and there weren't travel-battered albums to check. He had family questions, but there wasn't any longer a family to place them before. There was only Alex, a child of the New World, an adopted son of New York. Thinking of England, and a man named William Kessler and Kessler's faceless father, thinking of his mother but looking for Nella on the streets, he walked down Central Park West and then across 59th to Fifth, and then the seventeen blocks to the Main Branch with its palace steps and great stone lions. He flinched from the catalogue system but he crawled his way through it. He inspected the categories of his convictions and his dreads, seeking what might be—would have to serve as—the history of his dwindled family, which might be larger, perhaps, than he had thought.

In the enormous Reading Room, at one of the long oak tables, in the glowing green light of the lamps' glass shades, he read in the sparse available history of Barrow-in-Furness. Was it, he wondered, his mother's ultimate, buried story, even its possibility, that drew him? It was a gamble, he thought, to leave for awfully long. Each long absence by either of them was a bet against their continuing. He turned from them to a collection of reminiscences that had run in a Furness paper called the *Evening Mail*. He waited forty minutes for the book to be located and brought out, and mentally, he thought, he was panting by the time it arrived: the cover smudged-looking, the typography spiky, the paper thin and damp to the touch; this was a frail vessel to embark on, but he climbed aboard. Much of the prose felt, somehow, sepia in tone, with an affection for the fearfulness of the time, and deprivation, and reserves of what was called "British spirit." A man three chairs away from him insisted upon snorting repetitively at his mucus, which seemed to be choking him.

Poor guy, he thought.

But what he said, loudly, was "Jesus!"

He could imagine Nella's thick eyebrows rising. He could imagine Liz's stare. The man with allergies or ailments snorted and sucked. Alex read and dreamed, he dozed with his head up, he traveled through the language and the paper that composted as he handled it— he was in history's midden, working back against time—and he saw his parents' England and he followed his mother in the night.

Imagine how, in 1941, the Luftwaffe sent waves of bombers at the Vickers sheds in Barrow, where warships and cargo vessels, the frail nation's lifeline, were built. Streets were blown up, houses destroyed. People were heroic, and bus conductresses voted on whether to wear slacks while on duty. Their moderate decision: skirts in summer, slacks from November 1. The vote was seven in favor, one opposed. Alexander was born to Januscz and Sylvia that year. The German prisoners came in heaviest numbers at the same time—food was meager and bad—as shoppers were said to giddily report a sighting of Spanish onions in the shops. The moment of the apparition of onions was, according to William Kessler, the time of his father's arrival. In the room that had served as classroom for some of New York's great writers, under the ceiling high and broad enough to be the sky of a small village, and surrounded by the hidden books of entire civilizations, he saw the dark, wet cobbles of a cold Lancashire street, and he felt his father's puzzled silence, and saw the grim, familiar line of his mother's mouth as, in the blackout of a winter night in 1944, she made her way from their terraced apartments to join the fine-boned smiling man—conscripted Lutheran pastor and underground hero? Waffen SS, and a talented cocksman with a story at which she snapped?—to make a tiny dimple in history's skin.

According to some of these later versions, given in the sixties by disapproving witnesses, security was slack. One man who served in the Air Raid Precautions—"I was proud of my thin helmet, and risks I had to run in doing my duty"—claimed that as early as 1942, prisoners could make their way about Barrow without guards. But in 1944? Still: imagine guards. Imagine one who drank, say, and who was bored and ill-trained, who was issued with a sidearm, the huge Webley pistol on its lanyard, but who hadn't a rifle because there weren't enough to go around. Imagine that he could be bribed with whisky, with wine, with money for small beer, and imagine that the German prisoner or the Polish émigré wife would venture to buy the German prisoner's temporary freedom with drink. Imagine it done, and imagine Sylvia, then, leaving the dark brick three-story block of flats, the tiny terrace of their apartment overlooking Sloop Street, with its lightless, slick-cobbled cul-de-sac. And imagine Januscz, exhausted, bleary, perhaps suspicious, even, who remains to care for the child who, now, these decades later, creates his parents here in the glow of the Reading Room.

Imagine Sylvia on the wet streets that run behind the flats that are called the Eggerton Buildings. She smells the exhalations by the flats through the ground-level chutes down which rubbish is tossed from upstairs. She is wet already, in her men's cloth jacket, all they can afford for her, and rain runs down through her hair. Occasional lights blink through moving blackout curtains, and the Air Raid Precautions, the ARP, lenses of their battery-powered torches taped to thin slits of yellow light, whistle—per their instructions—to keep the neighborhood spirits up. Sylvia's spirits are down most of the time, but now they are high. For she is on her way to Otto. But she is on her way away from where she belongs, in the flat that smells of burned oleomargarine and mildewed bacon and soiled nappies and Januscz, not quite clean, because the harsh pumice soap is caustic on his skin and he uses it infrequently.

A round, bearded Barrovian helps her to board his little two-stroke launch that he grandly calls his ferry. They can't afford the shilling she pays, but she wishes to pay it. A woman who works as a barmaid and cleaner at the King's Arms on Piel Island, off the Walney coast of Barrow, in the last, trailing grasp of the Irish Sea, will be the other passenger. She will gossip about her, Sylvia knows, but she is afflicted with more than concerns for what these termagant English might say. Even if her chattering workmates at the garden hear the talk, she will not care. Her hungers are for a sustenance that cupboards cannot provide. She and the barmaid nod but do not speak. Fog blows in off the sea, and Sylvia closes her eyes against it, and against the blindness it brings. All day, she scrapes at the hard muck of the long waste ground behind the Hindpool Brick and Tile Works, the field now a large, hard-worked garden where she and Leslie and Tubby and Tina harrow and plant and cultivate beans and courgettes and achingly slow tomatoes and where she studies, as the sparrows and jackdaws must study, what they scratch upon. She studies her child when she leaves him and when she returns, examining his eyes for clarity and fearing to find them flooded with red.

She nuzzles him but also listens to his heart, his lungs, fearing the thick catarrh and then wheezing bronchitis that kills English babies. She studies Januscz to descry what he might be thinking while he smiles his forbearance, for he is the most hidden of men. And she sees, daily, the dull, dirty brickwork of the buildings, the worn, insufficient clothing of the men who walk in their fatigue to work at Vickers and then back to the small meal in the small flat and the small rest before they must march again to make the ships that the Luftwaffe will come to blow up with bombs or that the U-boats will sink. She sees the chirping women who are pleased to call themselves Land Girls and who chip away at the wintry earth to plant early, in hopes of persuading the brick and tile works field, its decades' deposits of packed earth and shattered roofing tiles, to yield an early crop of anything that anyone might eat. And above it, over them all, she sees the low, cruel sky that, when it clears, flowers bombing aircraft and barrage balloons, and, below it, craters filled with icy green water and rubbish.

So, no, she does not wish to stare into the harsh fog and blink back tears in the hope of seeing what—she perversely opens her eyes, as if to defy even her own injunctions—suddenly comes before them: Piel, with its ruined castle, its pub, its six houses. He helps them off and they wobble and catch themselves on the algae-coated, kelp-slippery jetty that slopes up toward the pub.

She permits the barmaid to climb quickly and to reach the King's Arms, so that Sylvia is alone as she walks past it, smelling the fire inside, hearing the low, throaty, tired talk. She circles the place of behaving correctly and climbs on, two or three hundred yards, to the ruins in the palisade above the sea. Two bony cows stand, watching her, underneath the icy needles of the rain. Sylvia walks on weed and excrement and stone to climb through what might be a five-hundred-year-old window frame. She crosses what is left of a roofless stone hall to find a recess facing away from the houses and the pub and the prevailing winds. It is the first even halfway hidden place, aside from Januscz's face, that she has seen tonight. Otto has blankets. He has a jar of soup that is nearly hot. He has a little whiskey, though most of it, he whispers in the only language they can share, the language of their hosts and captors, has gone to bribe his pistol-toting guard, the apparently stupid and very good-natured Leon Salthouse.

"I have thought of you all of the day," he whispers into her face. His breath is hot and he smells spicy. His hands are on her thighs, beneath her coat, working at her trousers. His hands are small and very powerful, and she closes her eyes, again with relief, and it feels as though she has stepped from the terrace of their flat or the wall of these ruins: she falls and falls, and she insists upon falling blindly, trusting Otto that she will not strike the ocean or the earth.

He has rations and drink. He has tactics they rehearse in their wandering, effortful English. He has the prisoner's sign: yellow diamonds stitched upon his sleeves and trousers. They collect what light is left in the night before he wraps them both in the stolen or borrowed blankets, then covers them with a rubberized tarpaulin. He has powerful, short fingers. He has cheekbones that are too prominent, she complains to him. "Like skull," she mourns. He kisses her to bury the mourning. She fears that he will die of this war, and she remembers to worry for her baby, little Alex, and Januscz with his patient, deep voice. Otto has the ferry schedule, such as it is. But he has no French letters. It is what the English call their contraceptives, he explained to her at the start. He claims that Parisians call them English letters.

"What," he asked her, "do Polish mistress call them?"

"Skullcap of Pope," she replied, and he laughed and laughed with his lips on her throat.

Sylvia didn't care and doesn't care about the protection. He is broad there, and powerful, hard a very long time, as ardent and energetic and, frankly, as cunning at love as he is philosophical and entertaining when their passion is finally fed.

He chats her up—though they are partly naked among the stones of a collapsed medieval castle in the cold English night—as if she is an English girl in a skirt and woolen socks and a thick jersey and sturdy shoes, sitting in the cozy of an English public house.

"How is good husband?"

"No," she says. "Not Januscz. Please."

"He is good man. He is loving you. I am loving you. So: I must love him, yes? Or not to be hating him. Wishing *I* could be husband, certainly. Is jealous, they say in English. You are hungry, Sylvia?"

"For . . . this. You. Yes. Food? I not thinking."

"I *am* not thinking."

"Of course," she says.

"You are thinking of large matters, of long times, as I warned you is devastation, Sylvia."

"Large."

"Naturally. You remember: war, no war, end of war, after war, live, die. All such. No! It is us tonight, Sylvia and Otto inside the blanket. You are feeling me, inside blanket?"

"Feeling you again. You return quickly."

"It is late and night."

"So," Sylvia says, "everything now."

"Exact. Beloved."

She smells the wet rock of the ruins, and the rubber of the tarpaulin, and the soaked, icy lichen on which their woolen blankets soak. She smells his breath, and she smells their sex. He speaks, now, of a person named Hegel. But she is thinking of his loins, and where they take her. She is waiting for the instant when, with a lot of him and a little luck, she will be, just that instant, beyond the reach of her mind and the vastness of what frightens her. And he—whispering, under the rain, and warming her with his body, and saying one word to this breast, another word to that, kissing her stomach, kissing lower—he knows how tensely she waits. And he wants her to. She knows it.

Why is he speaking of his church in Berlin? "Pastor Niemoller," he tells her, and she will not wait. She silences him by rising to surround him, to take him in, to take her away. She knows that he knew that she would.

And then the ferry back, the walk up from the docks onto Michaelson Road, and then Salton Road, and back, through the blacked-out city, the craters in the dark, the navigation through Barque Street and Brig Street, and the slow climb up the circling steps. In the darkness, in the rain, wet laundry hung out on ropes that cross the street three stories up droops lower and darker as it takes more water on. It isn't nine o'clock, but she has violated the curfew, she has violated Januscz, maybe she has violated herself.

Still. Hegel, she says to herself as she opens the unlocked door of their flat. Niemoller, she says. Januscz must be in the other room. She pauses, she removes her soaked coat to reveal the soaked clothes beneath. Beneath them, she knows, are the coarse undergarments that also are soaked, and beneath them is her cold, wet flesh. Within it is Otto.

Mommy, look. Here, on the floor, in my slatted bassinet. Here I am.

HIS PARENTS HID, he'd always thought, inside the cold stucco house with its porch painted the color of a battleship's deck, with its Norway maple on the small front lawn, with its rooms decorated (Alex came to think) as if for a civic theater's production of a play about American family life. There was Father, teaching his classes of freshmen and sophomores while his colleagues, some with degrees inferior to his, supervised doctoral theses. Father was mild and overwhelmed, and you might have thought that an early death would be his only form of advancement. Each evening, he kissed Alex good night on the mouth, and seemed, as Alex grew older, on the verge of saying something in Polish that was true to life lived in wartime on European soil. Or so Alex imagined. But his parents never spoke Polish and never spoke of Poland, even when he asked. They were Americans now, they said when Alex was an adolescent. They had given birth to themselves and, in their new life, the mother in the play made clear, they were not permitted a backward look. He therefore found it unremarkable that he fell in love, while he was in college, with Edward Albee's plays about family alienation. He thought they were the story of his life.

Januscz and Sylvia did, of course, look back, Alex knew. It was *language* that was forbidden. They could speak of the present. They could discuss the process of the present tense, so they were bound by each other, and bound from each other, in a webwork of insignificance: the boy in school; the repair of the two-door Chevrolet; the sullen, dark skies of southern Michigan; the list in the hand of Tailgunner Joe, and the need to remind one's colleagues how much one had hated the Communists, even those who claimed to be in the resistance. And there was more than imprisonment. There was his mother's sorrow, an almost physical affliction. It writhed across her pretty face, but was divorced from the source, and therefore a mystery: the flag, to Alex, of their small, stranded family's distress. And now, of course, because of William Kessler, he had a sense of her misery. Like her son, forty years afterward, she was separated from what she had to have. He wondered: did he look, to his wife, like his mother?

"My parents," Nella had said, "were survivors. The, you know. The camps."

"Which?"

"You're the first person to ask me that. Which camp?"

"Do you know?"

"Monowitz, it was called."

He shook his head to show his sorrow.

"Norwegians," she said. "Can you imagine?"

"Some old Hungarian Jew might ask you, 'Why not Norwegians? Because they have the nice bone structure?' "

She raised her hand to her temple, her cheek, then brought it down. She no longer slouched, but sat forward, and he watched her sweater shift, her skirt ride on her thighs, her calves bunch. Her hair was cut short, and he saw that her earlobes were long. Thank goodness, he thought: an imperfection. She smiled, he supposed, for his stagy Yiddish accent.

"My father has spent the last dozen years not talking. Before that, he *rarely* talked. But now—only to the man who comes to fix his radiator, and only if he has to answer a question. Say, when he goes to the doctor, which is almost never, until I nag him and nag him. He's young. Sixty-six. On the other hand, though, he's ancient. He's depressed."

"A good word for it."

"You think?"

Alex shrugged and smiled, but she didn't smile back.

"Probably," he said at last. Take a note, he instructed himself. Do something besides relish her. "Perhaps. Will he talk to you?"

"Hello, goodbye, you're welcome. I'm always afraid he's angry with me."

"But by speaking at all, he gives you gifts, you might say."

"Always. He gives me things that, when you present them, you should be smiling about. But he can't. His heart is broken."

"He gives you actual objects, then. And his relations with your mother?

"Dead."

"How long after the camps?"

"Twenty-four—no, twenty-five years."

"Natural causes?"

She stared at him. Her nose was red, her cheeks were flushed, and she was going, he knew, to cry. She shook her head, as if at her own reaction. "You knew, didn't you? She killed herself. She got into the bathtub and took a lot of painkillers my father used for his back. She took all of them. And—she never touched liquor. It made her sick. But she drank a good deal of cheap brandy. And then she used a razor, and she opened up her arms."

He forced himself to remain in his chair as she wept and wiped at her tears.

"And you want to know something," he finally said.

"Yes. Are you going to tell me what?"

"All right," he said. "You want to know what to feel guilty about."

She smiled. Her eyes pooled. And he despised himself. For, like a great, heavy hawk, he dropped through the sky to feed on her.

In his office, now, surrounded by his Indian pottery and African fetish figures, among the stones, shells, and prints with which he and Liz had returned from France and Italy and Ireland, Alex rubbed his tingling fingers on his temples, then on the flesh of his face. He thought of the rain on Liz the night before, and the storm blowing in over Barrow from the Irish Sea to soak his mother, and everyone, finally, hidden inside and as safe as houses. He slowly shook his head as if it ached. Finally, then, like a man who gives in to sleep, he closed his eyes and cradled his head in his hands. He breathed slower, and then a good deal slower. He tried, you might say, to compose himself.

2

LISTENING TO SLOWACKI at their second session, after watching him enter the office with his jaunty step—like many aggressive, short men, he bounced on his toes and swung his shoulders—Alex heard more than defensive annoyance, and more than a fear of being thought afraid; he heard the policeman's interest. Slowacki, he thought, wished to know about himself. He was brave enough to wish that, Alex thought with pleasure and a little envy.

It was late afternoon and he had switched on the lamps. And Slowacki, behind his tinted lenses and under the activity of his mustache, his large hands clasped tightly in his lap, like a man approached by a dentist with a needle, smiled as if to show that he understood that pain was about to begin. And, although he had not met the man, Alex thought of another Pole, Jerzy Kosinski, whose cruel novel of childhood suffering during World War II in eastern Europe, *The Painted Bird*, he had read. Two frightened men, and one betrayer of a different sort, gathered in the same brain at the same instant, he thought, abandoning Slowacki, in spite of his wish to hear the man's every syllable, and thinking instead of the story Liz had told them some time ago, before Nella and while you might have characterized the condition of their marriage as merely wounded but not dying.

"Normal stress," he said to Slowacki, who seemed startled. "But go on, please," he told him, remembering Liz at Teddy's place, where they were dining on a Sunday night in winter a couple of years before, four floors above Riverside and 114th. Liz wore gray silk that was almost black and, with her pale, oval face, the frame of her gray-white hair fanning back and out, she looked electric. Her ice-blue eyes drew the most cursory glance in further and further; she could not appear casual. Seeing her, you studied her, drawn to what might have been anger, or dark, uncomfortable knowledge. Even when she smiled, you studied the smile, making certain she was in fact pleased with you. He still reacted that way, and he was glad that he did, but also resentful. He knew that she was mild, and often meek, but she appeared, frequently, to be judging—harshly—what she saw. And he had come, more and more, to think that she was judging him.

"Slavic paranoia," she called it, trying to sneer, and—as almost always—failing: her face did not fall to disdain with very much ease; she looked queasy when she frowned, and more distressed than cruel. But he remained, he thought, frightened of her. Alex knew that he had loved his wife. He thought that he still had hopes to love her well. He wished, he was certain, that they could find a way to be in love. But he remembered how Liz had shouted, when he'd tortured her with assertions about emotions she did not, she swore, even begin to feel, "So what good does this famous love of ours *do?*" This was earlier in their marriage, and he remembered thinking that his heart would explode from his chest if he planted even one more sorrow in her.

And what he remembered now, as Slowacki spoke, was Teddy's place, in early January of maybe 1983, a dinner among three old friends. The possible lesser Vuillard above the Bauhaus sideboard behind them, a brilliant, casual meal on the light wood of the dining table, a second bottle of Châteauneuf-du-Pape uncorked. And Liz, very happy, as she always seemed to be at Teddy's, said, "It was at the Italian fellow's place, the agent with the imperious—you know: he brought that hideous French novel over, it was absolutely devoid of emotion but full of incest, and all the talk, so *much* talk, whenever they weren't screwing."

"*Gone with the Vent,*" Teddy suggested, saying in his impeccable French the word for wind. Then he repeated it with a hard *t* so that it was about venting emotions. He raised his brows, Liz pantomimed applause, and Alex gave his imitation of a man who hanged himself because of too much wordplay.

"And there was a mob," Liz said. "Some of them were not-quite-major-gallery people. That's how I got invited, through them. And Kosinski was there. All kinds of people with gossip-column names were there. So that meant that none of the Hunter painters would go because they were too secure to need that scene. Not me, though, right? I really wanted us to go. And we went."

Teddy served out more grilled peppers and fennel. "And Alex actually showed up? You went to that, Alex?"

"Liz said she wanted to go. I'm an easy guy. I'm not a hermit, Teddy."

"No," Teddy said, "you're a depressive and a chronic early night, but not a hermit."

Liz studied them, or felt some powerful emotion, Alex thought, as her glance rode over them. In the candlelight, and given the intensity of her eyes, it was hard for Alex to tell. He realized that he read significance— was it threat?—every time she observed him. So he chattered: "I really like this barley, Teddy. You're a great cook. And I don't think I ever ate salmon cooked with red wine."

Teddy smiled. Liz raised her glass, then drank. "So," she said, "Kosinski? Shall I get to the humiliation? I think he was wearing a tuxedo, or a really wonderful blue-black suit. He looked good. The rest of the men wore suits, you know, or sport coats. Except for the kid novelist—the one who didn't go to college?"

Teddy said, "Tell me he wore motorcycle leathers."

"Very smooth designer sweater," she said, "in a paramecium motif. With no shirt underneath. And jeans. Tasseled loafers. No socks. His ankles were tan, and the jeans had a crease pressed into them. They could stand at attention without anybody wearing them."

"What don't you see?" Teddy said.

"I see everything, Teddy. Don't you forget it." She drank more, and then she said, "Kosinksi, anyway, looked very good. Elegant, tough, like there was nothing that could hurt him any worse. He was in his own private movie, and I was gawking. He has this gold cigarette case filled with joints—"Join me, my dear?"—and all I could think of was his long, pointy tongue licking each one down the seam to seal it up. Maybe it was the boy writer's microbe-motif sweater, but I found myself thinking about germs. You know: infection. And Kosinski is holding this tall shooter of vodka in these long fingers of his. His fingernails were dirty. Not filthy or oily or anything, just not quite washed clean. I did notice that. We're standing near the fireplace in that long living room of theirs, and the domestic staff—I mean *staff*, you know? Indentured servants?—they're bringing drinks and very tiny hors d'oeuvres around, and I'm about to say something that is so middle-west and farmy about his book—"

"Except she really read the damned thing *hard*," Alex said.

Teddy flapped his hand to silence him.

"And he does this piercing cinema thing. His eyebrows almost merge under this brushy hairdo, the one Alex has by accident. You'd swear *that* guy never had an accident, once he survived the war. Everything's on purpose, you know? I'm guessing even the fingernails. And he looks out from under his brow and he says, very casually, 'I would adore to make you come with my tongue. Five minutes or a half an hour: you can choose.' He finishes his vodka and he continues the stare for *so* long until he says, 'Well?'

"I always promised myself," she said, "that if I ever told this story, I'd finish it by swearing that I asked him if he eats and runs. . . ." She looked at her plate. Her face was scarlet.

"It would have been clever," Alex said. "But the real story is why you never told the story."

"No," Teddy said, "the real story is why you don't want to let her finish it. Drink more wine and hush, Alex." He refilled their glasses. "Liz," he said, "I beg you: tell it."

She was chewing, and they had to wait. Finally, she said, "That's really the best part of it. I look like a real jerk if I tell any more."

"You cannot dine out on a story if you don't finish it," Teddy said. "And you're safe. There isn't a way for you to look bad. He's just revealed himself to be a joke about himself. Memorable, historical, monumental fool. Anything you said, short of 'No, thank you,' and you're home free. Tell it."

Her head drooped.

"No," Teddy said.

She shrugged. Alex wanted to embrace her. He thought Teddy did too.

"It was all I could think of," she said.

"Well, it was all he deserved," Teddy said.

When she raised her head, she said, "You're a dear man, Teddy." She sighed. "I told him, 'No thank you, Mr. Kosinski, and your famous foreign tongue.' I sounded like some American Legion xenophobe. He walked away, and he was laughing at me."

"He was humiliated," Teddy said.

"Do you think?" she had to ask.

Teddy said, "No question." He smiled at Liz with an undiluted pleasure Alex envied. Then he said to Alex, "We are about to have endive and red onion and orange," Teddy said, "and a lot more wine. I met Kosinksi once, did I tell you? He never made me any offers, though." Alex realized that Teddy was diverting their attention from Liz so that she could hide for a while. "Kosinski said, 'I knew a Levenson once. Oddly enough, he was a quisling from Chelm. Where are *your* people from?' A really classic bully. Classic victim, too, I would think, of childhood abuse. And it's possible that every word he writes is a lie. I don't mean fiction. I mean lie. He suggests the charming affect, the cunning, the utter lack of conscience you find in the true narcissist."

"I bought it," Alex said. "The book, I mean. I mean I believed it—a true story, not a novel, terrible stuff. I think it's an attack on the elders. All of the elders, including the readers of his book. He turns them *into* the elders who should have protected him. I think, instead, they let him be raped. Or they raped him. 'Nobody took care of me,' he's saying."

"Damage is damage," Teddy said, "fiction, nonfiction, who cares? It's part of the record. I mean, who cares if history's made up into fiction as long as the history happened? Which, in his case, I think it did not."

"Well, because you need a *record*, Teddy. You used the word. Because you need to know what happened."

Liz said, in almost a murmur, "And art?"

"We *are* what happened. In the case of people who bear witness, or claim to, it's up to the reader to discern."

"We—you and I—being the reader? Therapists? Analysts? We read the patient and we tell them where they've been?"

"We help them figure out how to tell us. How to tell themselves. Yes."

"But isn't there something wrong with saying something's made-up, fictitious, when it's true? Aren't you *denying* the truth?"

"There you go again," Teddy said. "True true true. What Kosinski believes, I would bet the month's food budget on, is nothing. He's a classic trauma victim. It's gotten worse and worse, I'd bet. He escapes by lying. He comes close to saying what happened, and then he makes it go away. He doesn't believe, Alex, in *anything*. Whereas you—you always want a guarantee. And you're ready to believe in something in order to *have* it guaranteed. If I told you your father was really as brilliant as Enrico Fermi, and that's why he was always depressed—because he couldn't disclose who he was to the world—you might seize on it. Because then, you'd be figuring, you would *know*. But there aren't guarantees, and you're perceptive enough to suspect that. So you are—what does Liz call you? A Polski Kafka? That's you, dear man: Alex K."

"I want a drink, please," Alex said, surrendering.

"I want two," Liz said, holding up her emptied glass. "And a promise that at another time, but not, dear Jesus, now, you will both apologize for having left out whatever it is that goes into novels and poems and paintings."

"Whatever that could be," Teddy said, pouring for her. "You may always have what you want."

"Promise me," she said.

Teddy looked at her and said, "I do."

"But why?" Alex asked Slowacki, forcing himself back into the man's language, forcing himself to see his patient, to hear him speak of his feeling about riding the subways for what he called the Job. Slowacki felt, he said, that if he closed his eyes he would sleep at once, and wake to strange stations with names he didn't know. "You're afraid of getting lost?"

"Not exactly afraid, Doc. I don't think I'd say afraid. I got pretty big stones."

"There's nothing *wrong* with fear, is there? It's a warning from us to ourselves. If you live near hungry tigers, wouldn't it be wise to be afraid?"

"Not chicken."

"You served in the war, Mr. Slowacki. You're a law enforcement officer in a dangerous place at a dan-

72

gerous time of night. You don't have to prove you're not afraid." Alex wondered if he ought to point out that his vocation and his tour of duty might be caused by that very need.

Slowacki said, "Well, that's the truth. I didn't know you knew about the war."

"You mentioned it."

"I don't do that, as a rule."

"You have a rule about the war?"

His mustache moved and Slowacki clasped his hands.

"What if—if you don't mind," Alex said. "What if I asked you, quickly, to tell me the worst memory you can recall from your wartime service? Could you answer?"

"I don't talk about that as a rule."

"You don't like to?"

"My wife's always asking me. Finally, she learned. I get—grumpy, you know? I get annoyed."

"Angry?"

"Why not? Even that. Sure."

"But what if you wanted to talk about it?"

"Not me. Thanks, anyway."

"What if you didn't *know* you wanted to talk about it. But you really did?"

"Could that be, with someone? They don't want to but they *do* want to?"

"Certainly," Alex said. "Most people are conflicted about something in their lives. And they want to tell their story, and they're . . . reluctant."

"You were going to say 'afraid.'"

"Who's the doctor, Mr. Slowacki?"

"You could call me Tony. Or Anthony, if you like. It would make things a little easier, maybe. More informal, you know? Like I don't have to stand up here at the microphone and, you know, perform?"

"Anthony. Please, if you would. Tell me something you remember from the service. Food? The value of cigarettes to the men? Leadership? The tension of the patrols?"

"You were there?"

"Many of my patients were. You're not alone in this."

"In this what, Doc?"

"You interrogate people in your work."

"Just like you."

"One small memory of Anthony Slowacki in Southeast Asia. Please."

"You may not care too much about this shit. This stuff. Excuse my French. It's pretty boring unless you were there."

"But you *were*. So it matters to me."

Slowacki sat silently, shaking his head. The little mustache jumped, then lay as still as his hands in his lap. "The goddamned water," he said.

"To drink?"

"To drown in. I saw a guy in the platoon—this was First Platoon, Company C, we were in the III Corps area. This is Vietnam. We're out on a search-and-destroy, and we're trying to sleep. Mosquitoes the size of birds, and leeches big as snakes. One guy gets one halfway up his dick—his penis. No kidding. The corpsman goes after it with insect repellent. Want to hear a man scream? Anyway. There's this black jive-ass guy named William Williams. His mother named him after some old-time disc jockey in the city. Williams is always talking like he comes from Jamaica the island instead of Jamaica in Queens. And he's always taking his own medicine, if you know what I mean. He's equipped with bennies, which are in very high demand since they keep you up when you need to be. On account of you got so tired from the fear, even the fear couldn't keep you from sleeping. He's got all kinds of stuff. Acid tabs, much powerful grass, naturally, and speed that could get you close to home, mon, which is the way he says it. He's always blinking his eyes, fast-fast. I hate that shit. There's enough spooks on the outside edge of the paddies without me needing a spook getting spooky. Which is what I told him one night over a canned peach. Also told him I would put a round up his ass, he came around me or my friends. He says, 'Thot's cool, mon. I find me way to trade wit somebody else,' and I really hated him.

"He said he was making money, according to him, to send Eugene, his baby brother—*You . . . gene,* he called him—out of town so he could have a life. Which is tiger shit. He loved the life. Probably Eugene did too. Anyway. Anyway," Slowacki said. "Anyway."

He crossed his legs and shifted his clasped hands in his lap. Alex waited, watching the mustache and the hands. The mustache slid, left to right, right to left, then sat squarely on his mouth and didn't move. Slowacki took a breath and exhaled it loudly, but sat

75

quite still. He was waiting, so Alex waited with him.

Then Slowacki shook his head, once, and then, as if prompted, he said, "All right. Right."

He took another deep breath and said, "All right. We're crossing a stream and I'm point. Thank you very much for making me point. You know the meaning of this? I'm a kind of walking lookout. Great honor, they tell you, because they're trusting you to save the detachment if there's trouble ahead. What it really means: you're primary target when some slant fuck with a full clip decides to deposit it inside of your sweaty little tits."

He recrossed his legs and took a breath. "Okay," he said. "I'm about fifty meters ahead of them, and the platoon starts crossing it—it's, I'm telling you, it's a flood more than a stream. It's an ocean. I get over, I figure, on account of I *can't* barely swim, I'm god-damned terrified of drowning, I go fuckin *through* it and I make it, and I send a rope back over for the machine gun team. We get it tied to trees, the MG guys get over, they set up, and the guys come across one at a time, holding on to this rope. They're coming across, and you can't see anything because of the rain and the fucking mosquitoes, they're like a flock of bats they're so big. And, anyway, I'm looking *out*, away from us, I'm security, being point. I hear someone yell. I turn around just in time to see this Negro person, Mr. Drug-store, William Williams, he's got his M16 in his hand and the big rucksack on his back, and he's in. That's it: he goes in, he's gone. I try to get into the stream to stop him. His head comes up and I'm trying to get down to grab him, and he looks at me, and he's gone. His head didn't break the surface again. I stayed there as long as I could, I figured the body might get pushed back up to me, everything in there swirling so much. But it never did."

"Did you talk to anyone about this? Later?"

"What later? We stayed there three hours looking for him. He might have been some jig asshole, but he was one of *our* assholes. The lieutenant colonel who's battalion commander—I hear his voice on the lieutenant's radio. 'Don't waste any more time,' he says. *That's* what we talked about later. The fucking CC's wasting-time thing, and the name of the guy, William Williams, and how his customers would start in sleeping on the job. It was a kind of a sick joke we all made."

"Do you feel responsible for him?"

"Somebody, if there was anything right in the world, could maybe have taken better care of him. I feel that. A guy's going by in the current under a rucksack and an M16 and boots and a tin pot helmet, you're not gonna feel responsible for him?"

"But it isn't your fault," Alex said. "You tried."

"Tried."

"You did try. Didn't you?"

"Wait a minute. Wait a minute. Are you telling me I *didn't*?"

"No. You were there. You know what you did and didn't do. You tried to catch him."

"I risked my fuckin *life* to try and catch him."

"But you don't believe that. You know what you did, and you know what you felt. And maybe you thought he was worthless, a drug peddler, a bad man. But you also knew he was a comrade of yours—"

"Comrade," he said.

"Buddy?"

"No way."

"Fellow being."

"All right," Slowacki said.

"And a member of your platoon."

"That's all it should take, Doc. He was one of us. He was our very own drug mambo artist dickhead, and we should of rescued him. And we didn't."

"Responsibility and guilt are separated by what you really know, inside you, about your feelings. You might feel better, one day, if you could tell yourself that he was an outlaw who would have gone to jail one day, if he'd survived the war. Who might have been killed in a drug deal. Maybe by a policeman. Maybe by someone you know. Is that kind of directness available to you yet? Or—"

"Doc," Slowacki said, "If I'm honest, I might feel a little better if I could forget the whole damned thing."

"Because?"

"In my line of work, everything gets down on paper. You write a report on every incident. You note events in your little book. You tell people what went on, they can track down witnesses, trace back important times you maybe didn't know, at the time, they were important. Understand? Maybe I could forget it happened. If it didn't happen . . . I mean, I know it *did*. It happened. A man went into the water and he never came back. But I'm saying: maybe I don't *think* I tried hard enough. I hated this guy, the fuckin jiveass walk, like one leg's two inches shorter than the other. I'd of needed him to cover my ass, no way he'd of been there. He constituted a clear and present danger to us all. He didn't *care*. Jesus. Listen to me. You'd think I killed somebody instead of endangering myself to try and rescue the skinny-ass, limp-leg, never-worked-a-day-in-his-black-life son of a bitch. Excuse my French, would you, Doc?"

He admitted he wept by taking a tissue from the table beside him and dabbing at the flesh just below his tinted glasses.

Lescziak, to himself: How dare you not listen to every syllable he speaks?

"But I really think I tried," Slowacki said.

ALEX ASKED HIMSELF again—How dare you?—but more mechanically, when Kessler returned. It was after Nella's call. He knew that Liz was in the house, that she would soon leave for Hunter, and that what he wanted to do was walk from the office, through the anteroom, and through its door into the corridor between the living room and their bedroom. He wanted to walk softly, and to come upon her from behind as she dressed. She might wear faded jeans and an excellent sweater, a silk scarf from Harrods, an old silver-and-onyx pin she had bought in Hawkeshead, England, all of it under a coarse brown-and-white tweed coat. She would smell of a rich perfume called Norell. And she would be lost in the contemplation of the interplay of texture and shade, and he would come upon her and stroke her throat from behind, and slide his hand down into her shirt, and kiss softly at the back of her neck. His eyes were closed, now, in the office, as he thought of closing his eyes as she, hers closed too, leaned back against him. This was who they were—had been. Their tension had become distance, and her discomfort had become certainty. He had betrayed her, she thought. And she could not detach herself from him.

Nella took him away. The telephone sounded, and it seemed to him like a fly in liquid, buzzing and buzzing its death. He listened to her breathing. It was hoarse. He heard traffic in the background, he thought. He thought, triumphantly: Still in the city! Then he thought that any city could sound like that. And so could any intersection near a strip mall. So could a truck stop—anyplace, anyplace. She could be any-place. He felt the hugeness of the continent as a panic that squatted on his chest. His own breathing sounded hoarse to him as he listened to hers, and he thought of their lovemaking, the rattle and echo, the dissonance, then sympathy, with which they breathed as her long legs pressed at him, as her toes jammed into his feet as if she sought to climb him to seize for herself what she wanted from herself, but pretended, he thought, to seek with him. The sorrow of their separateness at love was echoed by the hugeness of the distance in their separa-tion, now, as he listened to them breathe.

Nella.

Alex.

Are you ill?

Love's a sickness. You said so.

Never! I said I was sick with love.

That'll do.

I've called your office. I've been to your house. The superintendent of the building. Your internist. Nothing, Nell.

Here I am, Doctor. I know where I am. Don't worry.

All I do is worry.

Poor Alex. You have to worry about your patients. *The ones like me but who never got to take you to bed. Ridiculous! I've been assuming I was the only one. Could you reassure me?*

Will you believe me?

I believe you, Alex. I left a dozen clients in the lurch. They must hate me at the office. All those suburban garages with little old-fashioned cupolas. And the lawyer's office in Salisbury, with its Jacuzzi! Why would a lawyer need a Jacuzzi? To bathe his conscience, I figure. Let somebody else design them. I was a designing woman with you, dear Doctor, but I don't want to design any more tarted-up boxes. I want to get a good night's sleep. I always slept, when I slept with you. Dear pill. Dear pillow. Dear—what did you call it?—dear bromide.

Are you in New York, Nell?

Oh, Alex. Sweet, shaggy Alex. I'm there! I'm inside your head. Listen!

During their second session, toward the end, as she spoke of her silent, sorrowful father, Alex had asked, "Do you remember when your mother died?"

"When she killed herself? Some. Yes. Some of it."

"Do you remember what you felt?"

"Confused."

"Of course."

"Lonely for her. She wasn't always fun, because of the headaches and the cloths on her eyes and some-times—I told you—she would do this *stare*. In the middle of something. In the middle of nothing. She would look and look, and if I saw her, I would try and see what she was looking at. Because it was scary. I always thought somebody was *coming*. But nobody was. Somebody was going. That was the joke of it. My mother was going . . . going . . . gone. Yes, though. I remember that, all right. She was my mother, and instead of only not always . . . *being* there, this time she was gone for good, and *never* there. And I missed her."

Her long legs, the sound of her shoes against the floor as she walked to her chair, the sense he had of the weight of her chest inside the cream-colored silk shirt that her freed breasts moved against. He thought of her as pausing, say in the women's room of a restaurant on Amsterdam Avenue, to take her underwear off before she arrived for her session. She undressed for him, he thought. She unwrapped herself for him. She delivered herself to him. And he was supposed to deliver her from herself.

Hers was on the surface an understandable transfer-ence, he thought, given the violence of the mother's death, the sense—inevitable among the children of sur-vivors—of nonspecific guilt: the need to woo, from the parent, a kind of forgiveness.

He remembered writing notes and watching her, then not writing though he listened. He remembered wishing that he were free to move to her, and realizing, then, that he was. That was the curse of adulthood, was it not? That we can do as we wish? Even when we mustn't? That we *can*?

Her big, dark eyes, in the dimness of the office, looked liquid to him, and without personality. Then she said, "Do I sound to you like I'm bitching? Like a child?" And her eyes were familiar, friendly, for she was reaching toward him.

He offered the approval she sought: "You're haunted, Nella. We need to try to lay the ghost."

She giggled and shook her head.

"Send the ghost back to—wherever it came from," he said. "In this case, it's the unresolved ambiguities you feel about your mother: anger at her willingness to leave you, sorrow that she could bear to part with you, understanding—because you're perceptive, and you're intellectually *not* a child—that she could not bear life and was crushed by it. And then the not incidental matter of your need to be a suitor for your father's affections. He clove to her, not you—or so it might have seemed. We ought to be talking about these matters. These, I would say, constitute an agenda."

"I love your language," she said. "It's almost foreign. Is that all right to say? 'Lay the ghost' and 'clove.' I never heard 'clove' like that. Laying is something else. But I would use the word differently."

"About what I propose—"

"The agenda," she said. She was standing, now. "Yes. Absolutely. That's what we'll have to do. Whatever you say." She moved very slowly across the room, diagonally, toward his chair, giving him time to tell her to stop. He remembered how brave he had thought her, how willing to risk humiliation. Perhaps—he thought now, but hadn't, then—humiliation and rebuke and discipline were what she'd sought. She needed *rules,* he was thinking, though he hadn't thought it on that day as she came to him, across the room, across the dangerous border, to stop with one leg between his and to stand, leaning against him where he sat, and to let her leg press in on him, her trunk against his face. She shivered, as if she froze. His eyes were shut, and he knew how difficult it would be when he opened them. Now, though, with her, it was he who was like a child, in a distant place, and the world was in the nerves of his flesh and inside his eyelids.

Even today, thinking of them, and filled with fear for her and for his life, he had to remind himself that, although Nella had goaded them and drawn his body, he had thought of himself as residing inside the boundaries of his body and brain.

"Whatever you say," she had said.

And now Alex said, inside a mind that seemed to him as crowded and chaotic as Grand Central, as noisy and without a central purpose aside from motion, as vast and as filled with thousands of colliding cross purposes, Lie. You lie. You lie.

For it had been Alex who'd stood in spite of his belief that only in remaining seated were safety for them both and a governed life for him available. As for her, he knew, even as his legs flexed to raise him, that Nella was finished. He would finish her. She would fuck her father, her dreams would come true, and she would be destroyed. Worse, she would—could, he whined, now, in his office, only *could*—seek her mother's solution to what was unspeakable. But he had stood, and had walked across the room, his mind falling away from him like liquid carried by a small child in a heavy pot that was filled to the rim and splashing over with every step. He had stopped thinking and had watched her face, drawn by its bright pallor in the dimness of the professional room, and he had taken one slow step after another, trying not to frighten her by displaying his own hesitation, and watching her stricken face for permission. Her mouth opened, and he saw her tongue and her teeth. He knew that permission was granted.

He stepped between her legs and moved up toward the seat of her chair. Her skirt resisted his right knee. She brought her knees up behind his legs, and she pressed her head at him, resting it on his belly, resisting and permitting at once. He heard her release a great quantity of breath. It sighed from her, it sighed away, and then she released his thighs and buttocks from her knees, and then straightened her legs, and sat back. She lifted herself—he opened his eyes to see that hers were closed, and then he closed his own—and she brought her skirt above her hips toward her waist. He felt it move. He felt her skin, her hair; they were heated, and he was right: she wore no underclothes.

He'd squeezed his shut eyes tighter, so that he wouldn't see a drugged, dazed, helpless face, or one that was clenched in loathing for herself or for him.

They made love like that, as she raised her pelvis to him and he sank upon her, his knees bruised by the wood supporting the leather cushion of the chair. He propped his hands on the chair arms, he worked like an athlete for balance, dropping and resisting, pushing and letting his body go. As he fell upon her, she rose to him. And then they would not separate. He would not raise himself, and she would not slump down. Because, he'd thought—and he thought it now, as well—because they did not wish to stop the sensations: not those of the lubricated friction, not the screaming wish to let it all churn out of him, but the intimacy of harsh hair and hot skin, the being socketed together in midair, the touching so thoroughly, suspended together from the world. Love, he thought he'd thought as he had endangered his patient's health, and all of his self-respect, and whatever governance, as a doctor, he had known. Love, he had told himself. He had blurted the word in his climax, strangling it with his tongue but hearing it, anyway, escape: *"Love!"*

As if saying that word excused something. As if it excused anything, he was thinking in his office as William Kessler arranged himself for his second session in the chair into which Nella and he had packed themselves. And then, as he had thought it with Nella, he thought it now: love. And he thought it likely he was lost.

Maybe because they married late, he and Liz, he thought. Maybe because they had lived alone so long, had grown cranky and willful in spite of their feelings for each other, and maybe because they each were products of neurotic families. But who is not?

Teddy Levenson: "Family: that unit of domestic life which seeks to digest its members so that, by young adulthood, they are part of the elders' metabolism."

Alex, in reply: "The children are food?"

"Why Little Red Riding Hood? All the confusion between wolf and grandmother? Why Hansel and Gretel? It's a time of famine, so the parents lose the children in the woods, where they'll be eaten? By whom? By doppelgangers, those fierce creatures of the forest who devour them, standing in for the parents themselves."

"Jesus, Teddy, I thought you were joking. You mean this nonsense."

"All 'nonsense' is, of course, meaningful. But I *really* mean this. That's why I'm so pleased that you and Liz don't have kids."

"Because we'd eat them?"

"What's for dessert?"

Kessler appeared to have a set of cycles in which he would wear either his entire thick, dark brown tweed suit, of the first session, or the suit trousers with a black broadcloth jacket of muted dark stripes, as with this session. Alex made a note. But why? Why trivialize the poor man's wardrobe? And then he underlined *poor*, and put a question mark above it. Still, he made a note to check whether he would next wear the tweed suit coat with odd trousers. His ties, on the evidence of two sessions, matched nothing. The cuffs of his shirt were again burdened with amethyst stones set in gold cufflinks, and the cuffs were frayed. His shoes were earnestly shined. Nella was missing, Liz was on the verge, and he was studying this troubled, small person's wardrobe, Alex thought. Why was he worried about this sad man's wardrobe? He wrote and under-scored it: *transference*. Because it appeared to him to be going in both directions at once: danger. But what patient under his care, and what aspect of his life, was not in danger now?

"I would like to speak of our mother," Kessler said.

Alex asked, "Have we established that my mother and your mother are one and the same?"

"Oh, *I* have," Kessler said, and his smooth, small face was bisected by a smile, the teeth blue-white and small, as if that establishment had been the principal pleasure of his life.

"And it's very important to you that I understand this fact? If it's a fact? Or is it important that you speak about it?"

"Or both?"

Alex nodded, because the man was reasonable. "Yes," he said. "Is there proof?"

Kessler moved his left leg against the scuffed, heavy leather briefcase. "Indeed. And there are dates, places—those are the historian's proof. I do not speak, here, of interpretation—as, say, in the newspapers about the President's trip."

"To celebrate the warriors who staffed the camps."

"Some of whom staffed some of the camps," Kessler intoned with a sudden, heavy nasal tone that reminded Alex of Senator McCarthy interrupting a random Jewish victim his staff had summoned before his committee. "Nobody speaks of the children conscripted by the armed forces in the latter days of the war. These were small, terrified boys. They were chopped to pieces by the artillery of the United States Army, determined to plow the German body into the earth."

"How inconsiderate of them," Alex couldn't help saying.

"Facts," Kessler said, motioning toward his briefcase. "The dead children are facts. A wreath might not hurt their stripped, dead bones. And strengthening Chancellor Kohl, whose establishment is essential to a stable Europe: not the worst goal for a statesman."

"The actor playing President is a—never mind. Strike that. Never mind. So these particular SS did not march Jews off to be burned?"

"That canard," he said.

"The canard concerns—"

"The million or so who died of disease and starvation? The burning was of the corpses to save the rest from diphtheria."

"Could we, Mr. Kessler, address, for just a moment, the matter of your parentage? You began by speaking of your mother."

"*Our* mother."

"So you said."

"Sylvia Shber Lescziak. I was born to her on seven August, 1945," he said. "And you three, Sylvia and Januscz and you, were in the country—cozy at home by what? January? The deed done in December, let's say? I was a Christmas bundle of sorts. Surely you remember our mother's swollen tummy."

"Interesting," Alex said. "You think of it almost as though she'd devoured you. Do you think of yourself as food?"

Kessler sat up and smiled his good smile of great pleasure. "Wonderful," he said, "but surely you are beyond such cant?"

" 'Those who love fairy tales do not like it when people speak of the innate tendencies in humankind'— no: 'in mankind,' he said—'towards aggression, destruction and cruelty.' Actually: 'destruction and, in addition, cruelty.' That's Herr Dichter Freud." As quoted to Alex by Teddy Levenson in rebuke for his wish for an easier life, or smoother marriage, or heavier cock—Alex had forgotten which; but he had not forgotten the words.

Kessler said, "Quite wonderful, really, since you're speaking of Freud. You called him 'Dichter.' Wouldn't that mean 'writer'? Shouldn't you have said 'Doktor'? Is that what you experts call a Freudian slip?"

Kessler chortled. Alex was certain that his halfheartedly triumphant laughter could be called chortling.

"No?" Kessler said. "Well. Then Mother would have gone away," he said. "You were three, yes? And Mother went away round and came home slender. Are you recollecting? She was always slender, I've heard—except when pregnant with me. My father described her to fellow inmates—"

"Inmates, Mr. Kessler?"

"Later," he said, "if you don't mind. He described her, however, as thin. The result, I should think, of privations. Of their years in England under siege. But did she, perhaps, thicken here? When they prospered?"

He consulted his documents. The sheets were long, the continental size of bond, and they were flimsy, rattling in his fingers, and they were covered with typing that seemed to have been done with an old manual machine. The blackened pages were edited, or annotated, in inks. Alex saw bright green, a blue, a rusty red. Kessler gently waved the palimpsests, laid a sheaf on one of his thighs, pointed with a small, blunt forefinger at lines that contained, he said, "The simple truth. Pure facts."

"According to you, sir."

"I have it on excellent authority that she returned home from the hospital in the family auto, conveyed by Januscz. He is said to have been a decent man."

"He was." But, Alex remembered, she came home after an absence that seemed long, in a taxi, a black DeSoto with a rounded trunk from which the driver retrieved her small valise.

"And she returned," Kessler continued, "without the child who had left inside her. He was adopted. Given up, as one says, for adoption. Given up: surrender. 'I give up.' He became the bright and very well loved son of the Diamonds, Mom and Dad. *Magna cum laude* Indiana A.B. The M.A. and Ph.D from Chicago."

"Oh," Alex said, before he knew that he would, "you did complete your degree?"

And the small, tense Hansel, following back the crumbs of bread, stared at Alex in silence. The city's sounds drifted in. Alex thought he heard Liz in the apartment, but of course she was in school, he remembered. It was she he wished to hear, perhaps, but Kessler he was required—condemned, he thought—to attend. "I have you frightened," Kessler said, "haven't I?"

"Do you want to frighten me?"

"Well, a little, to tell you the truth. Surely. You're so smug, Dr. Lescziak, in your easy life."

"You think of yours as difficult? Despite the Diamonds' obvious love? Their generosity? Clearly, you were very much their child."

"Clearly," Kessler said, as if returning a volley, "I was born of Sylvia and Otto. That is the fact. That is the truth. It is that which I seek to establish as a matter of acknowledged public record."

"And your belief, you've said, that he was what? A pastor?"

"He was training. And he served in Bonhoeffer's Confessing underground Church. Indeed."

"A hero," Alex said, "not an SS interpreter. Not a man in a brown shirt with a gun and heavy boots."

Kessler smiled less of his smile and slowly shook his head. "The facts," he said, "are the subject of the book. The brown shirts, by the way, came earlier. In the thirties."

"You will write all that."

"Have written." He tapped the sheaf of papers on his lap.

"Because?"

"Because it—" His voice sounded flatter when he said, "Obviously, one—"

Alex, feeling like a therapist again, said, "Please. If

you can. It might be important."

"The truth," Kessler said. Like a child, he said, "You should always tell the truth."

Alex nodded, reassuringly. Kessler sat with his head tilted. He had, Alex thought, also heard the thinness of his own words.

"Or do you love a lie?" Kessler said, rallying. "Is it blindness you love?"

Alex did not close his eyes, but he saw neither Kessler nor his office. He saw Liz and him on what they called their honeymoon: two weekend days in the grimy whores' hotel off Washington Square Park. It was a small, hot room down the block from the Square's caged-in world of juggling, guitar-playing, singing, head-standing, drunken and dope-smoking boys and girls who seemed, to them, to have gathered before their window to celebrate their decision to close their eyes and jump from steady, unspectacular, separate lives into marriage. They drank two-dollar German May wine which they cooled in the stoppered bathroom sink. They ate a butter-cream layer cake purchased from a Greenwich Avenue patisserie. Liz wore his pajama bottoms rolled up into shorts, and a T-shirt tied beneath her breasts. Even then, her hair was graying, and he adored to burrow his face into it.

It was Sunday, and they were thinking of packing the suitcase to leave. Liz, very serious and almost naked and wholly thrilling to him, asked him about something she had read in *An American Dream*. "Norman Mailer," she said, looking at him directly, her face tense with interest, not embarrassment. "Did you ever read that? What I'm asking: did you ever *do* that? In her, the . . . other way? Do you know what I mean?

"Yes," he'd answered, suddenly breathless. "I mean no. I didn't."

"Would you?"

He said, "Would *you*?"

She'd nodded, as if she, too, couldn't draw enough breath for speech.

Dreamily, with those fierce eyes hooded and upon him, her face growing blank—perhaps with passion, he thought, and perhaps with concentration on herself, alone while with him—she had taken off the shirt, then stepped from the pajama bottoms, then slowly turned from him, as if for a long separation, to lie facedown on the bed.

"I want to do it," she'd said. "Are you watching me?" She drew herself up onto her knees, her head still down, and approached her buttocks, which stretched apart, revealing her, with her fingers. "Are you watching?" she asked him again. She slowly rubbed the lubricant in.

"God, Liz," he had said. He sounded boyish to himself, now, as he remembered.

And she, as if alone in the room, or as if the only adult, said harshly, "Now you."

Alex had reached for the lubricant.

"No," she'd said, "now *you*."

He remembered how he had furrowed, how he had dug, eyes shut with excitement and apprehension and the sense that where he went was not only into Liz, but into a place that existed because they closed their eyes

94

together and imagined it.

"Toynbee," Kessler said.

"Sorry," Alex said.

"I was referring to Arnold Toynbee, and you began to blink as if I'd spoken High Dutch. *Toynbee*."

"I haven't read him since college. Do people still read him? And—I don't know—Santayana? Ortega y Gasset? Are their studies important to your own?"

"I'm not writing a 'study,'" Kessler said. "I have written a memoir. Of the father I never knew."

"Doesn't 'memoir' have to do with memory? How can you remember what you don't remember? And why do that?"

"By doing it, I recaptured him. Or, as you would have it, captured him for the first time. It doesn't matter to me what you call it or how you judge it, Dr. Lescziak. I studied the documents, interrogated the witnesses, immersed myself in the history of his time. I know my father's life. It's actually an impressive act of animating facts long buried, I think historians might say."

"Excuse me," Alex said, "but isn't your coming here a testimonial to how much it *does* matter how I evaluate it? I've the feeling that I'm the point of your having become my patient, Mr. Kessler. Why do you wish me to know what you say you know?"

Kessler was replacing the papers in his briefcase, as if Alex had threatened them. He was orderly, and he worked in measured movements, demonstrating that he was not panicked, Alex thought. But the papers shook, he thought, in his patient's hands. Then Kessler sat up, arranged himself in the chair that was slightly too high for his short legs. He touched his toes to the floor and adjusted his hands so that each was palm down on a thigh. He took a breath.

"Because, Dr. Lescziak, you are the embodiment of the denial of what the historical data say. You seek— no: you *are*, just by existing, an attempt to rebut the facts."

"Logically, then, you would have to extirpate me to establish that you're right."

"No."

"As long as I'm alive, you're wrong."

"*No*. You're twisting the facts. You're twisting the language. As long as *I'm* alive, it's *you* who are wrong." His face was pale, but it shone.

"And President Reagan, and the laurels he will lay on the tombs of the SS?"

"Statesmanship."

"And the writing of your book?"

"Historiography."

"Denial? Of the murders in the camps? Of the Presidential trip? Of my life and my parentage?"

"And what of mine?"

"What of it?"

"Debating rhetoric. High school. You are not analyzing, Dr. Lescziak, you are defending yourself by attacking me. I believe that I've hit home."

"It's just about time for us to conclude for the day, Mr. Kessler."

"We haven't settled a thing between us," he complained. "And I haven't had your bill. There is, I assume, no family discount." He smiled for his own joke.

"My accountant takes care of that," Alex said. "And of course we haven't established that there *is* a family connection to acknowledge. *Or* that your subject matter is me, or, as you say, what's 'between' us. Perhaps we need to work on that. To define. And don't, please, worry about billing. The bills always come."

"It's what I've been trying to tell you," Kessler said. "The bill is always due."

"Next time," Alex said, "we can talk about which bills you mean."

"I'm not here, Dr. Lescziak, because I think I'm ill. This is essential. I'm here to heal the information. History's ill."

"And you're the doctor?"

He cocked his fine, bright face. Then, while Alex noted, *History ill. He its doctor,* Kessler stood to leave. He was smiling as he went.

ALEX, WHEN HE was not quite three, in Barrow-in-Furness—for he did, of course, remember that he had lived there, had been born there—became very ill. His affliction was a family story offered by Sylvia, as Januscz nodded, when Alex brought Liz to the family house for the introduction of the bride-to-be.

"You have a throat infection. No: had," Sylvia said. "And English doctors acquired from U.S. Army doctors a medication of sulfur."

Januscz, nodding, said, "Sulfa."

From somewhere, she had acquired a dirndl he could

not remember, broad, dark, and shapeless that she wore with flat-heeled shoes: the Polish mother in her native costume. Januscz, as usual, wore his rumpled wool trousers, his unshined shoes, his navy-blue cardigan over a wrinkled shirt.

Sylvia said, "So, then. Sulf-a. A tablet. Lozenge? Lozenge so large, the little boy have—no: had. Had no space in the throat for it going down. He choked!" And here, Sylvia laughed, imitating with her delicate taut face her son's, as he gagged and tried to swallow. "But it goes down," she told Liz, beside her at the kitchen table. "Down it goes," she said, patting Liz's hand. "He swallows. Sure. I am telling him, 'Down, or you die and go to hell.'" Sylvia laughed.

"You said that?" Liz asked, looking first at Januscz, then at Alex, and finally turning her head to the left, risking his mother's eyes. "You told him he would go to hell? Would a little boy under*stand* that?"

"Dying, don't forget," Sylvia said, telling Alex, across the broad table, and then turning to meet Liz's stare.

Liz shrugged. She pulled the neck of her cowled sweater as if to better wrap it around her. That night, when he had sneaked along the hall from his boyhood room to the spare bedroom, in which Sylvia had put the woman in her thirties who would be his wife, he had teased her about the drop in temperature she said she felt: take a New Yorker from New York, he'd said, and they shiver with fear.

But first, in the Ann Arbor dining room, among its souvenirs of states his parents had toured with him—

the bright red ceramic Maine lobster, the dark postcard of Walden Pond in its Woolworth frame, the yellow cowboy ashtray from New Mexico—they worked at eating something involving chicken gizzards, prepared by Sylvia as either information about the beloved's family background, or punishment for daring to marry her son. Alex could not remember her ever cooking it before. Liz chewed and chewed and chewed. And Sylvia supplied her with history.

Sylvia said, "This is what you procure—yes?—for the child when ill. So." She pushed her plate away. Liz moved as if to stand, reacting as if the clearing of places had been signaled. Alex motioned at her to sit, because he knew what came next. She sat. Sylvia, having waited, perhaps thinking that she had stared his fiancée back down into her seat, then went on. "He is having fever. Temperature climbing, and Januscz that night required at Vickers, the shipyard. No choice. Matter of steel on navy ship something-or-other"— thus dismissing all his work in the war—"and I am staying home alone with baby Alex in his catastrophe. Mine, too, make sure you know."

His mother's small, dark face under its dark brown hair—it stayed that color until a few years before she died—looked hot with her willingness to sacrifice herself for him, and with her pleasure in reminding him, once more, that she had suffered on his behalf.

"Januscz is away, I am home for few hours' sleep before back to the cursed farming in the wet slum. Land Girls, they called us! Slaves because Polska was me. I. Whoever it was. I must be at work, I must sleep,

99

I must attend my child, he shouldn't die. Problem? Sure. Solution? With ropes and string we save from holding together suitcases on boat, I am tying my hand to crib. One hand tied, one hand available for baby Alex. I am sleeping in chair, but always sitting up because of rope. Short leash! Like dog! But this is for baby, so who is complaining? Not me. All night! Tied into chair like prisoner. That is Sylvia: me! Prisoner of war! Prisoner of love! *That*," she said, turning to Liz, "is mother. You will see. Even older girl like you. Mother is prisoner of love."

She looked at them each as if from a throne or at least a lectern. Her nostrils were flared, and her eyes were enormous. She nodded. Januscz nodded back, as if he fingered the cello beneath her soaring violin. Alex thought this, in the Reading Room, about his father, who had known, who had to have known, about one specific prisoner of war and Sylvia, his wife, the boastful prisoner of love. Here he was, his long, sad, Slavic face the bottom half of which was curved up in a small smile, the top half of which, across the brow and around the eyes, was sagging downward, a flag of his conflicts. He had very large hands on strong arms. They were the product, he had told Alex, of scything hay for his father and stacking it, of hoeing potatoes and digging them up, of pushing the cows into place for the milking. At the dinner table, with Liz on her first visit, Alex sat and watched the big fingers as they held each other in repose. Why, he wondered in the Reading Room, had the fingers not curled into fists? Why had he not overturned the pine refectory table that night, on any such night, or ever, and vomit at her the years of swallowed insult?

"Prisoner of love," his mother had answered.

And in the Reading Room, remembering, he shook his head. Not good enough, Ma. He had to have wanted a freedom your treason enfranchised. You made something possible for him, but he never accepted the possibility for anger, for revenge. There had to have been a transaction between you. It can't just be about love.

Alex thought he must have whispered the "love," for a man in a stained, filth-smeared navy blazer, his white shirt gone nearly black with accumulated dirt, looked up from the newspaper he'd been reading or pretending to read.

He had determined to ask her as she declined. She was dying when they reached Ann Arbor, and was dying for several days, but he never did ask her. She had shrunken over the nine years since their first visit. Her face was like her younger face, but seamed, cracked. Her hair was gray and brown, not white, and her crepey, loose arms were like a junkie's, pitted with sore-looking scars from IV tubes, bruises from injections. Her physician, an old man who bore himself like the dean of a small, prestigious college, came twice a day. "Just wearing out," he said. "She held up and held up and held up, then—like an avalanche, it all came down. Some of them do that."

"'Them,'" Alex said. He heard the anger in his voice.

"Us," the old man said. "Us. She's not uncomfortable. I'll call it congestive heart failure. She's sedated past pain. She'll be all right. Just wearing out, you understand? Nice woman," he said, patting Alex's arm.

"Nice," Alex had said. He thought, now, in the Reading Room, of what had been lost when she died—Alex's childhood legends and truths, and the elder Kessler, the navel of his new patient's existence. With a sudden bite of sorrow he thought of what he never would know: the passion, and the hundred thousand transitory sights and feelings of the beautiful Jewish Polish girl who had loved a Catholic Polish physicist, perhaps, and who had probably, he thought, loved a killer, or saint, from Berlin. He was breathless with the loss.

His mother's breathing, then, grew louder, stertorous, and it followed him as he looked into bureau drawers and on the shelves of her double closet. He prowled, like a child, for secrets. He found none. He smelled the smell of old flesh and stale perfumes. He found no letters from the lip of the grave addressed to Januscz or to him. He did find, in a small yellow Whitman Sampler box, a patch of navy serge, about three inches high, about an inch and a half wide, with yellow embroidery. He kept his eyes away from his mother, whose face, over the three days he sat with her, collapsed in upon itself so that she bared her teeth and gums as if snarling, so that she leaked liquids from the mouth and nose, so that her high cheekbones were surrounded by brown, seamed skin that at first flattened her delicate structure, then sagged down past the face toward her ears, and made her look like a yellow-brown skull.

Oh, Sylvia, he wished to wail. But he had no idea what to say after that. He thought of her hard childhood in Cracow, near Blonia, where she met Januscz, who had come home from school to his father's farm to help graze the cattle in the common. He tried to say something to her about her mother, who, Sylvia swore, had never loved her, or about her hard, generous care for Alex, or even about the stillness in this large, unfriendly house as they waited, his father and he, for her to announce the detailed nuances of her dissatisfaction with what she called, as if they both were her children, their "behaving."

In the candy box under the garments in a drawer filled with stockings and underwear, at which he prodded but which he did not wish to hold, and which looked as if they would be slippery to the touch, and which the thought of touching made his fingers dismayingly dry-feeling, he found a newspaper clipping and a few large copper pennies with King George stamped on them. And he found the piece of blue serge cloth. It had been sewn onto something else, he knew, because dark threads looped in a running stitch formed a border at its edges. Embossed in its center with heavy yellow thread were three diamond shapes. It seemed like a sort of military insignia. She made a gargling sound and, like a child caught searching his parent's drawer—not a bad description, he thought, sitting in the Reading Room—he returned the patch to the box and, never having examined the newspaper article, he returned the box to the drawer. He saw it once again in his life, when they assembled her usable clothing to give to charity, and they threw out what he and Liz both referred to as junk. He often regretted his willingness to discard her belongings. He believed that he had felt forced to display his health in letting her go. Included with the garbage was the Whitman Sampler box, and, he thought, as he leaned above a collection of reminiscences of the Luftwaffe bombings of Barrow-in-Furness, he might well have discarded something about her lover—something, he could not help chanting to himself, that was old and new and borrowed and blue.

It must have been the greatest moment of her life. And time, in the form of her child, had shoveled it over, and it was gone. That was one of the reasons he put his head down into his cupped hands, at the long, glowing Public Library table, and tried to weep. He didn't succeed. But he sorrowed on his mother's behalf, and the sorrow seemed right. The man in the filthy blazer who was killing time and finding some ease looked at him with furtive, dark eyes, and, suddenly, he shook his head at Alex. Like Januscz, Alex nodded in return. It was time to leave, and as he walked on Fifth Avenue, staring at pedestrians in case one of them was Nella, he thought that in the library, tonight, he might really have mourned his mother for the first time.

ON THE FOLLOWING afternoon, in his office with a stocky, red-faced, attractive detective, Alex gestured at the patient's chair.

"Usually, they sit here?" Detective Rhys asked. When the blush left her features, her skin was milky and soft. She verged on overmuscular, as if she lifted weights and worked out with large men. Alex thought of Anthony Slowacki; she could take Slowacki in a street fight, he was willing to bet, and Slowacki could crush a man as large as Alex even before the fight might begin. And why, he wondered, was he thinking of hand-to-hand combat? Detective Rhys took off her dark tan twill topcoat and said, "You don't mind?"

"I'm sorry," he said. "I can hang it in the anteroom."

She shook her head. "Please don't take the trouble," she said, and he wondered if he was hearing how they spoke in Wales. "They sit here, do they, your patients?"

"Is that Wales I hear?" he asked her. "And, yes, they do."

"My father would be making speeches on behalf of the Welsh parliament if he could," she said. "If he weren't so dead. Yes, it's Wales. And then what?" she said, opening a long notebook and uncapping a fountain pen, shaking it to start the flow of ink—to start the flow of his words, he thought. "Then you talk to them?"

"No," he said. "Well. Sometimes. It's more important to the process that they talk to me."

"So this will be a bit of a change for you, then. You talking to me. You know: so that I can get what I need to know, and be of some assistance."

Her skirt was long, a dark blue that didn't quite match the dark blue sweater she wore. He was surprised by her tennis shoes, until he thought of films he had seen in which the police chase malefactors. Detective Rhys was ready to chase someone, he thought. That was why she was here. But she needn't be chasing him, he thought. His conscience would take care of any such pursuit. Her hair was very short at the back and sides but, somehow, one of her dark blond, or light chestnut, hairs had fallen upon her sweater. It glinted in the low light, and he wondered what her response would be to his standing, and approaching, and then leaning down to remove it from the sweater where it lay, just below her shoulder and above and to the right of her breast.

He sat where he was, and he said, "I filled out a report. A clerk, a lovely and efficient person, a tall black woman, took a statement from me. *She* filled out the report, and I signed it. Is this—"

"You could call it a follow-up," she said, writing something. "I read the report, and I've a question or two I'd love to have answered. If I'm to be of some use."

"So you're the person who investigates Nella's—"

"I am presently the precinct specialist in the life of Ms. Nella Grensen. Now, Doctor, you didn't poison her and cut her into pieces and feed her into the furnace of this palatial building, did you? Because I would have to follow you for the rest of your life and have the City's vengeance upon you for your crime." She smiled, as if Nella dead and dismembered were a story for children, a joke among the sturdier detectives, a cute anecdote for sweating psychologists. But she waited for him to answer.

"No," he said.

"Anything to add to that?"

"No."

"Aren't you outraged? Insulted? Horrified?"

"Yes."

"But."

"You've got me confused," he said.

"Oh, that's all right, Doctor. I'm here, really, to start the clarification of it all. You'll see. I've done this sort of investigation before. I didn't think, you understand, that you were some sort of monster. But it's best to have as much of that out in the clear light of day as we can. And so that you know how seriously I take the matter of a missing person. It's a terrible thing, a loved one gone missing." She looked up from the pad.

"Patient," he finally said. Her blue eyes seemed as dark as Liz's were light, almost black, and she stared from under long, dark lashes. "Patient," he said. "I like her. She's a—she's a good egg. And I worry about her. Because she's a nice woman and a patient."

"A good egg," Rhys said slowly, as if instructing herself in how to spell it. Then she said, in a businesslike, impersonal tone, "Suicidal?"

"She's the daughter of a suicide. Her mother. I don't rule it out. The children of suicides will, often enough, follow that path."

"Is it a way, do you think, of recovering the parent who abandoned them?" Her eyes were wide and innocent, her face slightly flushed, as if she were embarrassed by daring to explore, with any authority, the landscape that was his to patrol.

"No. In a word: no. I think not. Though it surely is a response to the parent's death and manner of death. It might be a way of *becoming* the parent and, as the parent, loving themselves—the child. It's tricky."

"Yes, and I've overstepped my expertise. I apologize."

"No need. No need. Anything that gets her back—"

"Back?"

"Well: anything that gets her unlost."

"Would you be meaning *found*, Doctor?"

He nodded, his tongue and mouth dry, his language, for the moment, evaporated. Then he said, "Found."

"Good. We're on the same page, then. Now. You know her well. Best of anyone whose name I have, except her employer—the thingy office, the architects', and of course her dad."

"I know her."

"Yet she's been a patient—she's been your patient—for how long?"

"Two months, or a bit more. Ten weeks, I would say."

"Did you see her weekly?"

"Oh, no. No. This was a difficult business, and it was five times every week—daily."

"My, my," Detective Rhys said. "Saturdays?"

"Two or three Saturdays, I believe."

"And so you believed at the time of giving your statement in the report."

He knew that if she examined his appointment book, she would see Nella Grensen entered three times each week. For the other appointments, that had not been noted, were scheduled by them for the Hotel Essex, on Central Park South, and the St. Moritz, and her apartment on Bleecker Street, and once at the cement-block Holiday Inn on Eighth Avenue—an evening of grueling sex for which he had suspected they would want a brutal room. His groin stirred, and he detested himself, thinking of her long body slicked with sweat, of his body slicked with her, and of the only words of hers he could remember from that night: Please. Please. Please. Please.

"And—can you tell me this?—what made her case so difficult?"

"Her mother *killed* herself. Her parents werc survivors of Birkenau. I'm speaking of the Shoah, Detective Rhys. The Holocaust. Their experience was unspeakable," he said, detesting himself more deeply because he lay beneath the bodies of the dead, cringed behind the motions of the walking wounded, because he had fallen from his marriage into love with a doomed woman. Why, necessarily, doomed? How far from the marriage? Love? Was it, heaven help them, love? "Her father"—he could not prevent himself from using any, using all, of it—"apparently never spoke. Apparently, he was not just a quiet man, you know, a brooding personality. He never *spoke,* once her mother killed herself. It is a sign, by the way, of the inferior care I gave this woman that I never found out whether she had had to endure that kind of silence as a very young child. If she told me, I can't remember."

"Is it on your tapes?"

"I don't use them. It would breach the seal I try to

establish between my patients and me."

"Seal."

"Proximity, call it. Chemistry," he said.

"Pretty physical, that word. 'Seal.'"

"It's a good thing you're not investigating me, then," he heard himself dare to say.

"And why ever would I do such a thing, Doctor? I'm here on behalf—it's how I think of it: I'm working on behalf of the missing person. I'm here for Ms. Grensen. We'll have to see you get your turn later on."

He watched to see if she meant it. He waited for her smile. Finally, it came, and he permitted himself to smile in return.

I did not make Nella disappear, he reminded himself.

And in Rhys's faintest of accents, he thought, to himself, Oh, no?

"The father has been contacted?" he asked her.

"I believe one of the clerks has been trying. We haven't had a reply. If he's as taciturn as you learned from her, it's no surprise."

"I might be able to visit him," he said. Then, faster, he said, "We were thinking of a trip upstate. I could stop off. Is that allowed?"

She put the capped end of her fountain pen on her lower lip. "Probably so," she said. "It would be a while, for us to do it. Contact the state police or the sheriff's department in—what county is it? *Up* there, for sure. I can't imagine it would hurt for her doctor to prosecute a few inquiries. This 'we' you mentioned."

"My wife and me."

"Mrs. Lescziak."

"That's right, my wife."

"Grand," she said. "That's grand. You'd let me know if there was any information I should have."

He nodded.

"And we'll be asking her employers, the architect fellows. We'll ask them about her. Did she have troubles there?"

"She was bored, she said. The men and the cute girls wearing glasses—her words, not mine. They got the interesting assignments, according to her. She got suburban garages. She didn't enjoy what she did."

"Not necessarily a reason to disappear."

"No. But reasons for disappearing . . ."

"Yes, Doctor?"

"Needn't be rational."

"No. And drugs?"

"Something to help her sleep. The doctor—that is, a psychiatrist I referred her to for medication. I'm not a medical doctor. I can't prescribe."

"Isn't that a shame for you. So burly and competent and all. I'd think you *could* prescribe."

"No, that's not allowed. But thank you. No. Anyway, she was never permitted to buy enough pills at a time to do herself harm."

"Actually, doctor, I meant nonprescription drugs. I was thinking more along the line of heroin, crack cocaine, or the good old snorting powder in its less ambitious form. Or methamphetamine, say, in all of its lovely variousness. That sort of a drug. Had she a habit? Did you ever see her bare arms?"

He saw her bare arms, long and muscled, as they

came up his own, and along his shoulders, and around his neck. She held him, when they kissed, with her hands at the back of his neck and head, steadying him for her lips, pulling his mouth onto hers—in that *seal*, Detective Rhys—so that her tongue could work in him.

"No. Well, maybe she wore a short-sleeved shirt. Blouse. You know."

"Men are no good to us in the clothing department, are they? But, then, why should they be? The species is oriented toward taking clothing *off* of the female, is it not? So. You never saw needle tracks."

"None."

"Scars of any sort? On her thighs or under her arms, between her toes. Of course not. Why would you have seen *there*? Strike it from the record, clerk." She pronounced it *clark*. "What, then, are the other things, Doctor?"

"Other things?"

"The ones that worry you. The ones that brought you to the precinct house and to the attention of what they so charmingly call the detectives' bullpen. Makes a bunch of brutes of us, doesn't it?"

"Missing appointments here. Not showing up for work. Her troubled state when she began therapy for insomnia, anxiety, irritability, possibly depression. The chaotic state of the early home life. Her father's disappearance into melancholy, perhaps a schizophrenia—well, that's a long-range diagnosis, and you mustn't ever rely on them. But there's enough, Detective Rhys, is there not?"

She was writing. "My goodness, Doctor, you're like

a lecturer giving notes. You're very good."

"I am?"

"One of the best."

"At what?"

"At talking. You're one of the great talkers."

"Will it help you find her?"

She closed the notebook. She capped her pen and replaced it, with the notebook, in her stubby purse. She laid the flap of the purse over its mouth without fastening it. And then she gathered her feet beneath her and stood. He could imagine a man wishing to venture upon her. "No," she said.

"No."

"We might have a grand stroke of luck. But she isn't violent. She doesn't do drugs. She hasn't stolen cash from the job, or kited checks, or conned old ladies, or rifled mailboxes in the projects. There's no trail, you see, Doctor. She's a handsome and unhappy woman of the middle class who came to see a fine-spoken doctor just a bit too late, I'd say. There are several million of them in the metropolitan area, aren't there?" She smiled, and the faintest flush came over her, as if she were wondering, Alex thought, whether to include herself among them. "So I haven't the highest of hopes. But I'll do what I can. We will make inquiries. Well, we have already, haven't we? Beginning with you? A bit unusual, you know, someone filing the report who isn't immediate family or a longtime employer. A married man such as yourself. Still, it's a fine civic act you've performed, I'd say—I *will* say—and I'm proud to know you."

She came forward, as she lifted her raincoat, and she

reached to shake his hand. Her fingers were short and very strong, her palm was broad, and her hand was as cool to the touch as her face now looked warm.

"On behalf of the City of New York, and speaking gladly for myself, Doctor, let me assure you that I will be in touch."

Teddy said, "So you're working with the cops, Alex. Alex the detective. Remember what Freud said: 'The false teeth led me to the governess.' "

"Is that a clue, Teddy? A riposte? A lesson?"

"A misquotation."

"She might well have killed herself," Alex said.

"Yes. Seriously speaking: yes. Given her mother. Poor bastards, all of them. Even you, Alex."

"Me?"

"How do you think Liz will react to your filing a missing persons report on behalf of a very good-looking, and considerably younger, female patient?"

"Oh, Teddy. Come on."

"Yes?"

"You're right, aren't you?"

"Just follow the clues. The false teeth will lead her to the governess."

"Pardon?"

"You don't need it from me, Alex. Though I'd grant it if I could." Teddy clacked his teeth a few times and smiled a sad smile.

3

HE THOUGHT HE scuttled instead of walked. He saw

himself inching sideways on Central Park West as he made his way downtown. He thought he must look like a madman, shabby and uneven at the edges—crewcut hair untrimmed, the hem of his topcoat maybe hanging crookedly—everything felt uneven—one hand in a coat pocket and the other swinging as he went south, toward the Public Library. On the other hand, it was entirely possible that he was straight- and proper-looking, perhaps a little squinty-eyed, like a sailor who peered through unremitting winds, and tall, and broad, and maybe a little pigeon-toed, like a former athlete who still could play a game of half-court basketball. Sure, he thought. Except the *real* city game is craziness, which is why you're a star.

He watched faces as they came toward him, for he *was* a peering sailor. He was a lookout on the mast. He was looking out for Nella. It was possible, he thought. It's one of the reasons the city is enchanted: you could meet someone, say a patient you'd betrayed by loving her. You *could*, he thought. And he meant to. He craved to. He saw faces chapped with cold and scrubbed, by drugs, of their oils. He saw hands that shook inside the pockets of coats and feet that dragged at curious angles. He saw stained trousers under thousand-dollar jackets of softest leather, and once, he could have sworn, a rose-colored silk slip that hung from beneath the hem of an ermine coat. Scarves, high collars, kerchiefs, turtlenecks up to the chin: he saw faces float above them in shades of black and beige and purple, nearly, and in liverish yellows, in pale orange-pink, in pasty whites so bleached by stress or disease that they verged on grayish blue. He didn't see Nella. But he tried to.

And, actually, he managed, on some of his downtown and crosstown walks, to find her more often than even he could have thought he would imagine. He projected as if on a screen—even while he sought her on the faces of pedestrians— the tight grid of the borough of Manhattan, say, or the forlorn immensity of Queens. And once in a while, there she was. She was tall and broad at the shoulder, with an elegant nose, long neck. Her hair was sleek and dark, sometimes drawn back and held by a metal clamp, sometimes pinned up as if she were fifty, and once, like Detective Rhys's, cropped very short, exaggerating the stretch of her pale throat. Of course, he stared. And sometimes the woman stared back, or angrily dropped her eyes, or, once, glared in outrage and opened her mouth as if to curse him while he saw how mistaken he had been and increased his gait to escape. Sometimes she seemed healthy. Sometimes she was very ill, a broken, tall, young woman who was used to living on the streets and who could not possibly recognize the shambling man who had been her lover, who had placed his large hands on her bony, naked shoulders, who had brought her into his embrace.

So he traveled, this man, and he looked down years as, now, he looked down streets. He walked the city and *was* a city. He teemed with the lives of those he loved, and with the lives of strangers. He lived the histories of him and his, and the words, the words, the words, the words. What can you do, he wondered, with a man who dreams of World War II, on the instigation of a Shoah-denying, or, anyway, -revising, attention-demanding, calculating patient—and who *is* treating whom?—a man who goes beyond the Primal Scene to imagine, in the creepiest detail, his flesh-maddened mother and her lover out of Grimm, *Liebschaft*, in, well, *action*?

Maybe he wasn't so out of control, he thought, now, in his destination, the Reading Room. He had stood on the steps near one of the great carved stone lions that guarded each end of the base of the monumental stone steps that led up to the lobby of the library's Main Branch. He had thought of himself as standing between the lions, and then upon, and then between the parallels formed by the long steps: like a soldier, like a scholar, caught between the lines, caught behind the enemy's lines. Who was the enemy? Which was our side? Maybe he was not responsible. Maybe someone was composing him on paper, he thought. Maybe William Kessler was his author, writing him on a ruled tablet, pinioned between one line and another, then another.

He thought he might be—to use the professional nomenclature—nuts. And so he thought of Teddy Levenson. Teddy would know. Teddy might not be sleeping with Liz. Teddy might. Teddy was, surely, the authority Alex consulted, the resource he mined, the witty commentator on the marriage's collapse. He was the person whose insight Alex prayed for, but also the person to whom he could not confess about Nella. For Teddy, possible adultery notwithstanding, was an honest man.

Sitting in the Reading Room, his pulse slowing, he breathed like someone who was not in a panic. He returned to 1944, and to another false alarm. Perhaps someone on the spotters' phone line from the coast is nervous. For no bombers arrive. But no one in Barrow seems to mind, in spite of the cold, for it is fair, and almost as bright as day under the full January moon, and families have wrapped themselves in blankets over their winter coats, and infants are swathed, while older children ramble and shout, in spite of their parents' best efforts and the barking of the ARP, who roam, nervous as Shetlands after sheep, and the air raid, minus raiders in the air, is an all-night lark. The entire city, you might think, is on the common at Sowerby Woods. The ARP have had to extinguish a campfire or two, and their commands tend to waken more people than, tonight, they protect—for there is no one aloft to be protected from—and families visit as if it were Boxing Day. The common, half a mile from the center of the city, is noisy with chatter and laughter and the singing of old songs. It is like a large room in a great, happy house.

Sylvia sits with Januscz, and she is holding Alex. The cold, or smoke from the cigarette, makes her sneeze.

"God bless," Januscz says, in English. She swore throughout Alex's boyhood that they had not spoken Polish together since 1937, when she had witnessed the riots against Jews. "As if Nazis hired Poles to do their work," she told Alex, in America. "Like we was their maids and their laborers. Their assassins." This was shortly before her fiftieth birthday, when she stopped speaking of their past, and when an anger for or about Januscz shaped her face when Alex spoke to her of his father. But Alex, now, is in the Reading Room and it is 1944, and Sylvia has sneezed, and gentle Januscz has blessed her.

"I did not close my eyes when *kerchoo!* Ah: sneeze," she says on the moonlit, brittle, yellow winter grass.

"Yes?"

"The word is 'no,' " she says.

"No?"

"No!"

"Oh," he says, bewildered. "You didn't close your eyes?"

"Yes, I did not. Most people closing eyes when they do that. I did not. Why?"

"I don't know," Januscz says, beginning to roll another cigarette of coarsest tobacco sweepings. "Why is that so?" he asks in his deep, slow voice as his large fingers work with great dexterity.

"Why is that so," she mimics him. "Because this *child* sleeping on my lap. Inside of my arms. I am holding the child."

"Yes," Januscz says, "you are."

"*Must not drop him!*" she whispers, her tone full of horror, as if her husband has begged her to do just that. He lights his cigarette.

One of the ARP, watchful for an opportunity, cries an exasperated, "Light there!"

"No," Januscz agrees, "you must not."

119

"If blinking, you could drop baby."

"Yes," he says reluctantly, "I suppose."

"So I did not. I made for my eyes staying open."

"You can do that? You did?" After a few seconds, he says, "I cannot."

"No," she says.

"Maybe, sweet Sylvia, nobody can?"

"I can," she says. She is looking across Sowerby Woods toward the little assembly of stretchers and medical kits, where the guards, Leon Salthouse among them, have gathered several of the prisoners at the verge of the Ulverston Road. "I can," she says. Among the prisoners who sit patiently, their knees drawn up and arms around them, perhaps huddling for warmth, perhaps resting the back with which they have lifted and pushed and carried all day, there sits Otto Kessler—so Alex fancies his mother thinking, while she studies her lover—too small for the labor they require of him. It occurs to her that Januscz may be studying her as she studies Otto. But she feels as safe from Januscz as she feels safe from, in the absence of protection, a pregnancy. She can safeguard her child by refusing the body's insistence upon closing the eyes when an act of sneezing requires it. She can introduce deep into her body the very essence of the life of a beautiful man, and she can require that his being be stored inside her, introduced by the motions of her walking, by her scratching at the hideous, hard earth of the tile works, into her bloodstream, into the hidden organs of her body. It will not impregnate her, she knows. She will not conceive. But he is in her, he is with her, and the saliva that she now licks across her lower lip, hoping that he will see her and be stimulated, is alive with the liquid he has pumped through her.

"I never have heard of anyone who could do that," Januscz says. Expelling the harsh, pale smoke at her, he says, "You can do it, though." He nods, as if agreeing with himself. "And here we are, so far from home, and the closest the Germans can come to you is the air so high above our heads. And even *there* they do not come tonight. I wish I could truly believe in a God so I could thank someone for your safety. England, yes? I thank England for your safety, and the boy's."

She cannot help herself. She wishes that with one of the hands supporting Alex upon her lap she could reach for her generous, nearsighted, gentile man who is made glad by numbing labor because it enables him to keep his Jewish wife safe from the Germans. And she wishes that she could lament the German interpreter, the pastor from whom Januscz cannot protect her. She wishes, too, that she wanted to protect herself from Otto—to belong to Januscz as a loving wife should be her husband's woman. And how she would pray, if she believed, that the ragged rhythm of Januscz at love, his great weight upon her, his hoarse breathing in her ear that sounds more like a complaint about his task than a celebration of his pleasure, were anything to her but an intrusion, an uncomfortable pressure, a noise. Januscz is a municipal band of flugelhorns and drums. Otto is the sound of deep, resonant woodwinds, and she can hear them by closing her eyes, she thinks, as on Sowerby Common she closes her eyes.

She opens them. "I *sometimes* am closing my eyes when sneeze," she can almost hear herself confess to her husband.

She thinks of herself, sometimes, as the greatest of fools, because she sometimes considers herself and Otto as victims in a stupid melodrama that has to end in sorrow. And she is a fool, she knows, because she only *sometimes* thinks of their unhappy ending. Of course, it awaits them every day, all day. They close their eyes and do not see it, but they know that it is watching them.

"What?" Januscz asks her. "What hurts?"

She knows that he has watched her in thought, just as, she knows, he has watched her in her sleep. He has described her face in sleep to her, and she has gone so far as to demand that he stop. Though he agreed to, and at once, she suspects him of continuing to spy—and that is her word: "spy," as in wartime, on an enemy—because she is afraid that he loves her so devotedly, so hungrily, that he will read her treason as, in her sleep, perhaps, she might bite her lips, or cup her breasts, or caress her belly, thinking of the German prisoner whose prisoner, she decides, she is.

"Only that I am actually loving you," she says, and Januscz's long, solemn face, with its great nose and broad mouth, becomes a boy's face split by a smile. The shouting, then chatter, then murmur of the night-time picnic goes on, although, at around three in the morning, most of the celebrants have fallen into sleep, or tired silence. The gulls wheel and flap at dawn, and infants in Sowerby Woods start to crow as if in response to the distant cocks, left behind, who scold at the sun.

Back in the flat, they fry stale bread in margarine for breakfast, and then the woman called Granny comes by for Alex, to care for him while Januscz and Sylvia work. When Granny and Alex have left, when Januscz is hastily sponging himself at the sink, Sylvia sits at the kitchen table, staring at the red and white checks of the American cloth covering, or at the old muslin of the kitchen curtains, yellow with cooking smoke and spattered fat, or at what she will tell Alex, years later, was "a same way of living. Every day, we are living the same. More or less." Perhaps she is staring at the sameness. Perhaps she is staring at the less.

Otto is the more. She has told him so. He has asked her, as if he were a teacher, as if he were a pastor at Sunday-school instruction, what she imagines they might have been like: the stern, beloved instructer, and the acolyte. He has asked, and she has told him, and he has asked her again, holding himself almost within her and almost out, steady above her on his sleek, strong arms. He has not posed a question with his language, but with himself, giving and withholding at once, torturing her. She loves to be tortured like this, because he is at her, upon her, attentive to her every motion, moving in response, teasing her and making her come, nearly, with his presence alone. Her eyes are closed. His, she knows, are open.

She answers him. "You," she replies, to no words of his.

"Me?" Otto says, quizzically. She can hear the smile

in his strong voice, a baritone that is higher than Januscz's rumble. He is a violoncello, she thinks. No, she thinks: he is the cello's *bow*. It extends deeper. *She* is the violoncello, she thinks, and he draws—he compels—the music from her.

Again, gasping, she says, "You."

In his choppy English, but with a tone almost merry, benign, an uncle's voice—if the uncle is naked and hovering upon you, with his thick penis moving inside of you, down and then back and then down—he says, this uncle, "Madame, you are the dream to me of Werther. Goethe's dream."

She rises, as she knows he knew she would, because she cannot wait. She demands him, she retrieves him, she surrounds him, and the gorgeous, mad blankness, like an English fog, is over and within her. Now she's safe.

And me? Granny and me, Alex thinks, forty-one years later in the Reading Room. He is with the baby minder called Granny, wheeled by her in his rickety wicker pram to the Indian Tea House at the intersection of Michaelson and Island Roads, with its great curved windows, all but one blown out by the bombing and replaced with old timber and waxed-paper sheets, the interior lit by tallow candles to supplement the nearly brown light of the small bulbs high in the rafters. He is rolled back and forth a few inches, kept in place and in motion by Granny as she chats with her lady friends of similar employment. He is going nowhere as they drink their long-stewed tea, bitter as bad wine, but almost medicinal because familiar and hot, and sufficient for the dunking of rock-hard, butterless scones. He rolls forward and back.

Perhaps one of Granny's friends, say the widow Agnes Plumb, says, "Like a little Polish doll, i'n't he? Big, bright eyes and all."

"His mother's eyes, I suppose," Granny says.

"Her. If she isn't swiving half the night, I'm the bucket. Of course, *she*'s the village pump."

"Oh, you're wicked, Agnes. And, after all, they're different, aren't they? I mean: she's foreign."

"To be fair," Agnes says, "I sometimes wonder how *I'd* behave if I had to leave the native land and live somewhere else, among alien people chattering on in their daft language, and different ways of preparing a joint or ricing potatoes."

Granny laughed. "You're hungry, is your problem, Agnes."

"Though swiving, I am told, *is* swiving. And that's the long and the short of it, any road and any foreign language. And him, the husband, such a handsome, hardworking man. *With* an education. A scientist at that. Always a cheery word, and a gasper hanging off his lip. You'd think him a navvy, or a stonemason. I like a man who looks like a man, don't you? Still. There she goes, at it, I'm told, and at it. So who's the cock and who's the fox?"

"Well," Granny says, "they've got the little darling here. That's my boy. Give me that merry little look again. This one could make her come round, if she thinks enough about him."

"And a little less of the other thing, Granny."

"Mrs. Agnes Plumb, I have no idea of what you're going on about."

And the three of them wave their hands and cackle in the Indian Tea House, while Januscz listens to English engineers who instruct him in what he already knows, although they use a language that sounds to him, when he is as tired as he feels this morning, like empty drums flung down a long, curved staircase. Sylvia chops at the hardpacked earth outside the Hindpool Brick and Tile Works. And Leslie, Christina, and Tubby scratch with her, Leslie teasing Tubby about her little girl, whom Leslie calls the Tublette. They farm in English, she thinks, and they chatter on as if their breathing required their mouths to make words. And they watch her with an affectionate distrust. They expect her to kill the crops, she thinks. English earth and German bombs do that without her assistance. Sylvia works at the hard soil because, every day, from too early until too late, she is required to. It is the price of her share of their safety. A detachment of the German prisoners in their navy serge with yellow triangles on the arm is made, this morning, to step and wheel in a sloppy formation by a raging guard who has already told them of his cousin, Brian, "Died in Africa of shelling from the tanks of your bleeding mates. One of you, I beg you, give me a bloody *glance*. I beg of you. Or water your horse without a by-your-leave. For I would then be required to fire, and with no warning. Do you understood, you conquering warriors? Heil bloody Hitler to you, and best of bloody days."

"I was slave," his mother had told him when he was

small. "I was agricultural slave." In a small field in Barrow-in-Furness, outside the brick and tile works, she hoed and tilled in the hard soil where for seventy-five years they had dumped and buried shattered tiles. Sometimes a bomb blew up their plantings, unearthing bits of tile and the buried seed. Sometimes something grew. "I am weeping on them, freezing fingers and my toes, turning ears and nose into ice. Sometimes I am screaming at that place and cruel people. One of them, she loses mind, creature named Leslie, Land Girls boss. Her husband is exploding in the war. She appears at the working place, she beats me with a rake. She is saying I shouldn't complaining no more. This was at the start. I made plenty noise, all I want. Nobody tougher than me. Bombs coming down, I am laughing. Then, I am remembering I carry you in me, and I am crying. But first I am laughing! They was pretty sure I am mad. Maybe, yes, I am. Probably am. Poor Tubby and daughter. Good woman, losing so many kilos of her weighing, skin comes to be hanging like tallow on candle made from sheeps. Fold over fold. Her they are torturing also. Still. What you would expecting in a war?"

Finally, Alex, thought, walking north from the library, you make history. You choose it. That is the lesson of Kessler, he thought, his probable half-a-brother. There are scraps and tatters, there are documents, anecdotes, testimony, half-heard and partly told stories, and finally you select. So: the German prisoner of war, after the bombings, after the false alarms, after the sighting of the surfaced submarine off Walney, after the Polish émigrés have moved to the lightless terraced tenements at Cavendish Park, where the children at play pretend that the drying, never-quite-dried, wash strung above the roadway is camouflage that protects them, after the backyard Anderson Shelters mounded with earth, after the wave upon wave of bombers with their undulant, low engine growls and then the higher-pitched, steady snarls of the English interceptors, after the stick upon stick of blockbuster bombs and the parachuted land mines, after Gracie Fields singing "Turn 'erbert's Face to the Wall," after eighty-three dead in the bombings and six hundred houses gone, all told, and after the birth of one long Polish baby to parents who—according to them, and so far as his experience concludes—never again speak Polish, or ever watch a film directed by the Pole Michael Curtiz, including *Casablanca*—after all this recorded, annotated, recounted history, or whatever you wish to call it—there come the blank several years. The marriage cools and hardens, like winter, like cement, and then the detachment of German prisoners arrives. They are settled in several locations in the Lake District, and some come west to Barrow. It is 1944, and Alex is cared for during the day by a hard, wily woman named Granny Buccleuch, while his father helps Vickers test the suppleness of steel in hulls, and his mother breaks her fingernails against the iron English earth.

HISTORY CAN CHOOSE *us,* Alex thought, walking downtown and staring at the faces of so many people who were not Nella Grensen. So here it is. This, then, is where the new, revised, revising history might be said to begin. With Liz, his wife, like a distant, cold moon that orbited whatever heat was left in him. She went out, she returned. She slept—having said nothing about the move, having heard nothing from him about it—in their extra bedroom. If they had been parents, it would have been their baby's room. They had not been, and it was not, and now it was Liz's. Sometimes they might coincide, might share a meal, the day's mail, the news they needed, in common, to know: Teddy called, or the hospital called, or Hunter called, or nobody called, and still nobody, and still. And then there they were, across the table they had purchased together, their silence suggesting that they'd little more in common, now, than the table itself. Untrue, he thought, and unfair to their life together. But they should have had babies. It was the unspectacular decision he made whenever they felt most estranged. And it removed him further from her reach.

This is Dr. Alexander Lescziak's confidential line, his recorded message told them. He returned their calls and noted their appointments, but he rarely answered the phone. It was better, he thought, that he was one step away from easy reach. As far as Liz was concerned, each of them was several steps away from the other. And the wintry silence of their apartment coiled about them, reminiscent of his middle western home and its emotional tundra. Nella was gone. And Liz would have to leave. Kessler was announcing the replacement of the story of Alex's life with something new, vaguely criminal, not unexciting, but so unfamiliar as to add to his fright. And the President, to make things complete, was also leaving, for Germany. He would not visit a concentration camp, he said, only the SS graves, because he did not wish to reawaken old memories: "Very few Germans are alive," he announced, "who even remember the war, and certainly none of them were adults and participating in any way." That was the actor who played their President, and that was the history—an untruth in every syllable, every serif, every space between each word— that he was writing for his citizens.

Everyone leaves, he thought, finding himself, at 80th and Broadway, at Zabar's, where a thin, shivering black man with elegant features pulled open the door so that shoppers might enter to put down $17 a pound for something smoked, imported, and fun to eat. He didn't go in. He stood before the man, then walked away, because he did not want to engage in the theatrics of giving the man some money to be spent on suicide by drugs or wine. His stomach jumped when he thought of suicide, because he thought of Nella.

"Strong men," he had said to Francine Sloan, the final patient he'd seen that afternoon, before he'd left for the library, "that is, men we think of as powerful and whom some might want to call—"

"Bullies," she said, surprising herself, Alex thought, with the promptness and anger of her response.

"That," he said. "Yes. Or leaders, perhaps. Dominant males. Alphas. That sort of thing."

"Type A," she said. She was pretty and mild, very

nearsighted, and exhausted by her marriage. Her husband had chosen the location of their apartment, the color of their walls, and now he was seeking to choose a course of action that ran against her every impulse. He wanted to know the sex of the baby she carried, and she wished not to know until she delivered. "I'm used to it," she said. "My girlfriends tell me I'm badgered. I think they're right, but I just don't care. I don't care anymore if he chooses the whatever-it-is, and I don't care whatever the whatever *is*. Let me have my life, and I'll be fine. I can serve this sentence out."

"Except: you're here. You came here. You called, you took the train, you came here. Don't you—"

She interrupted him with a finger held in the air. "I do not want to be rescued by you or by my girlfriends or by my sister, Stephanie, or by my parents. It's fine. Victor is a good provider. He's not always bad to live with. He's very strong, you're trying to get a table or a parking space—you know: *get*. He gives good get. It's a joke I have with my girlfriends."

"Really a joke?"

"Can we come back to that question?"

"Whatever you say."

"All right. Here it is. What worries me," she said, "is we're arguing about this. Because this is something I really do care about. I do not want some kind of a hold put by him on this baby. He, she, she, he—they're coming into the world with none of his expectations on them, no label, not one or the other sex . . . absolutely nothing. Soon enough, they're in the world and the world's jumping all over them. And Victor is going to have his way with their lives. I'm telling this to Victor, and—I have to confess this—I got a little violent. There's some crockery on the floor. Broken, if you know what I mean. I threw it straight down. I wanted it to smash into hundreds of little pieces, and it did. It was a gravy boat from his grandmother. All of a sudden—listen to this: he's blubbering! I mean, Victor, this big, strong man, the king of go-get-it, he's crying and crying, and he can't stop, and I'm hearing the Please and the Darling and the Oh, my God, and I'm going *nuts* with it. It isn't him! Understand?"

Alex waited, in case she wished to say more. He was watching the light that came around the edge of a venetian blind as it lit the smooth curve of a San Ilde-fonso pot on his bookshelf against the wall behind Francine Sloan. He said, "Yes."

"Yes, you do?"

"Yes. I do. Shall I tell you something?"

"I'm here to listen," she said, sounding not a little like him.

"Very strong men," he said, "dominating men—the kind of man we know as an alpha male. What you called a bully."

She sighed. "He does his best to be one."

"Often," he said, "not always, but, surely, often, they are very frightened people."

"Victor?"

Alex said, "You know how dogs bark when a stranger comes to the house?"

She shrugged.

"They're not, in spite of conventional wisdom,

132

guarding their master. They're protecting *their* home. Because they are frightened."

"They're scared? And husbands, too. The same?"

"Husbands, too."

"Of *what*?"

"The husbands? Of being left alone."

"That, specifically, out of all the things there are to be scared of, you're living in Manhattan and civilization is ending and everything is drugs and rapists and muggers, you could be laid off work tomorrow, and he's scared of being *alone*?"

"Yes."

"Victor Sloan is scared I'll leave him alone, by himself."

"Yes. Not rationally. Not consciously. He probably thinks—he probably would tell you—there isn't much that intimidates him. And maybe that's true. But subconsciously, where he lives, deep inside, where the dreams and the nightmares come from, that's what frightens him. So many so-called powerful men."

She had been on the edge of her chair, almost standing, and now she sat back and crossed her legs with, he noticed, shapely ankles under thick calves. He enjoyed the sound of the friction of her stockings. "Abandoned, in other words," she said.

He said, "Abandoned. Just so."

"Poor boy," she said, with no facial expression, with no inflection of voice. "Poor puppy dog."

After Francine Sloan, and before he had left for the library, Alex smelled the coffee that Liz had brewed before leaving for Hunter to teach. He went through the apartment to the kitchen to make a joke about sniffing her out. When she looked at him and flushed, he forgot the joke. She was in black jeans and a V-necked black cotton sweater worn over a white T-shirt. She looked at him as if compelling herself to do it, and he, daunted, stupid with what he thought of as affection, emboldened by what he knew was need, was confused enough to think only of words—he noticed, as soon as he spoke them—that would distance her.

'Hi," he said, "I had this woman in there—patient. You know."

"Was she good for you?"

"Liz. Liz. Disastrous choice of words. Sorry. No—"

She said, "And I was being profoundly bitchy. Anyway, no therapist should have to hear that."

"Thank you," he said.

"Why?"

"Just: thank you."

"Okay," she said. "But you look so worried. What? About this woman—the patient?"

"You should have heard me. I was telling her all about how strong men are frightened of being left alone, and no sooner was she out the door than I came in here"—she drew herself up, he saw; she narrowed her eyes as if against a bright light—"because I had scared myself."

"Because of what? Me? That I might—"

He shrugged.

"I keep thinking," she said. She cleared her throat, and he watched her powerful muscles work. "I think we keep leaving each other. We just never make it out the door." She sat, suddenly, on a kitchen counter stool. She laughed. "My legs gave way."

"Good," he said. "So you won't be able to run off."

"Alex," she said, "none of this—"

"This?"

"—is about us detesting each other. We both know that."

"There's a *this*?"

She said, "I think there is a this."

"And we don't know what it is?"

She said, "I think we don't."

"But we feel terrible about it," he said, as if reciting to a teacher.

"Yes," she said, "we do."

He leaned against the counter, sighing. "Thank you," he said.

She laughed and covered her mouth. "Thank *you*." She laughed again, and then, he saw, she couldn't stop. He laughed in reply, giggling at first and then belly-laughing, with tears in his eyes that matched the tears in hers, as her chest-deep laughter matched his. Blinded an instant, and lost in his hysteria, he felt safe for seconds, maybe half a minute. But then their laughter slowed, and then hers stopped, and so did his, and he remembered the safety as you remember a journey concluded long ago. He coughed, he wiped at his eyes with a paper napkin and handed one to her. She nodded her thanks and rubbed the napkin like a washcloth on her pale skin; the scrubmarks remained awhile, and he watched them fade as she bent to her coffee and he turned away to his.

He stood, now, sipping, as if he were a deliveryman granted a cup and a minute off the job, waiting to be signaled to leave. Tasting the coffee, and nervous about looking at Liz, he remembered a line he had read in a memoir by a pretentious and, finally, not very bright woman. He had told Teddy and Liz, one night, as they drank martinis and laughed and laughed. Everything had been all right, that night, he thought now. He had declared it the worst sentence written in English: "I drank the beverage, but I was consuming myself," the woman had dared to write. He remembered their laughter, now, and he smiled.

He said to Liz, "I'm drinking the beverage, but I am consuming . . ." She was blank-faced, but then she remembered, and she smiled. She wanted to smile, he thought. She wanted them to have a reason for smiling. It was a conscientious smile, and he wished he could see, now, the one of only minutes ago—the spontaneous grin, face full of teeth and gums and tongue and inner linings of the lips, oh, Jesus, let him see it before they divorced. But let her not divorce him, he thought.

All right, he thought. But then what?

So, after some syllables, after some words, after the sounds of very hot coffee tilted along the inside of a cup, and the silence afterward, and then a longer silence, companionable at first, but then embarrassed, it was he, backing, almost bowing, who left the room. And he worried, all the way downtown to the library, and all the way back, through clouds of language about wartime in England, about her sadness on the subway, about her sadness as she came home. And he thought, too, that he should have done what he had possibly forfeited any right to: he should have comforted her. He should have stood alongside her and cradled her head and hidden her tears from his own eyes—given her that, anyway—and he should have provided her with what large people ought to offer the small: shelter.

SLOWACKI RETURNED, the man whose beat was the subways and buses instead of the streets, but who was a man all about the streets—his pugnacity, his wariness, his willingness to grapple, his hard stare. Today, his bristly mustache seemed too large for his face, and his tinted, steel-rimmed glasses seemed too small; his anger was bursting out of his head, Alex thought, thinking too that it was a wild idea, a sign of instability in the doctor confronting—but why not say facing?— his patient. Alex thought that Slowacki was back because the process interested him. But it might have been in response to a superior's command, he thought. And it might have been that he sensed, if only from Alex and not yet himself, that Vietnam and the state of his marriage were related. According to him, reporting on their relationship, he had forced his wife, and more than once, to have sex with him. She had complained once, he said, but the complaint disturbed him. For, according to him, she had requested that he get tough with her. Slowacki's words: "get tough." It was likely, Alex thought, that she had complained to a friend of his, a cop, or even his superiors, and that he had been compelled to the intake session. But his return had been interesting to Alex, and even a happy note. This visit, his third, might mean a great deal.

Slowacki said, "I get out of here and I get home, and you know what she says to me? This is, well, you remember. You wrote it down. What I said about in-country stuff?"

"Vietnam," Alex said. "Yes. What did she say?"

"We're talking. Nothing physical, understand. We're sitting and I'm drinking a beer and she's folding laundry. She does so much laundry, you'd think it was a whole school instead of one kid. And she says something about a neighbor lady—this is out in Mill Basin, it's the direct other side of the universe from here. It'll take me two hours minimum, tonight, getting home. And she tells me this woman next door, down the block, wherever, she's talking about the Jews and the Germans."

"It's in the air," Alex said. "The President."

"That's it. That's the one. He's going over there for Germans, and we got guys in vets' homes dying, they fought in Europe, guys fought the war in Vietnam—don't get me started. Anyway, this lady, perfectly nice lady according to my wife, except for this. Lady says, it's all propaganda from the Jews in Israel, they want to raise money here, they talk about the camps, the gas, the usual. She and her old man, they're all for it. Except the thing with the gas. They have it on good authority, this woman says to my wife, the thing with the gas is a bunco deal. Elaborate fraud. Example: Oswiecim."

"Auschwitz?" Alex said. "The camp?" He changed the position of his pad and wrote. His fingers, as usual, were tingling. He felt his heart race.

"Doc," Slowacki said, "a couple of Polacks like us, we know from Oswiecim. Cracow. Like, the strip mall for Cracow. You like that? The little strip mall camp. You think they really used gas?"

"Do you?"

"Well, this woman points out the thing I always figured was bullshit, if you pardon my French. The thing with lampshades made out of skin. Talking like that has to cost you some credibility. The commandant making lampshades out of the dead prisoners' skin. I heard it was bad. Don't get me wrong. I heard it was terrible. They worked 'em to death. I heard the Jews got so hungry, they turned cannibal. You ever hear this? The poor fuckers ate each other. I figure that's where the B'nai Brith or somebody got the lampshade thing—all that skin lying around. People feel bad, they give money for the trees they want to plant in Israel, whatever they're doing over there. Now, you do this bullshit with lampshades, and then you try and get people to believe the Nazis were monsters, they don't believe you. All the exaggeration, you know."

"But what reminded you about it, Anthony? Anthony is all right?"

"Until they change my name. I told you." Alex nodded, but knew that he had failed to hear him say it. "You can call me Anthony, you can call me Slowacki, Tony, whatever you like."

"Thank you," Alex said. "Would you mind answering that question? About what reminded you of Oswiecim? And why you called it that?"

"It's Polish. We're a couple of Polacks, right? Brotherhood? All that. And plus the lampshades you got in here."

Alex didn't look at them. He forced himself to look at Slowacki, to neither hear Nella's voice, nor to see Liz's eyes, instead of the pale, immobile face before him. "The lampshades in here," he said.

"Yeah. They remind me of skin."

"Did you think it in Polish? Can you remember?"

"We're Americans, my people. I learned to think in English. I know, you know, maybe a dozen words in the old language. Like: *kielbasa.* Nothing sexier. No. Not in Polish."

"Yet you said Auschwitz in the Polish. And you thought of Cracow. You didn't mention Brzezinka, or Monowitz. Just the first camp they built, Auschwitz I. Do you know who went there?"

"Yeah. Jews."

"Poles," Alex said. "Good Catholic Poles. Jews too, of course. Later on, many many more, but in the early days it was the intellectuals, the resistance."

"You would have gone," Slowacki said. "Intellectuals." Alex tried to read his face. It was affectless, a statement in itself.

"I expect so," Alex said. "Why did you want to point that out?"

"Did I?"

"You said it."

"I'm not the perpetrator here," Slowacki said, "remember?"

"Anthony, who is?"

They sat for perhaps three minutes. Alex wanted to close his eyes. He wanted to sleep. He thought that if he did close his eyes, he would see, projected on the lids' soft linings, one of the women he had failed. So he stared at Slowacki, and suddenly his patient's eyes began to blink. He rubbed the back of his right thumb at the tip of his nose, and the mustache moved, and the blinking continued.

In a tight, ragged voice, he said, "It's possible that Rina thinks I committed assault on her person."

"Did she say so?"

"No. Not straight out. But you know women. . . ."

"How did she indicate it?"

"Not in so many words. The way she acted."

"How would you describe her actions?"

"Crying. Kicking. She kicked her feet."

"Did she kick at you?"

"No. On the davenport. She kicked her feet like a baby."

"Did you make love on the sofa—davenport?"

"To tell you the truth, I thought it would be—romantic, to tell you the truth. I come in off of a killer tour, it's late, I'm whacked, I'm completely whacked, I got a couple of beers in me, and she's sleeping on the sofa. She tried waiting up for me. Rina's a terrific girl. It's like I'm standing in the subway car and we're taking a curve—you ever do the curve standing up that goes from Bowling Green, you're on the 5 train going to Brooklyn? The way the wheels howl on the track? You grab hold of the stanchion or you fall. You could fall, right there. Same thing, except it's inside of me.

So I grab onto Reeny. I call her Reeny sometimes for Rina. This is short for Maureen. She's this terrifically cute little redheaded Mick, after a baby she still has this very good figure, believe me. I grab on to her so I don't fall down, except of course she's already down. A figure of speech, understand? So instead of down, I fall in, you'll pardon the details. She's still asleep, I figure out after. I thought she was reaching for me when I was pulling her pajamas down. But she was pushing *away*, she tells me. This is after. But during, there's all these arms reaching. Which, anyway, is what I'm *thinking*, until she told me the pushing-away part. Who knows?"

"Did you explain to her? Did you tell her what you thought?"

He was silent. Then he said, "Yeah."

"Did she accept your explanation?"

A shorter silence, then: "No."

"Do you know why?"

"No. I think—to tell you the truth, I think she wants to believe in the worst aspect of the situation. I think it makes her feel better if I'm a real shithead. I think she's maybe having an affair with some guy."

"Rina is looking for ways of blaming you?"

"This is what I think."

"She's blaming you."

"Yeah."

"So what's she doing to you, Anthony?"

"She's fucking me is what, Doc. Didn't I just explain?"

"Is she raping you?"

He smiled, his face crimson. He stood up, took a step toward Alex. "This is allowed? Moving around?"

Alex spread his hands to indicate that a patient could do as he wished. Slowacki walked to the drawn blinds at the rightmost window in the room and he ran his knuckles against their grain, admitting light in a fanning flicker. Then he returned to the chair, and then he sat. "It's like a word joke, right? Like Scrabble, except with people instead of letters? I say *fuck*, you say *rape*, so then I think about *rape* and I say *rape*. And I came in here, didn't I, talking about rape in the first place."

Alex said, "Not quite. You came here, remember, talking about human lampshades and Nazis and dead Jews, and the old country." Alex omitted, at least for this session, Slowacki's associational process that made his doctor a murdered Jew; his head would ache enough when he left. "Do you remember?"

Slowacki said, "Did I sound like a prick?"

"You sounded as if you didn't quite believe in the historical details of the Shoah."

"That's the Holocaust?"

"Yes, it is. Do you, Anthony?"

"Do I what? Believe in the Nazis making lampshades with the skins of Jews?"

"Do you understand that men and women and children—those not murdered immediately—were terrorized, humiliated, poisoned with gas and shot to death and worked to death, because they were Catholic priests or homosexuals or Jews. That murder upon murder was done. Four million, six million, eight—who knows?"

"Jesus, Doc, take it easy. No insult intended, you know? They worked them in camps, that's what I know. A lot of them died. The rest—"

"Why the camps at all? That's my question."

"I was wondering. You got a little excited, there."

"You said it: the lampshades, Anthony." But Alex knew Slowacki was right. Remember to be the doctor, he instructed himself.

Slowacki said, "*Why* is what you're asking me. Why I mentioned the subject."

"I am."

"That matters, huh?"

"It does. Because it isn't Scrabble. You're very clever about word association. But, as you know, there's no game. You said it—you raped your wife."

"Maybe."

"I think you know it's certain. Do you?"

"That I raped my wife? Or that, according to my doctor, my wife is raping me by fucking somebody else on the side."

"Anthony: quick! Off the top of your head! In your family, who's the Nazi? Who's the prisoner—the Jew? Tell me quick!"

"Who's . . . You're asking me who is— What kind of question is that to ask a person, for Christ's sake?"

Alex forced himself not to pant, to sit quietly with his hands clasped. He said, "All right."

"No," Slowacki said, standing, then sitting, as if his legs trembled. "No," he said, "that isn't the kind of a question you ask somebody. Jesus. I'm a fucking Nazi?"

"Is she?"

"Why does anybody have to be?"

And, to his own horror—call it disgust, he thought—Alex heard himself instruct his patient, "Everyone takes turns."

You can't believe that, he thought.

"Doc, I think this is over my head."

"That's all right, Anthony. Let's get off the subject. It's a disturbing one, isn't it? I find *myself* disturbed," he said, possibly crumbling the doctor-patient relationship, and maybe for good.

They sat, and no one spoke, and Alex thought that someone in the room was breathing harshly, from the throat, as if in panic, as if on its verge. His desperation, his own disintegration, led him, finally, to say, in a taut voice, "We spoke of Vietnam last time. Do you have the energy to touch on that again? Did you tell me you were wounded over there?"

Slowacki expelled the air he'd taken in.

Alex waited.

Slowacki said, "Yeah. I was hit a couple of times. You get hit by friendly fire, you don't get a Purple Heart. Did you know that? They don't like advertising we blew up our own. Why would you bring this up, Doc, right after the Nazi thing? Because one discussion we will *not* have is how the dinks in their black pajamas were like Jews, yeah? And the big, cruel Americans with their MREs and their cases of beer were fucking Nazis. Okay? That particular one we don't do."

"That wasn't my idea. I'm sure it isn't yours."

"I heard it enough from pinhead peace jockeys. *That's* not on the table, here."

"Okay.'

"You want me—I should tell you a war story, Doc?"

Alex said, "If you like."

"If I like," Slowacki said. "I guess even the Nazis told each other war stories."

Alex waited. He didn't know what else to do.

Slowacki closed his eyes. He cocked his head as if focusing, then said, "There was this pursuit. The lieutenant tells us a slant patrol wandered into our perimeter and got wiped out by our MGs. We heard the firing start and stop, then nothing. But two of them, it turns out, probably they got hit and they died, but maybe they were still in the area. Possibility. So the lieutenant gets our sergeant to tell off a detachment of us, we're supposed to hunt these fuckers down and bring back their ears."

"Literally? Their physical ears?"

Slowacki looked at him as if his doctor were a child. "It was a war."

Alex nodded. "Yes," he said.

"It's in the middle of what they were calling Operation Prairie, a lot of bullshit on account of nobody seeing any prairies there. We're supporting Marines. They had lost a lot of people to booby traps, so we're all jumpy, out on this hilly terrain with jungle highlands. Ugly terrain because you're always exposed out there. And we're chasing a couple of guys in black pajamas, following bootprints we pick up after a while. You don't need to be Tonto to find them. They're bloody. In all that mud and shit and brown water and fucking sea serpents for all we knew, we could see the blood. Seven of us after two guys bleeding to death. So we're standing there, an old sergeant who never got one day older after that, and six of us doggies with condoms over the muzzles of our weapons and dry socks in our helmet liners and nothing's working, we're wetter than the water, and Danny—I can't ever remember his last name: Danny is all I come up with— he's a specialist four, big motherfucker with the M79, it's a grenade launcher, he starts screaming, 'Grenade! Grenade!' I turn around, he's behind me, and I see one of those War Two stick grenades they got from the Chi-Coms, it's maybe a yard from my fucking foot. Lying there like a snake. I swear, to this day, I believe I heard the fucker *hissing*. Everybody says no, they don't make noise. I heard it, though. And we're standing like fucking tourists at the Statue of Liberty, looking at it. And then it goes off. No more helmet on my head, left pants leg shredded, left shirtsleeve shredded—I'm feeling myself all over to find out what part of me got blown away. I can't find my weapon, because the blast took it. You believe this? I cannot find it. I'm running my hands through the mud and shit but I'm afraid I'm touching my own blown-off toes or something. I hit the stock, I go to pick it up, and this guy Danny— Jesus, I wish I knew his *name*. Danny's screaming. He's screaming and screaming, and I crawl over to him, and I can't see any of him that isn't covered with blood. The sergeant's facedown, out, gone, he's dead. It turns out he bled to death through his foot. Pumped it all into the rice paddy. The other guys, they're all bloody and beat to shit and moaning, only me and the medic aren't wounded, and I was the one standing butt cheek next to the fucking grenade! They're shooting at us, the guys who're supposed to be half dead, and some of the wounded guys are returning fire, and I'm holding on to my weapon, which is covered with ox shit or something, wiping my hands against my chest, except there's shit and mud and blood on my shirt, naturally, and Danny: he keeps screaming. By the time I got a round off, the firefight was over. We never found their bodies. They're probably in business on Third Avenue, selling oversize Golden Delicious apples, two bucks a pop. Danny screamed, it felt like, for an hour, never mind the morphine. We pumped enough into him, I can tell you that. All I hear is the sound of the firing and Danny. He's always screaming. Like he never *wasn't* screaming."

He was speaking slowly by the time he'd finished, and more softly, and he looked directly at Alex, as if daring him to comment. "I was *not* hit, officially. Just a lot of scratches and scrapes from brush and flying shit, debris. I was not hit. You know what, though? I *feel* like I was hit. This kid, Danny, he screamed himself to death. He screamed his entire self away. There wasn't anything left of him after the morphine. He just kept crying and crying, softer and softer, and when they pulled us out, he was like this very soft towel that we wiped up everybody's blood with. There wasn't anything left except the blood. I don't remember the question. What—you wanted to hear something from—I don't know."

He sat with limp arms, his shoulders rounded, his mouth slack. He said, "That what you wanted to hear, Doc? Oh. Right. The Nazis and the Jews. So: that's what you get from a Nazi like me. Or am I a Jew?"

Alex opened his mouth, closed it, then leaned forward. He said, "You're a victim of chaos, Anthony. You were involved in a situation where you had absolutely no control. And what you need, now, is to assert control." How could he talk to this man after hearing his story? Because, when he was able to, that was what he did: he talked after hearing stories.

"Even when you make love to your wife," he went on. "Do you think that might be why you want to hold her down? To act in aggressive and what she might consider inappropriate ways? Guards, any kind of people in power, people *given* power, and people who decide to assert it: they could remind you of the warders in the camps. It doesn't mean you're a Nazi. You aren't. But you're perceptive enough to worry about it. The way, say, you worry about what she does when you're not home, I imagine."

"You imagine. Good imagination! She's fucking some guy, I guess I should worry. Wouldn't you? With *your* wife?"

"Do you know that she is, or do you worry that she is? Are you *afraid* that she is?"

"I don't *do* afraid."

"We're almost finished for today, Anthony," he said. "We ought to talk about control and anger and . . . worry next time."

"You wanted to say *fear*," Slowacki said.

"We should talk about it next time. Are you planning to return?"

Slowacki, on his feet now, rubbing his mustache as if to comb it into place, said, "Yeah, why not. We can trade war stories. Were you there, Doc?"

Alex saw an atlas, and then its maps, and he saw a finger—was it his?—moving from Eastern Europe, over a page, and onto a map of Southeast Asia; from there, it could trace his walks downtown, and Slowacki's ride into Brooklyn: the moving finger of despair's historian in wartime and in peace.

TEDDY WALKED AHEAD of him as they crossed Central Park, heading for Fifth Avenue, and Alex, tall enough, and with long legs, had to push himself to catch up. Was it, he wondered, that he resented being led?

"Teddy," he puffed, looking at the pedestrians for Nella, and thinking that he should say this, now, to his friend: Teddy, I keep trying to find her. "Teddy," he said, "the patient of mine who disappeared."

"The beautiful woman," Teddy said. Teddy wore a tan raincoat that billowed behind him. Alex thought he wore it open so that passersby could admire his hand-painted necktie under a gray tweed sportcoat that looked soft enough to want to stroke.

"She's more than a beautiful woman, Teddy."

Teddy stopped, and Alex did too, and they faced each other, two sizable men, one three inches taller than the other, men of bulk and bearing, one of whom, Alex thought, had a face gone crimson, the other of whom tried to look innocent and failed. Teddy said, "Define 'more,' please. Pretty damned quickly, please. State the nature of your involvement. And don't mess with me, Alex. I'm hearing lies. I'm hearing countertransference. I'm hearing—what? Malpractice?"

"You know she's gorgeous. You've prescribed for her."

Teddy nodded. "But I prescribe for a lot of your patients. And, except with her, I haven't heard that 'more.' "

Alex said, "When you say 'affair,' do you use the French word, with an *e* at the end, or do you say it in English?"

"You had an affair with a patient. You *slept* with this Cleopatra?"

Alex walked on, almost smiling, he knew, with what he thought might be relief. It lasted two steps, and then his mouth tasted sour and his stomach cramped. Teddy followed, then strode in front, cutting him off, and he stood before him. As if colder winds blew up, although they didn't, Teddy buttoned his long coat. With his hands in his pockets, he bent, as he often did, to peer into Alex's eyes, as if they led someplace. Alex said, "No."

"You're lying."

"No. I told you: I wanted to. That's bad enough."

"No, you're lying to me. I'm the only person in the city of New York with any patience for you, and I'm losing it."

"You're referring to my wife without naming her?"

"Good guess."

"Do you think she hates me?"

Teddy began to walk again, and Alex had to take two long paces to catch up. Then they walked in step, Teddy cutting through the damp grass of barely-spring as if to prove that his very expensive shoes were, indeed, waterproof; Alex's showed, with the spreading dark stain across each toe box, that his were not.

Teddy said nothing, and Alex, like a patient in his therapist's silence, had no choice but to speak. "I hate this, Teddy. When you take over like this. I worried out loud to you that my wife might hate me, and I know she talks to you, and you're my friend—I can tell this because you're always scolding me—so I need you to *tell* me something, not boss me around. All right?"

Teddy said, "How's this: I really don't want to see a Watteau show at the Met."

"Good. Neither do I. Too much light. I need darkness now."

"Name a hotel off Fifth with a bar that's dark."

"I don't know any."

"Let's go find one."

They sat in a booth and drank, at Teddy's insistence, single-malt whisky with an unpronounceable name that Teddy, of course, was able to pronounce. If the bar wasn't dark, it at least wasn't bright, and the booth was made of wood, and no music played. Teddy looked younger, Alex thought, in spite of his murderous work schedule—private practice, patients to see at one public and one private psychiatric hospital, teaching, and the occasional hours of hooky with Alex and, always, a wonderful woman. The women had been, and, Alex predicted, would be, different over the years; but each one stayed for a long time. He thought of Liz.

Teddy was looking into him again, his dark eyes squinting, the crow's-feet around them furrowed deep, the three wrinkle lines across his big forehead equally deep. His large hands were splayed on the table, suggesting that he suppressed a thought.

"So," Teddy said, "you had a crush on a patient. This—"

"Nella. And she's lovely. And the word, I'm afraid, is 'have,' not 'had.' She's hard to let go of."

"How hard have you been holding on?"

Alex shrugged. He sipped at the whisky and made a face.

"It's great stuff," Teddy said. "You can taste the iodine from the sea that washes into the peat. How hard, Alex? Alex," he said, staring at him, "you goddamned well *did* sleep with your patient."

"Only in my dreams," Alex said, looking away because he was certain that Teddy knew he lied.

"Tell me," Teddy said, "swear to me: it's a crush, and you'll pull away from it. Send her to somebody else."

"Oh, I would," Alex lied. "Except she really did disappear. Never showed up at work, she's never at home, she told me about no friends so there's no one to check with. She vanished, Teddy."

"This is the one with the father—"

"Who was in the camps. Yes, she's the one."

"And the mother who killed herself."

Alex nodded.

"I'm sorry," Teddy said.

"Me, too."

"But what were you *thinking*, letting yourself get involved like that? Then keeping her on as a patient?"

"You're so certain I was able to think?"

Teddy shook his head but then he toasted Alex and drank a large swallow. The whisky had been served in balloon snifters, and, as Teddy tilted his chin to drink, Alex studied his throat and chin—the only angle from which Teddy could look vulnerable. As Teddy's face came down into view again, Alex flinched from his eyes, and shifted his glance to his own whisky, shaking the snifter to make a play of light on the coal-colored surface of his drink.

"I wish you had an easier time," Teddy said, "you and Liz."

"I wish you could be my doctor."

"Suicide for both of us."

"The therapist can't be friends with anyone," Alex said.

"That's maudlin enough to come from a drunk," Teddy said. He signaled for more drinks.

"Liz may hate me," Alex said. "It's hard to blame her. Before it's over, she will."

"She doesn't. And you know it. And it doesn't have to be over. And you know I can't talk about what she says to me," Teddy said. "She's my friend, you're my friend, she's halfway my patient by now."

"So am I."

"That's why I need two heads," Teddy said.

"Think of what you'd need if we were parents,

Liz and me."

Teddy grew still.

Alex said, "She left home when she was sixteen because her father was a monster drunk and God knows what else. I'm the product of the most dysfunctional couple created by rise of the Third Reich. Breed? All my parents did was *brood*. No. Absolutely: no."

Teddy started his new drink.

Alex said, " But I did agree. We did try. We were plucky and loving and full of chipper, spirited commentary about our own biology, and we tried."

"I know."

"In vitro. In vino. All of it."

"You didn't adopt," Teddy said, as if reluctant to speak. "I hear it can be a lovely route to take."

"I have a brother, it seems," Alex said, looking away, and wishing that he could be confessing about Nella. "Half brother, he claims to be. The historical details seem accurate. This man called William Kessler, who my mother gave birth to, apparently. She gave him up for adoption, so that does take care of the adoption route, as you call it, for the family. And it's a major source of his aggrievement with me. Talk about inappropriate doctor-patient relationships—well, anyway, not so appropriate, even if it isn't anything I actually did. For a change."

Teddy set his glass down and he stared.

Alex thought he heard Nella's voice at the bar. It came from a round, sweetly smiling woman whose legs were so short she could barely climb up onto the wrought-iron stool. It had been Nella's voice, saying,

"If you do me the courtesy of pouring it, the least I can do is drink it." The words weren't Nella's, nor the tone, quite, but the compensation in the statement for shyness was hers, and it truly could have been her timbre.

"Tell me," Teddy said. "For Christ's sake, tell me."

Alex thought, as he moved his snifter on the shining table, of the great, greasy barrels he had read about, filled with filthy machine oil by the prisoners, to be lit by the ARP if bombers came attacking the sheds at Vickers. As Teddy awaited his story, Alex was thinking of Liz's lonely face, and of Nella's voice, and of whether he would tell Teddy that Otto Kessler was a conscripted clergyman and underground warrior, or an SS interpreter who had sold his mother a major league lie. Alex, as Teddy waited, was thinking of the barrels tended by the prisoners, and of the chimney cleaning, and of smoke screens.

Teddy's "tell me" sounded, now, like his own, Alex thought, as he had seemed to beg Slowacki for a story from his war. Alex thought, in his shame, that the question had been less therapeutic than evasive. A smoke screen, Alex thought, drinking the whisky that tasted like medicine. If only it were, Alex thought. But what, really, could you prescribe if the doctor was the disease?

WILLIAM KESSLER SAID, "Why would you choose *not* to read an essay by one of your patients?"

"I have to ask you to believe," Alex said, "that it's best for the course of a patient's therapy if his analyst does not study or admire or appreciate in detail or, frankly, take any very deep note of his patient's achievements, or, even, efforts. If you were a painter, for example—"

"As is your wife."

"Oh?"

"I am trained in research," Kessler said.

"I would not attend a gallery exhibition of your work, I was going to say."

"Just so," Kessler said. "I see. Pity. It's an estimable piece of writing, I think."

Kessler wore his heavy tweed trousers, in spite of the warming spring day, and his black broadcloth suit jacket. In its pocket, like ranked soldiers, were a green-, a red-, and a blue-capped ballpoint pen. He was speaking of the Association for Historical Accuracy, of which Alex hadn't heard before Kessler's last visit. A little research in the Reading Room had told him that the group, led by an English writer with a Jewish-sounding name, was dedicated to denying or mitigating German guilt for the Shoah, American guilt for the treatment of Native Americans and African-Americans. Its membership seemed small, and most were on every faculty except the history department of colleges of any distinction. He had heard of such groups and had read references to their work: not every German was a Nazi, not every Nazi was a murderer, the showers never poured out Zyklon-B but were all about delousing, to be followed by hard work, but no murders.

"Anti-Semitism," Kessler was saying, "is a petit-bourgeois bigotry. We are about the writing of history."

"And Otto Kessler? And my mother?"

"Our mother."

"If that's the case."

"Careful investigation, lucid writing, all will offer you the case conclusively. And that is what I have been writing."

"Your memoir."

"This is the age of memoirs," Kessler said. "But abundance does not diminish quality, at least in this instance."

"This instance," Alex said, "in which Sylvia Lescziak has the honor to be portrayed as unfaithful to her doggedly faithful husband. Maybe as an SS officer's strumpet."

"Strong, if antique, language, brother," Kessler said. He smiled at Alex, and Alex knew it was his mother's smile, the lips pressed tightly together almost in denial of the pleasure which the expression could be taken to suggest. "But, then, I bear you difficult news. So you cause it to recede by using a Victorian locution. 'Strumpet.' Charming, really."

Alex shifted his feet and realized that he was setting himself as if to try, once more, to undertake what was his obligation in therapy. He said, "Could you tell me why?"

"Patient to doctor? Brother to brother? Well, half brother, that is. Or man to fellow man?" Kessler's pleasure in pronouncing "brother" had been so clear: Alex felt like a schoolyard bully. And he wondered why he wanted to.

"Whichever you prefer," he said.

"So the question is why I have come to tell you about myself and my work?"

"About my parents," Alex corrected.

"About our mutual parent," Kessler said.

"About Barrow-in-Furness, and the war, and the German prisoner," Alex said.

"You're the person to whom people come when they need to tell things," Kessler said. "I'd have thought that was evident."

"So you *need* to tell this."

Kessler touched the cap of each ballpoint pen, green and then red and then blue, and he said, "Yes. I do. Very much."

"Do you know why?"

"It's who I am."

"And who are you?"

Kessler said, as if lecturing, his voice growing in resonance, authority, "I am the one she came here bearing. I am the one she gave away. I am the rest of your life, Dr. Lescziak. I am the part of the story no one has ever told. You might call me the secret refugee. I was, in effect, smuggled into and out of the story. I'm a sort of spy, you might say." He smiled, but he didn't believe in the smile, and neither did Alex.

"You believe that Januscz, my father, knew this story?"

"You know, I really don't care," Kessler said.

Alex, in spite of the pressure on his skull of Nella, of Liz, of Teddy's investigatory zeal, had kept listening— or, he whined to himself, he had tried to listen—for the story inside, the one closest to the nerve. He felt hungry for something direct from Kessler, who seemed always to be sidling toward him, somehow in disguise. His anecdotes were sub rosa agents. Alex didn't know whom they represented, or what, or what was most the matter with him, or what the matter was that meant so much. And he heard, instead, a weaving of information, anecdote, dramatic scene. You waited for a message, he thought, but what you got was artfulness. And *why* was this small, abandoned man so artful? Telling Alex was crucial to him, and understanding him, for obvious reasons, had grown important to Alex. So he asked, and Kessler answered, and they stumbled from exchange to exchange while—"*Here*," he heard in Nella's voice, "*sit down here so I can sit on your lap*"—he felt the weight of another past lean down on him.

"But Januscz," Alex said, "was a kind, gentle, very quiet, completely balked man. I don't think anything went well for him except at Barrow, in the shipyards, where apparently he became an expert on the tensile strength of what they called a destroyer escort's 'boss,' which I believe was some part of its hull."

"They built them for the North Atlantic convoys," Kessler said.

"I really don't know."

"Oh, I do. So much shipping bound for England, food but mostly weapons and munitions, was torpedoed. It was a shooting gallery for a while. That was what the U-boat commanders called it. The English used these little clapped-together variations on destroyer, quite insufficiently armed and armored, to race back and forth the length of the convoys, throwing a few depth charges over. It was futile, hysterical. They were as thin as the walls in their terraced flat, those escorts. They got sunk faster than the shipping."

"You know about the terraced flat, then."

"Really," Kessler said.

"Of course. You're an historian."

Kessler shrugged.

"And the sinking of those escorts," Alex said, "you make it sound like a personal victory for you. Is that the case?"

Kessler was flushed, and he sat back to push at his hair. Nella spoke to Alex, about an architect in her office who fancied her, she thought, and by whom she was disgusted. Alex sat back as if jolted, and Kessler studied him. Alex brushed his hair back and Kessler, as if emulating him, pushed at his own. "I'll never say you're not perceptive," Kessler said.

"Thank you."

"You're welcome."

"But that," Alex said, "was what *my* father worked on. While *your*—"

"My father worked on our mother," he said. "I think you can say that. Yes."

"You're proud of their relationship."

"I am," he said.

"It did no harm?"

"Oh. Well, not to her. Not to a man who had been conscripted from his pastorate and his underground work. A man who was unjustly imprisoned when he should have worn medals."

"As you will prove."

"As I will prove."

My father could not tell me the time when I asked him. He wanted to. He loved me! But it was like watching a broken machine at work, Nella said to him. *He made his mouth open, and it opened so slowly. He made his tongue lift, and it came up slowly. He made his voice come out, and it was like a horrible old recording of someone I almost knew. If I asked what time it was, I had to wait and wait. Then: 'Three-o-clock,' this dead, dreadful voice said. And then he made himself smile. Alex, he loved me. He did. He didn't know how to show me. But I know he did. Are you shaking your head?*

Alex said, "But I see—"

"Yes," Kessler said. "Time's up. Game over. The end is drawing nigh."

"Meaning?"

"I'll have to telephone for an appointment," he said. "I must fly to Lubbock, Texas, next week. A conference."

"Your historians."

"My historians. I still haven't had a bill from you."

"Patience," Alex said.

Kessler said, "I understand patience."

Do you? Are you stalking me? Are you saying that you've waited all your life for either me, or your life, or historical accuracy, or simple ease? And is that—is any one of them?—what you now possess? Oh, light the hearth fire and get the bricks smoking, he thought, envisioning a roofline of Victorian chimneys under a sky filled with sticky soot that clung to the faces below like dirtied snow. Wartime in Barrow. The chimney cleaning.

IT WOULD BE, he had thought as he turned off Lexington Avenue onto 39th, east and below any streets he had prowled for years, a Renaissance drawing of a man flayed of skin to show his nerves along his skeleton like vines on a long-dead tree. Or it could be one of those hideous paintings, *The Anatomy Lesson*, say, with the poor bastard opened up, while conscious, under some mustachioed fellow's scalpel. Alexander Lescziak: the horrible example. Watch this man carefully. Do *nothing* to emulate him. Maybe they could use him at one of the major psychiatric training hospitals, the way they used vagrants in the old-fashioned barber schools: let the students work on his living head as if it were not a portion of a live male. This, they could tell the students, is the man who did it wrong, every syllable, each step.

Begin, of course, with an affair with a fragile patient. Nuff said, he said to himself in the hoarse voice of an antique actor he could not name. Select for a rendezvous a hotel you have heard about from another patient who works there, on the theory that this patient is the night concierge and would never see you, and that his hotel, so far out of your way and Liz's, is somehow safer than the finer places on Central Park South you've been using. Have the room reserved in your own name, for the sake of being more easily caught—by whom?—and eat greasy gyros at a joint on

74th and Broadway so that your bowels are boiling by the time you arrive at what looks like an apartment house seen from a taxicab window in Sunnyside, but which is an old hotel.

The woman at the desk, tall and imperious in a flannel suit of dark gray pinstripes, had hair so blond that it looked white. Her face was long and expressionless, and her green eyes were filled, he was sure, with contempt. He paid with his credit card to be certain, he now believed, that an adequate trail of evidence—sought, he wondered again, by whom?—linked the afternoon and the room to Alex, who was guilty, though not yet openly charged, of adultery and of the abrogation of most other codes. The floor was a dark green marble clouded with cleaning fluid that he could smell, a mixture of citrus and peanut shells. The semicircular leather bench at what seemed to be a plastic palm tree was occupied by a tiny woman in a denim skirt and denim shirt and sneakers: a shabby, miniature Sylvia, he thought. She looked at him from above binoculars that hung about her thin neck. The day concierge was talking to a friend in Spanish. The woman at the desk called out, behind her, in what he was sure was Russian. The woman with binoculars spoke, to no one in particular, in what he thought might be Portuguese. He was reminded of fado songs, sung low by sensuous women in half-darkened rooms, about love that was lost or about to be lost. His bowels were fully liquid now, and he walked, tightly clenched, to the elevator around the corner. Alex, in his office between patients, forced himself to smile at this memory even if he wished very much not to. You deserve a condescending smile, he thought: you were the most complete of fools.

The room into which he'd sidled, carrying his large briefcase as an imitation of luggage, his single attempt at plausibility, was a large box of a bedroom, with a sofa, coffee table, and easy chairs at its far end, and, around the corner, a very small kitchen. He thought, for the first time, he believed, of living with Nella in a place where one cooked and ground coffee and corked a bottle of wine three-quarters consumed and later, before bed, washed up the dishes. He dropped the briefcase and scurried for the bathroom.

And there he was, in the stench of his toxicities, when Nella knocked at the door of the room. "Right there," he called, desperately scraping at himself with harsh toilet paper. "Be right there!"

He half-stooped above the toilet in order to flush away his wastes, hoping he would have a minute more to clean himself. He sat again, he wiped, he stood again and gritted his teeth, and he was washing his hands, smelling the wafer of hotel soap, when he realized that he had nothing with which to camouflage his stench. And were they ready, yet, for bodies with no pretenses? Were they prepared to admit, this early in their catastrophe, the ingloriousness of their flesh? Matches, he thought. You light matches, and they set the body gas on fire and burn the stink away. But he didn't smoke. He tiptoed, as he zipped and buckled, into the end of the room with the coffee table. There were no ashtrays in evidence and no matches. The door is a fan, he instructed himself, returning on his toes to the bath-room door. He pushed and pulled, pushed and pulled, and he succeeded, while Nella knocked, a little desper-ately, he thought, in scenting the air of the entire small suite with the smell of his stricken bowels.

"Hi!" he almost shrieked as he yanked the door open.

She stood before him with her mouth slightly open, her long, pale face vulnerable, almost frightened-looking, he thought. Then its somberness was lit by a big smile, and she entered, kissing his mouth as she walked into him and the room at the same time. She stood against him, and he tensed himself to hold her up. Her cold hands held his. "I thought you didn't come," she said.

"Stuck in the bathroom, actually," he said, sounding to himself like Colonel Blimp in a film about England in wartime. Which, he thought, he very much was, though he was uncertain of his rank.

"I always wondered if shrinks ever peed. I'm squirming there, swinging my legs because I have to go so much, and you're like a statue of some god, or a philosopher, sitting so still and listening to me."

"You were swinging those legs," he said, holding her against him with his hands clasped behind the small of her back, "because you wanted me to look at your legs."

"I did. You remember what I wore."

"God. Yes, I do. What are you wearing today?"

She pushed back, stepped away, then opened her long, camel-colored boycoat. "A little less," she said, flushing, closing her eyes, he thought, so she could stay in their dream of flesh and not see anything realer—thus leaving him, of course, he thought, to cope with the actual world. The chore filled him.

He went to her anyway, and he slid the coat from her shoulders. It was what he had wanted. It was what he wanted. She was what he wanted, he thought. It was she he wanted, he corrected himself. When they had shucked her coat, Nella's shoulders and chest were reddened, and he loved the strength of her torso, the accessibility in the blush of her strong body before him. He knew, too, that he was remembering how Liz's body warmed before his eyes this way. His superego, Teddy would say, was laying a trap for him, seeking to confuse his tongue so that he would call this woman by his wife's name. And then, as if it were a pang of memory, he felt an enormous pity for this tall, coltish child, as she probably was when she was alone in the house of dead parents. He wanted to comfort her. He wanted to sneer at himself. She wanted to bed him. He stepped from his shoes and dropped his trousers and underpants, hoping they were clean.

Kissing—she pecked at his nose and cheeks, the edges of his lips, before she extended her tongue and covered his mouth with her own—they moved toward the bed and went beneath the covers. She shivered as if it were very cold in the room. It was very cold in her life, he thought, thinking too that he was only bad for her. He had been thinking of the long run, kissing her nipples and chewing them gently, working his hand at her groin. But he was, apparently, going to be bad for her in the short term as well. He was soft. He was unspeakably, irremediably soft. She moved to his softness, swimming beneath the blanket and the coverlet to reach him with her mouth. She grunted and sighed about him, as if he were satisfying her, and perhaps he was. But he could think only of the failure he was about to be. He held the back of her head as gently as he could while he pumped at her face. She made pleased noises, and Alex felt nothing where he should have felt a good warmth, a moist generosity, friendly welcome. He was numb, from his nuts to her wide mouth. He thought he might weep. But he was male. He was all boy. He refused to say die. He extended his hand, its partly numb fingers, and she took it with hers, removed her mouth to say, "Do that, Alex. Do that," and grasp him as he grasped himself. And then he was, at once, a man of forty-four years and a kid of, say, thirteen. Powerful with desperation, enchanted and in misery, he made love to himself as Nella made love to him. It was a surprising eruption, and she hummed her appreciation of its volume and strength. And then, after sighing around him, after nipping him with her teeth in a kind of farewell, she worked up his belly and chest to kiss him hard on the mouth, to extend her tongue and its coating of himself and bathe his mouth and tongue with his own juices.

She slept at once, to waken while he watched her. He had looked at her long, delicate nose and at her cheekbones reddened by exertion and, apparently, pleasure, and at her broad mouth. She looked both infantile and cruel while she slept. And when she wakened, it was talking, as if they had not made love but had been holding a session and, after an interruption, had commenced, again, with the talking cure.

"Did I ever tell you about a boyfriend I used to have? A lover," she said. Then she snorted a sort of laugh. "Listen to me: 'lover.' Well, he was a male, he had a cock, and he was a pretty grown-up guy. I think he nearly loved me."

"Did you nearly love him?"

"Not the way I nearly love you." She moved her head on the pillow, then reached into her mouth with a long, slender finger to work at something in her teeth. "A gentleman's hair, I believe," she said, coloring, and watching him as he, too, reddened, he thought. Oh, he thought, we are such amateurs. It's the only quality that keeps us from being hateful. We might possibly, always, in some tiny, Edenic corner, be innocent. "This man, he was called Albert"—she pronounced it *Al-bear*—"was in some foreign investment thing with the Kaufman Fund. You know: money and all? He invested a little for me, and I made a profit! And he made me. Well, it wasn't like I was virginal and fighting him about it. He was very handsome. He was very good in bed. He always wanted, you know, to do it from behind."

And Alex at once thought first of Nella, bent upon a chair beneath some Frenchman devoid of body hair and perfumed by Chanel Pour Monsieur, and then he saw himself and Liz—her eyes flickering with what he'd thought of as the heat in her brain—as she turned from him but drew him to her, spreading her buttocks, moving her knees up to be more available.

"What?"

"I'll ask the questions around here," he said.

"You're the doctor."

Did you love him? Was he a good deal older than you? Did he like to hurt you? Did you like to be hurt? Who broke it off? Did you take him in your mouth and nurse at him? How much money did he get for you? Do you think of him because of me? In spite of me? Simultaneously with me? Was I just now, or was I not, an incredible failure in bed?

"I'm *your* doctor," he said.

"Yes, you are." She moved against him. "Yes, you certainly are. I want what's mine."

In his office, remembering how in bed with Nella he had thought of Liz beneath him facedown, he heard himself ask, grunting, his nose against the dusty striped-blue-and-white hotel wallpaper above the short headboard, "Why did you tell me? About this Frenchman? Why now?"

Nella retreated, pulling at his waist, and he followed. They were locked together, and she led him, it felt, for feet, yards, moving and moving. Her breathing was very fast and he, he realized, was holding his breath as if waiting.

"Questions, Doctor!" She changed her direction, moving toward him now, as if the coy retreat were over. He wondered how her face looked, but he kept his eyes closed. "Because," she said, "I wanted you jealous." She made a wordless noise. "Of my soiled past."

And he, of course, of course: "Soiled?"

And she, panting: "Questions!"

"Because I am, too," he said in her rhythm.

"Good," she whispered. "Good."

He thought about her teeth and tongue on her Frenchman. He thought of Liz as she had been with him and as she might be, now, but with another man. He heard his intestines gurgle. But then he didn't. Because he could feel himself in her. He could feel Nella beating against him like a heart.

4

SYLVIA KNOWS THAT Leon Salthouse lives in his mother's house, and his mother is in a place called Pitlochty, which, he has told Otto, is in something named the Grampians, a part of Scotland. Leon looks away from Otto's face when he addresses him, and when he addresses Sylvia he seems respectful. But she thinks that sometimes, perhaps, he is not. Otto says that she is embarrassed, but that it is wartime and anything can happen and they must—Otto, a scholar, says it is a term used by the Romans, who were wondrous lovers—seize the day, embarrassment or no, and they must not speculate upon Leon's motives. Had he wished to, he could have reported them to the authorities long before. Otto rubs his fingers over her head, squeezing and caressing, describing the reports of women with their heads shaved bald by the resistance of France, their punishment for consorting with Germans. And we, he tells her, cupping her breast so slowly that her flesh prickles to predict his touch, are consorting. Still, he says, slowly kissing it, on the other hand, Otto says, suddenly laughing and laughing, with a mirth she cannot understand, the French surrendered almost before there was a war for them to lose.

And she says, "I would be bald," as if she came to an agreement on a purchase in a cold, badly lighted shop in Barrow, with little to sell and little to recommend what she had bought.

Scotland is above them, Sylvia knows, just as they in Lancashire are over so much of England, in its far western corner. There are creatures, she thinks, suspended over creatures. Above the little beings on the ground are the barrage balloons tethered to their lorries, and over them the Hurricanes and Spitfires nosing angrily up or diving down among the German Heinkels that drop the land mines on their little parachutes, tilting them toward fragile creatures and turning them into bits of bone and smears of pulp. She and Otto, baby Alex, poor Januscz, sorrowful Tubby and the other Land Girls: like the mice in the fields outside Barrow, and over them the hawks, and old Mother Salthouse fled to Scotland, Leon has said, because her heart had threatened to stop on account of the weight of the notes from the engines of the German bombers as they pressed upon her.

"Like a ceiling fallen upon her, she feels, the poor old darling," Leon says as they walk the lane, walled with stone to contain the pastures on either side. Sheep nicker and run a few paces to stand in the mist and, looking away, wait for them to disappear or, for all she knows, and maybe for all the sheep know, eat them.

The mice in the fields, however, do not wait. She has seen it at home, near Januscz's farm, and she has seen it here. The farmers and their children and their cripples and ancient hired men as well as women not at work, all chattering, as excited as if it is a dance, forming into a square with the sides several hundred yards apart. They beat their way inward in crooked lines of a crooked, moving square, slapping at the grass with wooden flails and hay rakes, shouting, scuffing their shoes against the hummocks and the level meadow, the mice and rabbits panicking, fleeing where they were driven, in fact: to the center of the square, where the younger dogs might catch a few as the boys and girls hurl stones, all of them followed by the scythers, as the harvest of the grain begins, and the harvest, of course, of the little creatures. She thinks of the bombers with their grinding, metal music, herding them all toward the scythes.

Her feet ache on the uneven hardpan of the road after a day's farming at the tile works, she and Leslie and Tina and Tubby, the English women insistently cheerful and she, of course, the sorrowful foreigner.

"Lugubrious lot, the Poles, aren't they?" Tina had said, knowing that Sylvia heard her.

"They haven't much to laugh about," Tubby answered, "losing their country. You can't really blame them, can you?"

Tina, naturally, said, "But can't they just get on with it. Homeland lost, countryside ravaged, pillaged, looted, et cetera, very sorry, but life goes on. And there *is*, I'm certain you've heard the rumors, a *war* yet to be conducted."

She thinks of them as mice, and she thinks *mouses* because she and Januscz no longer speak Polish, so must fumble their way in English. Of course, she thinks, they have also agreed to be faithful to each other as well. Yiddish, she thought, would better serve the ironies of feeling some sort of loyalty as well as this thrilling deceit, and both at once. Suddenly, envisioning the driven mice, she thinks as she has not for years of Esther Lewkowicz, who lost an eye to a rock thrown by a small boy, egged on by his father when a crowd of anti-Semites drifted past the Kosciuszko Mound and then the Chapel of the Blessed Bronisława, which looked like a crypt for vampires, she thinks, seeing again its high, sculpture-covered walls: a prison without bars, Esther had often called it when they went together to her house, where Yiddish was spoken.

Better to speak English, as she and Januscz agreed. English carries no memories now. Though one day it will, she thinks, and she will remember Leon, sturdy and stupid and careless, so often drunk because of alcohol supplied with her help or Otto's. And she will remember Otto. She will be without him and she will be remembering.

Better, she thinks, to speak English and be out here in this chilling mist, the almost-constant almost-rain here, and inside her brain the teeming, uncontrollable thoughts about now, and about the true price she later on would have to pay.

"Is mother well?" she says as Leon guides her off the road and over a stone stile through the wall that separates his mother's house from the pasture. Grazing sheep start, run, then stand. Mice, she has no doubt, and voles and rabbits, run from them as well. Only she and Leon Salthouse walk, as if they have the evening to pass, and no demands on their time. He has always been respectful, she thinks, despite her uncertainties. She does not know that she will not remember him that way. And she wishes, suddenly, with a yearning that forces her hand to clutch her jacket above her heart while she fights for the next breath, that she can tell this slow-moving, mannerly man—already dead, now, in some future in which she will remember this lost night—how decently he behaved during the sordid, precious hours he helped her to steal from His Majesty's Government, and from her husband—and from me, Mother—and from respectability, and from what is, like the mist upon and about them all the time and everywhere, this almost-rain: from death.

"She's getting on, of course," Leon answers, walking beside her again as they approach the darkened shepherd's cottage. "But she's fit enough, for all that. It's the apprehension, isn't it? Will the Luftwaffe appear overhead today or won't they? And they rarely come these days, it seems to me. Times past, now! The raids were constant, especially at the south end of town. Lord. They did a mighty damage. A lot of citizens were, you'd have to say, shell-shocked. Poor bleeders, begging your pardon. Trembling and having fits and falling down, some of them. Not Mum. She's strong stuff. It's only the apprehension that's got to her at last. You can't blame her. And she does have only the one kidney, after all. Still," he says, like Tubby or Tina or most of these English, always shaving the thorns from disaster until with their words they can manage it. ("Lies," she says to Januscz. "Philosophy," he replies, drawing on his cigarette.) "Thank you, ma'am," Leon says, "she's tolerable well, you'd have to say. And your people?"

"My people," she says, halting their progress and standing an instant, like the sheep as, fleeing, they falter. She has managed to think so little of her mother and her small, dark, unhealthy sister, and the aunts and cousins in Gliwice. Finally, she says, "They are in Poland." And, as if she has provided an answer, she marches to the door beneath the slate roof in the field-stone wall. It is she who knocks, knowing there will be no answer, and it is she who leads them inside, to the rooms she has never seen before.

As if for Leon's sake, Otto, she knows, waits in a room that Leon will not use. Leon takes her jacket and his wet greatcoat and he hangs them on pegs on the back of the door. In the kitchen, where a low coal fire in the large stove doesn't quite warm the small room and its slate floor, its thick, white plaster walls, he brews a pot of tea, talking casually, as if not about to leave her, shortly, so that she may break so many covenants, darken so much honor, while Leon nuzzles at homemade blackberry brandy as if at Mother Salt-house's leathery teat.

"Freehold, and in the family for ages," he says, answering a question she cannot remember having asked. His face, she thinks suddenly, is quite unwashed, with dirt puttied into the seams and folds as if he has been working near a smelter or, she thinks, sleeping in the street. Has he done that for Otto and her? Is he so reduced, and are they so wanton, that, between them, they have this weak, decent man asleep with the dogs down narrow alleys?

"That is fortunate," she says, as if she knows what "freehold" means. She thinks she knows what "free" means, however, and she speaks because she must pass the time in a civilized way—they are, finally, at Leon's mercy—and because she waits with such difficulty, aware of how little of the night is left, aware of this endless English ritual of the hot water in the pot, the pouring out of the hot water, and then the arranging of the leaves and the pouring in, and then the steeping, and then the pouring into cups, and then the Here and the Lovely and the Isn't It. Tea, which can smell so sweet, and which can give you comfort, smells mildewed now, and on the verge of rot. She wants to lift her forearm to her nose and sniff, hard, to see if it is her flesh that stinks.

"Well, then," Leon says, setting his cup down and taking hers, almost filled with untasted tea, and placing them carefully in the shallow, lime-stained stone sink beneath the iron pump. He looks everywhere but at her face, and she is grateful. "I'll be getting on," he says, carrying a pipe and a rubberized pouch of the sweet shag he smokes, and shaking his matchbox, which sounds to her like an infant's rattle.

"Off I go, then," he says, not looking at her. He uses a door which she had thought might be a rear entrance but which she can see, as he lights a spirit lamp before closing the door behind him, contains shelves that hold a few potatoes and a couple of scrawny carrots as well as some glass jars, perhaps of preserved vegetables, and a number of broad, oval serving platters. There is a metal cup, she notices, and he will pour the brandy into that, she thinks, reading his newspaper by the orange light of the lamp. Or perhaps he will sit in the darkness with his bottle of comfort and his enormous patience.

Otto is at the door that opens from the dining room. He is a little taller than she, but not much. He is very capable. He smiles shyly, and then the smile closes down and his face is masterful, determined, full of business, like a doctor at his practice. He bows low and gestures her through. She did not see the fire laid in the dining-room fireplace. He lights it now, and it smokes. He was gathering wood, a difficult chore on these soaked, stony fells, she thinks, while Leon, deserting all semblance of duty, had left to fetch the German prisoner's whore. She thinks it in English, *whore,* and the abrasiveness of thinking it is pleasant. She will provide her own punishment, thank you. And she will take her comfort as she can to salve the wound.

He extinguishes the small lamp on the wooden mantel, and the room is lighted now only by the low light of the smoky, hesitant fire. He has danced to her—as if in the ballet, she thinks; as if in a dancing contest after school—and now his hand cups hers, his arm is around her waist, and, with his face against hers, his shoulders bowed toward hers, he is humming very low, almost sighing, a tune she does not know. It is too intimate for dancing after school, and she has not seen the ballet, has only heard it described by Esther's older sister. But it is dancing, and he leads her, and she follows, moving to this foreign music heard only by them, she thinks. The music is a secret, and it's theirs. It is them.

At first, she thinks that she is clumsy, for they bump instead of glide. He makes graceful, long, swooping motions, but their bodies collide. Then, she thinks, it is because she stares over his shoulder and past his face—his skin smells of woodsmoke and machine oil, his clothing is musty and it smells of sweat, but the sweat is his and, mixed with the harsh, clean odor of the American soap he receives from his captors, it is a kind of coarse cologne—and she thinks to herself that she sees wooden shelves with little carvings of stone. She sees dark paintings that seem to be of the local mountains. She sees one of a boat under sail on the sea. She looks for a picture of the Virgin, but there is none, and she is relieved. There is, however, a picture of their king and queen, and it makes her smile: no goddess of Christ, but the real gods of these English. She notes the yellowing plaster walls, though perhaps it's the low light of the fire that makes them seem unwhite.

She is memorizing the room. For it will be in a future room, which she will know better than she wishes to, where she will remember, will strain to remember, the Salthouse cottage and the dining room in which her German prisoner, Otto Kessler, invented the music to which they gracelessly, happily, seriously danced.

"Sylvia," he says in her ear, and he stops. She knows, then, why they have stumbled. He has been pulling himself close to her, he has been tightening his arm about her waist, pressing her hand back upon her shoulder, urging his groin into hers. She smiles and smiles, for she is used to his forcing her to wait, and then wait, and then wait, until she is desperate for him. But it is he who cannot wait, she thinks. It is a victory in what is and is not a contest between them.

"Here," he whispers. His voice shakes, she thinks. "Come," he says, and he leads her to a room around the corner from the one he has warmed and lighted like the corner of a café. Now, they are in the sitting room. He is too proper, she knows at once, to use the old woman Salthouse's bedroom. His coat is spread on the settee. The far wall flickers from the fire in the dining room, and she stares at the shadows, remembering, storing the sight against a time when she will—when she must—say to herself, if to nobody else, "Wall itself is lamp lighting room for us. He is being *so* urgent! He is taking his own clothing off at once, before I am undoing a button. So! And without his trousers, and I am seeing again dimples in his buttock muscles, over flanks. Did I tell you truly that I am putting tongue on each dimple that night? Like baby, with this dimpled bottom. He is having a giant pizzle, too, I must telling you without shame or hesitation. He is having me with clothing still on from day in field."

But whoever she might say it to, she thinks, and even if she says it to herself, the listener then would not be able to feel, as she does now, at this moment, in this war, in this cottage, the silken slide of his penis. And who will smell the sweetness of his healthy mouth as he strains—she knows this as he moves above her, between the bombers and her body—to wait for her to catch up. She thinks to torment him, and she halts the grinding swivel of her pelvis.

"Oh," he complains, almost whining. And he says, "Please."

And it is she who is tormented by his supplication. He has led her, he has mastered her, and now it is he who asks for the gift he knows she came here bearing him. She moves up to meet him, very gently, and gently he moves down. And for an instant that she begs herself to wholly remember, they are aloft, they meet in the airborne friction only, mating in the air, she knows she will one day think to herself, like birds who may be brought down in a second by the farmer with his gun. But they are, very briefly, aloft in defiance of gravity and every other law. And, thinking how she will remember this moment, she comes and comes, and so does he, and they collapse upon her, and then upon the settee itself. She is almost unconscious with this pleasure. Yet she is also so aware that, having felt it, they have therefore lost it. And, fearing that she will not be able to summon some of it, or any of it, even the sight of the fireplace lighting the sitting-room wall, she begins to weep.

He covers them with his coat and with a dark woolen blanket that was draped on the back of the settee. She silently weeps beneath her arm. As if from far away, he says, "This one was the best."

"You evaluate us? No. What is the word in English?"

"Rate," he says. "They say 'rate' for orderly evaluation."

She sniffs and squeezes her eyes, and she has stopped crying, nearly. "You are rating us, then, little Heinie?" She touches his flank to underscore the cleverness of her pun. "And how you are rating me? Bushiness of the foliage. Depth of the ravine. The canyon, is it? And moisture lining walls. And, of course, how deep can descend in it. Whether"—she moves her crotch to his hand, which has cupped her—"canyon rises up."

"An earthquake," he says.

"What is that?"

"This," he says, introducing a finger, then another.

She cannot speak. She works herself on him as he labors in her. They are silent, and the room flickers around them, the smoke is in the air, sweet now, as the moisture boils from the wood. And she has a right to this. It is why you bear children, she thinks, so that they may experience this.

Ah, she tells herself, you lie. You bear children because you must, or because it pleases you, or because there are children in you to bear. This, though, them—in the cottage on the fells, at night, in defiance of a war and of marriage—this you do because you can. Let the children fend for themselves.

And he cries out as if it is inside himself that his hand moves, this man of the cloth, this prisoner of the war. And she, with all of her body, all of her life, now, balanced on his hand, she, spitted on Otto Kessler, is a kind of prisoner too, she thinks. And she thinks that she must remember all of this.

ALEX LEFT THE Main Branch and stepped around scholars and bums and smokers who stared into the weak sunlight or into books, or who sat on the steps in an enchantment of fatigue. He moved ahead now, with what he thought of as a purposeful stride, enjoying the feel of New York beneath his feet as he looked into the faces of women who approached, in case one of them was Nella. He walked past the bus stop downtown from the library, at Lord & Taylor, and remembered that he was not to walk to the precinct but to ride the Fifth Avenue bus. Detective Rhys had instructed him, "Get on the bus at half past four, if you will, and I'll bet you I'll be aboard. I'll be on my way to the station house. And Fifth Avenue, I'd remind you, only goes downtown. A lot of West Siders don't remember that."

"I'm a New Yorker," he said. "I know the city."

"Was I mistaking you for a tourist, Doctor? And aren't you a proud fellow."

"Sorry," he said.

"No," she said. "Not at all. And thanks for humoring me, for I do prefer to see you outside your office. I'm sure you understand." She'd rung off before he could tell her that he absolutely didn't.

He counted the quarters twice and tried not to look like a man who hadn't ridden a public bus in twenty years. There was no room for him on board, but the driver gestured curtly, as if Alex were a little stupid, so he climbed into the smell of strangers' sweet, cheap cosmetics and sweated clothing and soiled flesh, into the airlessness and heat, and he forced himself a few steps along the aisle to stand behind a woman who smelled like a Danish cheese at room temperature. She turned, looked up at him, and stared. He wondered if he looked like the miscreant he suspected Rhys considered him to be.

A voice came over the mob, her tough, curt syllables on a rich, smoke-coarsened voice. "We'll meet on the street in four more stops, Doctor."

The smelly woman's head moved at the "Doctor," and when he mumbled his agreement over the congestion of jolting heads and shoulders, she turned back, this time to shyly smile with even, unstained teeth. He nodded as if they'd been introduced, then closed his eyes. When he opened them, she was still turned, awkwardly, and her smile still rode on the fetid air like the Cheshire Cat's in his boyhood edition—it suddenly came to him—of *Alice in Wonderland.*

"Never eating foods or drinking liquids from strangers!" his mother had instructed as he'd read aloud to her from *Alice* at night.

"No, Ma. Never *eat* the foods. Never *drink* the liquids."

"Of course," she said. "But *never* the drinking or the eating, yes?"

"Yes," he almost said to the dark, muddy, tinted hair of the woman beside him. He counted the stops. The bus grew less crowded. As they approached the fourth, he could see Detective Rhys, who sat on the aisle of the final seat. She waggled her eyebrows at him, as

Groucho Marx, in his movies, so often did at women he was about to victimize.

Rhys wore a brown suede jacket that came to her hips and a silky skirt in a chocolate tone and dark brown shoes with low heels. "You look nice," he said, stepping down first to offer her a hand, which she affected not to see.

She reddened up to the edge of her long-billed brown suede cap, and she nodded. "Let's you and me have a stroll," she said, "and we can have a chat about whatever it was that you discovered on the subject of your Nella."

They had crossed Fifth and were walking downtown alongside Madison Square Park, where, he thought, it was a comfort to be next to a sturdy, armed woman, for the benches slowly writhed with suffering addicts and rage-choked men who seemed capable of casual, purposeless violence: a detective and a middle-class outlaw on their late afternoon stroll. "I wonder, Detective, why you call her *my* Nella."

"Maybe, Doctor, I simply meant your patient. You know: Ms. Grensen, the person you did, after all, file a missing persons report on, and the one we interviewed you about, and the one you called me about because you've new information. The patient whose welfare you've been worrying at, Doctor."

"I have been worried."

They walked in the rhythm of a leisurely stroll, he adjusting his pace to hers and she, sensing it, keeping the rhythm slow but not mournful—a foxtrot if not quite a tango, he thought, and he wondered why he thought of dancing with this detective and whether it was the ritual or the contact, the sex, that had occurred to him. "What's that I've said that makes you smile?" she asked him.

He shook his head. "You're a piece of work, Detective." He risked a look into her dark, shining eyes, and his glance ricocheted. He was frightened, he understood, not only of her suspicions, but of her intelligence.

"I am that," she said. "I have to say: I'm interested in how interested you are. Surely, patients stop coming to see you. And they don't bring a note from home, or write you a Dear Alex letter—that's a play on 'Dear John,' you know."

"But that's what a lover sends to her lover," he said. "My patients aren't my lovers."

"No," she said, waving at a springer spaniel which had climbed to its feet in front of an empty baby carriage to which its leash was attached, had wagged its tail twice, and then had lain down again. "No," she said, "they oughtn't be." She sighed as if unhappy or fatigued, or as if disappointed with herself for taking his arm. But she did take it, and they walked as if they were friends. "So, then," she said, "what's the information you've unearthed?"

He wondered if, through his sport coat and turtleneck, she could feel his pulse—a Welsh lie detector. "It's not earth-shattering news," he said, "and I wondered if you'd think I was wasting your time—"

"But I get to have a walk with you instead of trying to frighten a baby raper—they're habitual, you know:

their soul cannot be repaired—or conducting a search of a nasty, decrepit building in the hope of finding something left of a six-year-old boy who's never come home. I can tell you that he never will. I can feel it, and it's true." She squeezed at his arm, and he felt himself harden his biceps as if this meeting were a date, and she were a girl, and he were a boy who hastened to impress her. "I'm away from the pen, and off with a dashing doctor, Doctor. So be a swell and tell me what you've learned. And from what or who—you know: the source."

"Oh," he said, "no source. Well, the patient. Something she said in an idle remark some time ago. I didn't note it, and I'm not sure what brought it back to me."

"Well, you've been thinking of her, haven't you? She's important to you, and you've been dredging your memory, trying to find me a couple of clues. You're the most cooperative of men."

Maybe, though, it was in fact a tango, he thought, and, as they danced it along the streets not far from Union Square now, about to descend to Greenwich Village, he could not help thinking of their being together in bed. She would provoke and possibly hurt him a little, but it would all be in the interest of bringing them to the risky precincts he was certain she inhabited. "Why the bus?" he found himself asking. "Why did I meet you on the bus?"

"Oh," she said, "I wanted to bring you a few socioeconomic pegs down toward me. And I was interested in whether you'd jump through a hoop or two, and without complaining."

"And I did."

"Yes," she said, smiling, then looking away, "yes, you did."

"And what does that tell you about me?"

"Surely, you know."

"What, according to *you*?"

"Oh, I'd best not be telling, for the moment, I think. I'm the cop in the couple, remember, and you're the—"

"Robber?"

"Cops and robbers? No, Doctor. I was going to say complainant. Unless you're guilty of a felony or two I haven't heard about."

He shook his head. "You're too fast for me, Detective."

"I'm not slow," she said. "Give us the information, will you?"

"She mentioned a boyfriend. Lover. Man she had an affair with. She made a joke. She said it lasted a fiscal quarter."

" 'Fiscal quarter,' " Rhys said. "He's a businessman?"

"Some kind of investment person. One of the mutual funds—Janus, I think. No, with a *B*."

"Berger."

"Yes!"

"Yes, I found some documents from Berger. She made good money with 'em. I was thinking of doing one of their no-front-load funds."

"I forgot that you looked in her apartment."

"Oh, I picked it to pieces. It isn't large, as you know. And you'd be surprised at what I found." He stopped, and he watched her walk a few purposeful steps away, then pause, as if surprised that he wasn't beside her. Her flush, as usual, betrayed her, but not her expression, which was a mask of patience, nor her stance, which was that of a soldier standing at ease. He jumped when a car on Fifth honked repetitively. "That's a fine for the guy if I have to walk over to him and remind him to mind his manners," she said. It was a cab, and it honked again, then moved on. "Didn't you think I'd give it a going-over after you convinced us that this person was, indeed, missing? We responded to your own conviction that there was a problem about her absence. It was really you, Doctor, as I'd thought you were aware. You're why we're involved. As you wished."

He nodded. Instead of addressing what he believed she was saying, he took up the dance again, walking casually toward her, slowing, then moving on; and she picked up his rhythm and walked along beside him. She didn't, he noted with some disappointment, take his arm again.

"She said his name once. She said it with a French pronunciation for Albert: Al-bear, she said it."

"A French capitalist, eh? Well, it's their time. We brought in the right President for capitalists. It's the time of making money if you've money to plant and money with which to water your money. The money's growing like grass, I'm told. Not that I have any of it. And Ms. Nella was panting in unison with Monsieur Al-bear. How do you feel about *them* apples?"

"How do I, as a person, feel? Or as a witness—complainant. Whatever it is that I am. What am I, Detective?"

"What you are, according to me, personally, Doctor, is slightly cute. I like a man who's grand and shaggy and who offers me a hand down off of the Fifth Avenue bus. I like the way you wrinkle your forehead, and I've had to resist, twice, actually, the inclination to rub my thumb along your brow to get the worry off of it. In a fleeting way, you could say, I'm curious about your relationship to your patient. And, as I said, I did find some items at her apartment that feed my curiosity. As does your reluctance to ask me what it was I found. Does any of that answer your question?"

Her face was scarlet, as if she were flustered. He knew that she wasn't. Her competence had nothing to do with her blood pressure or her propensity to blush. It should have made her a weak interrogator, but he knew that she was good. Slowacki would have applauded her techniques. He was close to shaky as they walked companionably to Washington Square Park, above which he and Liz had made love for the two days he had wanted, so often, to recapture.

"Doctor?"

"Sorry," he said, "I was thinking."

"Oh, I could tell you were. I'd love to know the subject."

"Sex, in a manner of speaking."

"In a manner of speaking, I'd have to tell you I thought that was the case."

They had come—too quickly, he found himself thinking, despite the danger of their walk—to the American version of France's Arc de Triomphe and they watched the readers read, the chess players play, the guitarists wail, the addicts nod, the buyers and sellers of the park's chief commodities—drugs, and aspects of the physical person—buy and sell.

"Where are the cops when you need them?" he said.

She punched his arm and shook her head. "I'm off, then, Doctor. Our business, you would say, is done."

"You already knew what I thought was news."

"I knew some. You knew some. It was pleasant to see you again. How's your marriage?"

"My . . . what about it?"

"You're married, but you never mention her. Was she friendly with our Nella?"

"My patients are my patients. The rest of the apartment, when I work, is a hundred miles away."

"A sizable distance," Rhys said. "So they didn't know each other?"

"Of course not."

"Of course. And how *is* the marriage?"

He looked at her heavy eyebrows, her hair poking unevenly from under the suede cap, her sturdy neck, reddening as he looked. He asked her, "Might I ask why you ask?"

"It's information," she said. "I'm in the information business."

"So's a librarian."

"Oh, I'm no librarian, blessed as they are as a race. I had a childhood because of one."

"My marriage is troubled," he said. "Surprise, surprise."

"Marriage *is* trouble," she said. "I've tried it. Murder is trouble, armed robbery is trouble, marriage is trouble. I've concluded that you get the greater scars with marriage. Although, in general, you do more *time* with the less subtle kind of killing. I'm off, Doctor."

"Why did we meet, really, Detective Rhys? And on the downtown bus."

"I had an appointment in midtown," she said. "And taking the bus keeps me out of the office a bit longer than wrestling some male detective for a car that works. And it gave me something to look forward to."

"Me?"

"Imagine that," she said. She extended her square, strong hand and gripped his, then released him, then turned as she strode and was off, across Washington Square Park, past the empty fountain around which schoolchildren sat while the drug merchandisers conducted their commerce. He walked the perimeter of the park, then cut across toward Sixth Avenue. He marveled at an exquisite, tall woman whom he understood, after she was gone, to be a tall, exquisite man. He turned to look back at him, or her, and he or she was looking back at Alex. He felt very happy and decided not to investigate why. He walked up Sixth to stand outside Balducci's, where street people sat with their backs against the storefront. The city was dying, he thought, squinting at the filthy men who seemed always to be cold inside their greasy rags. And I will not give one—or, as I should, all—of these dozen men some money for food. They'll drink it away. They'll shoot it up. They'll die, he thought. He went inside so as not to see the open eyes of those who didn't sleep, who simply leaned against the wall of their exhaustion.

One of them, a boy under twenty with a delicate face, lay with his legs drawn up. He wore a thin, shiny Yankees jacket, but he was no yankee. His brown, bony face, cradled on his arm, was filthy, and so were his hands. The skin of his wrists, which were thin, seemed to have cracked and then scabbed over. His small tan-and-white dog, some kind of terrier, lay against his shoulder watching Alex. This boy has a *mother*, he thought, as if the possibility were meaningful. The dog stirred, but the boy didn't.

Inside, in the smell of roasting meats and ground coffee and sharp cheese, fresh bread, he found contempt on the faces of the men who served up monkfish or muscovy duck breast or parmesan foccacia. When a thin, pale woman in a white doctor's coat, on the other side of a counter, demanded with her eyes that he order something, he bought a single bagel and, pushing it into his raincoat pocket, he turned uptown outside the store. Suddenly, feeling that his shoes were too heavy for his feet to lift, he caught a cab that was dropping a fare at 13th Street, and he headed for home. He looked back toward the sleeping boy.

But he was too restless to ride, and he asked to be dropped at Central Park South. He walked in front of hotels at which he and Nella had stayed, and then walked to Broadway, then up. He looked for Nella, told himself to stop, replied that if he stopped he would have to walk with his eyes closed. Please don't walk with your eyes closed, he advised himself, and he did not. But he stared, for a while, at feet, noting kinds of shoe or boot, width of calf, distance from hem to shoe top; each observation, however, also reminded him—especially when he saw a woman's long leg—that he was missing a chance to see if it was Nella's face above the feet. He shook his head, he stared at strangers, he walked, as if easy on the street, with his right hand clenched around his poppy-seed bagel.

When he came to Zabar's, the usual street person was opening the door, blessing each shopper who passed him, and shaking his paper cup with its few coins. Alex paused, looked hard at the man, forcing himself to see a person in the red-rimmed, squinting eyes, the joyless, weathered face, the gray hair. He held up the bagel.

"No food!" the man said in a thick, phlegmy voice.

Alex stepped back, then walked around the man, then cut over across Broadway and went toward Central Park West. He forced himself not to stagger. At 90th, he sat on the bench across the street from their building, his back to the low stone wall of Central Park. He still held his bagel, a bit softened and warm, and he looked up at their window. He counted the floors twice to make sure it was theirs because the lights were off; it could be anyone's place, and he was feeling sentimental, and he didn't wish to be a romantic fool about the wrong apartment.

He lifted the bagel to his mouth, then put it down. He was remembering how when he came home from school the lights in the Ann Arbor house were off, often, even though his mother was usually there. He used to let the heavy front door, with its oval glass window, beveled at the edge, slam behind him as he entered. The sound flushed his mother out, and, rarely smiling, but sometimes tender—she might kiss his cheek, or grip his arm as Detective Rhys had done this afternoon—she found food for him, as if hunger had stalked him throughout the day and at last, and at least, she could rescue him. She offered sandwiches, leftover soup or cake or, not unusually, cold, salted vegetables from last night's dinner.

Often, she would be wearing her dark blue bathrobe over gray or light blue pajamas. She would be in slippers, small men's slippers that flopped as she walked, and that made whispering noises against the dark yellow brick pattern of the kitchen linoleum. He ate, and she watched him, and he sneaked glimpses of her face as he could. It was bright and tight and without makeup. The crow's-feet and crosshatched forehead wrinkles and deeply incised frown marks, from her small nose to her broad mouth, seemed on some days to have grown deeper, while on other afternoons they seemed to have receded. Her lips were always reddish, though she wore no lipstick except on Parents Night or when she and Januscz felt required to attend university functions. Her dark hair, cut in a pageboy those days, had waves and ripples and looked like an animal's thick pelt. Her small, fine fingers worked at her mouth or chin, and were rarely still. She tried to smile for him, he knew; she did not seem to wish to be grim, he sometimes thought. And sometimes he was certain that her tensed mouth was a signal to him of his failure to live up to standards he hadn't begun to suspect.

He failed as a high school student in the first two

years and then, when his science teacher, Mr. Fialkoff, told him—saying *Lescziak, you know nothing!* to be sure he had his attention—that earning entry to college was a way of escape from his daily humiliation, Alex studied because his life, he understood, depended on his grades. Januscz smiled, reviewing his chemistry with him, when he correctly recited the formula for the hardening of plaster of paris.

"Smart boy," his father said. "You are a smart boy. Would you like to be a chemist?"

"Something," Alex said, sounding stupid even to himself.

"Yes," his father agreed, nodding, "it is good to be something. To be able to do something they need you to do. You will be something, Alex." He lit one of his unfiltered Camels and blew the smoke out while picking tobacco from his chapped lower lip.

"*You're* something, Daddy," Alex said.

"Some kind of something," Januscz said, smiling, but letting his eyes close under what Alex learned was an enormous fatigue. His life was heavy on his head. They sat in the silence of the living room, Sylvia gone early to bed and her terrible dreams, and with most of the lights in the house turned off. If someone outside had looked in, he remembered thinking, and they saw him and Januscz in the lighted living room with all of the other rooms in darkness, what would they have thought? Who would they think the Lescziaks were? They might never know, Alex thought, on his first day of college, sitting on a bench outside of Angell Hall while everyone else at the university, it seemed, all walking about at once, knew everybody else. They would never know, looking into the Lescziaks' on the night he recalled, how much that large, shy, quiet man, as close to inarticulate as an intelligent person could be, wished to give Sylvia and Alex his love. He wept, sitting on that bench in 1958, and now, sitting on a bench in 1985, looking through the darkness at a window, he waited to weep again.

He couldn't. It was a comfortable night at the end of April, and the breezes carried mild rain and the smell of wet earth from the park and, he thought, the sweet, rich smell of the carriage horses far away at 59th Street. He chewed the now cold bagel in small bites, nibbling like a man whose teeth and gums gave him great pain. Januscz was something, Alex thought. He was some kind of something.

So why, then, wish to weep for him? He *knew* how to love.

Because of Sylvia, naturally. And because his father could never tell them of his longings, or the depth, the complexities, of his love. Well, perhaps he told Sylvia. Alex suspected that he couldn't, though. He suspected that the German prisoner could. He imagined Otto describing elaborate emotional and physical needs, and he imagined her, imprisoned in both the lushness of his language and the impossible, grave grayness of her married life. She would have been excited, always, by what Kessler required of her.

And what, he wondered, excited Liz? And what imprisoned her? Was it his treachery that kept them in the familiar tension, the undersea silence? Or was it hers? Had she cuckolded him at Greene Street, in her loft? He thought of its high, bare, white walls, its stamped metal ceiling, her canvases leaning on the walls so that you saw only the braces of the stretchers and the underside of the canvas. She never displayed anything but the painting she worked on, and some tacked-up postcards, sometimes a clipping or two. The studio was furnished with a daybed, a table, a radio. There were a couple of closets, a rudimentary kitchen area, and electric space heaters high on the walls. It was a working place, where Liz listened all day to WQXR and, as she described it, moved paint. There's all you need there to live an alternative life, he thought. And Liz had never required much. She liked good clothing and she liked good food, yet she could live on toast and wear the same jeans for a week, he knew.

It was the jeans he'd found, one night, coming into the apartment late after seeing *La Ronde* at a MoMA festival; it was finding them on the floor of her room—the guest bedroom, down the hall from theirs—that had made him so sorrowful. He had come in to check on her, as if she were his child. He found her underwear and brassiere, her paint-stained sweatshirt and sneakers, her white athletic socks, in a mound at the door to the room. It was the way a lover would leave her clothing as she struggled with buttons and snaps to get herself naked and into someone's bed.

But Liz was alone in her bed, and she seemed deep asleep. He couldn't look at her undefended face yet. He picked her clothing up, folding each piece and stacking it on the foot of the bed, on top of the peach-colored comforter. When he lifted her jeans, he went through the pockets. He didn't think he searched for anything particular: he wanted to touch her life. He found a ring of keys; a thin leather sheaf which held two tens, a twenty, a credit card, and a driver's license; a folded piece of thick, possibly handmade, oatmeal-colored paper. He knew that he mustn't unfold it. He held the heavy page on the palm of his hand, where, in the golden light from a parchment-shaded lamp on an occasional table in the corner, it seemed to glow milkily. The flesh of his hand seemed as dark as the paper seemed bright. He replaced the keys, the leather folder, the piece of paper, each in a separate pocket. He folded the dirty jeans and placed them on the bed.

Liz woke. She turned toward him and her face, in spite of the daunting hair and eyes, was that of a girl. Her expression was worried. And of all the words that came to her, he thought, as he sat outside their building and remembered, these were what she said: "Oh! Alex! Are you all right?"

"Everything's grand," he whispered at once, and her eyes blinked, then closed, and she lay back. "You're safe as houses," he said.

She smiled sleepily, said, "Nice. Safe—" She was back asleep. He wanted to take his own clothing off, so that they might lie beside each other and, in the heat of their bodies under the comforter, feel each other directly. They might make the guest room their bed-room, he remembered speculating, and start again as visitors together to their old life. Guests could stay in the former master bedroom.

Yes, he remembered thinking. You can install Nella Grensen there.

"—as houses," he had said at last, finishing for Liz, and he'd turned off the wall switch that controlled the table lamp, and had backed from the room.

"YOU LOOK ABOUT as sick as a doctor's allowed to look," Teddy said. "You really shouldn't show up here, talking about Liz who looks like a baby asleep, with your skin virtually ashen, Alex. You look like an infarction in progress. Let me recommend someone very good who doesn't know you. Let's *work* on this."

They were in the Pyschiatric Institute, to which they both were accredited, Alex to run groups and see certain of his patients, Teddy to care for others, and one man they shared. Most were medicated into a trembling inertia, though their patient in common persisted in sleeplessness. He was almost yellow, as if in hepatic failure, and gangly, exhausted, silent. He had stumbled upon a solution to the problem of his doctoral dissertation that involved setting fire to the chairman of his committee. He had brought the lighter fluid with him to the hospital when he presented himself at intake, begging to be helped. He'd grown violent when they wanted his matchbox as well, and it looked like years ahead before he'd find any form of peace, if he ever might. Teddy had been inclined to medicate him heavily, and he probably was right, Alex thought. What good would talking to Alex do him, besides make clear to him how dreadful his prospects were?

"I think he's got an idea," Alex told Teddy. "I mean,

what else *should* you do with your thesis director?"

"Does Liz always sleep in the guest room, or only when you fight?

"You know the answer, Teddy. Come on."

"Why would I know?"

"This is farcical," Alex said.

"Possibly. But why? And why would I know what you want me to—or don't want me to. I'm not sure what we're talking about, Alex."

Alex said, "All right. All right. This is fine."

They stopped at the nurses' station on the ward as Teddy hissed, "*What* is?"

A woman in white with an unsmiling mahogany face and hair dyed chromium yellow sat on the other side of the counter and carefully read a chart. Her telephone rang without pause, and she permitted it to. Young men in sport shirts and khakis or jeans, with laminated cards hung on lightweight chains about their neck, shuffled past: they were doctors, though many looked like patients. The air, as usual humid and stuffy, smelled of old food. Signs taped to the walls announced the schedules of groups, including Alex's. The television set in the common room was, as usual, on, and patients who lit up their cigarettes from the chained-down butane lighter stood or moved about—a few sat, as if at rest—and watched what seemed to be *Naked City*, always in rerun.

"That's a little violent for them, isn't it?" The nurse didn't answer Alex, and neither did Teddy, who was looking at a chart. "On the other hand," Alex said, "maybe Liz is right to do what she's doing?"

"About what?" the nurse said, not looking up.

"Ask Dr. Levenson," Alex said.

"I don't have to ask," the nurse said. "He'll get around to telling me."

"He will? About my wife?"

"Anybody's wife," she said, taming a smile and leaning closer to the page of her chart. "This patient wants to package his privates in plastic kitchen wrap so he won't feel vulnerable to the rays from his self-defrosting refrigerator."

"Not Dr. Levenson," Alex said, "but the patient, correct? It actually makes some sense, considering how delicate everyone's privates are—excepting Dr. Levenson's."

"Particularly," Teddy said, "if he intends to live in the ice box."

"Or freezer," she said. "Can you imagine how that freezer burn would *chafe*?"

"He's a paranoid schizophrenic," Alex said, "right? This isn't funny," he instructed them.

The nurse said, "Who says?"

Teddy said, "That's right, Alex. Why isn't it?"

The nurse finally set the chart down and lifted the phone. "Third-floor nurses' station," she said, as if pronouncing a single word. Then she said, "Sure." Then she said, "Not unless she's a racehorse with a swollen hock, sweetie. You might try letting, you know, like, some *doctor* prescribe for her? Oh, sure. Uh-huh. Bye-bye."

"Do not let me learn her name," Teddy said.

"Give me her name," Alex said.

The phone began to ring, the nurse picked up another chart, Teddy signed his chart and put it down, pulled on Alex's arm, and moved them toward the staff elevator. "Rein that one in," Alex called back to the nurse, "the one who prescribes for them? Will you?" She waved goodbye as Teddy tugged him along.

He said, "She'll put the fear of a wrathful god into her, I guarantee. She's a wonderful psychiatric nurse."

"She's calm," Alex said, "I'll give her that."

They left the elevator and then signed out. Waiting for the woman at the desk to buzz them out of the locked streetside door, Teddy said, "Liz moves away from you because you've moved away from her, right?"

"I didn't say that."

"You say nothing for a week. Or you get surly and crazy with her about nothing, and you shout. You know, you're not a small guy, Alex, with those shoulders swinging around, and those long arms."

"Tarzan's ape," Alex said.

"Cheetah, right? There's a lot of you, I'm saying. And you can get scary when you're scared. Or panicky. Or full of rage."

"I don't panic," Alex said. "I worry."

"You panic more than you admit. You just don't think it's manly to panic."

"Oh, Teddy, I'm not worrying about what's manly."

"Because it wouldn't be manly if you did?" He stopped at a man who sat on the sidewalk, leaning against the coarse gray limestone of a foundation block outside the wooden walls and scaffolding erected for construction. The man's belongings were in a super-market shopping bag with a caved-in side. He wore no shoes, but seemed to be wearing three or four layers of socks. "No," Teddy said, more about the man than to Alex, "not at all. It simply won't do. I don't—here. Here," he said, putting some money in the man's hand. "Please," he said to the man, "buy shoes. Or food, anyway. Don't drink this up." The man, whose pale skin was black with dirt, whose eyes were crusted, and whose hands shook as he examined the money, cocked his head, looking up at Teddy, who stooped toward him.

"Jug muscatel," Alex said.

"Sure. Or crack. But also maybe shoes. Or another pair of socks and a sandwich."

"Teddy, since when were you an optimist?"

"No," Teddy said, "I'm just another guilty man."

They were near the restaurant when Alex said, "And I'm the *an* to your *other*?"

"If the sock fits . . ."

"Why don't we ever talk about *your* emotional life?"

"Hell, we do."

"I mean erotic life."

"Don't we?"

"No. You and Liz seem to. She knows about your women."

"I've never told her about the men, or the thing I do with birds."

"She does know."

"About the birds?"

"Come on, Teddy."

"We have different conversations, that's all. She isn't my patient, though I try to be—I don't know—helpful to her, in a professional sense. You and I are old friends, and I am trying to compartmentalize for every-body's sake. This isn't easy for me, Alex. Liz and I talk more about a variety of relationships and dynamics. You and I talk about, well, essentially you."

"And now we're talking about you."

"As part of our chat about you."

"Does Liz talk about me?"

"Yes."

"Does she talk about men?"

"No comment."

"Men other than me?"

"No comment, and you know it. Don't put pressure on me, goddamnit, talk to *her*. Please. Really: please do. Talk to her."

"Teddy, I do, of course. You know I do."

"I see."

"She says I don't?"

Teddy said, "I want a duck breast salad. And a spicy St. Joseph that's a little young. On the other hand, I'll probably have, given this joint, the hot and sour soup and some pork lo mein. Your order, Alex?"

"I don't have much order."

Alex, you're supposed to be strong. I'm supposed to hold on hard and ride away.

Where to, Nella? Where do you think we can go?

Someplace safe. Where else does anyone want to go?

I have to tell you: I don't know if I know the way.

"Are you with me, Alex?" Teddy said. "I'm trying to

give you a tip."

Alex wiped his face with his napkin. "Give me a tip," he said.

"Think of your mother."

"Do I have to?"

"Can you help it?"

"I can try to help it."

"Don't," Teddy said, leaning in over his menu, his dark eyes angry. He looked frighteningly serious. "Consider her," he said.

"Liz said that. Years ago. Or months ago. But she said something like that. She said I'd end up just like my mother."

"And you asked, 'Dead?' And, apparently, she shrieked something."

"She said, 'Alone!' But you already knew that too, I suppose. Liz told you?"

"No comment. God, I think I'll have to drink restaurant tea. There's no wine here worth paying for. I'm out of answers, Alex. I really only had this little clue."

"All your clues are from Freud and my wife, Teddy."

Teddy answered, but Alex was listening for Nella. And he was thinking of responding to Teddy's answers the way you think you're resting a moment when you've fallen back asleep. He was thinking of *The Answer Man* on the radio next to his bed when he was a boy. The radio stood taller than the bed, a piece of dark wooden furniture with a drawer in which he stored *Astounding Science Fiction* and *Galaxy*, and, above the drawer, there was a golden grille about a foot square next to which were the wooden tuning and volume knobs. He listened to *The Answer Man*, whose deep voice rose and fell with real authority. Someone looked up answers in an encyclopedia, and he read the questions and then the powerful information. And, on the same radio, *Helen Trent*'s heart broke, and *Our Gal Sunday* was plucky, and each was delivered to him by Duz or Dreft or Tide during the early afternoons when he was ill and home from school. And, later in the day, he heard *Bobby Benson and the B-Bar-B Riders* and *The Lone Ranger*, *The Green Hornet*, *Sky King*. Never had he listened to the story of a young woman named Nella and her questing, thrusting therapist. Though, in 1948, he had listened to the national madness as he stayed up all night, monitoring the Truman-Dewey returns, somehow convinced that the forces of mustachioed evil—he saw Dewey's mustache as a link to Hitler—must be defeated by the man who, his father said, had rescued the world by bombing Japan.

Teddy studied him.

"What?" Alex said.

"I asked you what was wrong with Freud and your wife?"

"Teddy," he said, "you're the doctor. You tell me."

"No comment," Teddy said, pouring tea.

SO NOW, HE thought, he was thinking of yet another woman. Detective Rhys, stocky and sturdy, with, he imagined, very powerful legs. He thought of her legs and he thought of them in relation to him. He remembered Liz's story about the novelist and his offer. He thought of Teddy's face and hers during the telling of the story. She had offered the story to Teddy, he realized. She had recited one man's fantasy to excite another. Teddy had known, for his face had gone soft. It almost never was soft; he was always alert. But then, at his dinner table that night, his expression had softened, and what Alex thought of then as pity for her embarrassment seemed, now, to have been a kind of yearning. Or: a kind of projection. Which could mean that Alex was the man who had yearned for his wife. So much the better, he thought. For that might mean that Alex loved her. And he wanted to love her. He wished to be guilty of Nella, and to feel guilty about her, and to wish to return—from where?—to Liz. If he could, simply, be no more and no less than a man gone wrong: a bad man. If he were bad, he might correct himself. If he were mad, he could possibly be corrected, and possibly with Teddy's help, and even Liz's, if she had the patience. But if he were neither, if he were a man who no longer loved his wife but who loved a patient who needed him, he was a cure and a disease—for Nella, and for himself—at the same time. He knew, only, that he was *right* to pursue her and to leave his wife. But he hadn't left Liz. He wouldn't. His hesitancy about their separating: he offered this to the jury as evidence of his goodness. Or was it badness? The coils of his logic strangled him, and he found it hard to breathe. He was panting. He heard himself panting in the restful, cool silence of his office, and he could think, suddenly, not about Liz and not about Detective Rhys in a bed or with her gun drawn—Jesus, with her gun and in bed!—but of flight. He was standing in front of his chair, his pen in his hand, and he saw himself in the building's garage, he heard himself asking whatever his name was, Anselmo. No: the daytime doorman was Anselmo. Angelo ran the garage. And he would bring Alex the soft-jointed old Peugeot and Alex would drive out onto 90th, go around the block and west, across Columbus, Amsterdam, Broadway, and West End Avenue, to Riverside Drive. And he would—he had put his pen in his pocket, was reaching to his pocket to see if he had traveling money—drive toward the George Washington Bridge and would exit at the Palisades Parkway and be heading through New Jersey toward the thruway named after the same Thomas E. Dewey whose defeat he had listened for all night on his boyhood radio. Nella's father lived in upstate New York, and Alex could find him. He found his way through the murkiest narratives, although, recently, not through his own. But he would find the father and, he believed now, Nella might well be there. Of course. Of course. He should have mentioned this to Rhys. Had he? He hoped not. Because, of course, he wished to get there untrammeled, to open his arms and take his patient in. But he thought of Rhys again, and then of him and Rhys, and some upstate motel. He could not see them now. He could see only the car outside the motel, parallel to other cars, and the darkened windows—he saw himself as he had sat on the bench across from this apartment, remembering himself on the bench outside of Angell Hall—and he knew that he and Rhys were inside. She had interrupted his flight. The word that came to mind for what she had done in his imagination, he thought sourly, as disgusted as if he had suddenly smelled his own excrement, was *arrested* him on his journey. He thought of Teddy and him, yesterday, in the restaurant: his wordplay, his fantasy would appeal to Teddy, at least as evidence that he was on the verge of decompensation.

He was forcing himself to breathe more slowly when William Kessler arrived. When Kessler said something he considered wry, according to his ironic, discourteous smile, Alex did not hear him. He was close to knowing, with whole certainty, that Nella was alive, that she had fled upstate. He was close to being torn like paper—he thought of the folded, secret page he'd found in Liz's jeans—between relief that she lived and dismay that what she had fled, along with whatever else pursued her, was Alex.

And what, he thought, sitting as if in command of the psychiatric hour, what if everything she fled *was* her lover, father surrogate, therapist, general salvation: him? What if the cure was indeed the disease, and Nella knew it?

Which, he later thought, was why, after murmurs of greeting from him and a few tense wisecracks from Kessler, Alex tilted the next fifty minutes away from what had ridden to his office in Kessler's brain pan by paraphrasing the President of the United States as quoted in the *New York Times*. "Morally right," Alex recited, and "I am not going to change my mind about that," even as bent, scandalized, tormented survivors of the camps were marched in and out of the White

House, "begging for the honor," Alex said, "of what you might want to call the ultimately dishonored. And then he says he was in uniform himself for years! But you know what he was doing—he was not fighting the SS who ran those camps. He was making training films! *For God and Country* he was making. And he says, 'I know all the bad things that happened in that war.' Like he fought! Of course, it's the fault of the press. They're like a dog worrying a bone, he says with profound unoriginality. Nixon tells us, and so does his fellow criminal Kissinger, it would be a sign of weakness for the President to cancel the Bitburg visit. So there's morality checking into the game." He snorted. "Some game."

Kessler wore the heavy suit of Donegal tweed. Alex, forcing himself to sit back in his chair, envisioned him in his furnished room, wearing garters for his long socks, and briefs and an old-fashioned undershirt, pressing the jacket and trousers of his suit at an ironing board that swayed beneath the steam iron's weight. Kessler wiped at his upper lip and consulted the papers he had withdrawn from his briefcase.

Unable to keep from goading him, Alex said, "Is your position on Bitburg firm? Do you think the actor in Washington is making history? I mean, making it the way you'd make sausages, say, or fruit pies? Baking a little confection—the Shoah's done, all is forgiven, what the hell, it was mostly Jews."

"He's got your goat," Kessler said.

"Well, it's dishonest. Isn't it? Can you concede that? That what he's saying isn't true? Isn't right? It should be *right*."

"Dear brother—if I may. We do know how great the distance can be between *right* and *truth*. No sophisticated man can think otherwise."

He would have to stop ignoring the matter of maternity and brotherhood, relatedness, Alex thought. He wrote down, *Shld focus on brother etc.* Suddenly, it was Liz he thought of. He saw himself telling her about Kessler. He wanted her advice. And he remembered seeking it before, about other patients, and how they might sit in the living room, or walk together in the city they had thought of, once, as their own, her hesitant, strong intelligence over them both in an early evening mist like an umbrella beneath which he took comfort. They had not been children together, but they had felt young.

"Perhaps," he said, interrupting Kessler, "perhaps the Association for Historical Accuracy has a position on this?"

"We actually have a paper. We're publishing it in the bulletin for summer. Almost all of the forty-nine SS buried at Bitburg were boys and old men sent as replacements. They were trucked in from southwestern France to help interdict the Allied advance."

"I know," Alex said.

"Are you—what's the word, Doctor? Are you obsessing on this?"

"Their detachment hanged a hundred people in the Auvergne while they were on their journey."

Kessler shook his head and smiled. "Ninety-nine," he said.

"Historical accuracy, of course," Alex said. "Strangled to death as a reprisal for a German death."

"German officer's murder," Kessler said. "Terrorism. This was wartime, I would remind you."

"These reprisals," Alex said. "Kill a German in or near the town, and everybody in it dies. Didn't these same bozos do in an entire town? A thousand people? Kids and old men, too, of course."

Kessler calmly said, "No. It was six hundred and forty-two. The town"—he closed his eyes and then opened them, having fished for the name—"was Oradour-sur-Glane."

Alex folded his hands to grip himself. "Sorry," he said, "off by three hundred and sixty-eight."

"Actually, three hundred and fifty-eight. And it was after that, in the Ardennes, that they took bad casualties. That's where the forty-nine were killed—those boys and old men about whom you're so exercised. They died honorably. A wreath would not be out of place, particularly since the placing of it would advance the cause of the Chancellor in the eyes of the world."

"In the eyes of his electorate. And your association equates forty-nine warriors, of whatever age, with six hundred whatever civilian victims?"

"The 'warriors' were victims too."

"You're equating armed soldiers with babies exploded by bullets?"

"That," he said, "is propaganda. I am speaking facts."

"History is facts? Who determines them?"

"That," he said, "is precisely what interests us. What compels my own attention. It's the facts—about Otto Kessler, for example—that I am trying to establish. It is what I was born to do, you might say. It's what I *have* to do."

Alex heard Teddy's voice in the Chinese restaurant: "Just how many minutes of your patients' time have you lost this month? Where do you go when you lose them, Alex? When they're talking to you about their lives and you phase out?"

Teddy, for example I go here: Januscz's voice, when he was old. "It was what you had to do. She got a little bit crazy, and I got a little bit sad, and I waited for her." Alex had never known where his father did the waiting, or how, or for how long, or why, or in which ways his mother demonstrated her craziness. He had seen more than a few of the postwar ways for himself. He was, even if an adult when Januscz told him this, a child, their child. Alex watched him breathe through the oxygen tubes that coiled up from the low, portable tank he wheeled with him from his bed to the solarium of the home, where they sat beneath glass beneath sky. Liz had gone to speak with his doctor. When she returned, Liz and Alex would drive his father home, and his father's breathing therapy would be concluded. This time, it was hoped, he might not sneak a cigarette as he slowly died from having smoked them.

He'd become smaller, and even his large head, filled with good brains largely wasted or ignored by a not particularly friendly world, had seemed to shrink. Only his hands and feet seemed large to Alex. As babies and puppies begin with big hands and feet and grow into them, his father seemed to be ending. The light in the solarium was golden, almost slightly green, like some white wine that Teddy Levenson would pour. Newspaper pages turned nearby, and a cart groaned, and his father's lungs, grown dark and inelastic, made little squeaking sounds as Januscz sat at seeming ease, while Alex waited for luck to descend, or inspiration to rise, so that he might know what to ask his father about his life that a son might preserve.

"You always loved her," Alex said. But he was asking a question.

"Sure," his father said calmly, smiling a little. "She sometimes—I don't know. You understand me? Sometimes you cannot know."

"If she loved you in return?"

"If, and if always, and if as much as before, and if more than before. It wasn't a steady state."

"You didn't mind?"

"Do you? Or is it steady, a given in the equation, always, with you and the beautiful hawk? That would be fortunate and unusual. That would be great good luck, Alex. I would wish that for you, child."

"It would?"

He felt—as he hadn't felt in years—like a son. No: like a boy. Januscz knew, and Alex didn't, and he needed to know, not only for the sake of his own daily life but so that he might remember his father's. Time rose, in that green-golden room, over the terrible small squeaks of his ossifying lungs, and Alex felt it, nearly saw it, as the vastness of its mass began to roar upon them, down, then further down.

His wife returned, compelling you to note her, then to watch her, and then to remember that you had.

"But she loved you, and you loved her," the son said, like a boy, almost whispering, rushing the words to get them said before Liz arrived.

"We did our best," Januscz said, smiling with what Alex now thought of as pity for him. His son knew so little, he must have thought. He said, "I wish—"

"Tell me," Alex said.

"Child. Alex. My boy. Love? Yes. Of course. Yes. But I wish, I have to say to you, I wish that I could smoke one more packet of cigarettes."

"In fact," he heard Kessler say, "it's even charming, if you can look at it that way. We use the school because the nuns don't charge us a lot. They keep a janitor there for us no matter how late the meeting runs, and it's warm, and of course cheerful. And Jesus, looking quite like a movie actor or a choirboy, wounds or no, is a comforting presence when you stumble in during an ice storm. It's the chairs, of course, that put some of the membership off. You know."

Alex made the sound of a man who listened. "Yes," he said.

"They're so small! They're made for elementary school children, naturally. I'm afraid we all sit there with our knees up, protruding, for comfort's sake, at odd angles, and we speak in the most dignified tones about matters of immense importance. I think of it as lovely. I'm happy to tell you about it! Yes. It makes me very happy."

"You're important in the association," Alex said, working again.

"One has a voice there." He smiled a tight smile, his face pale again, the papers beneath a palm on his lap. "I do wish you'd attend a session. It's your own brother, after all, in his world. And do you have, as part of your plan for my therapy, a sense of when we discuss the actual, er, brotherhood?"

"What would you say are the requirements for your treatment? No. Let me say it clearly. What brings you here besides me? Our parents, I suppose, and what you might perceive as an ailment. Am I the disorder to treat?"

"Well put. Lovely," Kessler said, beaming at the proximity of what he cared about, and giving, of course, the answer Alex sought. "The doctor as the disorder."

"It's a medical event, and it isn't unusual," Alex said. "It's called, by physicians, an iatrogenic disease. The doctor misdiagnoses, or even diagnoses correctly, but in the course of his therapy he brings on another medical event of real severity."

"As if, say, you drove me mad," Kessler said, nodding. In his pleasure, in its self-involvement and need, Sylvia peered forth from his eyes and then was gone. Alex found himself wishing he could call her back for an instant.

"I will try not to do that."

"I will try not to let you. But let me ask: do you feel a kinship? I may ask that?"

"It would be inappropriate to answer. Except, perhaps, to say, 'Is that important?' "

"How could it not be?"

"No man, let me say, would ignore the fact of a brother, half brother, suddenly presenting himself. It rewrites his past."

"And his present, therefore," Kessler said.

"Without saying," Alex said.

"Sorry?"

"I said that it goes without saying—past, present, et cetera."

"Et cetera," Kessler said. "You know, I feel suddenly as if we're really making progress."

Alex asked, "Toward what?"

"No," Kessler said, wagging his small finger, then pointing with it at his watch. "I think our time is up." And Kessler shook his head and smiled with deep pleasure, Alex saw, and then laughed one time with a triumphant bark.

HE WAS QUITE successful in groups, and he knew why. He could command. He could strut while sitting down. He could wheel his facts, parade them in ranks or columns. He could even be still: silent in his folding chair, as bloodless as his group members under the insect buzz of the fluorescent fixtures, flickering lamps set into the plastic panels of the low ceiling as inauthentically blue as the sky in a high school musical. He sat so still, he knew, they knew that he was silent on purpose; and, sometimes, his quiet—though it was never, he knew, a stillness—drove them in the direction he wished. In short, he thought, going on and on as he stood at the stone balustrade in front of the library, off to the side of the immense steps, looking onto Fifth Avenue and the Irish Sea and the soft inner skin of Nella Grensen's thigh and Liz Lescziak's eyes, which were the most authentic blue he'd ever seen, Alex thought he sometimes enjoyed the group sessions because he was permitted by their dynamics to show off. Still working for Mom, he decided, for Maddy Cohn and really for Mom. And he thought, then—not of going uptown from the library to review notes; not of traveling downtown, to Greene Street, and Liz, hidden in her work in SoHo—he thought of a bottle of Armagnac. It was in an unprepossessing bottle, and it wasn't particularly old. But it was Armagnac, a deep brandy with cruel edges to the aftertaste.

"Bring brandy," Nella had said. He'd carried it in his oversized briefcase when he checked into the St. Moritz, on Central Park South, and was taken by a bellman so casual about the charade of his carrying Alex's excuse for a suitcase that they both yawned at once in the elevator.

"Long day," Alex said.

The bellman's eyebrows met above his nose, and his face was chapped, almost seared-looking, so that his pink complexion clashed with his maroon uniform. The backs of his hands were covered with a thick, blondish hair. He smelled, Alex thought, of an unguent. He shrugged.

Alex said, as the elevator stopped, "I'll take it from here." He held out a five-dollar bill folded lengthwise, and the man handed over the briefcase.

"Have a pleasant afternoon," the bellman said. It sounded, on this man's lips and tongue, like an invitation to acts involving bare electric wires and sensitive skin.

It was, he was certain, the smallest suite offered by the St. Moritz. The tiny living room opened through french doors onto a balcony overlooking Central Park. You could look over the patient horses of the hansom cabs parked along 59th Street and into the park, pulsing with taxis and joggers and heaven knew what maniacs under which rocks. The bedroom was slightly wider than the bed. The mahogany-toned water-resistant wooden furniture was scuffed, the tan carpet was shabby, the mirror opposite the balcony was clouded, and the paint on the walls was either light mango or dark coral—a color of institutional glee.

Nella, as usual, came to the door a little late. As usual, she looked haunted—provocative and elegant and disheveled. He was her excuse to fall apart, he thought. He was a reason she fell. He was also the reason she wished to. And he was only the provoker of her symptoms, he knew, not of her terrible unrest. Her eyes were ringed with exhaustion and her long face was sallow. He held her, whispering to her that she hadn't slept, feeling her respond by falling against him. He literally held her up. She smelled of a day's work: salty flesh, and the pungent toner of photocopiers, and bacon from lunch. She was in tears before she was out of his arms.

"You make me so happy," she said, unbuttoning her dark blue suit jacket, "so how come I'm crying the second I see you?"

"You can be happy and cry."

"So am I really happy, then?"

"Certainly," he said. "You are really happy."

"It sounds like another language when you say it."

"Maybe we talk another language."

"No," she said. "You do."

She unbuttoned her sheer white blouse and it hung open. She wore no brassiere. She looked into his eyes so that, he suspected, he would know that she was offering herself unreservedly. Her arms hung loose at her sides. She had stepped from her shoes and she stood before him, waiting. He kissed her mouth and she moved her lips beneath his, and then she nipped him with her teeth. Then she closed her eyes and smiled.

She stepped back, unfastened her skirt, and let it fall. She wore no underpants.

"Where did you put your clothing, Nell?"

"In my briefcase. I thought I ought to be carrying something besides file folders and blueprints and sketches. I changed at work. I was meeting you, and I wanted to be naked, and I almost came when I was in the bathroom down the corridor from the office, when I took my things off. What do you think?"

"Oh, you know what I think." He moved closer.

"No," she said, "I never know what you think."

"Then that makes two of us."

"You lie," she said. "Did you bring the brandy?"

"You want to drink, or—"

"I want to get sexy with you. Then I want to drink."

And Alex did what he longed to, which was what he could—all that he could—and he was athletic, he thought, and not quite premature, and very, very generous, he noted, noticing his attention to his generosity while all that he wished was to be lost in her, in this fantasy—this Technicolor film—of her pale, gleaming skin, her dark, attentive nipples, and the goose bumps on her arms. She whined, almost whinnied, in her cry of triumph or despair. He knew she would have made that sound whether or not he was in the bed with her. He knew, panting, that he knew; and what he really wished for was that he could know nothing.

"Dreams come true," he said. "I *do* know nothing. Just not the way I wanted to."

She made an interrogating noise as she licked, almost lapped, at the sweat at the base of his neck.

"Never mind," he said. "Overexcitement. It makes men talk to themselves."

"Talk to me," she said, "I don't want you talking to any other selves. I'm the only self to talk to, Alex. Aren't I."

He nodded, as he would in a session, as his father did when he asked him about love.

Dusk dropped over Central Park, and in the hotel bathrobe, in the living room, lying on the sofa with her legs across his lap, her head propped on pillows, Nella sipped at her Armagnac from a thick water glass. She made a face, but she sipped more. It was as if she had determined to become drunk very quickly, and after this glass, her second, filled to the height of two fingers, she giggled and sighed.

"This is the worst thing to drink with pills," she said, not meeting his eyes.

"Oh, Jesus, Nella, *what* pills? What are we talking about?"

In his group, he had worked with two depressive suicide attempts, one a man who took a bottle of aspirin, because he couldn't stop drinking, with three-quarters of a bottle of Canadian Club, and the other a man who, afoot, had run headfirst into a car, ruining the car, injuring the driver, and breaking his own nose, right collarbone, and shoulder. Each had survived, and neither was certain he was glad, and each lived in a fever of rage. The drinker, Sidney Stone, chain-smoked cigarettes and coughed from deep in his lungs, turning dark as he did. The other, named Herman Tanner, used to write columns for the *Village Voice*. He still had a decent reputation, especially, he said, among college teachers of English, and he told them—not quite lying, he assured Alex—that his memoir was in progress. His wife had left him after nineteen years of marriage. Tanner was the unresponding member of the group: he barely spoke, he made no eye contact, he took notes, to the dismay of the others, and he chewed and chewed at his fingers as he did. Stone, a thick, muscled man with skin the color of the wooden furniture at the St. Moritz, was the policeman of the group. He whistled them to order, whether the group that night was made up of four or seven, and he reminded them of the topic— "Doc said we were talking *dreams*"—and permitted no interruptions, no matter how useful Alex told him some spontaneity would be. They sat in a rough circle of hard orange chairs with writing arms, and their smoke gathered on walls the color—according to Stone, a fancier of cars—last seen on a 1957 Chevrolet Impala. Sometimes a former scrub nurse, who had lost her career to methamphetamine addiction, sat with the group, but she hated Stone too much, and was too much drawn to Tanner, for the sessions to do her much good. One of the others, Tolliver, an electrician whose daughter had died when Tolliver's mother backed the car into her on a family vacation near Monticello, New York, was a good antidote to Stone because he was larger, angrier, more sympathetic to confusion, and built like, and facially resembled, the linebacker Lawrence Taylor. His enormous, bloodshot eyes seemed always to be in the corner of their sockets. He seemed, always, on the verge of violent action, and everyone watched him, whether he spoke or not—even Stone, who knew when he ought to be afraid. What Alex wondered, with Tolliver, was why he had *not* attempted suicide, given the rage he must feel toward his mother for killing his child; that kind of rage, almost impermissible against a parent, would be turned, by the son, in *on* the son, he thought, sooner or later. In the St. Moritz, with Nella, he realized that he hadn't seen Tolliver for two weeks. He should have been more worried, he thought, and right away.

Alex hated that he was thinking of his suicides, as he called them, because of Nella, whose elegant legs lay on his loins, whose bare flesh made him want to move from the sofa to his knees, on the floor beside her, so that he could kiss her cool skin.

"I read it, darling Doctor. That's all. Something about alcohol and pills. You know, sleeping pills. Maybe it was Marilyn Monroe. Do I remind you of Marilyn Monroe? Her chest was bigger, of course. And her thighs and ass were fuller. And we don't look anything like each other. Otherwise, though, I might remind you of Marilyn Monroe. Happy Birthday, Mr. President." She moued and looked ridiculous. He grew angry at her infantilism.

"Your chest is wonderful. Fine. But may I ask *why* you were reading about pills? And alcohol?"

"Would you give me more of this? It's delicious. This whatever you call it."

" I'm glad you like it. But I'm worried, Nella. Why alcohol and pills? Why care?"

"Well, for Christ's sake, Alex. Mm. Thank you. It's lovely. Why do you *think*? I'm this completely neurotic person who comes from a wrecked family, I hate my job, I don't have any love life that isn't *swiped* from your wife, I just about rape you in your office, I walk across town naked under my coat to see you, I worry about everything—my breath is bad, my legs are skinny, my apartment's filthy, my father's completely nuts, he goes for months in these miserable silences, this cruel, crazy stone face you can never get an *answer* from. I watch *To Kill a Mockingbird* on video and I cry and cry and cry because I want that man to be my father. All I *love* is possibly you. Are you going to save my life, Alex? I saw something, this Hemlock something—"

"Hemlock Society. Don't read that, Nella."

She was still. She held the tumbler and watched the amber level shift. "You worry about me so much," she said.

"Don't mix any kind of pills with any kind of alcohol. Please? If you feel—if you need me, you must say so. Call me. Get to me. But pills, alcohol: don't, Nella."

Her face might have relaxed, but her eyes seemed hard. "Thank you," she said.

"Don't do anything like that."

"All right," she said, "I won't."

"Truly."

"Yes." She sipped a little. "I worry too, Alex. I worry about you." She closed her eyes, sipped more, then slowly swallowed, then said, "About not loving you enough."

He heard the pain in his voice, which struck him as ragged, when he finally said, "You don't love me?"

She moved her feet on him, and he noted that he reveled in the contact. "No, I do," she said. "I do. As much as I *can*, Alex. But what if it isn't enough? *Is* it enough? Is it what you deserve, I mean. Is it what I *owe* you?" Her face looked stricken, but also young, and she was, he knew, as ill as when she had walked in. He had done her no good, of course. Of course, he had done her great harm. He was doing everyone harm. Why hadn't he sat down in *his* hot bath with Armagnac, with Valium, with a razor blade, with a plastic bag?

"Do you," he remembered Herman Tanner saying in a harsh, low voice many of the group had never heard, "ever contemplate doing violence to yourself or to anyone else?" His pen was in his fist, as if he were about to beat his open notebook with it, not write down what his doctor might say about anger.

"Out of order," Stone said. "He asks, you answer."

The columnist, too alone to care for his safety, Alex thought, stood suddenly, and said, his head waggling, his larynx pumping, "Fuck you, you bully long-shoreman. Fuck you."

Stone looked at him as if he contemplated a passing street dog. He said to Tanner, as if giving directions to the Holland Tunnel, "You could *be* discovering the hidden secret of how to die hard while old, you old used-to-be."

At the balustrade outside the library, staring ahead at Fifth Avenue traffic but looking back, Alex remembered Tanner and Stone, and he remembered the salty, dark smell of his and Nella's sex in the St. Moritz, and the rotten, floral pungency of Armagnac that rose to join it, and his sense, even as her legs were heavy on his lap, even as his fingers circled the pulse of her living ankle, as if to keep her with him, that she was lost to him and everyone.

5

ALEX WAS GLAD, even eager, to leave the office when a four p.m. appointment hadn't arrived. His fingers felt frozen, and although his legs had feeling right now, they often went numb, sometimes while he walked or even sat with a patient. This was either the start of syncope, or the process of a stroke, or an old-fashioned panic attack. He willed himself not to limp and not to shake his hands, as if they were wet, to erase the numbness of his fingertips. In spite of his anxiety, or maybe because of it, he was looking—as if he had left her, by mistake, in one of their rooms—for Liz.

He finally found her in what, fifty years before, would have been the maid's room, behind the kitchen, among piles of art magazines and partly collapsed antique dining chairs, and boxes of her family's photographs. Her fawn-colored corduroys were smudged with dirt where she had wiped her hands. Her face and her throat, under her brown V-neck sweater, looked sooty, and Alex realized that she'd been moving more than the canvas bag he watched her shove with her foot. The bag was brown, with straps, and it was very old. They used to carry it on trips, and he wondered whether she had packed it with clothing for the journey away he kept expecting, or whether she was thinking of what to pack, or whether to pack, and when.

"Liz, can I help you find something?"

She turned, startled, made fists as if she labored to calm herself, and the color, as he watched, returned to her face and neck. "I thought you were working."

"A no-show. Would you like some help?"

"No, no thank you. I just thought I'd clean the place up."

"It's like our brain, isn't it? The family recollection. All this stuff, these fragments, things I didn't remember we remembered. But I remember them now. We used to use that bag for Europe, because it was light."

"It looks useful, still."

"If we were going to Europe." He said, "You want to go to Europe?"

The pity in her face was worse than her evident belief that they would not be traveling anywhere together.

"I thought I ought to clean the room. I had a little time to kill, and I wanted to make something orderly. I was throwing stuff out when I began. You would say I was trying to forget stuff, I suppose, if this is the memory."

"What have you thrown away so far?"

"Nothing." She suddenly sat, as if exhausted, on a wide wooden chest they had bought on Ninth Avenue at the start of their marriage and had treated with polyurethane to use as a coffee table. Liz covered her face with her hands, and he knew that he would see her tears smeared over her face by her dirty hands when her face emerged. He did. He wanted to wipe her clean, and he didn't.

"Liz, honey, what can I do?"

She looked at him with something like pleasure, he thought. She smiled a little bit of her wonderful, wide smile. "It won't surprise you," she said, "that I was thinking about you. When you came in. That's why I jumped like that. You were in my brain, and then you were in the room."

"What were you thinking?"

"I don't want this to sound bitchy. Because I didn't feel that way."

"Please," he said, bending his fingers and rising on

his right toe because his limbs were tingling.

She said, "I was lamenting what's become my usual lament, I'm afraid—that I can't find you. Or: not that. That I get in there"—and she pointed to his head, then rubbed her own—"I get inside, and I look around, and I do everything but jump around and shriek because I can't find you. Then," she said, shrugging, "then I do find you. I get hold of you, and I tug. I pull you behind me, and we're getting away."

He opened his mouth to ask her where, then he closed it, because her eyes were shut: she was seeing herself as she led him by the hand from a dark place.

"Then it becomes so clear," she said. Her voice was hoarse with the honesty of her sorrow. "I suddenly understand that you want to *stay*. You're stuck in there, Alex. It's where you want to be." She opened her eyes and sought his glance. "You understand that I'm not complaining? Not bitching about you. I think maybe I'm beginning to know who you are. You're caught in the stories, Alex. Your patients', your own. Is there a word for this? A professional term?"

He said, "I'm afraid there would be so many, Liz. I—"

"Do you think I'm close? Am I saying something you recognize?"

"Absolutely," he said.

"Is it, I don't know, treatable?"

He shook his head at once, before he knew that he would. He was about to suggest a twenty-year analysis with someone brilliant and wise, but he would never— he was shocked to learn that he felt like this—subject himself to someone else's control in that way.

"It isn't?" she said, with real despair. "Alex, this is mostly garbage we never threw away because—what? We were scared to? You think some of it is everyone dumping their garbage in you? Talking and talking and talking and talking? So you're always filled with their rottenness and their despair? Is that any of it?"

He stepped closer to where she sat, and she looked up, stretching her throat, which looked so vulnerable. "Liz, what's the genuine '*it*'? Can you tell me?"

She dropped her head. "I thought I just did," she said.

"I'm sorry," he said. He deepened his voice to mock himself with melodrama: "The box room dilemma."

Liz sat on the chest and nodded once, absently, and stared over a dusty jade-green Art Deco bowl that sat on a stack of paperback books. As if she had only just now heard him, she looked up to say, "Box room?"

"One of my parents' souvenirs: an English expression. It's a little extra room. You might keep valises in it. Or even, if it's cold enough, store potatoes and carrots—like in a root cellar."

"Box room. Do you remember England?"

He shrugged. "Sometimes I think I remember an old woman who apparently took care of me. My parents both worked during the day. Sometimes at night. But, no. I don't remember much. I *think* I remember an air raid, all of us down in some cellar someplace and me being a charming baby, everyone applauding me."

"Beautiful Alex."

"Guilty as charged," he said, taking a stagy bow. "You remember—believe—that I love you, Liz?"

She stared at him, looking up and over to where he shuffled nervously and tried to restore the feeling to his right thigh, which seemed to have gone totally numb. He wondered whether you actually could start to stroke out in your thigh. She studied his face, and it was as if he sat, and lower than she, and she looked down and down, inside of him. He thought of a mouse that ran to hide as daylight poured through high grass into the nest in which he'd been trapped.

"What is the comfort in that word?" she asked him, talking very low. "I'm asking, I mean, what comfort will either of us derive from hearing you say it? Because, yes, I know—I believe—that you love me. And I love you back. But we're so unhappy, Alex."

Love? Yes. Yes, he heard Januscz say again, speaking over the whistle of his lungs.

Alex felt his head move from side to side, and it seemed that he was shaking it with slow, exaggerated gestures. He felt the distance from his head to his feet as consisting of yard after yard after yard, for he suddenly felt enormous, too tall to control the shifting of his shoulders, the drift of his body, left to right, while the head, like a barrage balloon that was tethered to a truck, drifted right to left. His voice, in a grave basso profundo, boomed inside his head as he told her, "I'm afraid I'm running out of words."

"You will never run out of words," she said. Then she said, "Alex? What? Alex!"

"The door bell," he said.

"No, we don't use the service door," she said. "Sit down. Here. On the sea chest. The coffee table. Why am I worrying what it's *called*? Sit down!"

Apparently, he did. Apparently, she had guided him down, and he was sitting on the chest. She stood in front of him, supervisory, attendant, and it seemed natural to him to lean his forehead at her stomach and groin, to put his arms around her buttocks, to pull her into his face or to bury his face in her. He felt more passion than comfort, and then he felt passion as a kind of comfort—if this had a name, he thought, it would be what his disease was called—and his left hand came around to press at her stomach and then at her crotch.

She said, "This is a hell of a time—"

"When would be a better time?"

She said, "You're right. It's the back-door bell."

"Which we never use."

"Fairway uses it."

"Did you order from them?"

"No. What happened to you, Alex? Just now?"

"I was . . . overcome?"

"You had some kind of an attack," she said.

"Panic overcame me, possibly. But so did—well, *you*."

She didn't move away, as he thought she might. She moved toward and against him, and they held each other in a knot of lust and comfort. He had not felt better in weeks. The door buzzer made its noise again and Liz said, "Something's wrong."

"How do you know?"

"It *sounds* like it."

She moved, so that he fell forward as she retreated. He caught himself and sat forward before he climbed to his feet and shuffled on the dusty linoleum to follow Liz, who had gone from the maid's room through its doorway into the kitchen to answer the back door, which was set down a long stretch of outside corridor from their front-hall entrance. He heard Liz's voice, flat and unresponsive, unwelcoming. And then she heard it rise and richen: "You're his *what*?"

Alex knew who it was—who had not, after all, skipped his four-o'clock appointment. He stepped to the little foyer of his kitchen, where William Kessler stood before Liz, smoothing his long hair with his hand, over and over, a little grooming animal. Alex put his hand on Liz's shoulder. She reached to touch his fingers, then she moved her hand away.

"This man, Alex, said—Mr. what was it?"

"Mr. Kessler," Alex said. "He's a patient, Liz. Sir, you are to use the usual hallway entrance when you come to your appointments. And you're far too late for us to do any work today. Telephone, please, for a new appointment."

"He's your brother, he says."

"Well—"

"You never told me about this."

Kessler said, "Now, that is compartmentalization. Highly ethical. My congratulations, dear brother." He turned to Liz. "Half brother, actually. It's a marvelous story."

"This wasn't an accident, was it?" Alex said.

He patted at his hair and said, "Of course it was." He didn't meet Alex's eyes. He said to Liz, "Mrs. Lescziak, it is a pleasure to meet you. Sorry about the contretemps. We're actually half brother- and sister-in-law, aren't we? Very sorry for—well, this. You seem to have been busy when I called at the wrong door. There are three in this corridor to choose from. Is one your neighbor's? I've not seen so many doors to an apartment! Goldilocks and the three doors," he snickered. "And I interrupted a family discussion, I see."

"Do you?" Liz said. Then she turned, and asked, "Is what he's saying true?"

"Please call for an appointment," Alex said to Kessler. To Liz, he said, "Let's talk in a minute, all right? Goodbye," Alex said to Kessler. "We'll have to reconsider if further work will do any good, given this." He waved his hand at what he thought of as debris that lay all about them. "Call, and we'll see."

Kessler's shiny, dark eyes seemed very pleased. His nostrils were wide, as if seeking air, and Alex realized that his bright, pale face, though no more infused with blood than at any other time he'd seen it, was excited. A moment like this was what he had sought. He had entered Alex's life as surely as if he had come upon him asleep and had driven a nail through his forehead. He was *in*, and he had done damage, and he was pleased because now he damned well mattered in what Alex had tried to keep from him.

Kessler apologized to Liz, who had been studying him with angry eyes. He looked at the floor between him and Alex and his expression was intimate, conspiratorial. "Goodbye, then," he said to them both. "Sorry. You understand." And he backed through the door, letting it gently close upon them.

Liz said, "Are you fainting?"

"I don't know what I was doing there. I'm sorry. I think you're right: I was panicking. I don't know."

"But you no longer require assistance," she said. "You aren't having a heart attack, for example? Or an aneurysm?"

"Don't be angry, Liz."

"You didn't want me to know about this—brother? Who appears out of nowhere. Who is pretty clearly stalking you. But why?"

"You're not asking about the stalking."

"No, Alex, I'm not. I'm asking about the not telling me. It is so painful to get shut *out*. When there are all those other people I never heard of who get access to you. They're allowed inside. It's what I was trying to tell you before."

"Liz," he said.

"That creepy little man is your *brother*? Your mother or your father did that? It would have to be your mother. Your father couldn't spawn something that small. Your mother, Alex. How does it make you *feel*? You must be so confused, and upset, and I don't know—amazed, right? And you didn't tell me, or couldn't tell me. Alex: I'm the person you should *tell* things!"

She was trembling, now, and her face was crimson. She was going to say something final, if what she'd just said was not it.

He took her shoulders and held them, squeezing. "Yes," he said, "I know that. You'd have tried to help me, Liz."

She stood in his grip, and she cried, looking down at the floor. He tried to pull her in, but she punched, with roundhouse swings, at his chest and face, and he finally backed away. Liz stayed where she was. He heard them panting over her sobs. They had, he thought, been running a very long race.

Liz expelled a gust of air, then took a breath, then blew air out again. She coughed and reddened further. She did not look, now, like the beautiful hawk. He waited for her to speak again as they stood near the doorway through which maids from Europe and England and Ireland, sick for home but excited to be born again in this vast building of the great city in the New World, carried sacks of food purchased for their employers into the kitchen before hanging their thin coats inside the room now filled with the collected wreckage of this life lived more or less together.

"MY DAUGHTER DON'T talk to me," he heard Slowacki say. He thought he had heard the telephone ring in their apartment, and he wondered if Liz would leave a message. She would not, he knew, and he was hearing Slowacki's voice dart and jump, because this matter of the daughter was a difficult one.

"We've not discussed her," he said.

"I don't like to mention her here. Or on the Job."

"Because?"

"It keeps her clean."

"You think of your work as dirty?"

"No, Doc. Because it *is* dirty. Not I think."

"And these sessions?"

"We're talking pornography here, aren't we? What I possibly did to my wife?"

"Which you don't do now?"

"Which I don't do now. I don't touch her. She's safe."

"And you're dangerous?"

"She's safe."

"May I ask: *do* you have sexual relations now?"

The mustache moved as he compressed his lips, then licked the lower one with a long, thick tongue. He wiped the back of his hand along his lip, then wiped the back of his hand with the other palm. And he said nothing.

"Are you angry about that?" Alex asked.

Slowacki nodded. Then he said, "I'm sad."

"Why?"

"We used to be friends, her and me."

"Wife or daughter?"

"Whoa," he said, sitting taller and raising a hand. "Whoa. The sex deal is my wife. That's Reeny. The one don't talk to me at all is Carol Ann."

"Your daughter."

"My fourteen-year old Polish princess who decides, ka-bam, from noplace: 'Daddy, you know how vulgar you are?' Excuse me, Miss Fashion Model of the Ninth Grade, I been a little busy dragging my life along the third rail. I'll try and ditch the vulgar parts the very next chance I get between people falling off of the 1 train or mugging a half-dead old lady on Bradhurst, she's waiting on One Five Oh Street and Frederick Douglass Boulevard, she's trying to get downtown to work as a maid on the night-shift laundry in the St. Moritz. You know that joint? Some spade kid, same color as her, he don't give a shit. And I'm telling the bosom of my family, that's Reeny, about my night defending the city from itself, which is what I do, and Carol Ann has to tell me how vulgar I am. I guess I am. But you see an old lady all beat to shit like that, sitting on the curb and shaking and crying—or a guy on the third rail . . ."

"Was he actually on it?"

"That's so much juice in there, Doc. It's what gives the trains the *power*. You don't go near it. Never. Ever. Do not. I saw this poor fucker lie down on top if it. He cooked himself." He rubbed his mustache as if he were calming it. "I see him when I close my eyes, sometimes. Straight, open-eyed, awake: I see him. He didn't say a word."

"As your daughter doesn't?"

"I'm exaggerating. She talks to me. 'Can I have my allowance?' 'I'll be home from school late.' 'Is there any salt on this table?' "

"How does your wife react?"

"She actually smacked her. Not hard, mind you. Nobody believes in hitting a kid hard. But—I have to say: she was siding with me."

"She wanted you to know it, you think?"

"I think she did. Yeah."

"Do you know why?"

"Because of this, with you and me. Some of the stuff you told me, or I thought about at work. This." He moved his fingers in the air. "Here."

"You told her?"

"I did."

"Why?"

"To get her back into bed without fighting, to tell you the truth. That part didn't work."

"But you'd be different with her, if it did?"

The mustache moved, then went still. "I would be. Let's say I *will* be. I got my hopes, still. Yeah."

Alex nodded. He had to say it: "Good. That's good."

"That's right. Except now, the Polish Princess don't know me from the guy delivers her mail and takes out her trash."

"She does," Alex said. "She will."

"You got kids?" Slowacki asked.

Alex felt himself go still. He searched for a next word.

"I'm not supposed to talk about you," Slowacki said, "is that the procedure with a shrink?"

Alex said nothing.

After what Alex knew to be a considerable silence, his patient asked, "Should I say anything else?"

"Last time," he finally heard himself mutter, "we spoke about the war."

"It beat hell out of me, Doc."

"Painful material," Alex said.

"Lot of pain in-country," Slowacki said. "Snakes—I hate snakes." He shook his hands as if to hurl moisture from them. "And land mines. You're lying there on top of your ankles or kneecaps, and you're praying somebody in your outfit has the balls to give you the head-shot worth more than gold. That's what we called it.

And some of those were given out, and that's the truth. And of course your basic ambush: death by small-arms fire. Before you get it, you hear everybody else get it, and it's a terrible noise. Our M60 guy was a spec four, a huge spade named Denny Lewis. Denny Lewis. We come under heavy fire on patrol, and I hear this thing—like Greg Luzinski or somebody picks up a thirty-six-ounce bat and whangs away at a watermelon. By the time I look, there's his tin pot —they're supposed to save you!—rolling on the ground. It was still in motion when I looked. Entrance hole in the front, exit hole in the back. Lewis is on the ground, he's nothing but old clothes. His assistant, Serious John, they called him, John Epstein, also a specialist four, he picks up the M60 and starts putting bursts into the jungle and *he* takes a round in the forehead. This is serious coincidental shit, now. I decide it's time to get killed, I guess, because I'm trying to pick up the fucking M60 by the barrel, and it is so hot I feel my skin cook. I fire it off for a while, hitting much plantain, I figure, and no doubt some vines and some trees, and by the time the fire fight's done, I have one burned barrel, one cooked hand, and this goofy kid called Dinky, on account of he's a Korean or something slanty, he's carrying both gunners' helmets with holes in them. Like he needs them for souvenirs. Guys there kept all kinds of souvenirs. I got this"—he held up a normal-looking, creased palm—"but I'd of left it behind if I could. And I did see a bamboo viper, just one time. Maybe—not quite a foot long. Most poisonous snake in Vietnam, somebody told me. He was on top of my rucksack. And I was *wearing* the fucker. Sergeant DiSimone almost killed me, pounding him into this snakeshit goo with the butt of his shotgun. That was worse than burning my hand. Burning my hand, now that I think of it, was easy.

"Hard was when this guy I'm teamed with, Larry Newkirk—Larry was a good man. He had my back. I had his back. We kept each other alive. You ever think about a safe time, on a nasty-ass patrol, in the dark, you got to take a shit, no choice, how you can dump without a gook he slides up and takes your voicebox out with a steak knife courtesy of some kitchen installed by the French Foreign Legion? That was me and Larry. We guaranteed each other's ass. He gets this letter from his wife. She tells him she's been fooling around with another guy, she feels guilty, she wants him to forgive her. We sit up all night talking, *whispering,* all night, it makes my throat sore thinking about it. And he writes her a letter when we're done talking. And he gives it to me. You know what that says, giving it to me?"

Alex, like a boy hearing ghost stories at a campfire, shook his head.

"It tells me he knows he's dead. What am I supposed to say? They didn't invent the words for that. I saw it before with guys, just not with me. I couldn't tell him it wasn't true, because I knew he knew it. So we just nodded our heads, like we said something. But all it was: he gave me the envelope with sweat stains on it, and her name."

Slowacki stopped. Alex watched him swallow. Then

he said, "We got jumped to shit. It was one terrible fire-fight. I went through maybe fourteen magazines before they pulled us back. I saw Larry go over. Just the same as usual, he's on my flank. But this time he's over on his side or his back. I saw him go over. I'm trying to figure out how to get to where he is, and how to get him and me back to Sergeant DiSimone, who's hollering for us, and this gook stands up. Hello. He empties a magazine in my direction, and I figure I'm dead, but every round misses me. He turns around to boogie. I'm on full auto and I let go. I saw every round hit him. I stitched his whole back, shirt collar to belt, emptied the magazine into him. Nothing's left but gookburger. Then I start shouting for Larry and running like hell for the sarge. I'm out of ammo, remember, and you don't want to get left behind when you're empty, so there I go. Now, we're about a hundred meters back, regrouping, and they're calling in the artillery support, I'm trying to fill up magazines with what I can salvage from loose rounds in my rucksack. Out there with no ammo: that's your heavy-bore nightmare. Understand? I roll this kid over, Reuben, the sergeant dragged him back but he died. I'm looking for full clips, and I turn him, and he's got no chest left, just ribs, the stumps of ribs. We got Reuben back, but we didn't get Larry. I knew this every second we were covering up and the fragments were in the air from the artillery rounds. Then air support arrives. They're dropping napalm, somebody says, and pretty soon we can see they're dropping it halfway down the crack in our ass. Everybody starts to pull back some more, dragging the wounded guys, maybe halfway killing some of them, and everybody's moaning, it's like a whimpering contest in nursery school. I start calling for Larry. I really wanted to go back. I saw him fall down in the fight, and I had to get back. But the sergeant grabs me to keep me from getting to him. No time, he says. No fucking time. No time.

"We go back after they drop their loads. There's no air left in the air. Everything's beat to pieces by artillery, then burned away by the jelly babies. You smell, like, this gasoline smell, and the heat. Ever go into a Chinese laundry? That kind of heat, except with gas in it. Jelly babies, the sergeant said. Larry died in the babies. Napalm burns the air you need, sucks it away, and your lungs collapse. He didn't look so wounded, considering. His hands were folded onto his chest by the corpsmen. Now, here's the story part, Doc. His ring finger was blown away. No shit: just the finger with his wedding ring, this guy whose wife was fucking somebody home while Larry's in-country, the ring finger is blown off of his body. The corpsmen find it. They put it between his hands, on his chest. His skin's all black. His eyeballs got burned out. They must of boiled. And I'm carrying the letter for his wife. You know what I wanted to do with his ring finger."

Alex waited. He did know.

"They wouldn't let me. If they'd of let me, I would of sent it to her. Here's your marriage, I'd of told her."

"How is it," Alex asked, "that he was separated from you?"

"Firefights," Slowacki said, looking away. "It's what

happens. Everything, everybody, gets separated. From everything."

"And guarding each other's back . . ."

Slowacki's voice rose, and so did his neck above his slumped shoulders. "Whoa. Whoa. You're telling me it was my fault Larry got toasted? Firefight, then friendly fire, and it's my fault?"

"No," Alex said.

"Yes," Slowacki said. "Yes, you are."

"How could it be your fault?"

"It can't be!"

Alex waited.

"It can't be," Slowacki said, lower. "It can't."

"But you think it was. You thought it was?"

Slowacki shook his head, the way an emphatic child might, his chin pointing parallel to each shoulder. He did this twice, slowly. "Cannot be," he said.

"That's right," Alex said. "But you thought it could be, didn't you?"

"I was so busy not getting shot to death and not getting toasted, I ran without him. I had *my* back. But I didn't have his."

"Anthony."

"I don't know if his wife ever got the letter. I mailed it. I never wrote to his parents, and I should of. I left him for dead. I saw him go down. I was sure he was dead. Then I wasn't sure. And I was so scared. You have to be. How can you be anything else? But I did want to go back. Sergeant DiSimone mentioned that to me, later on. He said, 'I remember how you tried to get back to your bud.'" Slowacki crossed his chest with his arms. He pushed at the open neck of his shirt. "But I never made it back," he said. "And I never made it out to his parents' place. He went home in a bag, and I went home outside a case of beer. That wasn't fair."

"It isn't your fault that you survived," Alex said.

"And that Larry didn't?"

"That's right. Also that Larry didn't. Men under the terrible stress of your service there, being asked to survive impossible circumstances, with so little chance to influence their fate—Anthony, did you ever talk to anyone there about *Larry*? I know you never spoke about William Williams. But what about your feelings after Larry's death?"

"Same thing. It's what happens. We rotated back to battalion, and we got new uniforms. Weapons check, ammo, gear, replacements, four days later we were choppered back not too far from the Junction City zone. We barely had the time to get hungover. One of the side gunners, when they took us in, told me they lost the same area three times to the NVA, took it back three times. 'Your turn to go in and lose it,' the guy said to me. Him, from inside of his dark goggles. 'Your turn to go in and lose it.' Hell, he's standing there on the end of his weapon, between the gooks and me, he can say anything he wants to. That's who I talked to. And the quartermaster, of course, telling the guy what size I needed."

"And, as usual, nobody mentioned mourning."

Slowacki laughed, the way someone might laugh at a smutty, shameful joke. It was a furtive sound, and ugly. "No," he said, "nobody talked about mourning. I talked about getting a letter mailed to a dead guy's wife. That was the talk about mourning."

"You could have used a little help," Alex said.

"Everybody could use a little help, Doc. Like, I could of done without getting into this whole thing in the first place."

"The combat, or the conversation?"

"You got it. Both. Right now, I'd say, especially the conversation."

"It isn't your fault, Anthony."

"Well, thank you, Doc. It isn't yours, either."

THEY WERE WALKING around the reservoir in the park, and Alex noticed that the high Cyclone fence that screened the water from the citizens seemed, today, to be walling the citizens in. If he looked to his left, of course, he would see that he was a free man, he thought as he did look to his left, where Teddy walked beside him. But then he shifted his eyes to the right again: the wall. The prison wall, he didn't say to Teddy, who was already, he knew, considering him clinically depressed. Depression, just then, seemed to Alex a normative response to most days in most lives.

Alex thought of Teddy, with his large hands, good for seizing, and his long, strong arms. Teddy's skin was soft-looking the way expensive pigskin gloves looked soft, and his voice—sizable, if not always loud—matched the span of his fingers, the length of his arms. He had large, dark eyes, though they were lighter than Alex's, and long lashes, and soft-looking hair that formed the dark beaches on the ocean of his bald scalp.

But why, Alex, wondered, was he looking at Teddy with such concern for the details of his flesh?

Because Teddy, he thought, was conducting an affair with Liz.

Which is nonsense, he thought. Teddy was his friend. He said, "Teddy, define 'friend.'"

"No."

"Because—"

"Because we're friends, Alex. If we start in with definitions, we're bound to get to the edge of them. When friends get to the edge, and then go over, they aren't friends anymore. I prefer to stay yours. Satisfactory?"

Alex shrugged. He said, "Sure."

"Besides, you're changing the subject."

"What's the subject again?"

"I told you it was obvious why your cop patient is such a favorite of yours—the only one, almost, you talk about. Surely more than the patient you did not go to bed with."

"Nella."

"I wish, Alex, that you'd named the cop the way you named the woman. Do you understand why?"

"Slowacki," Alex said. "Anthony Slowacki. Transit Authority. He rides the trains and buses all night."

"Right. We have the same man. And why are you so sympathetic to him?"

"Oh, you'll tell me."

"Because, of the people in your practice, he's the most like you."

They walked, two big men afoot in the city in daylight, dressed as for business but not conducting any—

people, therefore, of the leisure or the intellectual class, if you were to notice them walking in easy-seeming circles in the park. Alex found himself, despite the casual pace of their stroll, searching for breath. He felt a numbness in his left thigh, and he breathed deeply. "Because," he said, affecting ease, "he is primitive, anal-retentive, inarticulate, given to violence, sexually repressed, and deeply wounded?"

"There," Teddy said. "Now you're thinking."

"Not to mention of Polish stock."

"Q.E.D.-ski," Teddy said.

"You're not serious."

"Never more so."

"But—what about his raping his wife? I'm pretty certain that's happened, and so is he, and I'll bet good money that *she* is. His idea of making love to her has to do, at the very least, with holding down her hands."

"Maybe she wants him to."

"Jesus, Teddy. That's so unenlightened, it's primitive. It's— Is that what you do? Hold the woman's arms down?"

"When she asks me to."

"She *does*?"

"Who?"

"Whoever, Teddy, that you're in the sack with." And again Alex thought of Liz: her fierce features softened by passion, but her eyes demanding, even cruel. He saw the eyes go hooded, then, and the mouth shift from its frown to an admission, a vulnerability, as if the lips were about to confess, or somehow serve the man she lay, moving slowly, upon.

"If she'd like," Teddy said, with a casualness that infuriated Alex. A woman with rounded features—soft nose, semicircular chin, heavy cheeks—who wore a bright orange hooded sweatshirt over dark tights blew her nose into the air, as she passed them, by forcing a thumb against a nostril and expelling. "I was going to comment on the lovely shape of that woman's thighs," Teddy said, "but now, I think, I won't."

They walked on, Alex feeling that he lumbered, as the woman, farther along, cleaned out her other nostril in the moist air of early spring.

Teddy said, "Alex. Do you remember when my mother died?"

Alex nodded.

"You knew I was in a bad way."

"I worried about you. Don't, Teddy, turn this into a lesson about your worries about me."

"I thought *I* was going to die," Teddy said. "I didn't understand it, I didn't realize—this is the truth—that I was shocked by grief—no: *with* grief. I simply couldn't find the energy for rounds at the PI, for classes, for the clinic. Why do they have to keep jabbering at me, I asked myself. I couldn't pour a glass of juice without sighing. Without breaking the activity down into several small parts. Put the little glass on the kitchen counter. Pause. Open the refrigerator door. Pause. Take hold of the juice carton. Pause. Then *lift* it, and maybe set it on the counter near the glass. Pause. Then shut the door. Pause. You understand? I was physically ill, almost, and of course I was denying every manifestation. Nothing, I was certain, *was* a manifestation. If I saw no symptoms of depression, then I wasn't depressed. I was merely one of those men who had late-onslaught difficulty in pouring citrus fluids."

"That's the usual denial," Alex said. "Were you surprised by the denial, or by the symptomology?"

"Later on, by my having been available to neither. I succeeded in denying each: the depression *and* the denial."

"You found a censor. A camouflage."

"Of sorts. I remember standing in front of the juice carton and realizing that I hadn't the strength to lift it up again. It weighed a thousand pounds. It was deadweight. Trying to lift it would have been the same as attempting to pick up the refrigerator. And I stared at it, and I said to myself, 'Fag. You gay fucking *fag.*' Not, I'm certain, that I thought I was. Nor did I know myself to be frightened of gay men or concerned in any way for my sexuality."

"Not you," Alex said, thinking of Liz.

"Of course, with an outburst like that," Teddy said, "who can tell? It could have been a manifestation of what I'd sublimated. But I don't think so. And I didn't think so at the time. The point is that I had subconsciously found a symptom that was 'better,' in a manner of speaking. 'Better,' that is, than any truth. Gay men of vulgar stereotype, limp wrists and so on, the old etiology of prejudice and fear: *that* was why my body wouldn't function at its normal strength, I think I wanted to persuade myself. Never mind the mind. I was, apparently, what was repugnant to me. End of conversation with self."

"Did you leave it there?"

"What do you think?"

"You attacked it from another direction." And here she came again, lovely legs and sullen face, and the patently unstoppered nostrils which, nevertheless, at intervals, she blew.

"I made myself pick up the juice carton," Teddy said, "and I made myself put it away. I telephoned a woman of my acquaintance."

"Liz."

"Dear old Liz, Alex. But no. No, I called Sheila Cooper. Remember her?"

"She was—well, a few of us thought you were going to marry her."

"No, by this time we both knew I wasn't. By this time she didn't care. She was in the full flush of a love affair—I mean, you know, the full-time, long-time, much-awaited real thing. As close as you can get to it. I knew the man. I think he didn't deserve her."

"But Teddy Levenson did."

"No," he said, with real regret. "No. But I needed her. It was real need, and that was my problem, of course, but—"

"Wait. So you prescribed this person for yourself."

Teddy shook his head. "It was affection," he said. "We liked each other very, very much. She knew I was miserable, and she comforted me." He lifted his shoulders and sighed. "But with flesh as with orange juice," he said. "I got, in each case, nothing up. But what I did," Teddy said, with deep pleasure, "is talk to her.

We held each other—I held on for dear life, Alex. We talked all night and most of the next day. We broke appointments every few hours. And I cried like a child. Well: I *was* a child. And some of my mourning was because I was an orphaned child, and I would have to grow up. Sheila, who was my friend, knew how to be maternal with me, and she saved my life. It's basic stuff."

"Sure," Alex said. "I remember when your mother died. I remember the—it was almost a year. It took all of a terrible year for you to start to snap back. I still think of it that way. Liz and I were extremely worried about you."

"I knew that. It helped me, some. And I thanked you both, every day. At least inside what was left of my head I did. I never told you my thanks. As you know, the trauma is often an impossible subject. I wasn't much good at very much of anything, to anyone."

Alex looked at the fencing by which they seemed walled into the park. The woman came past them again. He said, "Teddy, we're walking counterclockwise. We're walking against the traffic here."

"Good," Teddy said. "We can roll some time back. You can tell me what in hell all these comments about Liz mean, and I can tell you why you're so invested, so transferring to, this Polish cop of yours. The violent one who can't express his pain in any direct way, so he finds sexual channels for his acting-out. And then you can stop walking, turn and face me, look right into my merry but knowing eyes, and tell me the truth about your missing patient."

"Oh, a missing patient," Alex said.

"The one with whom you did not sleep."

"Ah. That one. Sometimes, Teddy, as your precious Freud said, a cigar is just a cigar."

"All right," Teddy said, "and the circle in which this path is laid out is, therefore, not a clock, I take it."

"Not necessarily," Alex said. "Would you feel better if we did walk in the direction we're supposed to?"

Teddy said, "You and I are not supposed to do what people think we're supposed to do. We ought to keep on in the way we were going. If we're us."

"Who else? Except this, Teddy: how come, in all that awful year, you never said to me or to Liz—well, maybe you said it to her. How would I know? But *I* never heard it: 'Alex, help me, I'm dying.' "

"First of all," he said, "I did say it to Liz. She must have told you."

Alex shook his head.

"Strange," Teddy said. "That's a household matter, I think, more than mine. And, second of all, I really felt that I *couldn't* tell you. I was all but treating you. You were so very close to being my patient. . . ."

"Oh, Teddy, wait. The Liz thing we'll come back to. But this, about us: this is a *problem* for us."

"Problem for the profession. When to be half of a doctor to your friend, when not. When to try for objectivity in getting somebody healed."

"Who said I *needed* healing, Teddy, and especially by you? How could you be objective about me? I could *never* achieve anything close to that state about you. I'm baffled. I'm *hurt*."

Teddy said nothing, then, and they walked in their circle side by side.

Alex, after a while, said, "So you're telling me you laid my wife instead of Sheila Cooper, and you were able to lift up orange juice."

"No," Teddy said, "I'm telling you I laid your wife and then I switched to grapefruit juice." He looked ahead in silence, then burst into large, authentic-seeming laughter, and Alex was almost able to join him. "You silly sap," Teddy said.

"Thank you for the analysis, Dr. Mengele."

"Don't be angry, Alex. I was really trying to illustrate my own depression. I'm trying to suggest to you it's not unusual for the physician to need to heal himself. Or to find his own physician. And you are depressed."

"You could have taken a pill, you bastard, instead of my wife."

"Alex. You know what a joke is?"

"It's an act of aggression, Teddy."

"Is that why you called me Dr. Mengele?"

"It was a joke," Alex said. "The way a cigar can be a cigar, that was a joke."

"It was an act of aggression and you know it."

"You're right."

"Freud has taught us: there are no jokes."

"So how could you say you were joking about Liz?"

"Because you're my friend and so is she. Because I get to be tasteless about your wife whom I adore, and you know it, and you're my friend and I love you."

"You really want to screw her, don't you? Again?"

"I really wish I could prescribe a little purple pill for

you. I think I'd write the prescription if you'd comply. I intend to give you someone's name. This man was in the Special Air Services in England. I mean: he is tough. He's also up at the Psychiatric Institute. He's smarter than I am, therefore twice as smart as you. And he's tougher than anyone I know. He could help, Alex."

"Teddy," he said, "I want us to go in another direction."

The woman ran by them again, and Teddy said, "Right." He turned, in an almost military about-face, and he started to walk clockwise.

Alex followed and caught up with him. "I wasn't talking about a physical direction," he said, noting that each thigh now tingled, as if recovering from numbness. His breath was short. "An actual direction. I was talking about words, Teddy."

"Hardly," Teddy said.

SUMMONED BY A clerk who spoke on her behalf, and not by Rhys herself, Alex asked no questions, simply said that he'd be there. He needed to reschedule three patients; he was able to reach only two, and to post a note on his door for the other: not a responsible act, he noted, as if canceling the first two had been exactly that. He took a taxi down to the Village, although he considered the Fifth Avenue bus in honor of Rhys and her circular but increasingly menacing methodology. He had some doubt, and he breathed as much life as he could upon it, that he could be the focus of her investigation; but the doubt would not thrive, while his sense of encirclement did. She was coming at him from unexpected directions. Either he was paranoid, or Rhys was mistaken but very sure, and he would soon be charged with something.

Can you charge a doctor with not being able to find his patient? Could they—the Them, the looming authorities of his frightened envisioning—indict him for cruel and unusual fornication, followed by aggravated loss?

The driver let him off on West Fourth and he walked over to the angular jut of Christopher Street, and the little toy store at which he had no cause to shop, and the gray brick apartment house on the corner, where Nella lived, or had lived, or would live, or was deciding not to live. He did the declension of Nella's refusing to know him anymore and, maybe, anyone else. And he forced himself not to pause at the curb as he walked around a double-parked dirty black, unmarked police car. There weren't blinking lights, he thought, or the medical examiner's van, so maybe she was not upstairs, dead, or dying. He thought of her long, elegant body and how, he feared, it would fold in death, collapse, a construction of blue-white sticks.

But the black car, he thought, was a different ride from the Fifth Avenue bus.

Three floors up, he stood outside Nella's door. He had turned, at the entrance to her building, and had looked out over the corners, as if to see the city one final free time: the stubby woman in blue jean overalls, the straps crossed over a thick white sweater, who carried a large bunch of daffodils wrapped in green paper; the very tall man with his very tall Great Dane, the man circling the brushed-aluminum lamppost stanchion as the dog did, to keep the leash untangled, but who looked as if he, too, were about to squat, with his dog, in public relief; the truck from Balducci's; and the sound, from Greenwich Avenue, of children in the schoolyard, chasing each other and playing ball. And now, facing the glossy maroon door in the dim hallway, saying its name to himself—"Three G Three G Three G"—he waited for authority and consequence to fall upon him.

Footsteps came, in no hurry, to the other side, and the latch was thrown, and the door opened. The footsteps moved away as he reached for the knob. He heard Rhys's trailing statement as he walked in, wondering why he hadn't simply used his key, since there was no longer any doubt of what Rhys knew. He had known that she would know. But, playing out a delusional charade, he had insisted on not admitting a truth until she proved it to him. I've become a child, he thought. I'm my own son.

". . . unclear details, if you don't mind. I'm grateful for your cooperation."

There was a large hammered copper urn from Mexico near the hat tree. Nella had set it there for umbrellas. Her father had complained, once, she said, that contemporary life no longer made provision for the use of umbrellas. So, although her father had never visited this apartment, Nella had an umbrella receptacle ready, just in case there was a confluence of father, rain, and his daughter's dwelling place.

"In case of what?" he'd asked her.

"In case he misses me and comes looking."

"For what?"

"Me, Alex, I guess. I don't know. What else?"

"Did you hear yourself, though? 'In case he misses me,' you said."

She had let herself droop, then had straightened her shoulders. "Yes," she'd said, "I heard."

And now he and Rhys were in the large living room, the kitchenette on its right, the bedroom and bath around the corner. The carpet was gray, with maroon-and-blue Afghan area rugs atop it. The black piano was closed, the bench tucked under the keyboard. The two dark blue overstuffed chairs, the maroon-and-blue love seat, and the coffee table with antique brass corner irons were dusty-looking in the bright light Rhys admitted through each of the windows in turn—her equivalent, he was certain, of turning the bright desk lamp on and shining it in his eyes for the cinematic third degree. He couldn't remember the title of any film in which he'd seen that done, but he knew he had seen several. On the walls were museum prints in frames, and a muddy-looking painting of a farm. Alex knew that it had been painted by Nella's mother and was of a house in Torsby, in Norway, where she'd grown up. It showed, he thought, no talent whatsoever, only the normal urge of a child to recover what had disappeared. So Nella, by hanging the picture, sought to recover the mother who had chosen to leave her by killing herself; and the mother, as a girl, had sought to recover, with her inconsistent strokes and her untutored palette, her myopic eye, the farmhouse at which she had spent her childhood until the war had finished off the childhood and, probably, the farm.

Rhys stood at the window and looked the length of the living room at him. The sun behind her was a bright frame. He could tell from her silhouette that she had recently cut her short hair shorter. He was reminded of a moment many months ago when, looking at Liz in similar light—perhaps they'd been standing across from Lincoln Center, he thought, emerging from an early-afternoon movie, and he had looked at her as bright sun from around a Broadway building had lit the side of her face. She was glowing, he told her, and Liz had blushed. The simple pleasure of the moment had made him regret the terrible mechanics of their efforts to get her pregnant, and of the relentless battering she'd received as she sought a professional painter's career. Now, about to be confronted by Rhys, he realized that what he'd thought of as Liz's suffering was, in abbreviated notation, him. He was her disease. And he was almost in tears as he realized, further, that she, in spite of the disaster he had proved to be, would probably be relieved if the familiar Alex, who had cost her so much, would return. Yet, he thought, the familiar Alex, the real man he thought she might miss, is also just what had been afflicting her.

I'm here, he thought, as if addressing her. I'm still with you. And maybe *that's* the problem.

Rhys approached him, and by stepping sideways, out of the glare, he was able to see that she wore dark navy slacks and low-heeled shoes and a large, loose navy man-tailored shirt. He wondered if her weapon was in the black handbag on her shoulder or under the shirt, at her waist. Her hair, he saw, had been tinted a fiery red and was cut in a kind of a crown. Her neck looked strong, and she wore long earrings of lapis and silver that he thought might prove dangerous in a struggle. I won't struggle, he thought.

"So who's this Slowacki to you, Doctor?"

"Who?"

"The subway cop who put the word about that he'd appreciate a little special help for a friend of his, not on the Job, who was involved in the missing persons case of a patient he'd been treating. Pulling strings, are we, with people we've not heard of?"

"Oh."

"Oh."

Anything, Doc, he heard Slowacki saying. I owe you, and I wish I could do something more—ah, call it substantial. More substantial. I know we got a long ways to go, but you helped me. I feel . . . helped. Let me help you back.

It had been so easy to say, the lie about the missing patient that was not entirely a lie unless you counted omissions. And he'd talked on, about the woman who had disappeared, about how worried he was—a doctor's concern for his undefended patient. It had been easy to forget how easily he'd spoken to Slowacki.

"Oh," Rhys said, imitating his deeper voice, his tone of surprise. "It comes back to you now, does it? Do you think I appreciate your going—well, it hasn't been over my head, I'm happy to say, since that particular fellow is not particularly vertically advanced. Let's say you've gone *around* me. Shall we?"

"Sorry," he said. "I was worried."

"And I'm certain you'll be rewarded in heaven for your gallantry. Though not in this urban purgatory. If you would accompany me into the room around the corner, I would like us to speak further on the matter."

She walked past him, and he followed. He smelled a rich perfume and liked it. He had expected to smell sweat and something cheap. He consistently underestimated her, he thought, and it was time to understand that she was abler than he in matters of extremity. Which, he assumed, was why she led him into Nella's bedroom. It was dominated by the sleigh bed, the matching cherry bureau, and the framed architectural drawings—two by her, and done, clearly, in response to the third: Wright's Fallingwater house—austere, demanding, and somehow about Frank Lloyd Wright more than anyone who'd live inside it. Nella's work was softer than Wright's, and derived from his, and, since it was therefore so very out of fashion, her drawings constituted emblems of why she could not succeed in the trade to which she swore she was drawn. Wright, when old, had bedded younger women, Alex knew. He had groaned as if wounded, and she had sobbed as if struck, beneath these drawings.

Sitting crossed-legged in only a T-shirt, daring him to look at her naked lap, she had taken his hand, beneath those drawings, and had said, "Your fingers are just like my father's. He has big hands, too."

"So do you," he'd said, disgusted by his feeling of

achievement. For of course he had foreseen that she would find him, in certain ways, to be like her father. And, instead of being saddened by the truth of this easiest of predictions, he'd been pleased.

It was, he remembered remembering, like the moment that Liz, at the narrow front table of the Madison Avenue Bookshop, had turned to him bearing a book about Boris Pasternak. "He looks just like you," she'd said, smiling. And he had modestly shaken his head to deny it, needing to tell her that he hadn't an iota of Pasternak's talent or humanity, and needing, too, not to say it unless she did.

Here he was, then, with his self-loathing focused through a third female lens, Detective Rhys, who sat on Nella's bed and patted the ecru duvet beside her. "Will you sit, then," she said.

He did. His motion jostled her, and she slid closer. Their thighs were solidly in contact, and neither, he noted, moved away.

"Anthony Slowacki, the not-quite-cop, is a friend of yours?"

"Patient," he said, looking ahead at the closed closet door. "He asked if there was anything he could do for me."

"But by letting him serve you, don't you unbalance the flow of power as you'd want it to be maintained in your own office?"

"You've done some work like that before?"

"You don't get to be in the Job for very long without being ordered to see one of youse. I shot a boy on Morton Street. He lost his leg, thanks to me. They had me bawling my eyes out to a shrink for a month. The bitch. I kept asking her to look at his picture, from wouldn't you know the *New York Post*, and of course she managed not to. And only because I'd asked her, I'm sure. She wouldn't let me tell her the time, I swear— never mind, as with your Slowacki, do a good turn. At least as you and he, with your combined IQs not surpassing a hundred, might have thought of it as a good turn."

"I'm sorry," he said, conscious, still, of the heat of her leg.

"And when," she said, "were you going to tell me that the lass in question checked herself into *your* hospital, strangely enough, the Psychiatric Institute, all the way up at 168th and Riverside, one hell of a cab ride from the Village, where we've fine loony-bin care just down the street and, by the way, plenty of nutters to keep her company. And when," she said, "would you have mentioned that you called her insurance company to get their clearance for the treatment of a little spot of suicide attempt?"

"No," he said, "you always say that to make sure they authorize. They don't hesitate if it's suicide. Well, not so far. Let them crawl a little further into the pants of government, and they'll be turning them out into the streets in winter, bleeding from the wrists."

"Is that what she did?"

"Emphatically not," he said. He would not surrender Nella's whole self.

"You speak the English like a foreign language," she said.

"That makes two of us."

She patted his leg in agreement. He thought of turning to embrace her. But he simply said, "She was exhausted. She had . . . presentiments of death, not impulses to commit suicide. In other words, her own essential health was intervening. She'd think of others murdering her, so there's your wish for relief. Death. But she didn't fantasize doing it herself. Hence my belief that she was basically safe. Still, of course, she was harried and fearful, sleepless, her thoughts racing. She needed to rest. I needed to get an MD to prescribe for her—"

"The very suave Theodore Levenson?"

"As a matter of fact, no," he said stuffily.

She shook her head. "Because then he'd know. And he might tell the missus of your great concern for this—not to put too fine a point on it—piece you were having on the side?"

He shook his head, but could not bring himself to deny it—to deny Nella, to deny his guilt—once more.

"So she was alive one week before her disappearance. Because we have you and her at the PI, as they seem to call it up there. How I wish you had told me any of all of this, Doctor. Selfishly, as well as professionally, speaking."

Her brown-ringed eyes, the grayness of her skin, the weakness of her limbs, which she didn't move as he sat on the bed and touched her at the throat, the forehead, as he moved his fingers on her thin, loose arm, working his finger under the plastic identification tag they had fastened to her wrist near the bandage under which she had barely sliced the skin, much less the artery: alive. All right. Call it that. Say: breathing.

And then, at last, her voice gone husky from the drugs and from dehydration, telling him, somehow impersonally, "You're as quiet as he is, Alex."

He'd known who she meant. He had leaned to kiss her graceful nose, and to touch her lips with his, demanding nothing, promising support, wishing comfort for her, and seeing none to come. He found himself on her bed and at her body as if a physical embodiment of the psychic affliction he had proved himself to be.

"Do you," he heard himself whisper to Rhys, "do you think I murdered her because her dismay was uncomfortable? Because I committed several sins, professionally speaking, and would have felt better if I could forget that I had betrayed myself and my wife and my practice? So I shot her or something and hid her body in one of those hiding places all psychologists know all about, and then I called the police to go searching for her? The way so many criminal masterminds do?"

"I doubt you'd have used a firearm," she said.

"And that's *all* you doubt?

He wanted to stand and pace. He wanted to confront her. But he wanted, also, to feel her leg against his, so he sat where he was. He had dreamed that night of something rolling from his pocket as he lay on the floor. He needed to recover it, and he was panicked, he remembered, and he chased it, feeling like a child in a large room dominated by grownups.

"You don't got nothing like that," his mother, in the dream, had said.

"Don't *have*, Ma," he'd corrected.

"Of course," she had said.

Rhys leaned to her right and picked up a pillow. She held it flat on her lap. Then, slowly, she brought it to her face, which was crimson, but somehow placid. He watched as she sniffed it, heard her breath on the percale of the pillow cover. Then she replaced it on her lap.

"Is that you I'm smelling, Doctor, mingled in with her soap and her perfume?"

"There's always the father," he said, "upstate."

"The state police are busy, but expect to see to a visit one of these days. The sheriff's deputies would be happy to go out, but they wonder if the state might have jurisdiction in a matter crossing county and municipal boundaries."

"It's nonsense," he said. "This is about someone's life."

"That's law enforcement, Doctor. A lot of motion. Or a lot of not. What do you think of all this physical proximity, then?"

He could not help himself: he stood. Rhys laughed, with real pleasure, and she stood, too, shaking her head. "You're a boy in several ways, aren't you?"

He shrugged.

"And you're a fool, I'd say. And a man possessing a questionable sense of values. You have the foulest judgment, considering that you receive money for the exercise of it. You've aroused my suspicions, to say the very least. And, to place it all in public view, you've invigorated a germ of my own emotional self-interest." Her skin was crimson, but she spoke as if she felt no shame. "I don't know, frankly, that we're near to being compatible types. And *I* will, assuredly, not do a jug of pills because of you. Do you think that's what she's done, Doctor? Or is it purely evil, what's going on?

"Listen to me now," she said, touching his hand. "Pull back the dog Slowacki. He'll hamper us, he'll devalue testimony, he'll taint evidence, as surely as the commisioner is a despot. Tell me everything you know about the woman of your dreams—*they've* gone night-mares, I'm sure—and about the nature of your . . . well . . . relationship. Hide nothing. And work on getting yourself a night's sleep, by the by. You look terrible, poor fellow." She put a cold palm against his cheek and then, as if she were saying goodbye, she removed it.

"And make a note of this, will you? You ought to hope that I have short working days and long, stimu-lating nights. For you are one over-vermouthed mar-tini away—one underdone fillet," which she pro-nounced *filly*, "away—from a humiliation at the precinct, if you know what I mean. Consider yourself at risk. You're examined, from now on, with the coldest of eyes. Understand me?" She looked at him, then she nodded as if satisfied. She adjusted her bag on its shoulder strap, and he felt certain that it was heavy with her gun. She stood before him, her head cocked to study his eyes, a smile on her full lips. "Now," she said, "you haven't mentioned it yet, no doubt because I've been terrorizing you. But what do you think of my hair?"

ALEX HAS RUN out of resources at the library. The staff will help him by summoning microfilmed newspapers, but he is tired of the chipper tones that veil the sour daily sorrows and resentments of this community under duress. And, anyway, he can see and hear and smell the coal, the salty fogs, the sour flesh of the citizens of Barrow-in-Furness, and he needs no newspaper reports or commentary. It is in him now. She is in him now. She is trying to be born again, inside him, he thinks. And then he thinks that such a thought is inappropriate, to say the least, psychotic to say the most, but somehow about the survival of either him or his mother or both: about life, anyway, he consoles himself. Yes, and so is setting fire to someone other than yourself. And so is peeing on the fire in public. When is a crazy life less to be prized than a locked-in, festering death? Ask the assembled patients of Dr. Lescziak, he thinks. He smells the Walney Channel, like hardboiled eggs, and he hears, at the channel mouth, the tinny clang of the buoy off Dova Haw. Beyond it, to the west, past the watchtower, the Irish Sea is beating like a slow, heavy heart around Piel Island, where he imagined his mother with the German prisoner of war. What does it say about a man that he recreates his mother's most intimate moments? Shall we call it Oedipal, as Teddy surely would, and say no more? Or should we encourage the man to check himself into someplace more or less organized—say, the Psychiatric Institute—and permit Dr. Levenson or someone more objective, and perhaps less fully involved with the patient's wife, to prescribe a psychotropic, and encourage him to talk in a group, and help him to sleep and sleep and sleep? And would it matter to anyone in service of the patient that it makes a kind of sense to him? That, his mother having given birth to him, and probably to William Kessler, William should have his chance to give birth to her in his manuscript and he, Alex, apparently a brother, ought to follow through and bear her, by way of his imaginings, back again into the world?

Otto might have borrowed clothing from a civilian, Alex thinks because he cannot help it. Perhaps he borrowed some from Leon, trousers and a coat. Or they might have known someone who worked in the hotel laundry or its kitchen. He would have come past the grease and oil works on Ironworks Road at the southern end of the town, where so many craters had not been filled in. He might have struck through the alley bordering the sawmills, and from there he could have walked, as if he had a right to, around to the Hindpool and up and, through some arrangement, into a room.

Sylvia, this afternoon, free for her lunchtime, pleading family errands, could have come on Chatsworth Road and south, down Walney Road, which runs past the southern reservoir near the hotel. She is waiting for him, isn't she? And she is clothed. Even her sturdy shoes, which, she says, feel like iron by the end of the day, are tightly laced, as if to protect her. The jacket is buttoned to the neck. He must know as soon as he sees her unsmiling face that he is in for a trying hour.

"*Bog*," she says, saying "God," and then, catching herself, sets her finger across her lips.

"What is it?"

"I said Polish. I called to God."

"Hallowed be His name," Otto says. "There is no sin in calling out to the Lord."

"Here? Us? No sin?"

"None." He removes his civilian coat and stands before her in his blue shirt sewn with its golden arrows, and in thick woolen knickerbockers over tan wool socks, a pair of scuffed leather field boots she has never seen before. "Courtesy of Leon," he says. "England is fortunate that Leon does not serve in a munitions works or at Vickers. He is too willing to please, that one. Well: I should say he is just right in his willingness to please. And I am grateful."

"Willing-ness," she says.

"Being agreeable? *Complaisant*."

"You also speak French?"

He shrugs. "I am, after all, a translator. Interpreter. I turn base metals into gold and baser tongues into the language of Goethe. And back again." He smiles as if at applause.

Sylvia feels their tension, it is almost an odor, almost a visible cloud in the small, shabby room. He does too, she knows. He waits for her to reveal herself, either physically or emotionally, and he knows that they have possibly half an hour before they must leave. And they may be caught during any of the thirty minutes she wastes by sitting before him, protecting herself with clothes. Still, like a schoolgirl, she keeps her knees together and her brogans side by side, her hands flat on the legs of her stiff, baggy gabardine trousers.

"You are well?" she asks him.

"For a prisoner of war, I am wellest—would you say? Best. Wonderful. For a lover seeking satisfaction, I must say, I am . . . least. I would say, therefore, I am unwell. Did you ever consider that love could make someone sick? I am sick with love. To avoid the Polish and the German once more, per the Treaty of Barrow-in-Furness of 1944, I resort once more to the French: *Je crève d'amour.* I am bursting with love. And you sit before me like a statue, dressed in winter clothing, the trouser legs of men. And time is leaking out of the cloudy window behind us, and under that warped door."

She closes her eyes and almost raises her hands to cover her ears. His delicate face has gone dark with emotion, and she wonders if he might—and therefore she suspects that he has thought to—strike her. She might not object, she thinks. Under the clothing and under her skin, she is all liquid, she is certain. She feels that she trembles, or, if she is still, that the world trembles. Then he devastates her by sitting, in his shirt and trousers so many sizes too large for his fine bones and slender limbs, where he has been standing, on the floor.

She has seen the prisoners forced to sit this way before, at the behest of their guards. "Arses on the cobbles, lads," one of the guards might cry, and the prisoners would drop, soaked suddenly in icy, oily water that slicks the paving stones, their hands clasping their thighs, as her hands, now, clasp hers, their faces turned toward the guard with his weapon, waiting for a further command. Otto is his own weapon, and she awaits his pleasure. Yet it is he who sits, making her the armed guard and his warder.

"Tell me," he says.

"I am thinking we need more talk. Talk more, I am meaning."

"Oh?"

"I have to knowing your *thoughts*," she whispers.

"I have so few." He smiles, as if apologizing because he lacks a match for someone's cigarette. "But I will invent some for you. May I ask you why?"

"To remember them," she says.

"But why?"

"To remember *you*."

His face goes still. It looks petulant, as if he were an angry child. And then it looks dismayed, and then he is destroyed, and his sad, courageous smile says all of this to her. He shrugs, then shakes his head, then looks directly at her, and into her, his eyes enormous, his face very pale. "Perhaps your body will remember," he says.

She does not wish to lose the sight of his eyes, but she has to close her own for an instant as the ripples run through her. She is a vessel he has filled. He is filling her now. But they are going to lose each other.

And she cannot help asking: "What will I remembering you said to me? What will I recollecting I am telling you?"

" 'Recollect,' and 'told,' " he gently corrects.

"Of course," she says.

"I will remember your very slender vein, it is the color of a viola. Not the musical instrument, but an English flower." He closes his eyes to demonstrate, she knows, that he has memorized her body. "It runs from the left side of your neck and then, suddenly, it emerges there to run, almost like a little river, lazily, down the top of your left breast. And then it stops. I have traced it with my finger. I have followed it with my eyes. I have explored it with my tongue. When we are passionate," he says, "it grows darker, as if the river fills and rises. When we sleep—when you are asleep, if I am awake—it becomes almost blue, the color of the summer sky. Not winter. Not now. But of another season."

"You will remember that?"

"Yes," he says, "absolutely. Forever."

"Forever," she says. "Because we are being alive, and time passing and passing, it will running past and away, and we are being older. If we are surviving this time. Then we are old. And we—"

"—think of each other," he says. "Of course. Every day. Many times, every day. Each time I think of you, I will pray for you."

"And being united," she says.

" 'Reunited.' I do not know if that can be."

"Many things impossible can be," she says. "Look at us. The Polish strumpet and the German prisoner. Two people together in England."

"You are no strumpet," he says. "You know what that means?" He stands as if he has willed himself up: suddenly, he is before her, speaking through clenched teeth. "No whore. You are a woman who has blessed me with her love." He suddenly laughs, shaking his head. "And who has very few minutes left in which to prove it."

"Oh," she says, undoing her jacket buttons, "I must prove?"

"I must prove mine, and remind you of your virtue," he says. "Yes? You wish me to prove mine?"

"No," she says, opening her jacket and undoing her thick man's shirt. "No." She undoes the top of her trousers, and he pulls them down along her thighs. She slips from the chair and turns her back toward him as her knees touch the dark green carpet that smells of mold. He lifts the back of her shirt and she says, "No," raising her buttocks, forcing the trousers down farther so that she can spread her legs. She says, "No." She raises her hips and her back, her legs are almost straightened, and she wonders why she knew that this would be the position. She wonders how her body, now something separate from herself, can achieve that position.

She cushions her forehead on the backs of her hands, which lie on the wooden chair. She smells the high, gluey odor of furniture wax. If she survives this war, she will almost remember it, she thinks, in other rooms, when she is a very old woman. She will smell furniture wax and be unable to remember her legs apart, her buttocks raised against this small, strangely powerful man. But the scent of the wax will remind her, she knows, of pleasure and deceit, and she will sense a loss, but be unable to name it. She weeps now, as she gallops toward their pleasure, for that loss, and for her inability, decades from now, to properly mourn what is gone for good.

"For good," she laments aloud, as if already bereft in her future life.

Otto, grunting nonsense as if he answers someone else, or replies to a toast, or agrees with an incoherent pledge, says thickly, "For *Gott*. Of course."

Then it is afternoon, and the streets are solid with a smoky fog that clings to clothing and the stones of walls, the glaring windows of shops, and the wooden boards that seal the shops blown up, or made window-less, by the concussion of the blockbusters and land mines dropped by the Luftwaffe. She pauses at one battened shop because she thinks, peering through the sun-brightened fog, that she sees a swastika. It is very small, and it is painted on English wood—by whom? The German prisoners will be blamed, she thinks, and her chest aches for his endangerment. Anyone knowing his gentleness—except when they make love, she thinks—would know him innocent of any politics at all. In fact, she is dismayed to learn that it is her belief, held secret usually even from herself, that he would be incapable of resistance work, of political schemes, of performing anything but simple good deeds. Though he snuffled behind her like a beast, today, and his sex is large, his desires dark. Still, she thinks. Still. He has wept while describing an evening of opera in Dresden with his parents and cousins. *Don Giovanni* was performed with Jussi Björling, and he and his father smiled shyly, he said, as they discovered each other weeping. She walks away from the small painted emblem as if reacting to its power, as if she is preserving Otto from the accusations it cannot help but excite.

And as she walks stiffly, because of the abrasions on her knees and the ache in the backs of her legs, as she squints through the increasingly acidic fog that has blown in off the sea, as she listens to the shriek of train whistles and the chatter of donkey engines, the thumping fog sirens of the shipping off the Walney Channel, and as she looks at pedestrians to see if she is noticed so far from the brick and tile works—here, cutting through Bath Street, which is little more than an alley off Adelaide Street, which will run into Chatsworth and bring her to the edge of the stony field in front of the works where she must hack at the earth instead of lying in the warmth of a borrowed room and boldly touching her fluids, mingled with his, between her legs and her bottom—it is here that she runs into, physically collides with, her husband, Januscz Lescziak.

She cries out in alarm. He holds her shoulders and smiles from his height. He asks about her morning and she listens as he speaks of his. They talk of me—a little croup in the night, but with the raw weather and the damp, what can you expect? And Granny Buccleuch will see to some English remedy, tea and honey, perhaps: I'll be fine. And then, after only a very slight pause, he asks, as if he can think of nothing else to say, where she comes from, where she goes.

And Sylvia, as if the fog about them has filled her head the way Otto has filled her body, can think of no word to say in any language she knows or has over-heard. She looks into Januscz's eyes, which are, as ever, mild though shrewd—his farmer's eyes, she calls them, used to inspecting cattle and eggs, tallying pails of milk, assessing the moisture in bales of hay. She sees no anger, no suspicion. She looks again, though, because she realizes that she sees *nothing* in his eyes. And she cannot recall his having hid from her this way before. A pedestrian bumps into them, for the fog is worsening, and everyone apologizes and not-at-alls, as the English must do, and she, standing very close to him now, is reluctant to examine his eyes once more.

"So," he says, as if to prime the pump and release her answer.

She lifts on her toes and kisses him beside the corner of his mouth, a kiss of friendship and intimacy at once.

"I must returning to tile works," she says.

"Return from where?" He is holding the cloth of her jacket now.

"I went—I went to pharmacy the women at the field—Leslie, Tubby—are telling about. Special crouping medicine. Violas—the English flower? They are including in this formula for babies when they are coughing. But it was bombed."

"Bombed?"

"Oh, not soon. No—"

" 'Recently,' " he says.

"Of course. Not recently. Long ago. I suppose they are forgetting."

"Their memories, perhaps, are affected by the labor in the field," he says. "Bending down and bending up, bending down and bending up, the blood to the brain and then back to heinie end again." His broad mouth smiles and she wonders if his eyes do too. She does not wish to find out. It is war, she thinks: in an instant, you can lose everything. "Violas," he says, "they are lovely flowers. You know them?"

She can only shake her head.

"I have seen them," Januscz says, this large, surprising man.

The wind grows fiercer and a foghorn's repeated deep grunts, which seem to bounce on the fog, come in to them from the channel.

"They are lovely," he says. "Delicate and strong, with very deep colors of purple and blue. I wish that I could give you a bouquet of them."

She leans her head against his thin coat. She smells cigarettes and Januscz, a musky odor of sweat mingled with the deep harshness of the lye soap in which she washed his shirt. He pats her back, as if she weeps, and she does wish to.

"And what I am giving you?" she asks.

They stand in the icy fog of Barrow at the closing down of a vast war, not that great a distance from Europe, though very far from home—from Poland, she thinks, from Germany—and she moves her head on his chest while he strokes her back.

"Him," Januscz answers. Her head is straightened,

her back stiffened, by the thrill of fright that runs like electric current down from the back of her neck, and beneath his hand, down her spine and along to her thighs, then her calves, then through her heels. The bottoms of her feet do actually tingle. For she thinks, of course, that Otto is "him."

But it's me, Ma. Januscz embraces you in the battered English city, and he speaks to you of me.

6

IT WAS THE time of endings, he thought, screened from his progress up Madison by a moving wall of wide-beamed women in black dresses, their broad legs pounding down beneath the heavy, inverted cups of shiny skirting. They walked with a side-to-side stalking motion, ponderous on their ankles, the dresses tilting like bells above their clappers. There were three of them, sisters without doubt, or a young mother with old-looking daughters, all of them fat at the shoulders and waist, every one of them laboring. It was nearly seven, the night was humid, the lights of the shops were bright against the final brightness of the day. The air seemed smeared with purples and pinks from the stores and from a sunset that was more visible in reflection and refraction than it was as a presence on the air. The women wobbled and walked, slowly enough to keep him from passing. A man came alongside from behind him and made a sound Alex thought of as *"Tch!"* He walked around Alex and then, stepping off the curb and walking almost into the traffic of

Madison Avenue, he passed the women and worked his way between parked cars and back onto the sidewalk. Alex was satisfied with slowness. He didn't want to get to St. Agnes Ascension, although he was nearly there. He had lingered at Sherry-Lehmann at 61st, staring at the wines as if he were Teddy and as if he understood why a bottle of Château Petrus ought to matter. He had crossed the street to look into Pierre Deux, as if he understood why tablecloths in bold Provençal patterns should matter—as if he understood why France should matter. But France *could* matter, he thought, and wines *could* matter, to Teddy Levenson, for Teddy's life was populated by women who did not leave him until it was time for them to leave.

Slowly and helplessly making his way to the school in which William Kessler's historical association would hold its meeting—invited by Kessler's telephone message but, as Alex would say it, summoned—he is there, on Madison in the 70s, but also farther uptown, at the end of the bus run, over the Hudson at Fort Tryon Park; he is in the Cloisters, that transplanted collection of stolen chapels and abbeys and nunneries, with Teddy and his date, imagining them on a different day, at a different hour, but in the same month and same year. Alex sees them outside, in the garden of the Cuxa Cloister, and he listens as Teddy shows Liz the cherry tree, the crab apple, the hawthorn, the pear. The marble capitals on top of the columns glow reddish in the pale sun, and Alex watches Liz's eyes shift along the surfaces carved into lions that feed on humans, the man who leaps through the air, the mermaid, the apes. Stone heads peer down from stony palm trees at Teddy and Liz, and Liz stares back.

"It's the usual brilliant colonialism," Teddy says. "Like the Elgin Marbles. I don't know. And all those tapestries at the Met. The Frick, say, or the Pierpont Morgan. Robber barons and various mercantile pirates bring these things over and they're 'saved.' But for the likes of us. All these pieces of church and abbey, so cunningly pieced together. All this loot." He moves slightly, though not dramatically, closer to her. "Treasures," he says.

"Yuck, Teddy. You sound like an actor: 'treasures.'"

"I tried to ease into the woo. It sounded dreadful anyway. I'm sorry."

Liz nods, and she is clearly aware of him, and surely of the woo, but she is looking at art now, eating with her eyes, Alex could tell him. Though Teddy, of course, would know that too.

"But it *is* like being in a castle," she says, clearly unwilling to move away from him.

"Or a nunnery?"

"But I'd rather be in a castle. When they went to nunneries, they were tragic."

"And you aren't."

"I don't want to be, anyway," she says. "And you're a knight?"

"I'm Alex's friend. And you're his wife."

"'Wife' isn't always easy to figure out," Liz says. "Especially for the wife."

"Yes," Teddy says, "there's always that. Let's say

I'm Alex's friend and your friend, too."

"And by 'friend,' you mean——"

"Today's field trip," he says, "is the pursuit of that definition. Listen closely. Stay"—he puts his fingers on her forearm, and she lifts it in response, a child about to be led—"close."

The wind off the river drives bits of city grit, of riverside dirt, of stone, and the air of the city scours them. They move from the sunlight into the chill of wind and shadow, at Teddy's direction, because now, he says, he wants to show her the stonework of a Romanesque hall from the twelfth century, the Langon Chapel. Monsters are the writhing, carved capitals atop its columns, holding the ceiling up, and its delicate Virgin in her half a birdcage of stone altar looks through them. In the weak light of the chapel, Teddy removes from his silk salt-and-pepper tweed sport coat a maroon cotton handkerchief and he wipes as if at a smut blown onto her cheek. Alex would swear that there is nothing to daub, but it gives them an excuse to touch and be touched.

"It was a very hot day," Teddy whispers, since there are several families about, the children breathing through their mouths and bored, the parents bored too, the guards who watch them bored, the Virgin Herself, Alex thinks, bored beyond stoniness. "It was the area called the Entre-Deux-Mers," Teddy says. "Do you know it? Gorgeous wine country. The sun was very heavy on us, and we were alone in this mostly roofless place. The ruins of an abbey. The stones . . . shimmered. They were that golden tan stone you get in

France, and we were looking, it turned out, at Adam and Eve. The sinners were shining, and Satan was trying to tempt the souls of the not-quite-faithful, and the rooks, I suppose they were, kept calling and calling. They made things raucous. At the tops of walls and columns, high up on the towers—I don't know how the builders expected anyone but God, who did not need the lesson, presumably, to *see*—there, the capitals reproduced all the usual sins. And Job, of course. They had to have Job: Jahveh's nastiest, most selfish, most jealous bit of work. Well," he says, "these stones—"

He has taken her arm. The backs of his fingers around her muscle touch her breast. With his other arm, he gestures, sweeping the hand before them. "These stones we are looking at together, right now, are almost identical to the ones I saw in the Abbaye de la Sauve-Majeure, in the Gironde. The same monks who built it were commissioned to build *this*. You, madam, could just as well be standing where we stood then. You're standing in France."

Liz, now, is listening. She is more than eyes. "Who's the *we*?" she asks him.

Teddy stoops to look into her face, to inspect the enormous light blue eyes and the grand nose, the wind-scuffed russet of her cheeks. "Did you think I was corny," he says, as an alert dad looks up to check the force of cultural deprivation invading his children's lesson in sanctimony, "when I whipped out my hand-kerchief and rubbed you up?"

"Rubbing up," Liz says. "Is that like feeling up?"

Teddy turns his wrist so that his palm, which had lain about her biceps muscle, cups the side of her breast through her coarse canvas navy-blue shirt. "Feeling up is better," he says.

She says, "I agree." They regard each other, and then they start to stroll, walking over the cold stone and over centuries of what Alex presumes to have been real belief. The rhythm of their pace is easy, and they walk, he thinks, as if they have walked this way for years. "No," she says, "I didn't think it was corny."

"Good," he says. "And you, as well as anyone, must know that I have a melodramatic sense of—well, I don't know what to call it."

"I do. Gallantry."

"You flatter me."

"Gallantry flatters *me*," she says. "That's why it works."

"Does it, then?"

"You goddamned well know it, Teddy. You've known it for years. You're just too much of a gentleman."

"No," he says, "maybe too fastidious. Too fearful. It's such a *mess*, Liz. With—all of it. You once were virtually my patient. You're still his wife. You're both my friends."

They stand before a corbel that is disintegrating into a dark stone puddle because of pollution. Liz's eyes flood and Teddy, with a wry, self-conscious smile, takes out his maroon handkerchief and offers it to her. She ignores it, and he puts it away, and the tears come down her cheeks and curl toward her mouth. Teddy looks as if he's weeping too, but Alex knows he's not. It's sympathy that rumples his face. His hands are on her shoulders, and his head has drooped so that his chin rests lightly on top of her head."Liz," he says.

She shakes her head, and he permits her this silence.

Then they are in the Lescziak car, the old Peugeot, with Teddy behind the wheel and Liz angrily combing at her flared, curly, bright gray hair. Teddy drives so carefully you'd think he had never before navigated in the city. The Hudson on their right looks green, and its surface is broken into whitecaps. On their left, the old underpass stoneworks and railroad track arches, their stone a filthy gray, are covered with unreadable graffiti in black and white and yellow paint, declaring the secret names of the New World.

"I think about Alex all the time," he suddenly says.

"Then you won't be surprised to hear that I do, too."

"And . . . still?"

"You think I'm wrong, Teddy? *We're* wrong?"

He isn't a capable driver, and when he shakes his head, the car moves out of its lane. The horn of the car behind them blares and the driver keeps his hand down to scold them for a quarter of a mile.

Teddy says, "I don't. No."

Liz takes a breath and almost hiccups at its conclusion. She shakes her head, looks out at the river. "You want to," she says, "don't you?"

"Only for years, Liz. A decade. More."

"Then, Teddy, who was the *we* in the glorious Entre-Whichever in France? At the abbey?"

"Sure," he says. "Certainly. Sheila Cooper. She

writes poetry. You've seen some, I'm sure. In fact, you met her, Liz. At Books & Co., on Madison? Near the Whitney? I invited Alex and you to the reading."

"The tall one," Liz says, "with the fantastic scarf."

"I bought it for her in a tiny market in St. Macaire."

"Bastard."

"You were taken, Liz. I'd have bought you one. I *will* buy you one. We could go there. Why can't we go there? We can find the regional markets and buy me a beret and buy you a scarf. And it's a beautiful drive up into St. Emilion. You can get very good charcuterie with a liter of cold rosé in the square on top of the city. And I know places to walk on the Dordogne— Oh, boy. Listen to the chatter, huh? Like a kid."

Liz reaches out and rubs the top of his bald head, the curly fringes of chestnut and gray. He squints his eyes, like a dog being stroked, and she keeps her hand on him an instant longer—Alex can tell from the softening of her expression—than she intended. Still, she looks ahead through the smeared windshield. "This is almost more excitement than I can stand," she whispers. "Do—"

"Yes," he says. "You know it."

"I almost jumped you at the Cloisters," she says. "Hell. *You* know it. I've been on the verge with you for years."

"And Alex?"

They are on Riverside Drive, near his building's garage, and the turn signal ticks in the closed compartment of the car. "He misses me," she says. "And— well, I would say that I miss who Alex used to be. He probably does love me, although I can't imagine what good that would do either of us. I don't know. I don't know. I'm not saying this because of *us,* Teddy, whatever you and I might be. I've thought about this for a long while. He flares up. His face changes. I can't read it. I can't find anything on it to read. He just—he turns around, and he's a completely different person. I don't know who he is. I swear, I think his body smells hot, the way an engine smells when it overheats. He's frightening to me sometimes. And he's thinking of somebody else. That's easy to tell. And sometimes he *is* somebody else."

"The overheated engine, the changes: do you feel frightened for your safety?"

"No. Hardly ever."

"Liz: *hardly ever*? You sense violence?"

"Teddy, I don't know. I don't know. I don't even know what I'm trying to tell you. I do think, though, that Alex has thought for a long time that something was going on between you and me."

"He's smart. He's alert. He's been right. We've just been slow to act on it."

"You really think so? That there's—for a very long time?"

"Yes."

They emerge from the dark passage of the entrance and are in the cool, greenish light of the small underground parking lot.

And Liz at last says, "Good. Me, I took turns with it. Sometimes I would think so, sometimes I'd think not, then I'd think so again. I kept wondering: how come he doesn't notice? Then, other times, I'd think: why did he have to *stare* all night and make me blush?"

In the elevator, Teddy says, "Let's not try to be practical today, all right?"

"Not to worry," she says. "I am unimaginably incapable of getting pregnant. And I'm sure I'm on the verge of menopause. I get these temperature changes—"

He says, "I meant: let's keep our eyes shut. Let's . . . pretend. Let's not get into the matter of, well, I guess you could call it time. You know: before, or after? Could we just do *during*? If that's all right with you?"

Liz steps in and stands on her toes and kisses him. He uses both hands to pull her neck and head to his face. They say nothing, and then there is the sound of their lips parting, delicately, softly, moistly, the sound you may hear as a wife and husband kiss hello or goodbye and mean it, the sound you may hear as lovers reluctantly part.

"You're not some big, brilliant, psychoanalyst with a showoff taste in flowers and wine," Liz says into his face, "you're this huge romantic. Aren't you?"

"Ferdinand the Bull."

"Dreaming under his cork tree."

"Don't tell," he says. "You're the only one who knows."

"No," she says, "there's the poet, the tall one with the scarf. And heaven knows how many more. But if the word gets out, it won't have been me."

"No past tense, please," he says.

"Future conditional," she says.

"Painters don't know grammar," Teddy says.

"I know the past, and I know the future conditional. Those are my tenses."

"Nothing about the past," he says, "until the elevator down. Strictly present tense. As in 'am.' I am that bull beneath that tree. I don't want to even consider that anything with you and me is going to stop, Liz. Elizabeth. Liz."

"But my life does seem, these days, about varieties of stopping," she says a little cruelly. It is she who faces the facts for them, her tone says. She has taken over analyzing the case and announcing the truth.

Teddy says, "I demand the right to change that."

She touches his belly with the first two fingers of her left hand. She leans them against him and he presses his stomach out at her, as if to prove how hard his flesh is. She smiles for his boyishness. And then she looks away, facing the door as the elevator stops. "Then, you go ahead and try," she says.

In the small foyer of his apartment, there are four of them: Liz, Teddy, the five-foot-tall carving, in dark, oily-looking wood, of a fat mother bear, and the baby bear in her arms. Even in the shadows of the foyer, you can see that the mother almost smiles. She doesn't, quite, for her pleasure in the cub is almost painful. It says everything, Alex thinks, that Teddy greets the world with a mother at her most human; it says everything, as well, that he then withdraws responsibility for his statement by presenting a mother who is not quite human. *Not me*, the sculpture almost announces.

He is behind Liz, and his arms cross her chest, he

seizes her breasts and presses in at her back and buttocks and legs. Instead of kissing the back of her neck,
he bites in around the top of her spine, as if he would
tear her open. He bites gently and a shiver, Alex
knows, runs down her and then back up. She shudders,
and he moves his teeth from her, then kisses her neck
with a gentleness that makes the shiver repeat. It is
time, now, close to the sculpture of motherhood, for
them to remove each other's clothing—the lover's
privilege—but, apparently, they won't. Perhaps she
feels Alex watching? Absurd, he thinks. But she
cannot. Although they seem to be—you have to say
it—in love.

Absurd, Alex thinks: love. But they are surely in
something, and together. And it is worse than jealousy
he feels. It is envy for the energy of their feelings. He
thinks of Nella, whose face he has sought on the
Madison Avenue pedestrians and whom, he knows, he
will not see.

Teddy presses harder at Liz, but then he stands away
a bit, for he can sense her hesitation. Teddy, this man
who would make a meal of her, is also a gentleman.
But his hands are on her shoulders. She leans back at
him, holding his long right forefinger with her own
right hand, pulling his left hand down until it touches
the slope of her breast.

He moves his right hand to rub at her cheek, where it
joins the neck, at the jawbone, with the back of his
hand. She bends her head and his hand pursues her.
She turns her face, she leans her cheek into the cup of
his palm and his long fingers.

"Are you afraid to look at me?" he asks.

She turns. She pulls his ear, and he leans down, and she kisses him. This kiss takes a long time. When it is done, she pushes him back and takes a step of her own. She closes her eyes again, then opens them. Alex hasn't seen them fasten upon him that way for a terribly long time, the eyes of a painter who sees back through your bones and into the darkness between them. He wonders if Teddy has ever seen such a sight, for Teddy's eyes water as if he stares into the brightest light.

Alex followed the directions—two hand-lettered signs, neat capitals on orange-tan paper fastened with masking tape on the green cinder-block walls of St. Agnes. It was a small auditorium or large classroom, lighted by heavy glass globes that hung from iron rods. The lights floated in the yellow-gray dimness of the little hall. There were no folding-bottomed fastened seats; instead, the audience of thirty or so sat uneasily in rows of wooden straight-backed chairs built for smallish children, the grown-up knees raised high toward faces and chests. Before them, on an aluminum-edged strip of cork that ran above the chalkboard, which was foggy with bright blue chalk dust and on which the ghosts of old lessons were legible— he saw *JOSHUA–JESU–JESUS*—teachers had hung drawings made on the coarse orange-tan construction paper. The Triune God was envisioned again and again by children who, Alex thought, might once have been Anthony Slowacki's daughter. The drawings were earnest, they were bright, and they were predictable.

God the Father was immense and dark. His Son was beautiful, with a head and beard that were ocher, tan, or gold—never mere brown. And the Holy Spirit was either Casper the Friendly Ghost, an animated white sheet, or radiant lines connoting brilliance and power. On the cork strip to the right of the small, tilted wooden lectern atop an unpolished oak desk, neatly centered before them, Alex saw the work of a girl, he was certain, whose mother was powerful. For God the Father was short, burly, a reliable-looking dad just slightly shorter than the decidedly female-looking Holy Ghost: a mother worth knowing, he thought, nodding and smiling as he tried and failed to cross his legs in the squat, uncomfortable chair.

At the lectern, now, a stern-faced man with a haircut not unlike Alex's own, though pure white, adjusted a solid-red, silky tie that he wore with a red-striped shirt—the reds quite clashed—under a dark gray suit. He had been introducing William Kessler, Alex realized, to the several rows of grown-ups twisted into small-bottomed, short-legged seats. Alex saw dandruff on the shoulders of Kessler's heavy black suit coat. Many in the audience were holding legal pads or stapled sheaves of paper. Alex took a pocket notebook out as the welcome to the association's event was concluded and as the credentials of William Kessler, Ph.D., were recited.

Kessler's pale, shiny, small face was creased with pleasure as, nodding at Alex, to whom several in the audience then turned, he set typed papers on the lectern and, sometimes reading, sometimes speaking without reference to his pages, he spoke to them as if he were their professor.

"If you will indulge me," he said, speaking directly to Alex, "I would like to dedicate tonight's lecture to the memory of my mother."

Alex nodded once, as Januscz often did, to indicate permission to proceed if not agreement. Kessler could not know this, he thought. A woman separated from him by several empty seats to his right was studying him. Their eyes engaged. She wore a black suede pillbox hat with a furled veil. She kept her matching gloves on her lap beside her matching square handbag. Her shoes, he knew, would be dark suede. He lost Kessler's introductory comments. He was talking, now, about a novel Alex had never read, *The Confidence Man*, and, apparently, about what "confidence" meant in the 1850s when it was published. Alex was appalled to understand that he was jealous, in some fashion, of Kessler's assumption that their mother belonged equally to each. If they were brothers, he thought. No: they were, in all likelihood. They were. The conjunctions of time and place and what Kessler knew and what Alex himself recalled and had learned made it all quite likely. They were brothers-in-part. The woman wore a topcoat, although the school was excessively warm, Alex thought, and she looked, in spite of her age—thirty-five, perhaps—a good deal older because of her costume, which took him back to Mrs. Kennedy and the 1960s. Her features, though coarser, reminded him of Nella's, and his stomach jumped like a struck bell, resonating up through his body. She leaned to an older woman at her left whose lipstick, he would have sworn, matched the red stripes in the shirt of the older man who had introduced Kessler. This woman smiled at Alex, he thought. No: she was whispering to the younger one in the Kennedy costume. She said it again, and this time he saw that she was aiming her chin toward him, as if pointing a finger. *Jew*, he thought she said.

In a chapter of this book about faith in something, confidence in something, and, of course, Kessler was saying, confidence *schemes*—the stuff of conmen—a character apparently carried on at great length concerning the American Indians and Indian hating. "Naturally, 'Indian hating' is taken by liberal students of American history and, especially of the westward expansion, to mean the hatred of Indians. And so it can be and, often, should be, as we shall see. But it is worth considering that Mr. Melville also had in mind the hatred *by* Indians *for* white pioneers."

Alex heard what he thought of as a murmur. Apparently, Kessler had made a salient point. "Listen," Kessler said, to this, "from the thirty-sixth chapter: '. . . if in youth the backwoodsman incline to knowledge, as is generally the case, he hears little from his schoolmasters, the old chroniclers of the forest, but histories of Indian lying, Indian theft, Indian double-dealing, Indian fraud and perfidy, Indian want of conscience, Indian blood-thirstiness, Indian diabolism . . .' What if our author does not satirize? What if he describes the truth in this frontier educational process? As we sit in this classroom and reflect on the classrooms of our forebears, let us consider that they might well have been taught the truth—that Indians did rape the women of, destroy the homes and storehouses of, assassinate the parents and children of backwoods Americans. Is it not, then, conceivable that those stories—we shall hear a few tonight—of window upon window of railroad car bristling with long rifles, of citizens on board Mississippi steamers such as the *Fidele* in *The Confidence Man*, potting red men as if in a war—is it not conceivable that the stories are of self-defense? Or, at the very least, of retribution for malefactions past or present or impending? Let us consider, as Melville invites us to, that 'Indian-hating, whatever may be thought of it in other respects, may be regarded as not wholly without the efficacy of a devout sentiment.' It was a huge, dangerous continent upon which the Americans of European extraction embarked. And they were hated for their expansion by the people onto whose hunting preserves they expanded: Indians, ladies and gentlemen, Indians hating them, Indian haters."

Alex cannot see over Teddy's shoulder as he envisions them. The shoulder is ridged with muscle and he is as jealous of Teddy's back as, moments ago, he was of Kessler's appropriation of his mother. Now, though. Now he sees her face. It is flushed and going redder and she tears at his shoulder, then his arm, but his arm and shoulder are immobile, locked beside her just as he is sealed upon her. She pulls at him, she presses toward him, she revels, Alex believes, in his solidity, and then she gnashes, gasps, then finally cries out, and the sound—like a caught breath endlessly extended—

echoes in Teddy's bedroom in the late afternoon, the blinds not quite slanted tight against the light that beats against it off the Hudson, like waves, like gusts of river wind, like Liz, releasing herself and released by Teddy, crying into Teddy's flesh as Teddy shudders against and within her body gone tight and hard and holding, then spent.

And somehow Kessler has gone from the 1850s and a book, to 1942 and Jews in Vlodawa, Poland, who were Bolsheviks, alleged to have been deported to a labor camp, as he termed it, out of racial hatred. "So many of them were," Alex heard, although he had missed what it was they were. "It's a matter of record. And we are speaking—are we not?—of historical accuracy. The menace to German economic well-being was understood by the Chancellor as, essentially, the corruption of free trade and the Bolshevik movement as espoused and—mark this—*financed* by Russian Jews and by European Jews with left-wing sympathies; the two, in this latter European case, often being one and the same. Thus, the so-called war against them, a misnomer, an agit-prop coinage if ever there has been one, was in fact an extended effort at national self-defense."

He smelled sunlight, he thought, still seeing Liz's face and Teddy's naked shoulder. What did sunlight smell like? Like the absence forever of Liz, he thought. Like Liz's sweat absorbed by Teddy's flesh. Alex thought: This must be what you feel like when they tell you that the cancer is everywhere inside you, and untreatable. The body you took for granted has failed.

You are a failure. You are dead. In the parochial school room and so far inside himself, he was nauseated, afraid that he might retch. He smelled the bedroom. He thought, then, that he smelled himself. He smelled a barnyard.

> so much depends
> upon
> a red wheel
> barrow
> glazed with rain
> water
> beside the white
> chickens

Alex had submitted it to the former Miss Casey, their seventh-grade teacher, who made it clear, with a great smile he would now call girlish, that henceforth they were to address her as Mrs. Coyne, for she had married Mr. Stephen Coyne, known as Fighting Stevie Coyne when, in the Golden Gloves Tournament of several years past, he had "eradicated"—Mrs. Coyne's word— Horace (the Cobra) Diaz, the New Mexican entry, in the welterweight competition held in Portland, Maine. "Mr. Coyne is still tough," she told them, "he is a southpaw, difficult to figure out in a short fight, and gifted with a fast jab as well as a left hook to the rib cage that will do you some damage. But he will tell you that I am tougher. I ask him to take the garbage out, the garbage gets taken out. Am I understood?"

She was tall and very slender—skinny, they called

her—but with enough of a figure for the boys to study when she wore her pilled, thin, rose- or milk-colored sweaters with a straight skirt. She always wore penny loafers, and they made her look, from the knees down, like a girl. She hadn't that much of a chin, but Alex always found her compelling. And she knew about books. She gave him novels to read—who, among his few friends, read Rafael Sabatini's *Captain Blood* or Burroughs's *Pellucidar: A Sequel to "At the Earth's Core"*?—and she discussed them with him only if he asked her to, and only so long (she seemed to know) as he wanted to talk.

He thought of it, years and years afterward, as a wish to compel her deeper attention, as if shoplifting to satisfy a stymied child's needs, say, because he was angry that she had married; he felt not only jealous of the love she broadcast, but ignorant of the sort of love that made the tall, cool, competent, grown-up sisterly teacher—out of reach but, also, somewhat alluringly close to it—belong suddenly, and so exclusively, to the very mysteriously male and very tough and therefore dangerous Fighting Stevie Coyne.

The assignment, at the beginning of their poetry unit, was to write a poem about something that mattered to them. "It has to matter. It can't just be interesting. You have to *care* about it," Mrs. Coyne told them. "And if you don't care much, then I won't care at all."

The poems were due on an autumn Friday. He remembered how, that weekend, he heard the loss, on his tall, golden radio, of the Lions to the Green Bay Packers. He kept trying to figure out why Paul Hornung's last name was pronounced with an *ing*. He was supposed to be a playboy and a gambler, and Alex expended a good deal of imaginative energy on riddling out precisely what a playboy did. He had spent a lot of Thursday afternoon at the public library with a list of names taken from *Windows into Language*, the high, heavy textbook for their experimental advanced English course. He was looking for something special and he thought he had found it—verse he knew to be incomprehensible to anyone in class, and maybe even to Mrs. Coyne. It seemed serious stuff, and that was what he wished to submit. On Monday, after Home Room, and after Introduction to the Romance Languages, a course in French, Spanish, and Italian that began with a long unit on Latin, for sixteen gifted children and Alex, they entered Mrs. Coyne's room in bright October light. Heat rose about the shellacked pine desks and the chalkboard, the wooden floor that was dull from soapy hot water, the back-wall bulletin board with its thicket of clippings about famous authors—Steinbeck and his dog, Hemingway kicking a tin can—and heat beaming from a red-faced Mrs. Coyne.

She would not look at him, though usually she smiled a greeting, and often enough she might ask him about his weekend. She looked happily at Madeleine Cohn, however, and Alex knew she detested her. Maddy had bigger breasts than Mrs. Coyne, and she didn't seem to mind that a number of the boys nearly drooled when they studied how her blouse or sweater clung. Like several of the girls in the seventh grade,

Maddy seemed to Alex to be twenty, while the boys, for the most part, himself included, seemed closer to nine or ten.

"I enjoyed reading your poems," Mrs. Coyne told them as she handed them back. His had no grade. Three kids, he knew, had spotted the sentence written in her high, perfect hand, and they stared at him as if he wore several heads in the collar of his shirt. He started to perspire, and he knew it was not because of the glare of the early autumn sun. *PLEASE SEE ME*, Mrs. Coyne had written at the top of the page.

"One in particular," she said, "seemed to me to be— I suppose you might call it—professional. It's the work of a master, you might say. Alex Lescziak: will you read us your poem, please?"

He had entered a tunnel of short length. He could see light at either end, but there was darkness about his head and face and shoulders. Although the tunnel was small, his voice was magnified within it, and it sounded hollow. He heard himself as if from a great distance. "So much," he read, sounding to himself like a narrative voice on a slowed-down movie when the film slipped from its sprockets, "depends," he read, as if it were part of a telegram written in a single line, and he leaped into "rain/water" and collapsed among "white/chickens" and sat down, his head beating like a heart, pretending to study his creation anew.

"What's the poem about?" Mrs. Coyne asked.

As his vision cleared, he awaited his classmates' insights.

"Alex," she said, "I asked: what is the poem about?"

"Me?" he said.

"Stand, Alex, will you?"

"Yes," he said, standing with his hand on the top of his desk so that he would not fall over. "It's—farming. It's about agriculture. You need to have water to have a good farm, and you need to take care of the farm tools and all, and, you know, you need, you know, chickens and such."

Her mouth moved, and he thought, for a blessed instant, that she would give him a broad smile. She did not. "Chickens and such," she said.

"I was thinking about cows," he told her. "My father used to work on a farm when he lived in Europe, and he told me about cows. Lots of farmers choose to raise cows instead of chickens. But some," he said, swallowing a mouthful of saliva that felt hot and that seemed to sting, "will choose chickens. I'm not sure why, really."

"Interesting," Mrs. Coyne said. "An agricultural poem, then."

He nodded.

"And the lack of capital letters?"

He thought of an FBI story he had read in which the stalwart G-men caught a kidnapper with the help of their laboratory experts: you could trace a typewriter through the way it typed; no two machines were alike, according to the FBI. "The typewriter," he said to Mrs. Coyne. "It's my father's old portable from England, from when they lived in England after Europe, and the thing for capital letters doesn't work."

"The shift," Mrs. Coyne said.

"The shift," he agreed.

"As in 'shifty,' I suppose. And is there anything else we ought to know, Alex?"

He got cocky because untruth might have been working to set him free. "Well," he said, "the word 'glazed' is a pretty unusual word. When I used it, at first, I thought it meant like glass, you know?" He had, by then, turned to face his classmates, declaiming, moving his hands through the air as if he had something to say and a way he might say it. They looked at him as if he'd been sucking helium from balloons and talking in a Donald Duck voice. "But I figured I didn't mean that at all. What I was *really* getting at was how the water kind of *coats* the, ah"—he consulted the poem on his desk—"the wheel barrow. Yeah." They looked at him with amusement, but also with a kind of horror. He understood, then, that they were watching Mrs. Coyne's face, and it was commenting on his commentary. "I think that's all," he said, without looking at her, as he sat down.

She then asked Madeleine Cohn to read her poem. Even though it was Maddy and her pink oxford shirt, he could not look at her. He remembered her sweet, deep, lisping voice as it chanted something about autumn ending with winter and things getting cold, which is like your grandfather dying. His grandparents had died before he had met them, and he could not imagine winter now. He could not, in fact, imagine surviving the day. So he stared at his poem and its innovative use of "glazed," and then he looked at the ceiling. If one of the huge, milky glass globes that hung from its metal rod connected to the ceiling would only snap, he thought; and if it chanced to be the one that hung above the head of Mrs. Coyne; and if he could leap from the bench of his desk and dash across the room to tackle her, while cushioning her head from contact with the wooden floor; and if the globe shattered harmlessly behind them; and if she looked up into his face and understood that he had saved her—then something like one more day of his life might be attainable.

But the light globes shone, floating above them, and the danger in the room belonged to him alone. Class went on, then class ended, and the next group of students entered. Mrs. Coyne packed her zippered portfolio and motioned Alex to follow her. They went to a room he had only heard about, small and dark, where teachers sat in shabby chairs, like the ones in his living room at home, and smoked cigarettes and read newspapers or, like fat, short, smelly Mr. Delaplane, who also did this everywhere else, stared in front of him like he was watching a terribly sad television show. She led Alex to a little desk with a couple of chairs at it. Nobody sat there, and he figured it was the place you dragged cheats and told them they were getting suspended from the seventh grade.

She sat and sighed, reached for an ashtray, and lit a cigarette. He was thrilled to watch her crimson lips close around the end of her L&M, then slowly release and expel the stream of smoke. He felt as though he watched her getting dressed in the morning.

She said, "That was a brilliant defense in there, Alex." She let a big grin open, and then she shut it down and took another drag. "But you lied. You cheated. I read that poem, you smart little son of a bitch. I used to love that poem. And you spoiled it for me. And let me point out, if I may, that it was *not* because of its high agricultural content that I once liked it. We could have spoken with a great deal of profit about imagery and how you might try *not* saying the obvious in a piece of writing. Or about the importance of seeing the thing itself as a way of doing honor to the world. Because I think of you as having a gift, and I would have enjoyed discussing something that is not predictable doggerel and . . . Oh, Jesus," she said. "And young. If only you had written it, Alex. Do you know who did?"

"I forget," he said. "Double-u Cee Someone."

"And that's the third of your sins." The hand holding the cigarette, which looked long and glamorous to him, pointed at the fingers of the other hand. "You cheated. You lied to me. You failed to give a real poet, named William Carlos Williams, the credit, much less the praise, he deserves." Alex was thinking of the sleekness of her fingers as they danced to the tune of her condemnation. He did not care about a poet named Carlos Anyone. And he wondered, now, in the parochial-school classroom, if some of the amusement that tugged at her mouth was not provoked by her sense that he had possibly been sufficiently enchanted by her—even if he'd underestimated the range of her reading—to risk his academic neck in the theft of a poem that might impress her. All these years later, he was grateful, he thought, for the latent sexuality she'd both felt for and extracted from him.

He remembered startling himself and her by saying, "I hope that you and Mr. Coyne are very happy."

She had somehow understood him. "We are, Alex, thank you. And I would like you to meet him someday. He and you could be friends."

He nodded, having been shown his place. He was grateful, anyway, to survive, as he thought then he might.

"You must write a poem of your own," she said. "Tonight, for tomorrow morning, in my home room, at half past eight. It must be a very good poem. Do you understand what a very good poem has to be?"

"Not about chickens," he said.

She leaned her face in close to his. He smelled the perfume of her breath: the dark secrecy of her mouth, the moisture that made her tongue gleam, and the spiciness of tobacco. "No," she whispered, "not about chicken *shit*. I want the genuine article from you, Alex Lescziak. No lies. No trying to impress the teacher as if she were Madeleine Cohn with her . . . endowments. I want you to impress the *Muses*. To say something you couldn't otherwise say."

"Okay," he told her, although he was utterly confused.

"You do that all your life," she said.

"I will," he promised.

"Try, anyway," she said. She stubbed out her cigarette and reached to lightly slap his cheek. "Now: shame on you. Work honestly. And thank you for the compliment."

He said, quite brilliantly, "Huh?" as she led him from the lounge.

So what *then*, in light of his near-death experience in seventh-grade English, led him, later that afternoon, to kick through orange and yellow leaves on their short front walk, and climb the brick steps of their stubby stucco porch, and, entering the silent house, shuffle through the ragged-ended papers stuffed, but not yet fastened, into his three-hole looseleaf notebook, and climb the noisy wooden stairs to find his mother and show her his poem? He must have still thought of it as his. He had attempted with it to woo a teacher he didn't understand he wished to woo. But she had understood that he did. And she had signaled him all of that without saying so, quite. And the secret of poetry, she had told him, was to say something that he could never otherwise say. And there he was, more than thirty years later, trained and habituated to analyze statements unsaid. Toting a guilt that seemed somehow, by then, heroic, he went from one unavailable woman to another, bearing all that he then possessed that might pass for tribute.

His mother wore, he remembered, a very dark, full dress, perhaps the color of coffee without cream, fastened at the neck and somehow decorative in a way that had to do with pleats and folds. It was what she wore when his father begged her to accompany him to something at the university. There was a reception for graduate students, he remembered, and she ought already to have been there, serving tea from a samovar and smiling, according to her description of her responsibilities at these events. He was pleased to find her lying on her bed, on the left-hand side of the room, with a pillow over her head. She pulled it aside as he knocked at their bedroom door.

"A headache," she said, smiling a little. "The other pillow, you are thinking, why? Because it is cool on face, at top of the head."

"Forehead," he said.

"Exactly. Of course. You are well in school?"

"I wrote a poem," he said, standing beside her.

"You are giving it to me?"

"Showing it. If you like."

She sat up, making the furrowed face with which she always demonstrated her pain, her sacrifice in not submitting entirely to it. "Give," she said.

"You didn't go to the tea."

"The pain in head," she said, slowly shaking her head. "He is understanding."

"He understands, Ma."

"Of course. Give."

He handed her the poem, and she slowly followed its lines. He watched her finger trace the extra spaces of the breaks as Williams had carved them onto the page. And then her face brightened. She lost the sallow, sad tones he was used to. She smiled with the face of someone else. That person faded soon, but he had seen her, and he knew that he had seen something rare and would remember it. "*Barrow*," she said. "What is the importance, in a poetry in America?"

"Poem."

"Of course. '*Poemat*,' " she said. "*Gedict*."

"Huh?"

"Old words, foreign. Long time ago, when I was girl, nearly, and you were baby. A person giving me *Gedict*, he called it. We were saying in Polski *Poemat*. We don't talk it no more. Anymore," she corrected herself. "And this?" She pointed to Mrs. Coyne's crimson injunction.

"I stole the poem." He wanted to lay his head on her stomach, on the fancy, scalloped dress she was supposed to be wearing for his father at his school. He wanted to weep. He wanted to shout cruelties about himself, and about her and her blunted, staggering language which never, unlike his father's, had improved. "Somebody else wrote it. I didn't write it."

"Not Barrow?"

"I didn't write *any* of it, Ma! I cheated!"

She sat up higher, then leaned back against the headboard, wincing. "What you are meaning?" she asked.

He heard himself in school as he chattered his clever drivel about agriculture. "Nothing," he lied or confessed. "Nothing."

"Meaning bad? Good? Nice? Not nice? What you are *meaning*. At what? No: who. I am confusing, now."

"I don't know. You should have said confused."

"Of course," she said. The skin around her eyes looked moist now, and her face was softer than usual. "This I am knowing."

"What?"

"From long time ago. You are being good. You are meaning good, baby boy. Come. Come."

She embraced him at the edge of her bed, and he

smelled the lushness of the soaps and perfumes and lotions she applied to herself. As his body lay against hers, his feet still on the floor, he thought of Maddy Cohn, and he thought of Mrs. Coyne. He did not think of William Carlos Williams nor, with any understanding, of what, from the submission of the poem to his return from school, he had been meaning to mean.

"I am knowing this," his mother said.

"I *know*, you say it, Ma."

"Of course. Of course. But this: maybe is love in someone, Alex. Stealing poetry, giving to someone—"

"Maybe it's love, you say."

She said, "Of course." She rubbed the same cheek that Mrs. Coyne had pretended to slap. And she smiled. And she looked like the old ladies in half a dozen brown-black photographs his parents had taken with them from Poland and rarely examined. She smiled, and she said, imitating her child's brusque tones, his boy's cracking voice, "Maybe it's love, you say."

And grown-up Alex in the schoolroom watches them in Teddy's bedroom, dimmer now, so that their bodies look somehow phosphorescent, unnaturally bright. The long, powerful arm of his wife reaches across the sheets toward Teddy's. Her fingers lie against his wrist. Her eyes are closed, but not—as Alex has recently seen them—in anger or despair. She is partly asleep, but partly in a galvanized wakefulness; the lids are fluttering, and a smile appears on the lips he has seen so tautly compressed. Teddy draws his arm up so that his hand encounters hers.

"Hold on," he says.

"Like this," she says. "All right. I am. What are we demonstrating?"

"We aren't. We're holding hands."

"Yes, we are. And we're allowed to do this?"

"We can't do the rest until we first do this. We have to. It's a rule."

"I always thought of you as having rules in bed. Laying down the law. But I didn't mean to make a lousy pun."

"It's not so lousy. It isn't the lousiest I've heard."

"Is it allowed to ask what happens next? In the larger context?"

"Liz, we either never do this again, or we go straight *for* the larger context."

"I would rather not not do this again."

"Same here."

"No," she said, "I think you could do anything. You could figure out a way not to need anything."

"Oh," he says, turning onto his stomach, crawling along the bedclothes, and leaning his face against the cleft of her buttocks, kissing softly, then speaking again. "You think it impossible I might need you?"

She moves her legs apart and then together. She says, "I can't decide whether to clamp my thighs together and be spiritual, or spread them and, you know, do my imitation of being shameless."

He lowers his face upon her again and says, into her skin, "Be shameless, please."

"And we're in it for the larger context," she says.

"I really hope so," he says upon her.

So that Alex, lost in the loss of his wife to Teddy,

now knowing fully what he had thought to almost know, missed much of Kessler on the Chancellor, on the Bolshevik menace, on how many Jews were *Sonderkommando* and—here he surfaced to fully hear his half brother's rich baritone as he dipped and soared among the dead—now it was time to discuss the other dead, the forty-nine Waffen SS among those interred at Bitburg.

"Our President flies toward them, and his homage to the German nation, to the Chancellor of the new Germany, and to those boys and old men who died out of obligation, not fanaticism—out of loyalty, not hatred—marks a turning in our national ability to understand the ebb and flow of world history. For even if SS did compose some, though surely not all, of the upper echelon at certain labor camps, these particular children and oldsters, drafted into service in the waning of the war, were *not* among those who operated camps. It is a canard to say otherwise and—this must be faced up to, and squarely, by our nation as a whole—to repeat that canard is to manufacture propaganda for the machine that feeds armaments and unfettered funds to Israel. It is to force-feed guilt to the American nation in order that the Jewish state further aggrandize its colonialist expansion against the displaced and victimized of Palestine."

Thinking of bulldozed homes, of exploded school buses, and seeing Teddy on all fours, actually all *fives*, he thought, with Liz, Alex knew that while she had slept at first in their bed, and then in their guest room, and sometimes in her Greene Street studio, she slept for certain in Teddy's bed, and he in hers. Any bed, including his, in which they made love became theirs, he thought.

Nella had said that in the good and lesser hotels, and then in her own apartment: when they made love, they were in a castle, and she was a princess, and he was a knight. Or was that Teddy and Liz at the Cloisters?

No, Nella said, *it was me. It's me.*

"I only wish my mother, who fled the confusions and upheavals of that war, could be here tonight," Kessler crooned.

"Is that Mrs. Diamond?" Alex heard himself call.

"Oh," Kessler said, his face bright, his tone merry, "Dr. Lescziak. You are welcome, sir. No. I had in mind our Mrs. Lescziak, to tell you the truth."

Although when he looked away from Kessler's huge pleasure he saw the woman in the pillbox hat, her eyes wide with intensity and full upon him, it was Nella he heard: *I'm your lover*, she chanted, *I'm your whore. I walked to you naked in the streets.*

No, you wore a coat. You were conflicted. You were generous. And frightened. And you are no whore.

I'm not your daughter, she said, biting the side of his neck, nipping above the larynx, *am I?*

It was the doctor as well as the lover who asked her, *Do you want to be?*

Well, do I?

And then it is Liz in bed with Teddy, and he leans on an elbow to see her face. She closes her eyes, as if to escape him, and Teddy says, "Don't, Liz. I'm your friend."

"After this," she says, "you'd better be."

He bends to her, where the sheets meet her chest, and he kisses her. He kisses her again. She pushes him away.

"Let me, Liz." He kisses her, this time on the neck, and then on the cheek. "And for heaven's sakes, laugh. I'm being a funny lover."

"Can't," she says.

"Tough, huh?"

She nods, and the sheets echo raspily.

"Try?"

She gasps, or begins to give in to her weeping, then stops. "Jesus," she says huskily.

Teddy doesn't speak, doesn't move.

Liz says, "Are *you* all right?"

He laughs. "Thank you," he says, "I am. How are you?"

"Miserable," she says. "Happy. I don't know. I don't know."

IT HAS HAPPENED in an orderly, English way. Sylvia, working the soil with a hoe, has unearthed what looks to her like a pitted yellow stick. There is carbon on the wall of the Hindpool Brick and Tile Works, which, according to Leslie, was produced by the bombing. Something came over, lost or strangely alone—a Heinkel, Tubby said—and dropped two bombs so far from Vickers, ruining much of their farm garden and, farther in town, dropping two more. In the cold spring morning, Sylvia and the others have been chopping up the earth. They will ready the ground for more planting. Leslie, who works, as a rule, to Sylvia's right—they wheel in order, like puppets simulating birds, she thinks—is only too glad to step over and light a cigarette and observe as Sylvia now works with a small spading fork, its wooden handle fractured and bound with twine which will cause her blisters even through her gloves. That is what you do in a time of war, she thinks. You scratch like a farmyard fowl and you go home with blisters.

"Is that an important stick, love?" Leslie asks. She has a long, pretty face and her slightly bucked teeth make her attractive to a certain kind of man, she claims, the sort, she says, who tends to think with his thighs. Buck teeth or crossed eyes: you mayn't stay married, but you'll never want for company in bed, Leslie says.

"It is bone," Sylvia says.

"I don't *think* we've been asked to collect them, love, have we? Tina? Hallo, Christina!" Leslie summons the tall, broad-shouldered leader of their section, who always dresses in her husband's old trousers rolled several times at the cuff—he was run over and killed by a lorry at Dunkirk—and whose eyes are the blackest holes Sylvia has ever seen. To look at Tina is to understand sleeplessness. "Do they want us saving old bones?" Leslie cries. "Hasn't someone else been set to collecting bones and fat and such?"

Tina nods, looks at them with angry puzzlement, and then, with the tines of her long-handled rake, attacks the blown-up ground. The tile works loom ahead of them, all red brick and gothic turrets made to promote the achievement of nothing, only to look impenetrable; they succeed, and to Sylvia the structure forms a wall of the prison inside of which she is sentenced to serve. She wiggles the triangular blade beneath the far end of the bone, and it pops out and up, like a wine bottle's cork. She catches it in the air, she sniffs and inspects it.

"Well played," Leslie says, grinding her cigarette under her lace-up shoe. "Sodding weather. My feet are so cold I won't feel them until I'm in a bath. A luke-warm, slimy bath, I can assure you, after my mother's had a happy, hot soak and hopped out to complain of the rigors of having sat indoors all day."

These people will talk about *anything*, Sylvia thinks. She sees that Tina is marching over, holding her rake like a rifle slanted across her flat bosom. From the far end of the field comes Samantha Souter, once fat but now starved lean, except for the hanging wattles of jaw. They call her Tubby, and she reddens as they do, but seems pleased to be noticed, until Leslie refers to her daughter as the Tublette.

Sylvia has another, smaller, one loose.

"This is being graveyard," she says. No one seems to hear her. Leslie has lit another cigarette, Tina has set the haft of her rake against her foot, the business end near her shoulder, and she stares with her terrible eyes at the depression in the damp, dark earth where Sylvia works. Tubby, in her high, sweet voice, is commenting on Sylvia's wisdom in bringing gloves to work today, while Leslie has replied that Sylvia always seems to know how to take care of herself.

Again, she says, "This is *people*."

"Sorry, Syl," Leslie says. "Pipple?"

"Human beings."

"Yes. Naturally. Tina, what do you think she's going on about?"

"It's a ruddy old barrow," Tina says. "The explosions have unearthed an ossuary."

Tubby says, "She hasn't understood a word you've said."

"They're human bones," Tina says. "That's what she's going on about. She's found the bones of dead *people*. Why can't you understand that?"

"Well, of course I do," Tubby says. "Don't I?"

"*Pipple*, they seem to pronounce it," Leslie points out.

The fat silver barrage balloons float on hawsers that shift and sometimes twang as the wind bullies them. Fleecy clouds move quickly on the horizon, and the smell of the sea is taken from them; it is replaced by the stink of uncollected rubbish, due for pickup today, they've been promised, and by the smell of drains, which suggests that a low pressure front will settle, once again, leading in the fog and damp, then drizzle. For a while, though, Sylvia can feel the pallid sun on the back of her neck. She thinks of the heat of Otto's breath on the back of her neck. Three bones, now, are aligned on the earth near her knees. She has made it clear, she thinks, that nothing will deter her searching for more.

Tubby, as if she has been asked to instruct her, announces, "It's their house down there, Syl. Think of it that way. We oughtn't disturb them at home."

Leslie says, "Let the dead live with the dead. Isn't there a Latin way of saying that?"

"Still," Tubby says, "it's a bit eerie, now you think of it. A house full of bones."

"The house of the dead," Leslie says. "A bit like my place, isn't it."

"Safe as houses," Tubby says. "Gives *that* a new meaning."

"Last night," Leslie says, her terrible eyes on the ground, "on Schneider Street, one of those idiot errant bombs they dropped seems to have triggered a land mine that had burrowed under a bit of uninspected rubble left over from the bombings in '41." Her voice was flat. "Like a mole in the earth, it just hid there for all those years. It was waiting. And then the bomb set it off, the vibrations, I suppose. An old man and an old lady, in their bed, doubtless fast asleep. He had his pyjamas blown off him, arse winking at them when the fire brigades arrived, poor fellow. That final indignity. Both of them dead, of course. Killed by concussion, I should think. It took most of the slates of the roofing away, and left the walls up. They were caring for their grandchild. The old folks hadn't a scratch on their bodies, according to one of the wardens. It was the child took the worst of it, all sliced to bits by the flying debris, all running with blood. Apparently now, she can't see or hear. But she can breathe. Someone will doubtless tell you she survived. And *that* will be codswallop, from the beginning of 'she' to the end of 'survived.'"

Tina stands, staring at the bones as if they were her

husband's, then turns to carry her rake to the metal hut at the Holker Street end of the field to telephone for instructions. Leslie squats beside Sylvia, chirping small cruelties, and Tubby, from time to time, makes small wordless noises of agreement; together, they are curiously comforting, because they remind Sylvia of her mother and her aunt as they gossiped without any particular harshness, passing the time in the hot kitchen, not seeking to wound, while they peeled and sliced potatoes and dropped the pieces into a yellow ceramic bowl of cold water to keep them from turning black before it was time to dry them and grate them and fry them into cakes.

"Safe as houses," she mutters to herself as if it were an obscenity.

"That's my girl, Syl," Leslie says. "You sound down-right English. Home counties to the—well, sorry, love: to the bone."

It is the skulls, in fact, for which Sylvia searches, stabbing into the earth. There are people under the ground here, and she wants to look at the bone that held their faces together, at the sockets of their eyes and the roundness of their skulls, at what the mouths have become. For some of them, she is certain, were lovers. She has no idea how old they may be, nor what sort of lives they may have led. But, somehow, they are her ancestors, she thinks.

Leslie, talking on, whether or not she is replied to, whether or not she thinks she has been heard—speaking because speech, Sylvia thinks, is what the English use as fire when cold, as zephyr when hot, as armor when endangered—Leslie says, "Do you know, Syl, it appears to us that what you've stumbled upon, dug down into, in actual matter of fact, is what we born-and-reared English call, in our native tongue, a barrow. Did you hear us natter on about it earlier? I couldn't say, actually, where the term derives from or even if I use it correctly, now I think of it. Tubby, love? Do you know the origin of 'barrow'?"

Tubby shakes her head as she lights a cigarette, and her wattles shift. "I always thought it was why they named the old dear what they did. Barrow in the furnace, I thought. Didn't you?"

"Have to confess I never gave it a thought. We'll have to ask Tina. Or some man. You *know* she's sent for a man. Always sends for a man. Be sending for men until she dies, poor thing. And receiving precious little satisfaction for all the sending, I can assure you. Barrow, Syl. It's where they bury people when in ancient times. You've found a barrow in our Barrow."

Sylvia scrapes and tears. Her wrists ache, her fingers are cramped, her knees are cold and they are sore—and she thinks, of course, of herself on her knees with her face on her hands upon the cushion of the chair as Otto, behind her, wriggles and snorts and shoves. She works on because no one else will search with her, and she is desperate to release the people entombed below her, to look them in the face and find herself.

Like a girl afraid to offend, Tubby says, "Syl, they won't let you do much more of this. You might as well rest awhile. We've a long day ahead."

"Every day's a long one," Leslie says.

Tubby says, "It's the war, Syl. They need us for other purposes."

"The war comes first," Leslie announces. "It's the religion," she says in a voice Sylvia hasn't heard before, flat and strangled by anger.

She says, although she intended not to, "*They* coming first." She leans back, still on her knees, and she sets the tool on the scored, worked earth, flexes her fingers, shakes her aching arms.

"What's it to you, then?" Leslie asks.

Sylvia shakes her head. "I cannot say."

"You can't tell me?"

"Yes. Cannot."

"They won't let you do it. Tubby's right. We shall all dine out all week on what you've done already, you know. Assuming food enough in the shops or restaurants for us to dine on. You have to admit it looks peculiar, you snuffling about on the earth like a sow, if you'll forgive me, after truffles."

Sylvia raises her hands in surrender and smiles: she has no idea what Leslie has said.

"Truffles. A kind of mushroom, I'm told, that the toffs like to feed their ladies in London and Paris. I suppose the Nazis are eating all the truffles in Paris, these days."

"Not for long, they say," Tubby says.

"Yes, they say. But it doesn't seem to end, this war, does it?"

Sylvia has gone back to digging. She cannot permit herself to rest. And, although she cannot say why, she knows that her work among the bones of the dead matters as much as planting and harvesting crops. That is what she does, she thinks to herself: she harvests this crop.

That, she tells Januscz that night, is why she weeps when the tall officer rides his bicycle with the most awkward of pedaling motions over the bumpy, partly exploded field and stands beside her to say, gently enough, "I wonder if you'd stop that, please."

She looks at him, she looks back at the earth, at the fragments of bone, the bits of pottery that resemble bone, and the long, yellow, spongy pieces that come, she suspects, from arms or legs. She points at them with her bare hand—she has become so overheated that she's taken off her jacket and gloves.

"Yes," he says, offering a tentative smile. He wears metal-rimmed spectacles and fingers a narrow blond mustache. "Quite a catch, I suppose you'd call it. Or is it haul?"

She says, "Crop."

"Right. Right. Except, you see, we are required to get an *actual* crop from this soil. It's a very important aspect of Home Effort, and I must request—actually, it's my place to *order*, much as I dislike to be unpleasant. I must require, shall we say, that you return to work. That's all of you ladies, please. And the work in question is agricultural production."

Tina has walked over, this time without her rake, and her thin, hungry face with its burnt-away eyes is turned, after a moment, from Sylvia to the officer.

"Why aren't you in combat?" she says angrily. "If I might ask."

He touches his mustache and adjusts his glasses. "Was, dear," he says cordially. "At the start of the Italian stuff. Sicily. I dug up mines. Dug up one too many. Put my foot in it, as my corporal liked to say. The bicycle's supposed to be a bit of getting-adjusted, as well as the only transport they can provide. Rehabilitation, it's called. Left the better part of a foot outside Syracuse. This is the way they see me helping best, and wouldn't you expect it? Digging land mines, digging potatoes—all the same to them, digging. Just as this poor lady's doing. Digging things up. But bones? No. We've put too many bones down, dear, to ever start digging them up again. We'd never stop, you see."

The kindness in his voice makes her want to weep, she tells Januscz, as she does weep in their grim flat that reeks to her of sour food and cigarettes. "They are permit them being *lost*."

"They already were," he gently tells her. It is almost nine o'clock, and both of them are groggy, speak in monotones, blink against fatigue. She will not see Otto tonight, and she is terrified that he will be murdered by an angry veteran or the distraught father of a dead soldier, that someone giving orders—and there seem to be so many of them—will command his removal farther east, and maybe all the way to Yorkshire, which sounds to her like the hell of which this Barrow is the anteroom. The barrow with its bones has spoken to her, although she cannot understand precisely what it says, and she feels that she has somehow deserted him— abandoned *them*—by taking her instructions from the chain of command of the nation that does give them shelter, after all, even if in this cold, wet place. For her obedience has taken her from the lovers she sought to attend.

Leslie had said, "They're past it, love. They're all defunct."

Tina, making her tones final, had said, "There's a war on, for Christ's sake."

"It should not be," Sylvia says to Januscz.

He nods his agreement as his eyes roll with fatigue and he catches himself, lights a cigarette and focuses on her as she knows he would if the house were burning, if he himself were burning, should she command or require his attention. "But it is as it is," he says in his rumbling voice, "so many are lost in the ground."

"Still."

"Workers and scientists—boffins, they call them here. It sounds as if they are birds, very amusing. And Jewish babies in the camps. And lovers. All of them are lost. Cruel. Cruel and true, Sylvia."

"I want to checking on the baby," she says.

"Check," he says. "I want to check."

"I want to check," she dutifully repeats.

"Good." He nods his approval, and his cigarette glows.

"Jewish babies, you are saying. So now I need to check him."

"Good. Yes. And the lovers, I said."

"Somebody else," she says, "checking on them. I checking on our baby."

"I check," he says.

She does not say, "Of course."

ALEX WAS ABOUT to stand to speak to his former patient, his new half brother, the person who had shared a mother with him, but at other times, the way people sublet apartments and use the same intimacies—the toilet and the bed—and smell each other's lingering trace, even, but do not meet. He was leaning forward, his knees too close to his torso for comfort, his ears full of throat-clearings, laughter—and praise, of course, for William Kessler, who had addressed the way the world was setting down the record of its events. The Jew-sniffer in the pillbox hat turned to stare at him, and Alex smiled. He thought that someone observing it might say it was a sad smile. He suspected that she might find it a Jewish smirk. He took refuge in a crayon drawing of the Father and the Son and Holy Ghost. All three of them smiled toothily, and Alex smiled back, pleased for the child whose religion seemed not to be about terror. As he leaned forward, over his knees, and waited for his weight to shift so he might stand, he poked his face and head, as through a screen or membrane, into the night—the night before, his final effort, he knew, and hers—when he fell up the stairs on numb, exhausted legs, and through the door she'd left ajar, and into Liz's Greene Street studio.

The numbness in his legs, his trembling arms, compressed chest, blocked throat: a panic attack, he told himself, nothing of the cardiac in any symptom—

unless you were looking for a heart attack, he heard himself think but in Teddy's voice; because then it seemed a classic infarction, tingling of extremities to stertorous breathing to thoracic pressure.

They'd made a date, he and Liz. It could be their final date. He had come here, he thought, out of the cool spring night among the drinkers from paper-bag-wrapped booze, among the strollers come down from their studios, among the shoppers for unaffordable furniture at Zona, among the kids come downtown from the Village because the scene had drifted southward in Manhattan, among the cops who policed the rhythm of the walking of the long-legged women, and, doubtless, among the couples exploding apart with a terrible, slow certainty like him, like her, like the effort of their years together and like the pleasure of not being alone in the winding-down of the century into SoHo's golden rot.

He came off the street, away from scattered papers and cigarette butts and smears of dog turd, up through the smell of dark coffee, the heavy, sweet perfume of cakes and breads; he came into the industrial odors of thinner and paint, the almost barnlike smell of cloth, of heat in small spaces; he came on slow steps, like a tourist into an exotic place, not like a man who entered anywhere in which he was necessarily welcome. And he was in the sweat of his panic, or his cardiac incident, whatever it was that threatened to send him backward, down the steps, and onto his back, and out of this life.

He could smell, from the doorway where he panted,

that she had shampooed with something new. The discovery permitted him to smile. He thought of Nella's shampoo, a child's concoction with a strawberry tendency, and he bit his lip, devouring the smile. Her eyes were down when he saw her in the big box of a room. She had come partway to the door, then turned to lead him farther in. He thought that she looked shy. When she faced him at last, standing in the far corner, near her daybed still covered with coarse woolen blankets, next to a small pine table on which were pencils, a notebook, an overturned alarm clock, and used tissues, he noticed lines at her mouth, which he assumed he had seen before but hadn't registered. He found himself swept by a deep, undeniable pity. Not that he'd grown younger. Liz, nearly his age, but always youthful, was beginning to look *her* age. It isn't fair, he thought, that her skin, which he had known for twenty years, should have to be eroded. But that's the drill. Remember, he thought, when you counsel them, if you ever see another patient, what you prattle about: welcome the changes, learn how to live in them. Context, he said so many times a day, is everything: find a new context in which to be yourself.

"Hi," he said, feeling shy with her.

She looked up, as if surprised to be addressed.

"What do you think it means, Liz, if 'context is everything'?"

"Well, don't you know? You say it all the time."

"And suddenly I find I don't know what it means. What I mean when I say it. It still sounds smart as hell to me, but I wonder if it is."

She smiled thoughtfully, then looked very serious. "I always thought it was about learning from where you are. Figuring out how to be yourself in your situation."

"That's terrific," he said. "I hope that's what I meant."

She looked pleased. "Good," she said. "Good. You look a little tired."

"You know," he said. "It gets you, after a while."

"I've told you for years your practice got too big."

"Yes," he said, "I think you're right. But I meant— the thing that got to me—I was talking about us."

"Oh."

"Yes," he said.

"Us. That is such a huge topic, isn't it? Would you like some wine, Alex? I have some cold white wine."

He said, "Please." Then: "Do I sound nervous to you?"

"You mean like a man who's trying to have a blind date?"

"Maybe," he said.

She said, "Maybe a little. Drink some wine with me." In her clean white T-shirt and paint-smeared jeans and sandals, she squatted before the little refrigerator. She poured from an open bottle into a couple of tumblers which looked, he thought, as if they might recently have held brushes. Standing, she took a step to hand him one. She studied his face the way a wife studies an unwell husband. She inspected his eyes, the tone of his skin, his lips, then said, "So how do you feel? I haven't seen you all week."

He drank for the coolness, but then tasted the wine. "That's good," he said.

"A white Côtes du Rhône," she said. "It surprised me that I liked it."

"No, it shouldn't," he said. "Teddy served it to us. Remember?"

She reddened, and Alex thought of Detective Rhys. Liz shook her head.

He said, "Sure. He went on in that Teddy way of his about its surprising crispness and its big this along with its flinty that. You remember."

"No," she said.

"It was at Teddy's place. After—I think it was after a night in the garden at the Museum of Modern Art. The Modern Jazz Quartet, some summer night, I think. And we took a cab back to Teddy's, and he had this wine waiting on ice. It was a good evening, I remember."

"I'm amazed at what you can remember," Liz said, "considering how much you keep complaining about your memory."

"Well, that was a lovely night. We had lovely nights."

"Yes."

"Tough ones, too. But a decent proportion, Liz. Wouldn't you say? Thinking about all of it? A *decent* proportion of good along with bad. And then it broke."

She came closer. "What, Alex? What broke?"

"Sweetheart: *it*. The thing where he is not supposed to make her unhappy. And she is not supposed to want to go away. Or tell him that it's him—that he's been going away. So that there's, finally there's more *away* in their life than anything else except what they can remember."

"Is that us, Alex? Is that what we've got left?"

He couldn't talk and then neither, he saw, could she. He drank more wine. Now he couldn't taste it.

The daybed and the pine table were the only visible signs of disorder in the room. Her canvases were stored in their racks, and her brushes were in jars, the paints were in imprecise rows, and some sketches were tacked more or less straight on the walls near some postcards from museums. She used the brown Belgian linen, and a big stretcher, built with her hard carpenter's hands, was hung, plumb and true, on a far wall. It must have taken up eight feet. It was bare. Alex walked to it, and he stood and sipped his wine as if studying a finished painting. He smelled her new shampoo, something with berries in it, as she stood beside him. He reached for her arm and held it above the elbow. She permitted this, but he could feel the tension in her arm, and he let go.

"This is where it's hiding," he said, gesturing with his glass.

"That's where it is," she said.

"You'll find it."

"Yes," she said, "I think I will. I hope so. It's all I know how to do."

"You teach," he said. "You're a good teacher, I think."

"But this is what I do."

"What you want to do."

"That's right. Yes. What I want."

He turned to her with an ease that surprised him. He might be a professional at such encounters, but this was like losing an organ, he thought, something not quite irreplaceable which, through its absence, would ache and throb for all of every day, and weaken him, but maybe not kill him, at last. How, without these years with Liz, living so imperfectly but utterly, would he know who he was? Nella, he knew, could never tell him. She was necessary, but it was Liz whom he had known for so long; she was how he had known himself. He felt electric with panic as he thought about living without her. And when he looked into her ferocious eyes, which glared at him, but not with anger, he thought of his father calling her "your beautiful hawk." Liz's skin looked red at the cheekbones and nose, as if she were sunburned. He remembered when her hair was a very dark brown, almost black, with only hints of early gray, and those eyes looked even more dramatic when surrounded by it.

He had driven a borrowed Volkswagen bus from New York City, where he had a postgraduate fellowship year at Bellevue, to the Delaware Water Gap, in Pennsylvania, to where Liz worked for the owner of a camp for gifted girls. She had blossomed as a teenager at the camp, and she felt obligated to run their arts program for one final summer. They permitted her to live in what they called a lodge, at the edge of the camp.

"It's almost a private house," she said, studying his reaction as he approached the steps, at the top of which she stood. He had parked, against all the camp's rules, among the low branches of a spruce forest behind her lodge. She was wearing white shorts and canoe moccasins and a navy-blue T-shirt that said Mountain Vistas Camp. Her legs were dark from sun, as were her arms, yet her face had seemed white to him, perhaps because of the cool blaze of her eyes in the shadow made by her hair.

"How private would you call it, Liz?"

As he climbed to approach her, he remembered, he had reached out to touch her leg, and he had run his hand up the muscle of her thigh and then up inside the front of her shorts.

"Private enough," she had said as he encountered her nakedness beneath the shorts.

And of course, standing before the blank canvas in her studio, he thought of Nella, who walked across the city to him, with little or nothing on beneath her coat because she needed so much to bring herself to him as a gift. With Liz, it had been pleasure; it had been an uncomplicated lust. He shook his head.

"What?" she asked him now, in her studio.

"No, nothing. I'm—I was thinking of you in that girls' camp, and coming to stay with you. I was standing there, at your steps, when the goddamned bugles went off for lunch."

"I don't remember anything like that."

"It was the summer you were at camp, Liz, and I came up from the city to stay there awhile and then bring you down to our new apartment and marry you and sleep with you all that I could, and eventually ruin your life."

He turned as if to face her, but she was looking away. He kept turning so that he looked across the long room to the table and bed, the churned-looking sheets.

"You didn't ruin my life, Alex."

"I helped."

She laughed, and he remembered the pleasure they had taken in being each other's friend. Her laughter seemed unexpectedly girlish, and he loved its immersion in what had provoked it. "Yes," she said. "Well, we both did fine at that for each other. You know: I'm as sorry as you. I am."

She was standing beside him, both of them turned toward the front of the room, and they faced across to the bed.

He saw Teddy in it with Liz. This time, as he watches, she is on top of his friend, she looks small on Teddy as she clutches powerfully, desperately, as if it were she who would penetrate him. He hears her breathing. Conscious that Liz was staring at him, he heard his own.

"Are you all right, Alex?"

"Never better," he said. "The wine was terrific, and so was seeing you, Liz. I mean here, in the studio. I haven't been here for weeks, I guess. We should have looked at some of your work, maybe. If you'd wanted to show it."

"Another time," she said.

"Another time," he lied.

She leaned over and kissed his cheek. The sisterly distance struck him as if a taller, stronger man had thumped him between the shoulder blades. But he knew how to lean down and kiss her cheek in reply. He forced himself not to nuzzle her cheek, or to try to smell her skin as he went. He turned, and he left. He'd carried the tumbler of wine with him, he found, down the stairs and out to Greene Street. While he waited for a cab, he drank the white Côtes du Rhône and remembered how he and Teddy and Liz had listened, on a summer night, to the controlled emotion, the avoidance of sentimentality, of the Modern Jazz Quartet as it played *Django*.

Now, in the parochial school room, at the end of William Kessler's presentation, Alex reached his tingling feet, thinking of Liz in her shorts when they were young, and how she had offered her cool, hard body when he reached for it. He thought of her the night before, in her studio, and how he wished, now, that they'd made love a final time on the Greene Street daybed where, he was certain, Teddy and she had been happy together. Say it, he thought: in love.

THE POEM IS called "Break of Day in the Trenches," and William Kessler's father has printed it on a page torn from a ledger, perhaps the book at the front desk of the old hotel at Back Strand Street. The horizontal lines of the page are a light, dull green, with red vertical lines at the left-hand side. Standing to speak with Kessler the son, Alex imagines the work of Kessler the father as Sylvia tries to read it. His writing slants hard to the right, as difficult to read as if the characters were in another tongue. Some of them possibly are, Sylvia thinks, returning to the lines she believes say this to her:

> Now you have touched this English hand
> You will do the same to a German
> Soon, no doubt, if it be your pleasure
> To cross the sleeping green between.

What, she wonders, is a sleeping green? She has no doubt that the hand that touches the English and the German is hers. The poem, she knows, is written to her. The fear of death and terrors of war intrude. He thinks of the dead, but he also thinks of her. No one ever wrote a poem to her, she thinks. This encounter with his cryptic hand is a new kind of excitement; she studies the mystery of his thoughts as she has studied his fine, mysterious body. For all his brilliance, for all his clarity, he is a puzzle, she thinks. She recalls herself on her knees, digging at the blown-up crust of the tile works field, unearthing the dead and mourning their passage. So: they have been thinking alike while kept, by circumstance, apart for this week of weather turned cold and tempers grown short. Even Januscz, the most patient of men, has narrowed his eyes and raised his voice from its pleasant low notes when addressing matters he once might not have thought to mention— the harshness of Alex's nappies, for instance. It is the soap, she recalls herself explaining. It is the mineral content of the water. It is the war. It is the almost sun-less English world. But, all the while, she thinks, looking at the shapes of his letters on the page, they have each, she and Otto, been thinking similar thoughts about the fierceness of love and the dread of passing time.

They aren't to meet tonight, and it would be her preference to go early to bed and shiver and finally sleep. After supper and before they go to bed, she will play with her baby. This is her plan. It is her duty. But how, she wonders, do you play? She thinks of her grandmother and a dreidel. She thinks of Aunt Gussie and the game of clapping palms, of Gussie singing and Sylvia imitating her words, breathing in her breath, which is always scented with cloves. But how, now, in this world, with these long shadows on these yellowing walls, and among these odors of salted fish and dirty fog, in all these noises—the static of a radio drawing in no words; the endless crying and crying of a colicky or hungry infant; the muted, repetitive, seething chants of a man who is seized by rage—how do you play?

She refolds the page and places it in her cosmetics case in the grimy, cold bathroom with its cracked, short tub that is sandy from the scouring that never cleans it. The toilet, of course, is in the barely lighted hall, and you can smell it from the street. You sit, in its narrow closet, among the odors of people to whom you barely speak although their leavings climb into your lungs. In the kitchen, now, still in her woolen stockings and men's trousers, but in soft slippers instead of the hard shoes she must wear to work, she heats beans in tomato sauce, which they will eat on toast. This is not only nothing of a meal; this is not food. The baby will eat this gluey pulp because it will fill him and she will cajole him into eating it. Januscz will eat it because he is hungry and because he enjoys it. He enjoys the taste of almost anything, including her when she occasionally permits. She does not apologize or explain. Januscz is too gentle to insist, too embarrassed to speak of it, too tired to force her. It is as if they were very old, and, since she has thought of Januscz as old since shortly after their marriage, she has persuaded herself that little is missing from their intimate life. They live in this dark, damp place, and they do not very often touch.

"You," she says to her baby in English so that he will speak only in English, "you I am touching."

They sit together on the chilly floor, the beans in the pot and the toast on its rack, forgotten, stiffening as it cools, and they sing the little song about his being a teapot, short and stout. The lights go out, and she thinks that the works have been bombed. There is no sound in the sky except the gulls and the incessant swallows and the doves, of course, who fly in shifting, dark clouds above the block of flats; they land, then complain, then fly off, gobbling their fright, then they settle again. "This is my handle," she sings to Alex, "this is my spout." The lights come on again, the angry man downstairs raises his voice to cry that it is a bleeding outrage and then he settles down to his murmurous chant. The crying infant still cries, and boat whistles thump in the channel, and she and Alex sing that you must tip me over and pour me *out*!

Januscz brings home two varieties of news, which he shares with her after kissing Alex hello and then kissing the cheek she has offered him. Two nine-year-old boys, exploring the strand, have been blown up and killed by a land-mine explosion. "They should not have been poking about," he says, slowly shaking his head. Oh, yes: and a German prisoner was exposed, last night, reciting poetry in a neighborhood talent show at the Craven Park Restaurant.

"That sad little fellow," he says. "Saltworm."

"Salthouse," she says. "Leon Salthouse."

"You know him?"

"I saw him at the tile works. He is speaking with Tubby."

"Your farm friend, Tubby. So. It should be 'speaks,' not 'is speaking.'"

She says, "Of course. And what of Salthouse and the German?"

"One of the prisoners he guards, of course, the one they call the Reverend. He is always claiming—he always claims—apparently, to be a clergyman and not SS."

She nods. She looks at Alex and swallows and nods.

"He was reciting poems," Januscz says. "Why would anyone do that? Reciting like that in a restaurant where the others played the accordion or danced with the metal bottoms of their shoes, or sang songs to raise the morale?"

She shakes her head, forcing her eyes wide. The baby protests her hand around his little fist, and she releases it.

"But they do it," Januscz says, "and the German, the Reverend, says he will say aloud to them some poetry he has written. So. Apparently, he says the poem.

And—listen to this. Of all the people in the Craven Park Restaurant, of all the people in the world, this sad fellow, Leon Salthouse, with his large pistol and his long feet that make even mine look small, this man interrupts to tell them in his schooldays, when he was a boy, his teacher had a heart broken by the death of a sweetheart in the first war between Germany and England, 1914 to 1918. She demanded of her school-children: they must speak to her the poetry of that war from their *heart*. So. They forced themselves to remember poems of that time. They were required to, you understand? This poem, he announces in the restaurant, is by a very famous English poet who is dead! I cannot remember the poem. But Leon Salt-house can. He tells them, from his memory by heart, every word the German has not yet reached to recite! So: the dead speak out to the living. They cry from the grave through the mouth of Leon Salthouse. And the German prisoner is disgraced. And in the midst of war, some honesty shines through. Some truth."

The silence goes on. Januscz doles out beans onto cardboard toast. Finally, she says, "He was prisoner before poem, he is prisoner after poem."

"This is true, Sylvia."

"Maybe such a beautiful poem, he is feeling he have to say it anyway. It talk for him."

"Listen," Januscz says: " 'feels,' not 'feeling'; 'has,' not 'have'; 'talks,' not 'talk.' "

"Of course."

"You have sympathy, then, for a thief of English poetry?"

"Maybe he steal it to give," she says.

"'Steals,'" Januscz says.

"Of course," she says, lifting the baby and wheeling with him toward the table.

"He is heavy," Januscz says.

She thinks of the weight of his body upon her, insisting, insisting. "Not too much," she dares to say. "He is small."

"He is three years old soon," Januscz says. "Big boy for three, I think."

"Oh," she says, "yes, then, pretty big. But I am strong."

He squints through the smoke of his cigarette.

"Sylvia," he says, "I am confused. For heaven sake: who would he steal the poem to *give* to? A German prisoner. An English poem. *Who*?"

Smelling the acid of tomato sauce and the sweetness of the beans, shifting her long, watchful child on her lap, and bringing a spoonful toward her face to blow it cool, she says, "This not nothing I know."

She looks, now, not at her child but at her husband. He looks back. She waits to see if he will correct her, but, watching the spoon move from her lips toward their baby's, he does not. He smokes, he stares, he finally nods, and then Sylvia, feeding Alex, smiles in his direction.

AND ALEX MOVES from there, from inhabiting Barrow, to the schoolroom inhabited by God and His Son and the Spirit that tugs against the weight of the world. He is standing with the German prisoner's son, surrounded by the evidence of things unseen.

"Are you impressed?" Kessler asks Alex. "Tell me honestly," he says.

"What I understood," Alex says, bending to look into Kessler's face, "seemed to me a lot of clever rhetoric. Indians were hateful so that hating them was acceptable. These particular men may or may not have guarded Jews, so the outrage of Jews over Bitburg is somehow inaccurate. Maybe I didn't understand you?"

"You were in a reverie, I'd say, Doctor. Brother, if I may. You believe *that* part of it, I sense. About our relatedness. No small matter, that. And you do."

Alex shrugged. He felt that he was smiling, though Kessler's response was not as if to a smile. He took a backward step. Alex followed. "You've rewritten my life," he said.

"I've said it accurately."

"So you say. So you say. Well, I'm here to offer you congratulations on your talk."

"That's praise, indeed. I'm grateful. I accept it. I wanted it. But that you came in the first place . . ."

"Consider it a failure of the practice of psychology. I never should have come. But I came because I knew I'd failed. I thought to say it in person," Alex says, aware that there are so many persons here, so much history in him, that he could not find the time or pages or words or the thousands of characters with which to note it all. He is swollen, his skin feels stretched, by it. "I needed you to know— Look. For your own good, consider this. You're writing a book that will establish your father as a bona fide hero, as I understand it.

You're reversing history's judgment on him. I don't pretend to understand how you've established that you are his son, that my *Jewish* mother is also yours, but I am perfectly willing to accept your conclusions. All right?"

"Shh," Kessler said, gesturing downward with his hand. "We should be someplace more private. Permit me to buy you a brandy."

"And I don't know if you need to make the case as strenuously as you think. It's acceptable as fact: Otto Kessler, a German prisoner of war in the Lake District of England, fathered you. If you say that his mother was Sylvia Lesczak, a *Jewish* refugee, and you seem to have evidence that convinces you, then fine—taken as read."

"A good English locution," Kessler said, looking at the remaining few historical accuracy buffs who lingered. "We are brothers, and we share a fondness for them."

Alex allowed him the "brothers." Why not? "No," he said, "here's what I want to tell you. That you are making a profession of professing your own validity. By battling for the historical truth of your conclusion about your father, you battle for the social solidity of you, yourself. You are validating William Kessler. You are rewriting the part of your life that has you the child of the Diamonds. You know that you're a revisionist in no flattering sense. You choose to associate yourself professionally with people who have Hitler giving teas for the Jews at Bergen-Belsen. And these colleagues of yours must be in heaven, with Reagan standing at the graveyard in Bitburg—no Jews allowed, lest they make a fuss and embarrass the German hosts, and the actor who plays the sorrowing part. Some guy from a panzer division gives him the Nazi heel-click of welcome and, I figure, those colleagues of yours are purring. And the Jews aren't even spinning in their graves. Do you know why? Because the Germans turned them to ashes. They turned them to smoke. They used the ashes to compost the commandant's garden in the spring. And here it is, William, how wonderful: spring."

"You oversimplify. Because this is about *you*, isn't it, brother? Not so much about me as about you?"

"And you live on the Diamonds' money," Alex said, "spending it to erase their dedication so you can celebrate someone who was maybe SS so that you, in turn, can be more than you're afraid you might 'only' be? It's a mistake, William. You could be an estimable man. This—you ought to listen hard. This is common with some adoptive children. It surely is true of you. You might want to stare that one in the face."

"You came here to tell me this."

"Think about it, please."

"I live very frugally."

"All right. And what about the rest of what I said?"

"Preaching, I would call it."

"As you say, Otto was a preacher."

"Have I talked about his preaching to you?"

"Actually—"

"*You* have fixed on this. Because you are persuaded, a little. So try a little more, Brother. And patronize a little less your younger sibling as you give the advice you have never permitted me to pay for. Another canon of your profession violated, yes?"

"The advice, good or bad, is on the house, William."

"Because we are brothers?"

"I accept your story," Alex said.

"It is not a story. It is my life."

"It is a *version*," Alex said too loudly. The Jackie Kennedy anti-Semite, now at the door, looked over. A short man in a plaid blue suit, his face dark with hypertension, glowered. "We all choose a version," Alex said. "We do that every day. William. Find a job. Something you can go to that is not entirely about you. If you live so intensely with these preoccupations about your birth, you will find yourself stuck in your childhood, a grown-up baby."

"And if I make a face, my face will freeze in that expression?"

"All right," Alex said. "I tried."

"As do I—to shine some light on my father's story."

"But, you see, the world is doing all right without much more of him."

"It does make you uncomfortable, I note."

"So I think it's time for us to end." Alex thought of so much that was ending. What, he wondered, might he start, or simply continue?

Kessler sighed, because he understood. "I would urge you to send me a bill," he said. "For the sake of your professional pride. For my own pride's sake."

"I'd just as soon not. If you need help—a referral, say, to someone in the profession—you're welcome to leave a message to that effect. I'll get some names to you. But let me ask you a question. Your name. Is it really William?"

"It's what they named me. I thought you'd like it better."

"Than what?"

"Wilhelm. The name I chose, for obvious reasons. And please spare me the lecture about that. It's *my* night to lecture."

Alex stepped back, and then he made for the doorway. Kessler hurried behind him, almost whispering. "You're the only person alive in my family whom I know. It seems a shame for us to never see each other again."

Alex stopped. He turned to the little man and put his hands, which seemed so large now, on the small, bony shoulders. "You won't get lost, William. That's what frightens you." Alex said, " I promise. You won't get lost. Find some of the Diamond family. There may be some of them around. That's where you can live, William."

Kessler, very pale and very small, said, "Right. I'll be absolutely fine. And you, I see, must be off. Then, goodbye."

Alex found that he had no more assurances. He tried to smile as he left.

7

SLOWACKI, DRIVING A large maroon-and-silver vehicle, something like a station wagon but broader and longer, with a winch on the front bumper, stopped for him at 90th and Central Park West. They rode in what Alex thought of as an easy silence until Slowacki said, "Doc, wake up a minute, will you?"

"I wasn't asleep, Anthony."

"Snoring and all. You must be wiped out."

"I'm a little wiped out."

They went up the 72nd Street ramp to the Henry Hudson Parkway. On their left, the river was surly, a heaviness of grayish blue. Through Alex's squinted eyes, it looked paved over. They drove past stripped, burned cars, past grown men playing basketball with children on the blacktop courts where chains instead of ropes flapped when the ball dropped through. Slowacki shook his head. "As soon as the game's over," he said, "they'll be dealing to the kids they just played hoops with. Welcome to the twentieth century."

"Not our finest hour," Alex said.

"You want to talk about Detective Rhys?"

"You spoke to her? You weren't supposed to."

"After what you told me she said? Come on. This is me. This is you. A couple of law-abiding Polacks not quite on the run. I talked to parties who know parties, let's say. Let's say, the word is she likes you for it."

"Likes me."

"Thinks you're involved with this patient who disap-peared."

"I'm involved with all—"

"I know. I know. I don't want to know anything. All right? Nothing. So if we *do* run headfirst into more rules and regulations that I maybe broke already, I can tell 'em the truth: I don't know anything. As Reeny will tell you, that *is* usually the truth." Slowacki brought them into the middle lane as they approached the George Washington Bridge. He looked at Alex and smiled tautly. "So this Rhys is a ball breaker. Let her be. It's her job. It's how you have to do it. Don't worry. We'll find this woman's father, we'll work him, and we'll find the daughter. She'll be all right. We'll make it all all right."

Alex looked out his window at the steelwork of the bridge, at the cars too close, he thought, for safety.

"You asleep again?"

"No, Anthony, no. I was thinking."

"Me too. Listen to this. Before we go over the information. It's about your favorite cop patient. Me. Who else, right? We're—we're in bed, understand? Reeny and me. But she's still—I don't know."

"Wary?"

"That's it! That's the word. She's wary with me. And this is a pretty long time, now. And I figure, go for all of it. What can you lose? I'm about to tell her, 'Look, you can hold *me* down, or something.' I really want her to trust me. This woman, I'm thinking, I'm looking into her face in the light through the window, and I'm seeing these lines on her lips and the corners of her eyes, down from her nose to her mouth. She didn't use to have those, understand? I put them there. She was at home, waiting for me *two years*, waiting to hear I'm blown up over there. And goddamned if I don't start to cry." He smacked the wheel, the horn sounded, and Alex jumped. "Like that. Doc: you call that a breakthrough, or what?"

Alex nodded. His rescuer, his investigator, the only patient he hadn't recently ruined—unless you counted suborning a Transit Authority policeman to violate law enforcement procedures or whatever Rhys might decide to call it when she had them arrested or arraigned, detained, whatever was involved— Slowacki gripped the wheel and leaned back hard, as if he were pushing himself away from the windshield. He looked determined, grimly pleased, a man on a mission he knew and approved. Alex nodded once again. But he was, inside his skull, turning to peer behind them. His eyes now shut in the fast, heavy car, Alex felt his ears block up they way they did in a descending airplane. He heard their motor, and noises from the road, as if from a great distance. It was psychosomatic shutdown, he thought. The thought didn't help. Even with the strong soldier Slowacki, he was alone. He was alone except for Liz and Teddy, except for his father and mother, except for his half brother, and except, of course, for Nella. He leaned his head at the window to his right, he let his eyes flutter and then close, hard, and he remembered, he remembered Nella's appearance, a week before she had disappeared, when he came onto the ward, telephoned by a night-shift nurse he didn't know.

She was in what Alex called the suicide room. It was diagonally across from the nurses' station, where they could watch the patient who had been processed in for a suicide attempt, or fantasies of self-destruction. The swinging door had no latch and was half shatterproof window. The room was little larger than the narrow bed. It flickered with yellow fluorescent light. The yellow-painted cinder-block walls were dirty from food and had been scratched with plastic spoons—no one there had access to anything useful for stabbing, slicing, hanging, or suffocating. The floor was filthy because patients in the room dropped food, saliva, hair, even urine on its green linoleum tiles. Alex stood behind the nurse and looked at the chart in its brushed aluminum clipboard. *Rhapsodizing on self-aborted fetus*, the admitting doctor had written. Beside the notation she—Dr. Padma Bahl—had doodled a couple of eighth notes. *Fears suicide by pills and alcohol. Took none—is certain. Wanted to. Frightened. Checked self in. Why here?* The admitting nurse had circled the last two words and, in the margin, had written, *Dr. to call insurance co. for clearance.*

"Is Dr. Bahl on the ward?"

"No chance, I'd say," the nurse told him. "We have, count 'em, three psychotics they consider homicidal. Each one has his own large guard. It's a war zone up there. We might not see Dr. Bahl for a solid shift and a half. This one"—she gestured toward Nella, a long, flat shape under cotton blankets too short for her—"she won't get a bed upstairs for days, I bet you. We might have to transport her downtown."

"I'll look at her. I want to thank you for calling me."

"That's all right," the nurse said warily. She knew that he was troubled by, or even *in* trouble with, this patient. He was being humored, he thought, just a little less than the woman who had stood in the hallway of the ward near the locked doors when he came in. He'd seen from her plastic ID wristband that she was a patient, though she was wearing street clothes and a thick, if shedding, fur coat. She smiled, working at her chewing gum with an active, rhythmic grind, and her eyes sparkled with the deep, plumbless delight of mania.

"Hey, babe," she said.

"Yes," he said. "Good evening."

"Now," she said, staring up into his eyes and challenging him with her smile, "exactly who are you and who do you represent? No: who do you *claim* to represent?"

"I'm Dr. Lescziak. I claim to represent my patients. Who are you?"

"I'm Laverne of the Laverne and Diana Coalition. You know me. The people who claim to represent your patients know me. Got it?"

"I have it, and I'm glad to hear it from you. Laverne, I have to see someone down the hall."

"You go ahead, babe. I'll wait here. I got time. Later, all right?"

She popped her gum and smiled, the sweat of her speeding metabolism a golden glimmer under the fluorescent fixtures and the yellowish hallway tiles.

Then he was in Nella's room, smelling ketones on her breath and telling himself to ask Dr. Bahl, if she would listen, to check glucose levels. He was saddened by her pallor. She looked like a car-wreck victim in shock, her face taut and bony, her complexion a grayish-white, almost blue. The lips looked dark, like

350

those of someone who had killed herself with carbon monoxide. But she wasn't dead, she was breathing very slowly with the deep, lagging breaths you get with thorazine. Stick 'em, stack 'em, let 'em sleep: the key to running a compliant ward. He touched her neck, as if to check a pulse. He reached inside the heat of the covers for her pale, cold hand, and he forced himself not to run his fingers up to the muscular, round upper arm he had always enjoyed touching, its miraculous animal strength. Her lips were slack, her nostrils were crusted with dried mucus, her eyelids looked raw from weeping. He remembered her questions about Armagnac and sedatives, and he remembered his begging her never to—never to die, he had meant, whatever he had said. He watched her sleep as, he supposed, parents watched their children. He was certain he'd watched Liz, in her sleeping secrecy, from this same interior place. Now he was watching his lover. He knew her long thighs, the slight protuberance of stomach that embarrassed her and that he loved to cup, to fondle, to gently bite. He knew her very long toes. He had bitten them as well. She slept as if she floated, her slack-mouthed face a mask of childhood. But there was only one way, he knew, to remain afloat: you die, and you rise from the world. Choosing that way, having labored to achieve it, she had been balked by her own fearfulness. But she could practice to combat her fears. That's what suicides do: they learn the skill. And she was willing to leave. Admit it: leave *him*, he corrected himself. For he was nothing more, this moment, than one more jealous lover.

As if she knew that he was there, Nella turned so that her face and shoulder trapped his arm. He moved to one knee so as not to wake her. He stayed that way a little while, in touch with her flesh, remembering through the touch of his fingers what of hers, and how, he had touched in the past. And then, whether the duty nurse saw him or didn't, he leaned toward the back of her neck, where the hair was sweaty and a little sour-smelling, and he kissed her once, then, pushing his face farther, once again, on the smooth, young cheek.

Was it so simple, he wondered, standing now to look down at Nella. Was it as simple as the need for her youth? For he had been her father as well, he thought, in a certain sense of the word. He had been her adviser. He had been a usable older man. There are fathers all over the place, he thought, and children too, and none of them belong to each other.

You fucked a child, Teddy would tell him. You fucked your patient. You're an outcast. Would Teddy cast him out? No: Teddy had slept with Liz. Alex was sure they were lovers. And even Teddy was hamstrung by guilt.

"There's a sappy love song," Nella had told him in her apartment as he planted his fingers on the furniture where, Rhys had let him know, they would soon enough be checking for fingerprints. He wondered if they really did that when someone was reported missing. She was sitting on Alex, who sat on a heavy old brocaded easy chair. She wore a jumper and T-shirt, he remembered, and high-heeled shoes that strapped around her ankles, but no underpants or bra.

The jumper surrounded them, but he was out of his trousers and she had been naked underneath, waiting, she said. She wished, always, to be naked while presentable, naughty while looking nice, a rebel of sorts, a bad girl who managed to look good. She was upon him, and he shifted upward because he could feel her hair against him, and the heavy, hot liquid interior of her, and because she winced but with real pleasure, he thought, when he did that. And he loved her pleasure in him—*in him*, he remembered thinking.

"God," she said. She kissed him, then she slowly bathed his upper and then lower lip with her tongue.

"The song," he said.

"Yes, Doctor. Oh. The song has this line in it, and I always thought it was so sappy. Except now I go around singing it to myself. The people at work think I'm nuts. And they *know* I'm full of sex. Somebody sings that she *honestly* loves somebody. I think. Oh, it's dumb. *Oh.* Yum. And I thought: Does that happen? It has to happen, right? People love each other honestly. You know, they say it and they mean it, and that's what they're doing. It's more or less simple. So is that the way it is for us?"

And Alex—because, he thought, he had always been Sylvia's baby, though not, apparently, her only one— Alex had to say, "You told me, one time, that you loved me as much as you could. But you were afraid it wasn't enough."

"You never forgive me, do you?"

"For what, Nell?" But she had risen, driving herself with her hands on the chair arms so that she rose from him like a board pried up from a nail.

Her face looked drawn and full of shadows, then, in her living room, as she stood before him, sneering a kind of anger he had sensed beneath the surface but had not before seen. She raised her jumper, slowly drew it by handful and handful so that it came up her legs, until, when it was level with her groin, she spread herself and scrubbed with the fabric at her crotch as if to dry herself.

"So sorry," she said, almost whispering. "Still not good enough, I guess, you bastard."

He stood to reclaim her, but had to stop to shove his damp, softened sex back into his pants.

"You look absurd," she said.

He said, "People in love *are* absurd. They're vulnerable."

"And you are," she said, "to me."

"I am."

He approached her. He took hold of her shoulders and then of the back of her neck. He drew her in to him. He wanted, he found, to devour her. He wanted to inhale her. He had to take care not to bite through her skin.

"How much do you need me?" she asked into his mouth.

"How much can I have?"

Wrong question, he thought in the hospital, and wrong answer. But none could have been right. When she offered herself, you should have locked your legs the way grown-ups do—or ought to. You should have kept your clothing on, and your fine mind to yourself.

When you knew that she might even consider the offer of herself, you should have sent her to somebody else. He shook his head, watching her in the drugged, deep sleep. He inspected her slender, strong wrists again, and, seeing no wound, he leaned forward and kissed her throat. Fathers should not kiss their girls this way, he thought. As for doctors kissing their patients, you, he said to himself, are the reason for license suspensions. They write laws in case people like you are born in Barrow-in-Furness to come over here and break them.

"Doc, you want a bathroom break?" Slowacki asked as they entered the Palisades Parkway.

"No, thank you, I've stopped putting out urine," Alex said.

"That happen a lot?"

"Only as the organism approaches death."

"A doctor joke," Slowacki said.

"Exactly that," Alex said, "a doctor joke."

THIS, NOW, IS what, in his sleep or—what did Teddy call it?—in his time travel, Alex sees as Slowacki steers them upstate. It is a few minutes before curfew, and the exiled family returns from a walk along the pier near the Vickers launching stage, which overlooks the Walney Channel. A glare remains on the horizon, and whipped edges of cloud hang upon it like hair hanging down in a vast, cruel, blue-black face with yellow eyes. The baby, in his brown wickerwork pram on its hard tires, has finally fallen asleep. He has been mildly unwell, crouping again in the damp, cold nights, drawing rasped breath. Not any of them knows that Januscz will sound like this at the end, so many years and miles from here. Alex sleeps with his head hung back over the curved edge of the pram, and Sylvia pulls his arm in so that his hand won't be caught in the spokes.

Januscz has been speaking of his wish to emigrate as soon as the war, which might be starting to end, ends. He has put in papers, he tells her, and she tries to understand what they say, and into what he has put these papers. They must leave, he tells her. He has spoken to someone from the U.S. Consulate through intermediaries at Vickers. In America, he says, he can be a scientist, not a boffin for a shipbuilder, although, he adds—Januscz always is fair—he is grateful for the work. He would assist them, in America, with their research, if he could. He knows a little about what they are calling heavy water, and he has made his knowledge seem greater than it is to someone from the States. He thinks that he knows much to teach, he says, if they do not wish him for the research.

She hasn't replied because, although she respects his scholarly ways and the slow, steady tread of his mind, she cannot imagine, tonight, under this bitter sky, that anyone knows as much—about sorrow, or entrapment—as she. A lone street dog, all snout and ribs, watches her. She wonders whether, if the war goes on for very much longer, they will roam in packs, taking down children and tearing them open to devour their soft inner organs. She must stay alive for her baby, she thinks, although the only real threat, tonight, is from the sky; and the Luftwaffe, according to the radio broadcasts, has mostly been elsewhere, in its declining attacks on London, in its sporadic bombing of the Allied troops in Italy and France.

Then, outside the flats, in the rotten breath exhaled by the building from its rubbish door, Januscz removes the baby from the pram and hands him over. She carries him in as Januscz hauls the carriage through the door and up the stairs. Despite its bulk, he is well ahead of her, and a man who has been waiting on the third-floor landing at the entrance to their flat might hear their labored breathing as they push up in the darkness of the unlighted stairwell brightened only, at the small window of each landing, by the yellow glare from the sea. But Leon Salthouse hasn't heard, for he squatted on the floor with his back against the wall, then stretched his legs out to wait, and he has fallen asleep. Januscz is waiting near the top of the steps as Sylvia catches up with him.

"A soldier, asleep," he says. "It is that Saltworm, the guard."

"Salthouse," she says. "They are keeping soldiers in the flats, of a suddenly?"

"'Keep,' not 'keeping'; and you should say 'sudden.' And I do not know why he lies down here."

"Of course," she says to the corrections. Then: "Wake him up."

"Maybe he is tired," Januscz says.

"Of *course* tired! Why to sleep except tired? Now, *wake*!"

"Soldier," Januscz says gently. "Hello? Leon,

good evening."

Sylvia takes hold of the toe of his long, oiled boot, and she shakes him. Salthouse's eyes open, he sees them, he smiles, and he wearily climbs to his feet by pushing with his boots against the floor and sliding, with his back along the wall, until he is vertical. It is as if his smile triggers someone invisible who tugs on the strings that lift him smoothly up.

"Evening, Mister and Missus," he says. "I see the laddie's still asleep. Isn't *he* a lucky chap?"

"What?" Sylvia asks him. "You have what?"

"I have news, Missus. Mr. Lescziak. How are you, sir?"

"Thank you, I am well," Januscz replies.

"What news?" she asks. The baby murmurs, and she forces herself to stand still, to hold him without pressing him uncomfortably against her. In the darkness of the landing, she can see from beneath the entrance to their flat the light of the sitting-room lamp, which they forgot to extinguish. Another rule broken, she thinks. And then she thinks: We have broken every rule. And this soldier, with his weapon and his dull, scratched, broad leather belt, his clipped-on torch and his bayonet in its canvas scabbard, and his well-shined boots, has been sent by the State to deliver its punishment.

"The Reverend's scarpered," Leon whispers, as if the flight were a secret to be kept from everyone but them. "The German prisoner as swore he was a preacher. We've been searching for him, silent like, for the better part of two days. But that lad's gone. As near as we can reconstruct, he went over the stone wall that his detachment was resting at, near the sewage works just above Cistercian Way. He must have got himself to Levy Beck—it's where the dogs lost him."

Sylvia thinks of the hungry dog she saw outside. She sees the flash of their teeth, the stiff, protruding tongues, as they hungrily follow his scent. She smells the sourness of small beer from Leon's mouth as his own tongue dances at his teeth and he exults in his story.

"Of course, these dogs aren't much good except with sheep. And that's a lad's no sheep, I can tell you. He could have got into South Ulverston and out the other end by following the Beck. Not too many know how far it winds on. He could have gone to ground all the way out in Dalton, I reckon. Everyone, you see, looks out to sea for raiders. Or up in the air for them with their bombs. Who among us bothers to examine the very ground we tread upon?"

He sounds desperate. Sylvia assumes that Leon was drunk, whether sleeping or awake, when Otto ran.

When Otto ran without Sylvia.

It is an officer's duty to escape, she has been told. But Otto never wanted to be an officer. He was a clergyman. He was resistance. Otto was her lover. Why does a lover escape? From *what* does a lover escape?

Clearly: from love.

So she is abandoned. Sylvia, across the small landing from Leon, in the rising smell of his damp woolen uniform, his perspiration, his beer, leans her back against the wall and slides down, pressing her feet, hard, to brake her progress until she sits, holding her baby, between the two tall men. As he rose, as in a Punch and Judy show, she now descends. She does not look up at them. She looks into the darkness at their feet, at the slate she suspects to be littered with mouse turds, and she looks further, while Januscz inquires and she reassures him—"Only, at once, tired from the walking," she says—she peers into what they call a beck here, a stream, where a small man crouches, panting.

She hears his harsh breathing, and then she thinks that she is hearing her own. In fact, she realizes, she has heard Januscz. His deep tones thicken and drop into what she knows is his anger.

"Why is he telling us this?" Januscz says to Sylvia. To Leon, then: "Why are you telling us this?"

In the darkness, the white oval of Leon's face turns to her. She looks back up at him now. She is waiting for the rest of her life to be decided, she knows. She is waiting for the strings to be tugged by someone above her. This is war, she thinks, and everyone waits for this every day.

"Recollecting past events, sir," Salthouse says, "I recalled you showed an interest when I mentioned that ill-fated talent contest at the restaurant, and how the Reverend gave out with what you would have to call a bogus poem. It was you made that joke, sir, you'll recall, about the bogus poem. You do recall, don't you? So I thought, as I happened to be delivering a message to Old Barrow Farm, just up the way, that I might call in and keep you informed. And I'm blessed if I didn't fall asleep! I'm right nackered. They've had us out all night, searching. Quite embarrassing, I suppose, to the officers. Well, to me and to the men, as well."

He gave you drink, Leon, she thinks. Standing, she smelled the sourness of drink on his breath. Down here, she smells the mice.

He gave you drink, and he ran away from love.

It is an officer's duty.

But what is the duty of lovers?

It is the beloved's duty.

"Januscz," she sighs, "help me, please." He extends an arm and then he tugs, and she is up. He is a strong man, she thinks, with a powerful body and small imagination. But you can live with only power if it is gentle, and Januscz surely is that. They must be joined tonight, no matter how tired. That is the duty of the wife tonight, she thinks. So that the timing, if he calculates, will be correct. Januscz is a man of numbers.

Duty, she thinks.

"And so you have told us," Januscz says.

"Though it appears you didn't want to be bothered," Leon says, edging now toward the stairwell, in a defiant, almost bitter, tone.

"I thank you," Januscz says, "for coming because you thought I wished to know."

"Even if you didn't," Leon says, moving again, and carefully looking only at her husband. It is as if her baby were suspended in the air beside Januscz, but she were not there. I am not here, she thinks. I am not here. She thinks: Please. I am not here.

"Ma'am," Leon says.

She doesn't reply.

"Very kind," Januscz says. "Isn't he?" Januscz stares at her.

"Kind," Sylvia says.

She has heard enough of them discuss escape, townspeople and Land Girls and prisoners and guards. She knows that, miles away, beyond Barrow-in-Furness, there is a savage place called the Duddon Valley. It is like the Valley of the Shadow of Death in prayers the English recite. Northwest of that is Hesk Fell, and beyond it—maybe the prisoner can steal a horse; she thinks of Otto galloping through the hellish valley, across the fells, on the back of a horse; she thinks of Otto galloping on her—after hectares and hectares of what she envisions as boulders and then swamp and then broad, icy rivers: finally, the sea. Whatever it may look like as it slices between Ireland and England, it is not hell for every German. U-boats rise to charge their batteries in the slop and swell of that sea. They might look for German officers escaping, she thinks. She thinks of Otto, soaked and shivering, exhausted, sleepless, peering about with his large, soft lashes blinking at the cold rain. She hears the sound of sirens, of dogs, of shouting men who will crush his skull, stamp his ribs in, break his thin arms before they haul him unconscious in a jolting lorry, to a hard bed, and pneumonia, and a wheezing, feverish death.

She sees the jagged end of a cracked bone protruding from his fair, penetrable skin. She sees the blood about it, and the bone she imagines is a sharpened, whiter version of the dulled and yellow bones she has unearthed at the Hindpool Brick and Tile Works. She was not mad when she wept for the bones, she thinks. She was reading the future. Did the wandering farm-workers at home—do gypsies here?—not read the future by interpreting arrangements of bones? She was right. She was right. And now she sees Otto's blood geysering up from the skin and fragile vessels torn by the broken bone. She cannot see his face. She strains to see his face. But she sees only his fractured limb, and his blood as it pools on the stones to which he has fallen. She is afraid to imagine the dogs now, for she fears that, having discovered him for the angry pursuers, they gather beside him to lap, as he watches, at his blood on the rain-blackened rocks.

Leon stands, now, on the stairs. Januscz lifts his head so that his jaw juts upward. She hears his deep, troubled voice. And she thinks: What if he escapes? What if he somehow escapes? She sees him saluted. She sees him decorated. She sees him in a dark gray uniform with epaulettes on which there is a lightning streak. She sees him banging the heels of his hard, black boots together and crying German words. What would he say, the fierce, small man who cried his pleasure in her ear and on her flesh?

And what—it is this question she has sought for weeks to evade—what if his love for her, his love *with* her, has been unimportant? If he lied about a poem of death and passion, has he lied to her about his passion in the face of death?

Among men in uniforms, she sees him, bathed and uniformed himself, smiling his triumph, the man who was naked with her, naked *within* her—her hand has gone, she feels, to the clothing above her navel. She clutches herself, and Januscz has seen.

"What is it?"

In the darkness, she shakes her head.

"Nothing?"

"Nothing," she says, remembering that she must lure her husband into her body tonight.

Leon Salthouse has seized the railing and begun descending the stairs. "I'll be saying good night, then, Mister and Missus."

"After bringing me the news you thought I wished to hear," Januscz says.

"There it is, then," Leon says. "Missus."

"Good night," she tells him. "Thank you."

"Although the news," Januscz says, "was for me."

Shifting the baby, she says, "Although."

Januscz opens the door of their flat, and the light is brown, leathery, rolling out like an unspooled belt along the unswept boards and onto the smeared slates of the hallway. Their sitting room looks smaller than usual. Sylvia nods to Januscz, whom she will seduce, walking in before he does—Januscz is a gentleman, always—and she carries both of her children in.

IN THE CAR, his head against the window, Alex heard the engine's noise and Slowacki's voice as if through a filter of ocean, as if he were a child under water, rolled by a busy surf. Teddy would say it was the great oceanic mood. Teddy might be saying it now, he thought, to Liz.

Slowacki had spoken of his Vietnam service, and

Alex tried to surface to acknowledge him. "I enlisted," Slowacki said. "I *joined* the war."

As if sharing the cost of gasoline on their journey, Alex pitched in. "Do you regret it?" His own voice sounded distant.

"When I was scared. Which was basically all the time. So: yeah. I did."

Alex saw that Slowacki's glasses had gone dark in the bright sunlight. Alex thought to study the mustache to see how it moved, but the glare closed his eyes, and he spoke in darkness and heard muffled sounds. "Do you regret it now?" he heard himself ask.

"What it cost Reeny. What, I guess you'd have to say, it still costs her. And who I lost, the people who died. But—I just now thought of this. I was an honorable warrior. Like the GIs in War Two. To tell you the truth, what I heard from the older vets at the VFW post—I heard the German troops they faced were straight-on soldiers. So the President goes and throws them a salute over there, a wreath, whatever: okay. That's where I come out on it. Now, I'm not cheering on the Gestapo here. Just the German GIs. And they're okay. You understand me?"

And of course, he barely does in one sense and in another doesn't at all. He manages to ask, "Why raise the issue now? Or, really, at all?"

"Because you nailed my ass with the Jewish lampshade thing. You shamed me, to tell you the truth. I'm no anti-Semite, here. And I have to tell you: I think I'm really what people call fearless. I pride myself on it. You can't intimidate Anthony Slowacki. I carry a piece on my ankle, and a full set of balls, mentally speaking. And you should know, while I am giving you a little backup here, I'm going up against a cop with bigger balls than me. This lady detective, Rhys. She got cojones, in a mental way, she don't even know about yet. This is a woman, Doc, who stood up so big, she got a full-scale operation on in the Gowanus Canal. She went straight up the chain of command."

Alex, with his eyes closed and his ears clogged, with his fingertips and toes gone numb, felt like a swathed child to whom a grown-up was telling a tale. He was only a receptive consciousness, processing no information, lulled by the rhythms of a story chanted and crooned. He tried to open his eyes to encourage Slowacki with attention, but Slowacki seemed to need only the road, the low-level combat of fast traffic, and his therapist beside him.

"You know Brooklyn? Everybody says they know Brooklyn. Maybe. Maybe Flatbush, Park Slope, maybe, now maybe Greenpoint. But nobody knows it that well. Big place, full of Jews from the Middle Ages, Haitian drug-fiend cab-driving maniacs, Russian cannibals—half of them used to be cops over there, I hear—and your basic living-death blue-haired people who cash the pension check, or the welfare check, watch the tube, and never talk any kind of English we would understand. That's one changed town. They always had the Gowanus Canal. Goes way back. You hear of it? Nobody heard of it unless they know Red Hook. One stretch of this canal, they used to use it for shipping in the heydays, goes to the Buttermilk

Channel—they'd use it to bring these cargo ships right inside of Red Hook. Also, it was how they flushed the stinky water out of the canal. It's all gravel yards down there, and cement yards, foundries. Terrific place for doing anybody needs the extremely long vacation, and very, very popular with the old-time Frank Sinatra Fan Club.

"And our cop, Rhys, she's—this is a couple of years ago, it's a story I heard. She's catching on a missing persons thing, a child, one of those deals where you *know,* on account of the last-seen-with report from a pretty solid witness, the kid's holding hands with a baby raper down near the canal. Rhys breaks down her lieutenant, and this lieutenant reaches out, reaches *up,* that's the thing of it, and convinces the Detective Borough Office to reach out for the Chief of Detectives Office to call over to the Special Operations Division to activate the scuba team which comes over from Harbor Charlie at the foot of 33rd Street—this is Brooklyn we're talking about, not what you Upper West Siders think is 'the city.' And there it goes. Divers in the water, a Harbor Unit boat, detectives from all over the place, and many cigarettes adding to the pollution, and bow-koo coffee cups. One of the divers was a guy used to be a SEAL: those are men. He comes up with an old canvas U.S. Postal Service delivery bag filled with a tire iron, a jack, and a couple of smooth stones. It's strapped around one broken, bent, folded, spindled, and mutilated small kid. I don't know if Rhys ever cleared the case. But she filled the canal with wet suits. The woman will not stop. So, what I'm trying to say, she likes you for it, I'm in this borrowed monster GMC vehicle—I will not drive a Ford—and I'm heading upstate where I cannot believe the state cops never turned out for us. What I'm saying: you're born with balls, you use them. And I'm telling you directly, Reagan wants to salute the German GIs, he's my commander in chief, even if he does have a face like an old rabbit, and he's got my support."

Alex could rouse himself only to say, "I don't kill people. Or kidnap them. I *help*," he said, distrusting his own tone.

"Yes, you do," Slowacki said.

"Why suspect me, then? If she really does."

"Oh, that's no if. And why? Because you were—you have to excuse me, Doc, but a dick is a dick—you were porking the lady, apparently. This is what the detective says. Intimates are suspects, they tell me. Of course, the only intimate suspects I have conversation with are puffy-eyed crazies on subway trains late at night who are porking people against their will. But the general rule is cherchez whoever. Understand?"

"Porking."

"There it is," Slowacki said.

"Hopeless," Alex said. "It's somebody's nightmare. I'm in somebody's nightmare."

"The exact words of a college kid I could have nailed down for drunk and disorderly conduct one night on the B train. Nightmare et cetera. He didn't puke directly onto anyone, confining his public nuisance to the end of the platform, so I let him go. It was close to the end of the shift."

But Slowacki's voice was fading almost away. Alex was imagining Liz in Teddy's apartment. Teddy would be making her a meal, and Alex could hear references to baby potatoes coated with cumin and paprika, roasted at a high heat. Tuna steaks are to be seared in a ridged pan. Liz is tearing lettuce for a salad and Teddy is opening a bottle of what he has announced as Yamhill Pinot Noir.

"So finally," Liz says, "just to make sure I was impossible enough to torture him, I *wheeled* around and pointed like some actress in an old movie—"

"Silent?"

"Unfortunately, no. No. Out loud. I said—I pointed at his head, and I said—I sounded to myself like some horrible owl. I said, 'Who?' "

"Good question," Teddy says.

"Not that good. I was a shrew. I mean, he's so troubled, and I'm shrieking, 'You ask questions. You elicit answers. You ask and ask and ask and *ask*. But what about *you*, Alex? When do we get to hear about you? Who's *in* there?" That kind of thing. And I'm pointing, of course, at his head."

Teddy is chopping a shallot for salad dressing. He stops and walks to where she sits, on a stool, at his counter. He embraces her from behind her, his arm around her waist and his head on top of hers. He says nothing, but holds on, until Liz lets her hands go loose and then leans back into him. "Anyway, it was the right place to point," he says. "Did he answer you?"

She nods. She cries. She whispers, "He was so mild, Teddy. I'll never forget it. I never should. His eyebrows went up. He looked—I don't know. Vulnerable. He looked the way he must have looked when he was a boy, in that house of theirs. He said, 'Oh.' Just like that. And then he said, 'Why, everyone.' Teddy: like he thought I *knew*."

He kisses the top of her head, and he kisses the back of her neck, lifting her wavy hair and clutching it in his fist as he kisses her. She leans back against him, and he says, "Comfort, too, can be a handmaiden to lust."

"You sound like a man making dirty phone calls. Handmaiden." But she laughs, and she continues to lean against his stomach. He shifts against her, and she says, "Don't get your hopes up. Handmaiden."

"You will have noted," he says, his voice still oily, "that it is not only my hope that has risen."

"Well," she says, leaning forward, "tell the hope and tell the other thing to go away. I want something for dinner that has no implications." She shakes her head. Teddy steps back, then returns to the bits of shallot he has cut. He adds olive oil and vinegar to a mixing bowl and works at the mixture with a small whisk. "All those years I couldn't have a child," Liz says to him.

"Why not say all those years *we,* meaning Alex as well as you, didn't have a child."

"Well," she says, "except I actually had one, didn't I? Alex was my child."

"You are raising two subjects. You raise them together often. They're connected by guilt. You ought to think hard whether you're right to appropriate the responsibility for either one. It was not your fault there weren't children. It is not your fault about the marriage going bad. They go bad, and often."

"What about you, Teddy?"

"Because of us?"

"Obviously."

"Obviously," he says. "Liz. I wanted you all of the time."

"All the time that you knew us," she says.

"Of course. You knew it then, years ago. You know it now."

"Even when you were lolloping and lolling with the skinny poetess?"

"Sheila is a gifted, tall, but hardly skinny poet. And she would never permit a lollop."

"A loll?" Liz asks.

Teddy adds mustard and the shallots to the vinegar and oil. He looks at her and says, "Liz. Childlessness is not what did the marriage in."

"I don't think it helped," she says, not looking back at him.

"You may not be more, as a couple, if you don't have a child. A child could do that. That could be. Of course, I only *was* a child. I wasn't ever a parent either. But the couple, if there are large emotional resources within them and shared between them, can grow, can be healthy. Can be content, maybe, Liz. And if they do have a child, if they are jointly or singly selfish in toxic or even slightly more than ordinary ways, they can ruin the child, and each other, and the joint relationship. Babies are a guarantee of nothing."

"Then what are *no* babies? Besides emptiness."

"You aren't empty. You're full. And you're also full

of me, these days, and that's *not* nothing, I hope. And babies guarantee nothing. Liz: *we* won't have babies."

"We're a we, you keep insisting."

"I am prepared, within limits, to beg."

She sighs. She shakes her head.

"Don't do that, Liz, until you've tasted my marinated tuna steaks."

She says, "And the wine had better be special."

ALEX HEARD SLOWACKI speak and he felt himself as if in a dream heading from the sandy shore where the riptide had splayed him underwater, up now, toward the surface of the sea. He felt himself break into the light and air and gulp a huge breath, and then another. He felt the air in his throat and lungs, but he had to sink again, so he took a great breath and then he closed his eyes and dived.

He sees his mother, who is in hell, which is in Barrow. She scrapes, she plants, she wheels with the other farm fowl in their men's clothing under the weak, fog-screened sun and under the thick mists and under the Lake District rains. Januscz is civil, even when in bed she makes certain that the child she has started to carry will be thought of as his. He is urgent at love, but in private: he pants, but softly, and he says nothing and, coming into her with thrusts that do not jolt her as Otto's did, he does not utter sounds of triumph or satisfaction. He plants his fists on either side of her, at the shoulders, as if to keep her in place, and, with his eyes closed, a small smile you could mistake for a smirk, but which she knows is embarrassment, masks his face. He hides within it, and within Sylvia, and he has his wife, or whatever it is that he has by the time he is done, on his terms alone.

Perhaps, she thinks, the prisoner has fled somehow to Canada. Does he prove, thus, that he lied to her and was a Nazi in his heart? She has felt his heart, pressed upon it with her fingertips, her sore breasts. Very well, then. Say the German prisoner lied and say he made his escape. Perhaps he finds work on a cargo vessel returning to North America from Liverpool. How does he get to Liverpool, so far south of Barrow-in-Furness? Never mind. He gets there, say, past Morecomb and Preston, and—she has taken to reading a map of England at night, instead of newspapers; her English will not grow, but she will grow old knowing Blackpool and Ormskirk and she will call the Isle of Anglesey "The Isil of *Ang*-a-less-ee," but her mouth and memory will possess the place—and say he gets past Formsby to Liverpool, and what she hears is vast, busy piers where the high-riding, emptied vessels are docked. Say, then, that he survives the primitive seamen, and the German submarines, and the waves that are higher than the high masts of ships. Otto alive in Newfoundland! She will not see him again. But she will know that he lives. And she will live a tragedy that no one can be told. She weeps above her maps.

Or perhaps, she thinks, he wanders the narrow English island to Kegnes, and a merchant vessel traveling to America, where Januscz wishes to ship them, into another version of this slippery way of speaking. In America, he says, there will be more for the baby to eat. Will there be Otto? In a place called Detroit, or San Francisco? It is a large place, she realizes, moving her finger from Idaho down and over to Texas. Otto in Texas! Could they meet? She does not ask if he might wish to. But he escapes, she thinks. He does escape. She sees the immensity of the Atlantic Ocean, its high, green swells chopping white, then crashing into the hull of his ship, which is moved sideways, in a kind of a skid. She sees a sky almost black in the darkness of its blue, and the sun is a dimly lighted coin. Still, she sees the sea shine with its own luminescence and with the froth of its waves, which break against the deep troughs into which the ship falls. There is the roar of the sea, and then there is the wind, a kind of moaning, a sorrow that carries to the horizon at which the look-outs stare for periscope silhouettes and pray to find none. Otto could lead them in a prayer, she thinks. He knows the Lutheran liturgy, of course. And the strong, small man, driven by the energies of liberty, and resisting the exhaustion of exile, which she knows so well, works his way to what she must think of as freedom. But what sort of work can he do? Will he speak to the sailors of his Hegel? Will they betray him to the officers? Or pitch him into the sea?

And if he is achieving freedom, she thinks, it must include his freedom from her.

Unless they meet. In Canada, or America, in twenty years, they meet. She hopes that she isn't fat. Several of the women in her family are large—were large, before the war—but many are not, and none would you call fat. You would call none of them fat, she reproves herself. "Of course," she says aloud, and Leslie looks up from the worked earth at the Hindpool. In twenty years, she is a prisoner someplace else, and Januscz, not suspicious, is a kind and gentle, boring man. And her babies are gone from the home.

She worries about her life with this new child. How *can* she endure to live with, squabble with, discipline, and teach a girl with Otto's delicate face? And would she court the madness of incest with a boy who looks like him? Januscz, if he learned of it, might smother the infant in its cot, she thinks. Perhaps *she* would. There have been mothers who killed their babies, she thinks, cutting into the packed ground. In this world, where you pant and cry and scratch at the bone-filled earth, you do not bear more children, she insists. Yet they are born, and two of them from her. In twenty years, then, will Sylvia be childless, perhaps with Januscz, perhaps without, and probably not fat? Where, in that continent of the New World, will she live?

Up near the top of the world as it occurs in North America, she imagines, Otto will live in a house surrounded by reindeer herds and evergreen trees. He wears leggings and a jacket made of deerskin, and he will tirelessly saw and split wood for his family home. She sees him married to a tall, heavy woman with a broad beam and lots of thigh. She sees him climb upon her and bury his head between mammoth breasts on which, at night, the sweat collects as he drives her, with his fingers and his tongue and slowly, at last, with his organ, into the explosion Sylvia almost feels now, as she stoops over chilly Barrow.

And will he? Yes. He will think of her as he pumps and pumps into his vast, satisfied wife. Will he see them at the ruins on Piel, or—she must never forget this, she thinks—with Sylvia bent upon the hotel chair? Or will he, she wonders, be free of her? Is that what freedom finally means? To be safe from what has driven you? Which means that love is a bondage. So here, then, is Sylvia, not bound. I am free, she thinks, prodding at seedlings. I am sentenced to be free.

It is afternoon, and the spring is warming Lancashire, with occasional sun, and no fog beating in at them for hours as Barrow settles down to coming off the shift and going home and thinking about gathering the scraps and tatters for the preparation of tea. Tubby has reported that a famous stage actor will appear at His Majesty's Theatre as Jack the Ripper. Leslie ripostes with the news that his tour is postponed until summer. Tubby trumps her by announcing that three Russian singers, in their native skirts and blouses, will sing songs in their own language at the Boys' Grammar School.

"Will you understand them a bit, Syl?" Leslie asks. "Given how close your country is to theirs?"

Sylvia has stopped working. She doesn't answer, and Leslie calls to Tubby, "Give her a prod, will you, and see if she's awake?"

But Sylvia, on her hands and knees, is watching Leon Salthouse lead the horse and wagon in. He pulls at the mare's bridle, and a German prisoner holds the reins. Another sits beside him, two shovels propped against his leg.

Tubby calls, "Oh, good. It's time for tea."

Leslie says, "Oh, no, dear. That isn't the tea. That's the latest government-issued news from the European front. Though I suppose you're right, in a way. We are supposed to swallow it."

Sylvia is on her feet now, and she is absolutely still, her eyes blinking in the pale sun, her hands clasped just below her waist. Leon looks only at her, and she stares back. Then he falters, drops his eyes, looks at the prisoners, stumbles, catches himself by the bridle, annoying the tall, old chestnut-colored draft horse with her thick, pale mane, who digs her broad hooves in and stands stock still.

"I'm terribly sorry, old girl," he says to the horse, patting her neck. "Over here, Missus? That where you want it?"

Sylvia looks at him, his sad, long face, his enormous hands and feet, his eyes, which glide toward her, then dance, blinking, away. Tina stalks toward them, her rake at port arms, and she says, "Back here, if you please," redirecting the wagon and the three men by a dozen paces. "Thank you very much," she says briskly, and then she marches off.

When the wagon brake is set, the German prisoners, in their blue uniforms with golden arrows, their feet in high, rolled Wellingtons, walk back through the muck in the wagon, let down the gate, and sullenly begin to shovel.

"You all right, Missus?" Leon asks her from the corner of his mouth. He is near enough, now, to be heard by her but possibly not by the others.

"All right. Yes," she says, not moving away.

"I've been worrying about you, with him run off and your mister so riled."

"Everyone fine," she says, her tongue still thick with the news, less able than usual to curl around the illogical idioms and modulated, sliding tones of this oily language.

"I worried about you before that, of course. I don't suppose it ever occurred to you, the amount of concern I've been taking on your behalf. Do I need to declare my interest, Missus?"

"Interest. Is like money in bank, interest. Yes? I am your money in bank?"

"Jews and their money," Leon mutters. "I mean *interest*."

"Maybe I know this, what you mean. Maybe not."

"Right. Right, right. Listen. I gave up my mother's own cottage to you and your German prisoner."

"Why?"

"Certain rewards, you think? I say: ha! I say: think otherwise. I say: think of this—that I gave you what you wanted because it was you and you wanted it. No other reason. Even if it was to be you with a German prisoner in my stead."

"Stead?"

"Place."

She shakes her head. "*Why* you are doing this?"

"No," he says. "Why are you doing it, you say."

"Of course. Please. Tell?"

"It occurred to me that one day you might wish to

return the favor."

"Return."

"Same bed, different man, I'm saying. Me."

She studies him, looks over at the horse, which seems to be studying her, and then Sylvia watches as the prisoners shovel the fresh, ammoniac, fungus-colored rich horse manure onto the earth. It is too fresh, she knows. Januscz, the farm boy, could have told them. It will quite possibly burn out the crops it is intended to nourish. Life is this, she thinks. They say shit. All of life, including the new one inside her, is shit. The stench of the manure surrounds them. It wells up from inside the earth, she thinks.

"You. Me. Mother's bed," she says.

"That's it, Missus. That's my hope and expectation. I'm a lonely man, but capable to the occasion, I can assure you."

"You and German prisoner's whore," she says.

"Now, Missus," Leon says. Sylvia advances on him and Leon retreats. Leslie, the sharpest-eyed of them, has been watching. Now, she turns to study, unabashed.

Leon backs away, and Sylvia walks toward him until they are at the side of the wooden-walled wagon, and past the high wooden wheels, and then at the back. She walks around him as if he is not there, and she dips her hand into the thick gravy of slopping muck. Hatred moves her arm and keeps her eyes open though they water from the powerful stench while the manure sits on her outstretched palm. Her arm moves, then, as if in contest with the rest of her. Her hand drifts toward

Leon, who leans back. It returns toward her, as if she would paint herself with feces, and then it moves toward him again and, at last, seems content to turn itself over and slowly spill the muck upon Leon's well-oiled boots.

"German prisoner's whore," she says, not whispering, to Leon, whose hand dances on the butt of the big Webley, then slaps against his thigh. "This your payment," she says. "Interest."

Leon's mouth is open. His hand is hard against his thigh.

"Everything," Sylvia says, "everything in world is made of shit."

WHEREVER SLOWACKI HAD taken them on this visit to Nella's father, Alex could not find the way again if he had to, and he had no idea how to navigate home. His chest and stomach filled with the pressure of being lost. This was panic, he knew, and he waited for the numbness and deafness, which had receded, to surge through his body like blood. It was as if he were a child, and the adults had driven him upstate, along Route 17 and then the smaller, two-lane roads past towns with odd names—Deposit and Sidney—and then, with two stops, one at a convenience store and gas station, one at a small-town post office that looked like another gas station, off onto single-lane roads that twisted and climbed. The big motor of the borrowed vehicle growled, and so did Slowacki. They were heading west now, and the glare of the sun darkened Slowacki's glasses and blinded Alex. He rode with his eyes closed, sitting erect as if he were one with this tough and cocky, troubled man who, Alex knew, had errantly decided that the prince of malpractice was owed his devotion.

Alex searched for a way to tell him otherwise. But Slowacki said, "Could be up that one," as they drifted to a corner.

They had come slowly down a rocky, rutted dirt road, trailing dust. As he looked behind them, Alex thought the dirty plume made the car appear a damaged airplane leaving a long cloud of fire and smoke. Welcome to another country, Alex thought. A state forest bordered the narrow road, and they were closed in by huge old evergreens. Sun filled the road they would turn onto, but now they sat in the shade of the trees as the reddish-brown dust subsided.

"It should be up there—we hang a right. You ready?"

"I haven't been really prepared for this entire journey," he said. "As you could tell."

"You seemed a little tense," Slowacki said. "I served with a lieutenant, once, for a couple of weeks. He got the runs before we went into action. Of course, there was always action, or it was on its way. It was like the weather, you know? Or those big goddamned leeches that dropped onto your neck. So it was all around the place, big-time, most times. Which meant the kid was shitting himself every other hour of the day. He got quiet when the hooches looked empty or a woman with a kid came up the road, smiling on account of being scared—probably. Unless—this was always the deal—unless she had an antipersonnel mine taped onto her tits. Or the kid was dead and had a grenade up his ass. So he gave off this very heavy quietness. That's what I've been sensing. You thinking combat here, Doc?"

"Fear. Only fear."

"Big only," Slowacki said. "You really think this girl capped herself?"

"Capped. You mean killed?"

"Close enough. Yeah."

"It's a possibility. It has to do with her father. I can't talk too much about it."

"Confidentiality," Slowacki said.

"Exactly. But the father—he's a man who has suffered terrible extremities. His inability to communicate with her could be causative."

"He don't communicate."

"Not at all."

"I hate that. Reeny gives me the big-league frost, I end up nuts, I'm shouting, I'm throwing chairs, throwing dishes out the window, you name it. I guess that's pretty violent."

Alex found himself smiling. This man, somehow, made him happy. "I'd say it does the job."

"Anthony Slowacki does the job. You can put *that* one on my gravestone. I'm guessing a right-hand turn, and we start looking on the left: little white garage near the road, big white house up behind it, stream with a stone wall to the right of the garage. These people up here know how to give directions. Good habit to get into, since the poor sons of bitches don't have streets to go by."

Alex nodded his agreement. Then he remembered.

"What was the outcome with your anxious young lieutenant? Did he survive?"

"Jesus, no. No way you can make it, you're all wound up like that. Somebody killed him."

"Some—you mean an *American* killed him."

"I didn't say that."

"Because," Alex said, "he was a threat to his men? He would be, wouldn't he—unable to cope. And they actually murdered him."

"This was a kid died in the war of wounds sustained in combat. Too young to be in command. Too young to die. Like most of the rest of us who died. End of story. Just don't go getting *too* quiet on me, Doc. None of this quiet, sweaty staring up your own asshole, you hear?"

Alex said, "You mentioned carrying a gun in an ankle holster? Is that really done? And *are* you?"

"You don't want to know," Slowacki said. "Don't worry. You're safe with me, Doc. Nobody's safer. I'd of thought you'd know that. And it's a joke, about the piece, about the lieutenant."

"A psychiatrist of my acquaintance has told me that there are no jokes."

"Maybe he was making a joke," Slowacki said. "Hey. You hear that? I think that was very clever, if you're asking me. This patient's father here, this Grensen, he gives us the big silence, I'll joke him into submission. Here we go. Right-hand turn, and then we're in the cornflakes, we're swimming for the edge of the bowl."

Half a mile or so along, around the potholes and

stony corrugations over which the big car waddled and jolted, past a small aluminum trailer with broken windows and an enormous television antenna that slanted from its roof toward the partly emptied sacks of garbage piled near its steps, on the left-hand side of the road, they found a white-painted post on which a large aluminum mailbox sat. It was near a small white garage to the right of which flowed a little river—a beck, his mother's fellow farmers would have said—and behind which was sited a two-story white house that faced away from the road and looked over a valley that went on and on, much of the land a deep green but some of it still sparse and even flax-colored, as if spring had just begun to settle in. There were daffodils in clusters at the side of the house, tightly clenched and waiting for warmth. Bird feeders hung in the lower branches of a broad tree, and birds went up as they came from the car and slammed its doors. Alex was sick with anticipation. He thought he might bend over and retch. He leaned back, took in air until he grew dizzy, noted how he seemed unable to cope even with breathing, while Slowacki, at the garage now, looking in through a side window with his hands cupped over his forehead for shade, seemed able to cope with so much. Except *his* life, Alex thought.

"Pretty amazing old car in there," Slowacki said. "They stopped making the Silver Hawk so damned long ago. Studebaker. Beautiful thing. Like me: ahead of its time, and very sporty. Somebody here knows about transportation. You think your person would be driving a vehicle like this?"

"She knew nothing about cars. I can tell you that. She got her driver's license only a few years ago. At her father's insistence."

"That's this guy don't talk, but he insists about a license?"

A black bird with red bars on its side scolded them from the thick tree that was only beginning to leaf out. A door slammed on the front porch, at right angles to them and the road, which curved and dropped out of sight. Then Alex saw a man in business slacks and loafers—he made out light tan socks under pressed trousers—who wore a white shirt with the sleeves rolled up on the forearms. He waved, although he was close enough to speak. Alex waved back.

"Mr. Grensen," Alex said.

"The same."

"I'm Dr. Lescziak. This is Investigator Slowacki." Alex noted that Slowacki's brows went up in response to the designation, part lie and part evasion.

"Is it Nella?" He was before them now, white hair cut *en brosse*, though slightly longer than Alex's, and taller than Slowacki, broad-shouldered, big-bellied, very pale, in need of a shave but dressed as if for the office, with a necktie designed like a piece of maroon-and-blue Persian carpet tugged down to reveal the undone topmost button of his white oxford-cloth shirt. He looked as though he wished to stoop but refused to. "Is she all right?"

"Actually, we're looking for her," Alex said.

It was Slowacki who thought to say, "We don't know anything bad about her, Mr. Grensen. We can't find her, but we don't know she got hurt or anything. Okay?"

Grensen was rubbing his jaw with a closed fist, a gesture Nella had used when puzzled or afraid.

"You okay?" Slowacki said.

"Maybe inside," Grensen said,

"You want to go in and sit down?" Slowacki was in charge, and Alex was grateful. Grensen embarrassed him. "Let's go in, Mr. Grensen. Remember: far as we know, she's all right. She's not showing up for work, though, or— This is her doctor. Dr. Lescziak. He's a shrink. Your daughter's, ah, *head* doctor. Therapist? She's a no-show on her appointments. That would be his involvement in the case. Investigation. Really— just seeing what's up. You know? Want to go inside?"

In the foyer, near the door, was a high blue-and-white ceramic urn that held two dark umbrellas. Alex thought of Teddy's possible comments on the erect, black shapes and their repetition in the daughter's apartment. The room that opened off the foyer was bright, with many uncurtained windows on the valley side of the house, and the objects on glass shelves at those windows caught and transmitted the light. There were large, pearly shells and Italian glass paperweights, lacquered dishes and glazed pots, stones that seemed worn to shininess—whether by hands upon them or by the sea, he couldn't tell—and the paintings on the walls were bold and colorful, not the doleful, dark smudges Alex expected because of Nella's comments, and which he also expected because of his own childhood house, so gelid and dark.

The kitchen to which Grensen led them opened off the left of the living room. He pushed buttons on a coffee-making machine which ground coffee and heated water while he sat with them at the long, narrow wooden table alongside the kitchen's four windows that looked down at what once must have been a pasture.

"Magic," Slowacki said.

"German," Grensen said. "Their ability knows few bounds. They have loved the industrial revolution. You know: the assembly line. They are capable of producing anything, I think. They are brilliant with coffeemakers and murder. But tell me of Nella. Please."

Slowacki sat back and folded his hands on the edge of the table, signaling Alex to become responsible. Alex thought of the pistol that, he suspected, really was fastened to an ankle that remained, somehow, not irritated by its chafing or burdened by its weight. He wondered if it felt like a fetter on the leg.

Grensen folded his hands, as if in response to Slowacki's.

"Your daughter is my patient."

"You are treating her for what?"

"I can't say, in any detail. I'm a psychologist. A therapist? We talk. Nella came to see me several months ago."

"Yes, but for what?"

"I can't, as I told you, say in any detail. This may seem ridiculous. But confidentiality between patient and doctor is essential to the process. To any health care. Let's say that Nella felt anxieties and urgencies that are not abnormal, given our times, given the issues prevalent in contemporary life."

Grensen shook his head angrily, then caught himself. His pallor was replaced by high color. "This is nonsense, Doctor, with all respect. Don't you hate it when somebody insults you and then says 'with all respect'? Pardon me. But you are offering flatulence and wary phrasing to a concerned parent. I use the English language, an adopted tongue I have learned with care, professionally. I hate to hear it abused. Except, of course, when I abuse it for a profit."

Alex raised his brows and Slowacki took out a long, thin notebook with a dull black cover. He said, "Notes?"

"Fine," Grensen said. "What would you like to note?"

"Abusing words," Slowacki said, "which is not a crime."

Grensen grinned like a mischievous boy. His hair was receding, but not nearly so far as Teddy's, who was far younger than he. His pale skin seemed healthy, and his hands didn't shake. Alex had expected failing health, clinical depression, a grim or even absent affect. What he saw was a man in his early seventies whom he would have described as healthy—though, now, greatly concerned.

"Perhaps it should be," Grensen said. "I write corporate reports. That's the extent of my abuse. Well, and of course my poems. Nella told you?"

Alex could only shake his head.

"Too bad," Grensen said. "Well, I'm not Ted Hughes."

Slowacki said, "Who?"

"Do you send them out to magazines?" Alex asked.

"I've published them, yes."

"Right," Alex said. "That's wonderful. Well, I was treating Nella. She came several times a week."

"So the poor kid must have felt terrible," her father said. "I knew, of course, that she was troubled. Who wouldn't be? Anywhere, I mean. Anyone. It's a nasty time. It's a bad time." Alex could hear the lilting rise in his statements, the heavy dental *t* of Grensen's original Norwegian.

"Do you write about the camps?" Alex asked.

"So she talked about that."

"I'd rather not comment."

"A nicety, given that by raising the question, you comment."

Alex shrugged.

"Certainly," Grensen said. "Yes. Not camps: a camp. The one I was in. The one her mother was in. You know, I take it, about her mother." Now he seemed paler. His large fingers worked in their knot on the table, and he spread his hands apart when he saw Alex study them. "The coffee's ready. Let me—"

While Grensen gathered white cups and saucers together with milk and sugar and spoons on a tray, Alex saw Slowacki, his eyes very large and glistening, as he cleaned his tinted glasses on a bone-white hand-kerchief. He remembered Slowacki and their discussion of the lampshades. He looked stricken.

"Birkenau," Grensen said, setting blue cloth napkins before them. The coffee smelled very rich. "This is from your own backyard—I have it shipped from upper Broadway. Zabar's. It's their espresso bean. I hope you like coffee. The camp they transported us to was Birkenau. Then, before they could net us in a selection, and before they sought to kill us in other ways, we were caught up in the siphoning off to Auschwitz III—Monowitz, they called it. Labor, labor meant to kill us off in months instead of weeks, and of course diphtheria, starvation, the madness. But there, they did not do selections for the gas. They murdered you through work. *Arbeit macht frei*. Or you lived in spite of them. We were large people. We were strong. She was a nurse, and they used her with the women. I was handsome, and two of their *Kapos* fancied me. They vied for me. So there were favors, and so we lived. We lived. That was what we were, at the end. The Allied soldiers told us this: You are alive! So that was that: we were alive. Her mother—" He tilted his head toward Slowacki. "You might want to note this, sir. She killed herself. In 1969. It is not, you know, uncommon among survivors of, as you would say, the camps. Attempting suicide there was forbidden. Did you know this? They reserved for attempted *Selbstmord* the cruelest punishment—a torture refined beyond the daily tortures, the same as the punishment for attempting to escape. Then *they* gave you what you had craved, but on their terms, because only they could. It was as close to a reason for any of it as I have come. They could, so they did. But suicide? You arrogate to yourself, merely because you are accustomed to owning your life, the right to dispose of it, to dispense with it. Forbidden. I have never learned how to define it further or with any more elegance. It ought to be available to language, I continue to hope, but I have not been gifted with a way to find it.

"I would love to ask you how she speaks of me. Spoke? Are we in the past tense?" He put his cup into its saucer very gently. "You are here, of course, because of urgency. emergency, perhaps. Has *she* threatened suicide, Doctor?"

Alex took a breath. As he breathed out, he thought, he was expelling his license to practice, and maybe his freedom. "Yes," he said, reserving the details of her Thorazine dreams on the suicide watch. "She—let's say that she indicated thoughts about it. I mustn't say more."

"Poor child," Grensen said. "Poor baby. We had her late in our lives. We hesitated because of our experiences, and because of these times. We wondered, you know, about offering this world to a baby. Of course, one ends up offering the baby to this world. And it is a cruelty, I think, that we did. Poor Nella. Sweet Nella. She was the gawkiest— That is a lovely word, is it not? 'Gawky.' She was the ugly duckling. My wife, who was called Ula, Ula Grensen, often, she stroked those long arms, those legs with their bony knees, and she told her, 'You will be a swan. If you are patient, you are finding yourself a swan.' And Nella would snap at her, a sorrowful child: 'find,' Mamma, not 'finding'! And Ula would tell her—"

"—'Of course,' Alex said.

He saw Slowacki's head turn very quickly. Grensen's white eyebrows, tufted and thick, went up. "She told you," Grensen said. "Good. It should be remembered. It should not disappear."

"It should not," Alex said, not knowing what he remembered and what he made up.

Slowacki said, "Has she been in touch, sir?"

"Not for this week. We are in touch, of course, but with no rigid schedule."

"Last week?"

"Yes."

"Anything out of the ordinary?" Slowacki asked.

"Nothing. Oh. She had discovered the pleasures of brandy, apparently. I teased her about a wealthy beau with elegant taste. A man she saw from time to time— so she said: I thought she had some real interest in him—this man had bought her, or given her, Armagnac. A lovely French invention, yes? She took pleasure in it. I hoped it meant pleasure in him. I would like her not to be alone." His face, as he said this, became very still and seemed to set in a mask of pleasantness. But the muscles beneath the skin appeared to grow tense. And Alex saw another face, the one that responded to loneliness, to loss: the face that Grensen wore when he confronted himself. "I ought to have sensed something, I suppose. Of course. I should have been more venturesome in asking her about—about *her*. One tries not to pry, you understand. But is she considered to be in danger? Might she be dead? How"—again, one hand clasped the other, as if to give comfort, or as if in search of it—"how shall I think of her?" her father asked.

He stood, suddenly, and he went to the coffeemaker as if to touch one of its switches. But he was looking, Alex saw, for someplace to hide his eyes from theirs.

"Sir," Slowacki said, "there someone you'd like to call? Have us call for you?"

When Grensen turned to them, a smile nearly shaped his mouth, and Alex knew that it would have been mirthless. It disappeared and, at the vanishing, the father looked like his child. Nell peered out of her father's eyes for an instant, the way a child peers out from beside a curtain at the upstairs window of an old house.

"Whom would I call?" Grensen asked Slowacki.

"A relative someplace? Any friends in the area?"

Grensen shook his head. "There are no relatives. There is Nella, or there are none. As for intimates in this area, I confess that I befriend people with difficulty. Nella, or nothing."

Alex agreed. He wished that his ears might fill from his hysteria once more, that he might seal himself in deafness.

"Doctor," Grensen said, leaning now against the counter of his kitchen, "what can you tell me of my child? What, that is, are you *permitted* to say?"

Slowacki said, "How about local places she might visit? Some bar nearby? Men she's been involved with?"

Grensen stared at him as if Slowacki had spoken in an unknown language.

"Women?" Slowacki said, shrugging at Alex and shaking his head.

Grensen said, "Doctor. What can you say?"

"Devoted to you," he said in a hoarse voice that didn't sound, to him, like him. "Not fulfilled by her job. A bit at odds and ends. Do you know the American term 'the blues'? Sometimes she was unhappy, she complained, for no apparent reason. She woke up 'blue.' Suffered nightmares, not surprisingly."

"Nella was neurotic, you are telling me," Grensen said. "I suspect you are being unspecific whereas she would have been very specific. She was—we called her the Judge. She had a somber way of addressing one, with a kind of magisterial regret: 'I'm afraid, Daddy, that you have been a disappointment to me and my class.' This was in your third year—second grade? I was requested because, no doubt, of her promises of my charm and that of the doggerel rhymes I made for her bedtime stories. Her class and teacher invited me to sit on one of those miniature chairs and tell them about being a poet. I was not very interesting when they asked me where poems came from. I pointed to my less snowy but equally dense head and smiled stupidly. 'You have been a disappointment to me and my class.' But, in this age of enormity, is neurosis not the only appropriate response, Doctor? What is normative in an age of enormity?"

Alex said, "I suppose you're right. What we used to call neurosis we now know as paradigmatic behavior. You search the crowd at Grand Central because it is the *norm*, now, for someone in a raincoat to take from under its skirts a military rifle and begin to pot people from the Vanderbilt Avenue balcony. In that sense, yes. And, yes, Nella was unhappy."

"Was," Grensen said.

"Transit Authority personnel would interdict such an action in Grand Central," Slowacki said. "We're trained. There's a chance, anyway, of interdiction."

Alex said, "I don't imply that anything has happened to her."

"Your visit, the long trip from New York, this is implication—this is *denotation*—enough. It is storming in heaven."

Alex cocked his head.

"From my childhood in Norway. You know we came from Norway?" Alex nodded, and Grensen said, "My granny used to say it, when there was thunder in the spring. 'Storming in heaven, so why not down here?' She never intended very much reassurance, I think, only a sense of . . . justice. No: aptness, perhaps. A cold logic. Granny was what the English would call cold comfort. All I meant, just now, was that I hear thunder in my brain. The blood pressure, doubtless. But why not hear storms? What you are telling me is enough to bring me to my knees and lower, yes? Like a child. Thunder inside, thunder out, in heaven and here, in hell."

"The police in New York are notified," Slowacki said. "In case you were worried everything wasn't in line. It's all in line. Nobody contacted you from the state police barracks outside Binghamton, though? Or the sheriff's department?"

Grensen shook his head.

"Bureaucracy," Alex said.

"That is merely a reason for something necessary not having been accomplished," Grensen said. "Knowing it is no palliative."

In response to Slowacki's expression of puzzlement, Alex said, "Painkiller." Slowacki nodded and wrote some notes.

"Give us a prescription, Doctor," Grensen said, smiling with his teeth but showing no pleasure.

Alex saw her pallor as she lay in the little room on the ward. He remembered how he kissed her throat and held her wrists. "Mr. Grensen," he said, "I would give anything to—"

"No," her father said, "I intuit that you already have, perhaps, given much."

Slowacki, Alex saw, was taking notes on their exchange.

ALEX SEES HER—sees his mother, Sylvia—as she sees Otto while she labors on the shard-rich soil of the farm at the Hindpool. For what if Otto has not escaped to North America? What if he has made his way to France, to the southwest, where Vichy reigned and where he might expect to find Germans or their sympathizers, and a way to safety—even if his safety lies at home, and very far from the German prisoner's whore?

But is there safety in Europe? For they have heard the stories, have they not? They know the reports, she and Januscz, from exiled Polish fliers in the RAF, a few who escaped the roundups and who live in London and speak and speak and speak of it to, apparently, no one's understanding aside from that of other Poles. The Poles say it as they can, and it is known but somehow not known: the facts are the facts, but also aren't. So some of the English, many of the Poles, and Sylvia and Januscz know of children taken from mothers to be murdered, old people killed with injections, diseases at the mass toilets large as community bathing pools, the beatings with clubs and rifle butts, the cold and the hunger and the shame. There are rumors of poisonings. Sylvia thinks of shame again, and how it might kill someone small and weak and proud. She recalls the perfectly respectable farm boys and guest-house girls who hurled stones and clumps of dried manure at them: *"Zyd! O ty zydowko! Jewboy! Girly kike!"* And the camp near the railhead—how far from home? Fifty kilometers?—about which her aunt, through the Red Cross, wrote before the letters stopped. It was rumored, her aunt said, that members of the resistance would be sent there. A question her aunt posed: how could they build so large a camp for so few people? Sylvia had read the sentence twice, in an earlier flat in Barrow, dimmer and colder, even, than this one. And then she had asked Januscz what he thought it meant.

"It is a joke," he told her, lighting his cigarette. "Your aunt's sense of humor has been darkened by the war."

"So few resistance, though," Sylvia had replied. "How can there be so few?"

"Because you and I fled. This is another joke."

"There *is* no resistance, Januscz?"

"Was," he said. "Now, it is dead. Everything is dead. Everyone is dead." And, until Otto, she has believed him. She is tempted, now, to believe him again.

"Everything," she repeats in the silence that surrounds the Hindpool field. Then the horse led by Leon Salthouse moves, the wagon shakes with the prisoners' motion as more excrement flies toward the earth, and Leon, watched by Tina, retreats toward a distant standpipe to clean his boots.

She has been out to Oswiecim often, of course, but she has difficulty in imagining the camp. And there are other camps, she has heard, to which he could be transported after the capture. Why capture? Because of what composes the world. She smells it. She is certain of Oswiecim, for it is the place to which they haul the resistance workers. And, whether he has lied or not, whether his poem was true, he has been inside her so far, from every direction, and has filled her so full in every way, that she knows him. You know no one very well, she thinks. It is not possible. But for human beings in this war that is waged upon a world made of shit, Otto and she have known each other.

Still, it is possible that he escapes, that he makes his way off the island of England, and that he is free in Europe. In France, perhaps, and she knows no words in French, knows only a basic French geography, so Alex's mother cannot imagine the places in which he sleeps or eats or runs, runs. She sees fields beneath his feet as she saw the fields at home. Why not? All fields, finally, must be the same. They are hilly or level, they are yellow and blighted or fertile and green. It is possible, she thinks, that the Nazis have poisoned the earth. She smells the fresh fertilizer on the Hindpool garden and she can therefore smell the stink of what they doubtless have done to France. She has heard lavender mentioned in connection with France, and *rosmaryn*, which the English say as "rosemary." So: the sweetness of herbs as their fragrance collides with the oily stench of German sewage, and she sees the small, strong man with his fine, bony face and his thick hair—she tugged upon the richness of that hair, pulling it toward her, raising her body toward his face that he might devour her—and she watches him run from the culvert next to a field, and then over the stony, narrow road, and onto the drooping, blighted vineyard. They grow wine in France, she knows. He kneels between the orderly vines, their unhealthy leafage supported by rope and wires, and he pants for breath. His mouth is dry, his lips stick together. He cannot find drink in this hot southern climate where the Vichy coordinate the patrols and, from what Januscz has read and reported, where they are only too pleased to cooperate in turning over Jews, resistance, and Allied spies for deportation to the east. *The east.* They are, in English, cruel noises, those two words. And they are her home.

So, despite the foreignness, it is simple to envision the sorry patrol, three or four partly drunk and very bored and sweaty Frenchmen, very old or very young, who chance upon the brave, frightened man who has dared to escape from the ease of Barrow-in-Furness, and Sylvia, to work his way north toward where resistance might most be needed.

She sees them kick at the man as he lies curled on the brittle, yellow grass. He is bruised, and his lovely face is brown and yellow, swollen, gashed bloody along the line of the jaw. They have broken soft organs inside him, and she can feel it. And now he is required to endure weeks of living in camions with broken springs and unforgiving wheels so that his body is pounded and pounded. One more slam of truck against the ridged and rocky road, she thinks, and something might rupture, its fluids leak away. She fears, seeing his face, to see it go blue-white, then bright crimson, as his spleen or liver dies inside him.

She wishes for Otto that she could pray. You cannot trust the god of this world, however. He is a god of lies and murder. He has constructed his world entirely of dung.

Up through France, then, and she knows enough to imagine how he might travel: Montpellier to Toulouse, then Aquitaine, and then Bordeaux. How did he get to France? she wonders. Never mind. He made his way, by ship, to France. Perhaps he docked at Marseille and managed to travel to the southwestern fields in which they captured him. But they have taken him, and he is shipped, like a damaged cargo, from Bordeaux, by train, and then by other trains, to Oswiecim. According to an American journalist who has outraged London, Januscz says, by urging that the Allies drop their bombs on the railroad lines to this place, the Germans are calling it Auschwitz.

Reading aloud to her of home, Januscz looks up from the newspaper and says, in a whisper, for I have just fallen asleep, "It is the language of Goethe, and yet it makes the old place sound so ugly. *Auschwitz*."

And this is what she says to herself: "Auschwitz," the place they have taken him. She cannot imagine what a camp would look like. She thinks of men in leather shorts and women in dirndls who cook for them. She thinks of the men chopping down trees, repairing country roads, and singing in unison as they work. This, though, cannot be what the sound *Auschwitz* means. It sounds like barren earth, everything upon it dead. It sounds like victims—she does not dare to imagine of what—who howl their pain. It sounds like dark, poisonous air where once the evergreens scented the wind. It sounds like the smacking of wood and metal on flesh.

It is at the entrance of this place, outside the snorting train, that her brave, small Otto stands, perhaps squats to ease the pain of his damaged inner organ. Yes. He tries to stand, falters, then manages to stay up: he is so powerful, even now. Others do fall, and they are dragged away, are soon out of sight. Whistles blow, and the guards bellow. Otto was transported in a carload of Greeks, and they look to him as the German commands crack like whips among them. Otto tells them to hurry this way. Then he realizes that he has said it in German. He searches for his scholar's Greek.

As he does, he sees two old men who cling to each other for support. They seize the other's arms and shoulders like children in terror. But one, he realizes, is the child, and the other is his parent. They wear filthy black garments, one has no coat, and one wears no shoes. A guard, shouting at them to line up to the right, seizes the head of the old man as if it were a melon, and he hurls it at the ground. The old man falls, crying a single word over and over, and when he strikes the cobbles of the railhead, his arms and legs shoot upward, as if he were a baby clutching for the mother he was torn from. The son moves to his father but is held by the throat, the guard's wrist pressing at his larynx, and is driven to the line of weeping, shivering men. The children are elsewhere, and Otto hears them. He hears the wailing of women. And then the line of men moves, then moves again, and the son disappears, and then the father is dragged by an ankle, and he disappears, and then Otto lurches after the line, attaches himself to the moving queue, and is, himself, about to disappear.

Before he does, Sylvia sees his face. She searches for it in the shades of brown and black that are his world now. And his face is the color of the ledger page on which he wrote her poem. She thinks it likely that he wrote the poem. Leon Salthouse lied because he wanted Sylvia: his interest. The pain of Otto's injury must beat like the pulsing of a heart. He must be thinking of her, she thinks. As he walks through the gate in his line of prisoners, Otto is in his freedom. He is free of everything except pain. He is free of Sylvia. She cannot be free of him, however, unless she forgets, and she is terrified that one day she will.

Is that the sound, from the sky, of Allied bombers, arriving as part of an effort to rescue the prisoners? No. It is Sylvia's heart, which growls in her chest and echoes in her ears and which sounds, as Grensen told Alex, like thunder in heaven. For this is not a god of rescue, Sylvia remembers. This is a god of false hope and of women who are pregnant with death.

A guard shouts words in the cruel language, and Otto turns toward him as if in politeness. He is always a man of dignity, except with her, when he displays his secrets, upon her, within her, panting like a beast, nakedly and truthfully himself. He and Sylvia have known each other. They will know each other no longer. Again, the guard calls out. Again, Otto listens. Now they move off. And, as they pass through the gate, Sylvia listens. She hears their footsteps in the mire through the frightening din composed of high, crying voices and, in the lower register, of groans, and of the engines' churning, of the whistles of the guards and their often incomprehensible instructions, and of dogs that snarl as if to emulate their masters. Sylvia, somehow, hears the sucking sound that is made by the world beneath Otto's feet as he tries to walk, to lift himself free of it and to move, as instructed, forward. There is no freedom now, she thinks. And that is because he has told them all the truth: he was of the resistance, he is a man of the cloth as well as of the flesh. He is here because of truth. Sylvia somehow hears the thick and liquid breathing of Otto as he labors to walk where he must go. She holds her breath in order to listen more carefully. The throbbing of engines rises on the air, as if a dozen vehicles are about to begin a journey—lorries, perhaps, or omnibuses. Is there nothing not a part of this vast, shaking engine? Men shout, they make the sound of the brutal assurance of those in power who cry to those they control. She hears the muddy suck of Otto's footsteps, his rasping breath, and then she hears him clear his throat.

Otto knows that she listens. Somehow he knows that somehow she listens. It is an eastern spring, and the wind that carries the stench of the camp—ordure and rancid flesh and a harsh, stinging smoke—feels very cold. Somehow she knows that too. Otto shivers, and so does she.

She is listening.

His strangled breathing becomes his voice. She knows it, whispering, so well. Her fear is that she will forget its sound when she is old, but young enough to know that she has forgotten it.

He says her name. Is that what she heard?

It is what she has waited for. Otto says her name— yes?—under the gate of Auschwitz camp. Then he walks, or limps, inside. They do not shut the gate against her imagining, but she cannot see further. She hears nothing more of him as she stands, her eyes tightly closed, in the freshly fertilized field of the Hindpool Brick and Tile Works while Alex imagines his mother and imagines, as well, that his half a brother—alive inside her at this instant of the waking dream—imagines her too.

Otto, limping into death's hotel, spoke her name. She is certain he did.

IT WAS ALMOST dark in the hills of Chenango County, and Nella's father had spoken of the iced aquavit, the smoked fish, the brown bread, the boiled potatoes now chilled that he would serve them if they stayed. Slowacki telephoned his home to speak of his dinner plans, and he sought occasions, Alex was certain, on which he might drift through Grensen's rooms to search for signs of his daughter.

When Slowacki had left for the bathroom a second time, Grensen, at the butcher-block counter beside his refrigerator, said, "There is nothing for him to ferret out. I suppose policemen think that way."

"No one knows where to look," Alex said.

Grensen looked down as if something moved slowly between his hands along the counter. His voice very low, his breathing audible, shallow, he said, "What terrible things must I imagine? I have a tendency to see the worst. I write annual reports for capitalists. They send me what they call 'data,' and I—frankly, I lie on their behalf. I interpret, to their benefit, the way their stockholders will see the management's decision over the fiscal year. I end the year in, let us say, July when of course it actually ends in the January ice storms. I interpret the loss of money and the laying off of workers as 'restructuring.' I am excellent at this because I have learned, over a lifetime, how to make a language obey. Yet I am, by nature, a man of the north. You are little different, I think. You, too, yes? You know what I mean by 'north.' I am speaking of the realest of the ice storms, the worst of the cold, what occurs inside ourselves. Now I believe that I must imagine the worst. Dr. Lescziak, what is the worst?"

Alex thought of her pallor when he saw her on the

ward, and he imagined her ending as he feared: bled white in a white bathtub, tones of gray and purple in the water that would not for long stain the porcelain of the tub. Someone would scrub it away with an abrasive cleanser, he thought. He thought of her arms slightly supported by the dyed water. He thought of her mouth agape, her teeth mere lengths of bone, her tongue a tube, her body no more than flotsam made of fat and slackened muscle in an expensive place where they had stayed together. He thought of Liz beneath him, yet commanding him, in their Greenwich Village hotel. He thought of Liz and Teddy in a bed, and Liz at her love or half in sleep beside his friend, smiling. It was the smile he coveted. He thought of Nella as she told him how this man of so many words, before him in this upstate kitchen, never spoke. What else had she lied about, or reconstructed? he wondered. What, when she said it to him, had been true? And how could he require that she, in her torment, know what might be true or, if it was, how to live with it?

"We'd have heard if something dreadful happened," was all that Alex could think to say. "The chances are we'd have heard."

"Is that what I can do, Doctor? Tell myself that no news is merely no news instead of bad news? Impossible. A woman leaves her work, her apartment house, her therapy sessions . . . and her men? Have the police examined the men she knew? Dated? Is that still the word we ought to use?"

Slowacki, entering the kitchen, called, as if in a foreign language, " 'How well you knew how long to make the bleeding last.' Excuse me, sir, but could you tell us which bleeding individual we're talking about here?"

Slowacki held a small book before him so that Alex could see it. *The Birth* was its title.

"You poor man," Grensen said. "The line you read is the only decent language in the whole poem. You know nothing of poetry, though, do you? Or of how long it might take for a miserable poem like that to get from manuscript to set type. Read the dedication."

" 'For Ula,' " Slowacki said.

"My wife."

"She bled?"

"Sir, she did," Grensen said. "She did bleed. You may keep that copy."

But Slowacki was setting it down, gently, on the far end of the counter. "Sorry," he said. "You were asking the doctor here about your daughter and sex, even if you didn't like to, you know, snoop. I was doing the same thing. Trying, you know, to help."

Grensen raised his chin and lowered it, a parody of nodding in agreement. "Help," he said, "of course."

"Sorry, sir," Slowacki said. "Doc here will tell you I'm pretty much a straight-ahead Polack. All I mean is that certain lines of inquiry are obvious, if you know what I mean."

Grensen had returned to the preparation of their meal. He said, finally, "I do. Just as you must look in my rooms to see if I have—what? 'stashed away'?—hidden my daughter from the authorities. Am I the Bluebeard among fathers?"

Slowacki looked his inquiry at Alex, then said, "The pirate?"

"You are quite wonderful," Grensen said. "I am sprinkling on some dill weed that I have dried from the kitchen garden. You might wish to dig it up to see if I have hidden my daughter beneath it, and the lemon-thyme. Or the larger garden: I am planting early lettuces, I grow starter sets of peppers, the tomatoes, which take forever in this climate—four heirloom varieties. You can buy anything in America. Lie to them about their corporations, then cash their check and purchase whatever you wish: fruits, vegetables, gardening tools, coffees and teas, recordings on tape of spiritual lectures, carpets from Assyria, antique American milking stools, Impressionist masters. As you wish.

"But my daughter is in neither of my gardens nor anyplace inside my walls. The first room you entered so stealthily would have been upstairs on the right of the staircase. It is the room Ula and I slept in. After her death, I closed the door. It sounds heartless, but it was, believe me, heart*felt*. Nella and I then agreed to relocate, she to the guest room, which is one door down from the old bedroom, and I across the hall and down the little corridor, to what had been Nella's. In none of them at the present time is anyone but ghosts. And each of them abounds in those. Do you believe in ghosts, Detective Slowacki?"

"Straight Mister does it for me, sir. And the answer is affirmative on ghosts. Yes, sir. I got a lot of dead friends."

"One of the wars?"

"Southeast Asia."

Grensen said, "Very bad. You had no chance to win, the soldiers. Nor, I suppose, the people who stayed at home. But the soldiers lost their life. The people who protested lost their mind, I think, a lot of them. Or, anyway, their ease. But you men died."

"Yes, we did," Slowacki said. He closed his notebook and jammed it into the hip pocket of his jeans. "Reeny, that's Mrs. Slowacki, she asked me to tell you she's saying a prayer for your daughter, Nella, and for you."

Grensen bowed his head over the counter and kept his back to them. When he straightened, it was as if his back had grown stiff. He looked ahead and said, "She is kind, and I am grateful."

"She *is* kind," Slowacki said. "Me too on the grateful."

Alex had to smile, and Slowacki shrugged as if embarrassed by his doctor's pleasure.

Grensen put cloth napkins, large and creamy white, folded narrowly, at three straw place mats. He brought them each a large white plate on which were slices of very dark brown bread, a pool of yellow-white horseradish, a pool of what Grensen said was sour cream, and long strips of smoked trout, he said, that he purchased by mail from Maine. The potatoes, in thick slices, looked moist, a little gluey. The bright green dill lay over them in a fine powder. He added pepper and salt to his food and pushed the pepper grinder and the shallow glass dish of coarse salt across to Slowacki, who took some of each and imitated, Alex was sure unwittingly, each of Grensen's gestures.

"Oh, my," Grensen said. "How to forget *that*?" He stood, a little effortfully, and went to the freezer compartment of his wide refrigerator and brought them a frosted three-quarters-of-a-liter bottle of aquavit, from which he poured into slender glasses about four inches high. "This is how they live, at home, to be a hundred. *Skoal!*" He drank off an inch and shook his shoulders and head, and Alex thought of Nella's shoulders again, and how he had been thrilled by their simultaneous freedom and restraint, their stasis and motion. He thought of her naked shoulders under his hands, how careful he was not to bruise her as he demanded with his fingers and palms that she move to the rhythm she'd inspired in him. Grensen's hand was still in the air, the glass aloft, when his face lost the burlesqued pleasure into which he had twisted it. "I cannot," he said.

"No," Slowacki said. "To tell you the truth, I think you might feel better if you just enjoy this beverage and the food, but don't try and convince yourself you feel any better. Just take another step. When you're someplace that was mined and swept, or they tell you it was swept, or they *think*, pretty sure, somebody's been and swept it, and you have got to get over there from over here, you take a breath, you take a step, and then maybe you get there. If you wanted my advice."

Grensen moved his glass in the air and then set it on the table. He nodded. "Good," he said.

Slowacki said, "Good. But I always thought it was a chewing tobacco. Some kids, when we were in-country, chewed some terrible stuff out of a can that said *Skoal*. Your people do a lot of that?"

Grensen smiled as if actually pleased and he lifted his glass again. Slowacki lifted his in acknowledgment. "In a word," Grensen said, "no."

"No it is."

"It is a salute," Grensen said. "A toast. *Skoal!* Here's mud in your eye, it says."

"You too," Slowacki said, and he drank down the glass.

"And you, Doctor," her father said, refilling Slowacki's glass and his own, adding an oily drop to Alex's. "How shall we resolve this visit? Otherwise, if we do not, you will never feel that you can leave, and I will be reluctant to see the last of you. I have no doubt we could all become friends and live here together with pleasure. But the business of the day, the reason for your journey, and now"—he shook his head and gently pushed his plate an inch away—"the cause of this terrible headache, the hollowness in here"—he gestured toward his chest—"I cannot imagine what to say or do. You will help me? To contact the proper authorities? To . . . I *must* act. You understand."

Alex tasted a tarriness in the bread that responded to the aquavit. He knew now that he'd been waiting for this mortally wounded man to demonstrate wisdom, to offer a clue. What was Teddy's joke about clues concerning Freud and somebody's teeth? Liz had always laughed at that, showing her own teeth, wrinkling her eyes and nose, releasing herself because of her pleasure in Teddy. She hardly smiled except with Teddy.

Clues, Alex thought. Everyone wanted a clue, a hint, a gesture of wisdom, a scrap of knowledge, a tattered half an inch of something smart. Liz had found it: Teddy, tall and broad and wise. Nella had thought to find it in Alex, Alex believed. But her interpretation of this man across the table from him suggested that either she was delusional or the man was a brilliant actor, and psychotic, and, maybe, his daughter's seducer if not her killer. Facts are facts, he thought. They're what happened. Find the facts. But how do you learn from these people what a fact is?

"Yes," Alex lied, "of course I'll help."

HIS MOTHER WOULD not know these particulars, if ever, until later in her life. But Alex knows them. As if he might will the information through her bloodstream into Otto's son, Alex's half brother, he thinks that facts are facts. And the facts to which it all reduces are that the body is a machine for producing waste. He wills her, now, to know it *then*. And Sylvia, tears on her face as she works at the garden they have made in 1944, sees Otto, broken inside his body, a feeding ground for microbes, feverish, weak from the diarrhea against which he must clench his buttocks. If it runs slowly down inside your trousers and they do not smell or see it, you are alive for the day. You squat and shit when permitted to. If you cannot regulate yourself, you are too ill to work, and then you are selected out, and you are dead. They cull you on this farm for corpses. Somehow, you must find enough water in your filthy bowl, you must find enough energy at night, you must find enough strength to withstand the poking in the ribs and the slaps against your head from the shivering man beside you on the wooden bunk—he wishes you still, he wishes to sleep—so that you may rinse the frail cloth of the trousers and sleep a little and wake without having fouled the bed and use your bowl for the luke-warm gruel and go, again, to work. His detachment hauls logs to which rusted chains are affixed with spikes. Their hands bleed as they tug the cold chains to drag the logs to random locations in a field that seems, always, to elude the sun. Sylvia remembers the giant draft horses hauling logs at home to be sawed into lumber. Now, little men who stink of decay do the work.

In the latrine, yesterday, a man wept as he squatted at the iron rail and squirted black and bloody water into the indoor concrete channel but also onto his own ankles. Otto squatted on the other side of the channel, grasping his knees, leaking thin streams of excrement until he thought that his raw anus had turned inside out. He grew dizzy and leaned forward to save himself. Then he stood and, a few feet from the edge, turned back to look across the channel at the man who wept. The second-largest of their *Kapos*, whom another pris-oner called Der Drache, the Dragon, because of the flaking scales of crimson skin on his cheeks, stood behind the weeping man. Der Drache shrieked, in his native German, which the little prisoner clearly could not comprehend, "Stand when I address you!"

The prisoner looked behind him, then in front, at Otto, who now faced him across the ditch of the latrine. The weeping man's eyes were enormous. His hands, palm up, asked Otto: *What? What did he say? What must I do?*

Der Drache said, "No, on second thought. Continue. Good, small boy. Shit yourself, go on. Please yourself. Why not swim with yourself?" He raised his foot, and Otto shuffled backward from the edge in the stink he thought of as tangible, and Der Drache pushed the man, too swiftly for him to have said a sound, into the river of excrement. He sank, he rose, and then, as if his disappearance was an escape, he stayed under.

Even so, Sylvia thinks, in that place, with no dignity, he is himself. Otto is himself. She sees him as he peers into the stew of vanities, the logical conclusion of the philosophies he has spoken—so, she thinks: Hegel—or of their lust, or of Januscz's comforting smile and icy eyes. This is the compost of being human, she thinks he must have thought, as he gave praise to his god that he had not drowned, and that another man had been compelled to swallow the truth.

This world, Sylvia thinks in Barrow-in-Furness, as William grows inside her, as she breathes the mild, salty fog and the farm animals' dung they have spread along the ground, as she dreams the dream that Alex dreams, is made of shit.

SLOWACKI WAS IN the car, in the dark, and Grensen, a kitchen towel over his shoulder, a plate of potatoes in his hand, saw them off. Alex stopped at the screen door of the hall to say, "I'm as worried as you are, of course. We'll all keep looking."

"Isn't it astonishing," Grensen said. "You can get deliveries of smoked trout or navigational charts for the Mississippi River. You can get a therapist to your house! I am so grateful, Alex. This is not the usual service provided by psychologists."

"Nor do most poets dry their own dill and serve it on potatoes to the likes of me."

"Potatoes," Grensen said. "They are the essential food. Potatoes and bread: they are the earth," he said, moving the dish. "And, anyway, I am not a poet in this . . . situation. I am her father. Just as you are—?"

"Her doctor," Alex said.

Slowacki started the car. Its deep rumble threatened everything.

"And possibly the provider of Armagnac, I think. The man in the city. Is that so?"

Alex shook his head. He looked down at Grensen's brown loafers. The old man's feet looked young in them. Alex's feet felt tired in his shoes. His stomach ached, and his fingers tingled. "It was wrong. From start to finish—to wherever we are now: wrong."

"You love my child? Does she love you? Or think she does?"

"The definition of love," Alex said, as gently as he could, "is hardly a simple assignment. As you know. Whose understanding should you trust? Can you rely on your own? Would you accept mine? Or hers?"

Grensen's eyebrows rose, but his face collapsed. He opened his mouth, then closed it. In a husky, strained voice he said, "Rhetoric, now—*banter*—is beyond me."

"Yes," Alex said. "Me, too. I'm sorry. There have been important feelings, it's safe to say."

"Safe," Grensen said. "Do you promise?"

"No. I want to. I can't."

"No. Haven't you been unwise," he said. "Cruelly, carelessly unwise."

Alex said, "Yes." Grensen held the platter of potatoes as if it were an illustration of his point. Seeing that Alex looked at them, he did too.

"Ridiculous," he said, lifting the plate a little. Then he shook his head. "I don't know anything else to say." He tried to smile, but looked only ill.

Alex said, "I'm sorry."

Grensen shook his head.

"I'm sorry," Alex said. "I don't— Look, I'll be in touch if you like. I can phone you."

"Perhaps we'll have a little luck."

"You deserve it," Alex said.

"Nella does," her father said.

SLOWACKI, DRIVING ON the dirt road, said, "He's a hell of a man."

"He's had to be," Alex said. "Do you know the way?"

"He gave me directions. Imagine him being a poet."

Alex didn't answer.

"I didn't do any good for you, did I, Doc?"

"Just as I didn't do any for you, I'm afraid."

"No, but I got puffed up on knowing procedure and being trained and just general ballsiness. It's what Reeny says gets me tripped up every time. I think I'm bigger than I am."

"Anthony, if it's material to you, I think you're bigger than life," Alex said. "Did we come this way? I can't tell."

"No, the father—Mr. Grensen gave me a quicker way." As they bounced into a turn, Slowacki said, "I almost called him 'your girlfriend's father.'"

"Did you."

"Doc, everybody needs to feel good. Am I judging you? Not me."

"Not you," Alex said. "And I'm not judging you, Anthony. But I wonder: the business with your wife—"

"—Reeny."

"Yes. You didn't know she was having an affair, did you? Or even suspect it? I mean with any conviction. That was what? A diversion? An excuse?"

"You're a piece of work, Doc."

"Yes," Alex said, "I really am. And your—Reeny's affair?"

"Feeling sorry for myself, I suppose. I'm good at that."

"Were you feeling, in some way, unfaithful to *her*?"

"That's what I mean about you. You're a very wise man."

"Except for my choice of girlfriends."

"I don't feel like I should be talking about this."

"Good," Alex said. "Excellent. Let *me* talk about something. Your dire warning about my suspected involvement in the disappearance of my . . . let's say 'patient,' if I may. I might not have made this trip, no matter my worries about the patient, even if I'd been

417

contemplating the possibility of such a journey. I believe that somehow I acted, finally, because you helped me convince myself that I was thought to be involved. Guilty of something. Now, I made my own decision, and all it's cost is a day. And what was left of my self-esteem. But you really wanted us to be here, didn't you? Driving around upstate in the darkness? On a mission? A couple of boys playing war?"

Slowacki said, "This Rhys is supposed to have a theory. This is what a guy tells somebody I am in touch with."

"Well, fine, Anthony. She has a theory. Everyone should have a theory. So?"

"It's about you, though. Because you filed the report. You know: you made the fuss."

"Why? To divert attention away from myself? To cost the police department bus fare? What a mastermind I am."

"Doc, I don't know about this bus business. What I told you, it's what I heard. I know a person knows a person. It's what *they* heard."

"A lot of not-too-much."

"She's worried about the girl. The patient. I also heard that."

"Yes," Alex said, "and I'm worried too."

"She's pretty lucky, when you think of it. All these people worried about her."

"Except you never talked to anyone who knows Rhys. Did you?"

"Who?"

"*Rhys!*"

"Easy. Easy. Here it is." He turned onto the state road and said, "Now we look for 12, heading south. It's simple now."

Alex said, "So Rhys never really said I was . . . guilty of anything. Did she."

"What? No. Not in so many words, exactly. No."

"And you don't know anything about the Gowanus Canal, do you, Anthony?"

"I was demonstrating about the chain of command. That's how it would work."

"Yes," Alex said, "the chain of command." Slowacki was driving very quickly, but Alex didn't care if they wrecked and turned over or were stopped and issued a ticket and held overnight. Sooner or later, he would be home, and alone; he was alone tonight, at seventy-five miles an hour, as he'd been alone at a walking pace or standing still, and as he would continue to be. They passed through a little town where Christmas bunting of silver and green still writhed on the streetlight stanchions, and then they were in darkness again. Their headlights brought up listing fences, occasional bright, asbestos-sided Victorian houses, and weather-scraped barns, and then they left them behind, as if they were escaping. A powerful, thick stench surrounded them and didn't diminish for a mile or more.

"Skunk," Slowacki said. "We hit some killed skunk and the ventilation pulled in the stink. I hate that."

Alex's voice sounded grave and unlike his own when he said to Slowacki, "And all those times in Vietnam. And all those detailed stories of gunfights."

"No, I was there, Doc. I was there."

"Where were you, Anthony?"

"Saigon, mostly. Tan Son Nhut. I was attached to the 483rd Tac Air Lift. I was fuckin day *and* night labor. We unloaded matériel off of Caribou C-7s. They brought in a lot of important shit. Listen: we took *fire*."

"Yes, but what you told me, Anthony. The stories you told me. Night patrols and ambushes. Men disappearing into the water. People bleeding to death and screaming, and the heads coming off."

"You wanted war stories, Doc. I think about that shit a lot. And I do carry a piece in an ankle holster. Look." He lifted his knee and pulled at his trousers. The car drifted and slowed a little, and their tires tossed up gravel and twigs at the margin of the road. Slowacki's thin, pale ankle, between his denims and his clean, white sneakers, was at the level of the dashboard. Alex looked at Slowacki's weapon and then looked away.

"Yes, you do," he said. "But the stories, all those terribly moving stories. The drug peddlers and blown-up men. Those poor men."

Slowacki's foot was on the accelerator again, and they moved more quickly than before. He drove with authority. His mustache was not still, and his jaw muscles moved in a steady rhythm. "Pretty soon we're at 17," Slowacki said, "and it's a straight shot home." Then he was silent, and Alex lay back in his seat. He thought he heard Slowacki say, "Whoever heard of a shrink yells at his patient for being fucked up?"

He thought of Grensen's demolished eyes as he asked about Nella, and then he thought of Nella's face looking out at him from those same eyes, and of Liz's large canvas and her knowledge that something was inside its blankness for her to discover.

Slowacki coughed a long, strangling, artificial cough designed, Alex thought, to waken him. They were passing the outskirts of Monticello. He said, "We need to stop for gas and coffee. I need coffee." Alex didn't answer, and they drove on, not stopping. Half a dozen miles on, slowing for a service station, he said, "I really gotta stop, Doc. And you need to know this: she won't arrest you. She maybe don't approve of this relationship with the kid, sure. It's always easy to find somebody don't approve of your weakness. That's why it's a problem to have a weakness. But as far as law enforcement and jurisprudence goes, you're all right. You're fine."

Slowacki pumped gas and they took turns in the men's room and purchased coffee separately, not speaking to each other. They were silent for the rest of the ride except for Slowacki's "Mother*fucker!*" when a scarred, black car next to theirs in the George Washington Bridge exit lane seemed to drift dangerously close.

When, at a little before two in the morning, Slowacki stopped at the entrance to his building, they sat in the silence that had overtaken them. Finally, Alex said, "I should thank you, I suppose."

"I can't say, Doc. You tell me you wouldn't have made the trip except I conned you, then you shouldn't."

"No. But I wanted to go, I think. And I'm glad I met him."

"You learned something."

"Plenty."

"Then thanking me would be the proper thing, to tell you the truth."

Traffic was light on Central Park West, mostly slowly cruising cabs and vans from wholesalers. The night man stood motionless, holding the apartment house door ajar, just as Alex kept open the passenger-side door to Slowacki's borrowed vehicle. Small tan birds, in the artificial daylight of the street, worked among the beech trees of the park across from them. Alex looked at the bench on which he had sat, studying his apartment.

"Thank you," he said.

"You're entirely welcome," Slowacki said. "Could I ask you something?"

Alex waited.

"Why do you think I do that? With the war stories?"

Alex laughed, he thought, although what he heard was a wordless shout. He shut the door and walked into his building. As the elevator slowed, he felt very dizzy, as if his brain were still ascending. He let himself into the office and found the lights on.

"Nella?" he said. He should have called for Liz, he thought. Nobody answered. The furniture looked dusty, as if he'd been away for weeks. He found eight messages, none from Nella and none from Liz. The latest, left at four that afternoon, was from Detective Rhys, whose voice sounded tense and unhappy. She said, "Call me, Doctor," and rang off as if she tossed her headset into its cradle. It had to be news of Nell, he thought. But of course it was too late to get hold of Rhys. He would have to wait for morning. Her news, he thought, could be dreadful.

He crossed his rich rug and sat in the patient's chair, but it felt wrong. He moved to his own, and, though it didn't feel better, he stayed there. The office smelled strange but familiar at once, from steam heat, which of course was not on, and flesh, a peppery combination. The air conditioner was off, so perhaps it was the plumbing, he thought, that made the sound of someone who whispered words he couldn't make out.

He picked up the weekly schedule book and moved its pages, finding it difficult to focus on his handwriting. He wanted to drink something powerful, but he would have to enter the apartment to do that, and the prospect seemed less happy than remaining where he was. And it was as he stared at the ruled pages of the book that he thought: Januscz had to know. He must have found out. He had to have acted.

Sylvia might have worried about being haunted by her lover's child. But, more than anything, she must have wished for Otto to continue in her life, long after the war. She would have kept that child, Alex knew it. So it must have been Januscz. Alex knew in his stupor, this revery or exhaustion, and he knew with certainty: it was Januscz. The wily farm boy, the slowly but powerfully reasoning man schooled in the behavior of matter, had at last deduced or reconstructed the details of the truth. Januscz learned the facts. And he had told his wife, in his deep, rumbling, undeniable voice, that she must yield up her stay against time.

Alex closed his eyes and listened for his father's terrible requirement. Instead, though, he saw Dr. Bahl's leftward-leaning scribble: *Rhapsodizing on self-aborted fetus*. Nella had not been pregnant. She had never mentioned a pregnancy that occurred during her adolescence or her early twenties. Was it she, herself, she referred to—she, the ruined child, destroyed by her mother? He thought of Nella pregnant, he thought of Sylvia leaving the house in Ann Arbor, though this time with Januscz. That was how it happened, he remembered. He remembered. They had left him with a sitter, Meredith, a college girl, his father's brand-new student, who drank his parents' slivovitz and taught him to play gin rummy. He remembered them returning to Alex and Meredith in the black taxi, and how his mother climbed slowly up the stairs to his parents' room, how Januscz stood at the foot of the stairs and watched her go, then turned with a smile of greeting for his child. "This is a difficult time," his father might have said in his heavy voice, if it had happened that way, the way he remembered it now.

"This is impossible," Januscz might be saying, in the weeks before they are to leave for America. He confronts her in the stale English kitchen that has shrunk about Sylvia until it is the size of a closet, a closet with vermin that fearlessly march along the floor at the edge of an exhausted tenant's vision. And then he lights his cigarette and says, around the smoke, "You will carry this child?"

"Ours."

"No."

"Yes."

"No. Do not say this insult again. It is not my bed, you understand, that you *now* insult. It is my mind. No. Once again: you will carry it?"

Sylvia stares. Inside her, a tiny Otto floats, and she is the safety about him. She feels sleek and broad. But she is in extremity, she knows. Lovers in war are endangered. And now the authorities have come for them. The door has shivered from the blow of the heavy fist. She stares back at Januscz, and he looks wily at the eyes, his nose looks flared, as if he smells her lover on her clothing, her baby in the sweat of her pores and the breath from her mouth that is carried to him, when she sighs, "Of course."

"So," he says. "So then. Someone will want a child. Many men have died and someone needs a baby. Someone will languish without a baby to feed."

"No," she says.

"Exactly so, in fact. Yes. You will renounce. You will renounce everything. Or you will be alone—Jewess, Pole—in a filthy world. This world will stew and devour you."

"*You*, Januscz? *You* are saying this to me? *You* are meaning this? *Jeste's pewny ze chciates to powiedziec?*"

"Saying by mistake? Accident." His face falls as he supplies the English. He looks as if he is about to pass out. His eyes begin to roll toward his forehead and he closes them, hangs his head above the smoking saucer where he stubs and stubs his cigarette. He crushes it flat and rubs the ashes with his finger. Then he studies the finger and speaks. His language is as fractured as his composure. "All an accident. Airplane falls from sky upon hospital. Lorry collides with crocodile of schoolchildren. But not this, Sylvia. This is my purpose. Even you. Even me. Yes."

"Then world made only of—"

"Exactly the case," he interrupts. "That, you say, is the world. That is what you believe, I know. But let me tell you something worse." He speaks slowly, he composes for her. "This world is made of invisible particles. Even the great hulls of ships, with all that they weigh, are of particles so tiny, we never will see them. *Ever.*

"Sylvia," he says, "they do not care. Can you understand?

"Now. This is what *you* must care about. You and I, we have created one child. If you wish to change the number to two, then we have a process of subtraction. I will keep Alex by myself. And you will be alone. *Jak Cie zostawie to zdechniesz glodu bezemnif. O ty zuydowko*: this is what the world says. You will be not this family. Nothing. Only German prisoner's—"

He sits unmoving. He licks his lips. Then he slowly cups his large hand about his mouth and chin, as if he silences another man. He shakes his head.

"Whore," she says for him.

And so his life with Januscz, the son thought, had been constructed on the foundation of a long mistake. For he had believed, with a smug knowingness, that Januscz had been defeated, was somehow complaisant in his servitude, and had lived in permanent thrall to

Sylvia, whose sorrows and afflictions and dismay had been the weather of their home.

He knew nothing. He was the man who sent his patients away, who dismissed his wife, who lost his lover, who could not keep a friend, who deserted his new-found brother. He was the man who, beginning in his youth and continuing now, composed a life. He could say goodbye in many languages. And he knew nothing.

He thought of Grensen's aquavit and he wanted a drink. He straightened in his chair and looked, at eleven minutes after three on the fifth of May, over his commitments. Slowacki had been scheduled to return in two days. Alex had an intake appointment with Steven Lind Stern, a high school sophomore his mother described as always enraged. His anger fed his father's own, and his mother—Alex knew this before meeting the boy—was their mediator and mutual victim. Howard Dance would be in, the pale, insomniac pharmacist who had wished to become a physician, and who, when he was required to sell condoms, felt that he would gag from the smell of latex, which, he swore, permeated the heavy wrapper of every brand he carried. And he was to see Ed Barbarosa, the not entirely successful trial lawyer who was divorcing for the third time. He was a robust, handsome man who hid behind the neutralities of law and its obfuscatory jargon. He was incapable of intimacy, at once a swaggering and frightened man whom no doctor would make well. Alex thought of him as the crouching, intimidated small fellow behind the large, frightening mask: the Wizard of Oz.

Soon, he thought, in a minute—in a couple of minutes—he must walk from the office to the apartment and check two rooms. In the stillness of trapped, dusty air, he must look in the maid's room for their old canvas case. He would find it gone, he thought. And then he must walk through the kitchen and out, left, through their foyer, and around to the left once more, and then down the long corridor to the room in which Liz had been sleeping. There he would open closets and drawers and detect the absence of certain garments and toiletries. Liz would be gone. He hoped for her—maybe also for him—that she would be gone. It was sad, and they were sad, but it also might be right, he thought.

But he wasn't ready, yet, to go into those rooms.

He must find a doctor for himself, he thought. Damaged people must do this. He, for example, sometimes had helped such people. He sought to name what it was they would go about healing, he and his nameless new doctor. But he couldn't say.

He remembered a time when Liz had placed her hands on his chest, her strong fingers seizing at his shirt and pulling him toward her. "And what about you?" she had cried. She moved a hand from his chest to touch him at the temple. He'd flinched, but her hand had been quite gentle. "Alex," she'd said, "honey, who's *in* there?"

He remembered that he'd answered her, and what he said seemed very important to her. It had meant something, he knew, for she in turn had flinched. But he could not remember his words.

He did remember Nella's.

I pretend to be an adult. I have affairs. I walk around half-naked like an Eighth Avenue whore. I shout at associates in the office, as if I know something and they don't. I know the words to use to blame my father for what he should be blamed for. But who says I have a right?

What do you think your father should be blamed for, Nella?

Did he or didn't he kill her is what. Do we love him or do we hate him? Thumbs up on Daddy, or down?

If someone dies, are they murdered?

How else?

Well, we've talked about—you remember: suicide, for example.

But there's a reason for it. Isn't there a reason? Isn't somebody there behind the reason?

In the case of your mother . . .

In the case of my mother. Exactly. Exactly! One of us killed her. Daddy, in the conservatory, with the umbrella. Or the wicked daughter with her periods and her twitching little ass and her nasty undercover practices. You tell me which one's guilty. Quick!

May 5, he realized, and the President would be in Germany to lay his wreath. The child of Sylvia Lescziak and the German prisoner of Barrow-in-Furness would undoubtedly be making notes, sitting in a weak-jointed straight-backed chair at a desk to which it wasn't matched, watching the news reports on a black-and-white television set with tinny sound that burred against its little speaker. Alex knew he owed the small man more.

The upstate trip, a vain, ridiculous quest, he thought, had been a boy's dream—his or Slowacki's, his *and* Slowacki's: an imitation of responsible action, but only, at last, just a little more make-believe. Because Nella, he knew, was dead. She had aimed to be. And he, who should have been useful, had used her.

Well, certainly, he thought. Of course. Go ahead and call it love. Call it enchantment. But what you do becomes the facts. And you know what you did, he thought.

He pressed the open pages of his broad, heavy date book against his chest. Its weight where Liz's hands had clutched his shirt reminded him of how he'd answered her: "Why, everyone," he had told her. And she had started, and her great eyes had filled.

Tell me which one's guilty. Quick!

But he had thought of the war.

He and his doctor could start with the war.